Kiery

RAIN

Bobby,
Mel says she thinks you're
a tough cookie.

— Kieryn

**Shakin' up
Young Readers**

QUAKE

quakeme.com

RAIN
A Quake Book
Shakin' Up Young Readers!

First Quake paperback printing / July 2010

Cover © Nathalie Moore
Artwork © Henry Ziegler

QUAKE
is a division of
Echelon Press, LLC
9055 G Thamesmeade Road
Laurel, MD 20723
www.quakeme.com

13-Digit ISBN: 978-1-59080-792-7
10-Digit ISBN: 1-59080-792-8
eBook: 1-59080-671-9

PRINTED IN THE UNITED STATES OF AMERICA

10 9 8 7 6 5 4 3 2 1

For Henry,
whose rare compliments motivated me to finish.

Of course, I'd like to thank everyone involved in encouraging/helping/forcing me get through the writing, editing, and publishing process. There are some people I want to mention that I'm especially grateful to, or who are just great in general.

I'm lucky enough to have what I call my "Review Board", or on some days my encouragement/helping /forceful minions. They're kind of like the caffeine of my writing process, giving me the ability to proceed, mostly by demanding the next chapter. They are:

My awesome cousin Henry, who always provides me with honest–painfully honest, at times–feedback.

Brynna, the best sister ever, and my #1 cheerleader.

My Grandma Barbara, who was the first to provide an adult perspective, and the techno whiz behind my website.

Katie, who is 1) the inspiration for parts of this book, 2) the amazing model pictured on RAIN's cover, and 3) the best.

Natasha, who read RAIN's first draft in one day, can use more exclamation points in one sentence than anyone I know, and who is an amazing friend.

Beth, who pointed out both the good parts and the parts that made no sense.

Tess, my writing buddy who always provides me with a dose of enthusiasm.

There are many other people who have made an impact. People like:

My mom, who read RAIN after the first draft was complete and was crucial in filling in plot holes and encouraged lots of rewording. My dad, who read the story a few edit rounds later. Both my parents are extremely supportive–I couldn't have done it without them.

Professor Kellerman, Dani, Julianne, Nicole, and Vince– these people taught me how to really revise something. In the no-comma-left-unchanged, no-sentence-left-unmarked, take-no-prisoners kind of way.

The Heiningers, who are extremely awesome and supportive.

Mr. Rockower, who gave me the best school year of writing I've ever had.

Rosie, my e-pen-pal and Australian consultant.

Thank you, Mary the super-editor, and also Karen, the super-publisher, for making everything possible.

Prologue

The stars spin.

They fly in and out of focus as I attempt to draw air. *Breathe*, my head chants, but I can hardly hear it through the sharp pain wrapping around my skull. The asphalt presses into my back and the concrete walls of the alley frame my vision. A ringing sounds in my ears. As I struggle for oxygen, other injuries come forth, the feelings blossoming in my spine, my ribs, my shins, my arms.

I should be getting up, preparing to defend myself, to make some sort of attempt to resist my attacker. But I can't get my body to listen, I can only lie here and wait....

For a moment the agony peaks, and my lungs stutter. When I regain semi-awareness I urgently try to focus. At Watson they teach us to concentrate on something, anything that will motivate you to fight. Anything that will give you the strength to get up.

My mind lands on Ray. Immediately I'm lost in memories, one's I've been suppressing for years, and they flash through my mind with more clarity than the pain in my body.

That's where everything started, anyway. *At the beginning,* my mind says, as if I'm telling myself the story, which cues the first memory, the first time I saw him...

1

The first time I saw Ray was when he walked into the lobby the day he arrived at Watson. He was called Anthony back then. I was supposed to be at lunch, not squeezed behind a large cement flowerpot, but I didn't have to worry about getting in trouble. I was more a part of Watson than half the teachers. Oh yeah, and the principal was my guardian.

Two men accompanied Anthony. The first was a thin, pale fellow who dug his fingers into the kid's shoulder to support himself. The other was Mr. Syme, the head of Watson Institute. I called him Shadow because he always seemed to be right behind me, especially when I didn't want him to be. Everyone at Watson got into trouble–right into the middle of trouble, actually, and then to the bottom of it. That's our job. But I was more trouble than the rest of the students combined, so he kept a close eye on me.

I had been reading in my position behind the flowerpot, but I decided this was the perfect time to practice some of those stealth observation skills we'd learned in class earlier that week. Ten-year-olds weren't taught many real techniques. Other than a few simple defense moves, we were basically instructed on how best to report to our seniors in case of a real event. I couldn't wait to be in the Red Group, the highest group, the group that got to do real stuff.

Red Group was a few years away. Right then the stealth observation seemed like good practice. I positioned myself on the balls of my feet, crouching behind the ferns. Rule #1: Never kneel. Always position yourself in a stance from which you can easily get up and run.

Anthony carried two duffel bags. His dark red hair was sort of curly and jumbly, and he had his head bowed, making it hard to see what color his eyes were. The gray Jersey City sweatshirt he wore looked old and slightly damp around the cuffs, and his jeans seemed a size too big. Nothing at first glance would tell me exactly what was going on with him.

I was especially curious because this was such an interesting occurrence. Watson Institute never got new students his age. Parents–usually former students themselves– enrolled their children around age two or three, *sometimes* as old as age five, so the kids could start learning at an early age and accelerated rate such crucial skills as *noticing* things. I myself had been enrolled at age zero. I assumed Anthony was ten, as he seemed about my age.

Shadow addressed the man who'd arrived with Anthony. "We've got lots of paperwork to do. Maybe Anthony could take his things up to his new room while we get some matters straightened out? I'm sure *someone* would be glad to help." His eyes slid around the room. "Isn't that right, Amber?"

I grumbled under my breath and stood up. It wasn't that Shadow actually saw me. He just expected me to be wherever I wasn't supposed to. He raised one eyebrow, but I could tell he was more exasperated than upset. His cheek always twitched when he tried to mask anger. It wasn't doing that now. I crossed my eyes at him in reply.

"Anthony, this is Amber Rind. Amber, this is Anthony Luther. He's going to be in room 716. Would you kindly lead the way?"

"I'm supposed to be at lunch," I told him, eyeing Anthony. He was avoiding everyone's eyes, staring off to the side.

Shadow sighed. "Anthony, Amber will show you to your room."

I scowled. I didn't mind the job, but I minded being ordered around like a Labrador. Sparing the adults another glare, I turned and strode down the hallway. Out of the corner of my eye I saw Anthony hesitate and look back at the man with Shadow. I wondered if the man was his dad.

"In here," I said when Anthony caught up with me by the stairwell. "Hope you don't mind walking a few stories."

Anthony stared at me for a moment, then looked away and began to climb. "Don't you have an elevator here?"

I took a second to process the sound of his voice, then dashed ahead so I was leading the way again. "Of course not, stupid. Elevators are too easy to stop, essentially trapping us inside. We always use stairs. This is the second floor, where the nurseries are, as well as the Green Group rooms. All the other dorms are on floors seven and eight. The classrooms are on the floors in-between. The first floor, where we just were, that's where the lobby and cafeteria and gyms are." I tried to improvise a tour guide tone.

"So what is this place?" Anthony asked, looking around as we reached the first landing. I waited impatiently on the next flight. "Dad didn't exactly say. I mean, what's the deal with the no elevators and stuff?" I sensed the curiosity and apprehension behind his words. "Are we training to be in the CIA or something?"

"Do you think the only secret agents are with the CIA?" I scoffed. "Sheez, what's your problem? Adults can't do all of the work all of the time. In fact," I said, "kids are better in some ways. Who's suspicious of children? That's why we're so good. We're good at helping *people*, not just dealing with international arguments and stuff. Like, if a thief is in town, we're the ones who'll get them. And we can pick up on so much more detail–" I stopped, aware I was starting to ramble. But I hated it when the new kids assumed that we were all just training for when we were adults. I only had to wait until I was fourteen, or sooner; if I was good enough, I might be in Red Group when I was thirteen. I *intended* to be good enough.

Rain

Anthony was looking at me in surprise.

"What?" I asked.

"Girls train, too?"

"What, you think I'm Shadow's *daughter* or something? You think *that's* the reason I'm here?" I said, anger flaring inside me. "Of course girls go here! We're just as good as boys!" That was another thing I hated—when boys assumed they were superior. To prove my point, I stomped hard on Anthony's foot. While he was distracted, looking down, about to protest, I gave him a neat shove and pulled off his duffel bags, dislocating his center of gravity. He toppled over. I tossed the bags on top of him with a smug grin. I'd seen something like that when I was spying on a Red Group the week before. I'd been dying to try it out. Maybe this Anthony guy could come in handy.

"Chill!" Anthony yelled, scrambling up. "What's *your* problem? I was just asking! My dad made it sound like it was boys. That's all. I don't know very much."

"Sorry." I turned away so he wouldn't see me smirking. "But I do rest my case."

"You never needed one! I wasn't arguing."

True, I admitted silently. But it felt good. There were some boys who treated me like I wasn't as good as they, even though I could kick their eyeballs to Timbuktu if we actually did some real combat training. "Are you coming or what?"

"Or what," he muttered. We climbed another flight of stairs. At about floor five he stopped and switched his bag arm. "That was pretty neat, though," he said, not quite meeting my eyes. I was shocked, but didn't say anything. "Do you learn that stuff here?"

"Yes, but not until we're older," I told him proudly. "That was a Red Group move. I'm only in Yellow Group for now. Red is the highest."

"Well," was all Anthony said. I showed him to his room.

"How do I get in?" he asked.

"The key's tucked under the door trim."

"Why? Isn't that obvious?"

"Yes," I told him, "but that's the point. It's so obvious no one would look there."

I turned to leave as Anthony fumbled for the key. Ten feet from the door I stopped and looked over my shoulder.

"Anthony?"

"Yeah?"

"Who brought you here?"

Anthony was quiet for a second. Then he said, "My dad."

"Oh." I couldn't find a way to reply to that tone, so I left.

The next day at breakfast, I stood in line fuming. I'd told Shay to stay in my room last night since Lyvia was showing signs of the flu. But she hadn't listened, so now both girls were sick. Classes weren't as fun without them. Plus, Shadow had pulled me aside that morning and asked me to baby-sit Anthony. Well, he didn't say it in those words, exactly. What he did say was, "Amber, you're practically a member of the faculty, so I feel I can trust you to help Anthony adjust to Watson Institute." And then he added some other stuff, but I didn't pay attention, knowing it was going to be just blab about how I could be a great role model if I wanted to and blah-blah-blah, which I got every day.

I took a piece of French toast and two glasses of orange juice. Vitamin C was my main food group.

I hesitated before I sat down when my eyes caught Anthony hovering at the edge of the room, obviously unsure where to sit. Sighing, I walked over to him.

"There's an empty table over here." I nodded to a small round table in the corner of the room. Anthony shot me a grateful look and followed me to it. I flopped down in my chair. Anthony sat down across from me, then seemed to decide that didn't work and awkwardly shifted ninety degrees to my left, his back to the wall. I drizzled syrup on my toast and began cutting it while waiting for him to say something. He stared at his food, picking little bits out and chewing very, very slowly. At first I wondered what his problem was. Then I saw his hand clenching the bottom of his new uniform shirt.

"Oh, are you nervous?"

I startled him and he jumped. He turned to me, slowly relaxing his grip.

"No," he said after a moment.

"Really."

"I'm not."

I rolled my eyes. Boys who pretended to be tough drove me insane. "It sure looks like it to *me*."

"I'm not," he repeated, then added in a whisper, "Terrified is more like it."

I felt the corner of my mouth twitch. "Scared we super spies'll kick your butt?"

"Sorta."

"Huh. You lucked out." I sawed at my thick toast. It was like trying to cut down a tree with a baseball bat. "The teachers have the Yellow Group learning observation right now. And in science we're doing *weather*."

The instant those words left my mouth, Anthony's eyes lit up.

"Weather? Really? I've always wanted to be a meteorologist," he said excitedly. "I'm telling you, it's going to snow today."

"The weatherman said it wouldn't. It's going to pass us by," I said, contradicting him. I rolled my eyes, unable to help feeling irritated. The one subject in school that I wasn't the best at was weather, and what do you know, it's my little charge's favorite.

"But look!" Anthony pointed to the window. "See that dark gray line? That's the storm. And on my walk over here I found the wind was coming from the northeast." He opened what I'd thought was his watch and showed me a compass. "This was my mom's," he said quietly. "She was good at meteorology too." I didn't say anything as I gazed at the gold and blue instrument.

"But anyway, the wind was moving pretty fast. It was gusting around, maybe, twenty miles per hour. And a cold front's coming, and the jet stream should be moving the speed of the wind." Anthony finally stopped jabbering and leaned back, looking pleased. I scowled.

"If you *know* everything about *meteorology* already, why are you *here*?" I demanded. His face fell.

"Because my dad's getting too sick for me to live at home," he said quietly. "And he'd worked with Mr. Brothers, the previous principal, so he knew about Watson. For some reason he thinks this place will be good for me."

"What about your mom?" I asked, then I wished I hadn't. Maybe he was like me, maybe his mom died when he was young. Or maybe she was an ax murderer or a psycho. It was probably painful for him to talk about her.

But Anthony just shrugged. "She and my dad got divorced when I was four. She was a weather-channel host until then. But after the divorce she quit and went off on some big project. She moved, and I haven't seen her since. I get a few letters now and then. But that's it."

"Sorry," was all I could think to say. He didn't respond, only worked at his breakfast. I continued my attempts at hacking through my own meal.

Suddenly Anthony raised his head, eyes narrowed in my direction. "Wait a minute. What about *you*? Why are *you* here?"

"Sheez. You have fairness issues." I finally managed to

tear a corner off my toast. I put it in my mouth and chewed slowly, eyes on Anthony, grinning as he started to scowl at me. I swallowed the gooey mass and put down my fork. "Okay, fine. I have my mom's last name–Rind. She went here when she was a kid, then went on to an adult espionage life. But when I was born she obviously couldn't keep me. Shadow's her old friend so I came here really early, when I was a baby. And then…it's been almost five years…since she died." I said it as quickly as I could. I hated telling my life story. The only part I didn't mind was letting the listener know how long I'd been at Watson.

"Who's Shadow?" Anthony asked, not making a fuss over my mom. I felt a rush of gratitude.

"Mr. Syme."

"Oh." Anthony kept his eyes on me, obviously waiting. I scrunched up my mouth, gratitude gone. If he was waiting to hear about my dad he could wait a long time, partly because I couldn't tell him anything. My mom had to keep his identity a secret from everyone, because of, duh, her line of work, so my dad probably didn't even know I existed.

I bent over and continued eating. Tired of trying to cut through the toast, I just picked up the whole piece, syrup and all, and bit my way through the meal.

Anthony was really, really good at predicting the weather and anything to do with air pressure, relative humidity, static electricity, whatever. Ms. Keen fawned over him the entire fourth period. He wasn't half-bad at the other classes, either. Miss Blume, the Inspections teacher, said he was the most observant first-timer ever, and according to his performance in scenario class fifth period, he was a really good judge of when was a good time to report back to older agents.

To top it off, it really did snow. When it started halfway

through lunch, all the students flocked to the windows and started cheering. Anthony gave me a triumphant look. I crossed my eyes at him and shoveled grapefruit into my mouth so I wouldn't have to say anything.

The next day Shadow asked me to continue keeping an eye out for Anthony, to help him out whenever I could (read: let him tag along everywhere). So, with Lyvia and Shay still sick, I sat with him again for breakfast. I hadn't for dinner since we were allowed to eat in our rooms in the evening.

"It's going to rain," he said in greeting when I sat down in the vacant seat ninety degrees from his spot.

"Well, no duh, Einstein." I rolled my eyes to the window where dark, rolling clouds lined up on the horizon.

"Yeah, but do you know how much?" he countered.

"No."

"I'm guessing about a tenth of an inch, enough to wash away the snow, unfortunately. But the rain won't stay too long. It'll get turned back by the colder winds coming from that cold front I was telling you about."

"The rain's not with the cold front?"

"Come on, Amber, really. Those clouds are coming from the south!" Anthony pretended to hold a microphone and spoke in a deep news anchor voice. "In our next segment, we'll cover the arctic blast coming into Rochester, New York. Reports say the cold weather is heading north from the Caribbean, since, as everyone knows, it's freezing at the equator."

It was so stupid, I had to laugh. Anthony shook his head.

"Hey, well, how was I supposed to know it was the south?" I demanded.

"A good agent always knows what direction they're facing," Anthony said, quoting Ms. Keen. I stuck out my tongue at him and he shrugged. "It's important."

"Yeah, maybe. But I'd rather be doing something real."

15

Rain

"You have to be good at the basics before you can be good at anything else." Anthony swallowed a bite of cereal while staring down at his tray.

"Since when are *you* an expert?" I said, annoyed that his remark made sense.

"I'm not. That's just something my dad used to say. He was a tennis coach."

"Was?" I blurted it out before I could catch myself.

Anthony didn't respond.

The next Monday, when Lyvia and Shay were feeling better again, we sat at our regular table by the vending machines. At first I started catching them up on what they'd missed, but then I saw Anthony sitting by himself in the corner.

"Would you guys mind if someone else sat here, too?" I spoke before considering the consequences.

"Who?" Shay asked.

"The new boy, Anthony Luther." I quickly added, "Sha– Mr. Syme asked me to look out for him, you know, since he is new and all."

Shay shrugged. I could tell she didn't want to hear the whole story. Lyvia nodded as she paged through a recent magazine.

I stood up and headed for Anthony's table.

"Hi."

Anthony looked up. "It's going to be cold today. Maybe cloud cover with some flurries in the afternoon, but don't believe the weather reports about an inch of rain."

"I won't," I assured him. "I was… Are you *really* eating that for breakfast?"

"What's wrong with it?" Anthony glanced at his tray. It held a cinnamon roll, a bowl of cereal, and a glass of milk.

"There's no ascorbic acid! Ever heard of Vitamin C?"

"Oh." Anthony examined his plate again. "Why is Vitamin C so important?"

"A lack of Vitamin C can cause scurvy," I told him. "But I just came over to ask if you wanted to sit with us,"

Anthony shrugged. "Sure. If it's okay with all of you."

"It's fine," I said.

Anthony picked up his tray and followed me to our table. Shaking my head disapprovingly, I set my second glass of orange juice on his tray.

"Drink this," I ordered. Anthony obligingly took a sip. Lyvia and Shay looked unabashedly at him. I suddenly wished they wouldn't. He seemed uncomfortable enough.

"So, Anthony, what do you think of the weather prediction for tomorrow?" I mentioned the weather only to get some sort of conversation going. "Is it really going to stay snowy? Because Carrie proposed a ski trip at the last staff meeting and she wanted it to be sometime this week."

"Who?" Lyvia sounded exasperated as she slammed her magazine down on the table. "I hate it when you do that! Who's Carrie?"

"Ms. Keen."

"I don't really know yet," Anthony said. "Probably. Maybe another one or two inches tomorrow. That would be good, only I think it's going to be really light and fluffy."

"Oh. Why?" I asked.

"Well, for one, it's getting colder, and the colder it is, the smaller the snowflakes." He said this like it was obvious to every person in the world.

"Of course." I gave up trying to understand the weather and instead listened to Shay and Lyvia talk about how much fun a skiing trip would be for the last fifteen minutes of breakfast.

I noticed Anthony was fidgety during seventh period.

Rain

We changed classes seventh period depending on the day of the week, and that Monday we had a cooking lesson. Not anything stupid like how to make microwave soup (we'd done that in second grade), but a real survival cooking lesson. Mr. Barton gave each of us four random wild ingredients and, with the help of a knife and a stove (in a weak representation of fire), we had to make a substantial meal.

I'd gotten the inside wood of a tree, ten heads of morel, eight ounces of chives, and two robin's eggs. Mr. Barton said my meal was amazing. I fried the eggs with chopped-up chives, but I didn't fry the morel so less water substance would escape. Mr. Barton also added that it was good to make the meal appealing (like I did) since it would help anybody else who might be with you to eat more. "Except for the disgusting tree wood, of course," he added. "But you could always eat that yourself." Then he'd moved on to Lyvia, who'd gotten a dead squirrel as one of her ingredients.

I had enjoyed the lesson, but Anthony seemed like he wanted to get out of there as soon as possible. The moment Mr. Barton told us to clean up, Anthony dumped his already gathered garbage into the trashcan and was out of there. I'd been done for a few minutes, so I picked up my workbook and followed.

"Hey! Wait up!" I called. Anthony stopped ten yards down the hall from me. I sprinted to where he stood, but as soon as I reached him, he began walking again. "Why are *you* in such a hurry?"

"I want to check my email."

"Why?" I asked as we started up the stairs.

"To see if my dad has written. I haven't heard from him in a while."

"Oh." Anthony often left me little else to say. I climbed the stairs two at a time to match his pace. He didn't object when I trailed him into room 716. Watson didn't have strict room policies. Mostly it was no boys in girls' rooms or vise-versa after eight in the evening. There were a few other restrictions, but it was mainly how lenient the teacher was–*if* he or she walked in on you. No one was going to make a fuss over ten-year-olds. Anyway, ew.

Anthony booted up his laptop and I sat on the edge of his armchair. Apparently Anthony, like me, had his own room.

It felt weird sitting there and not talking. "So what ingredients did you get?" I said to break the silence.

"Ingredients from in and around a deciduous forest. I was lucky. Horn of Plenty, parsley, brook trout, hazelnuts."

"What'd you do with them?"

"I made the parsley and hazelnuts into a salad. I didn't cut up the mushrooms, so I'd save the moisture."

Hmm. Smart kid. Wait a minute! "What about the fish?"

"Chopped it up raw," Anthony said, almost grinning. "Quicker, easier, less moisture wasted."

I made a face. "*Raw?*"

"Yeah. Ever had sushi?"

"Nope. Never felt the appeal to risk disease to eat a slippery piece of pathogen-ridden mush."

"It's good in restaurants."

"Never had it," I maintained.

"That's because you've never been anywhere but here."

"Not true! We go to the beach in the summer, and skiing, and…" I trailed off, seeing his point. I'd never *known* anything else. Everywhere else I'd gone was with the school. So? It didn't matter to me.

Anthony turned his attention back to the computer screen. After a few minutes he bit his lip and closed the laptop.

"What's the bad news? Fire? Bankruptcy? Moving?"

Anthony shook his head. "Nothing."

"Something."

"Just shut up, okay?" Anthony pressed one hand to his forehead, hiding his eyes. I raised my eyebrows.

"Sorry."

He shook his head. "I didn't mean that. I meant...nothing. He didn't write. No big deal."

I almost said, "Really? It sure looks like a big deal", but stopped myself in time. He obviously didn't want to talk about it.

Anthony was great at everything that had to do with weather, but he was best at storms. Ms. Keen would ask a question and Anthony's hand would be the first in the air. Or if we were doing games or speed-question rounds, Anthony would have the perfect answer in less than a second. We timed him. His best was negative two-tenths of a second from the time the question ended to the time he started giving the (correct) answer.

"What kinds of clouds have thunderstorms?"

"Cumulonimbus."

"What is thunder?"

"The sound created by the fast expansion of air suddenly heated by lightning."

"True or false? Lightning bolts can have temperatures hotter than the surface of our sun."

"True."

The Thursday of that week Ms. Keen explained to (the rest of) us how humans could sense lightning before it touches down.

"It's the weirdest sensation, a prickling, almost, on the back of your neck," she said. "Okay, who thinks they can demonstrate the position to get in if you're, let's say, in a field during a storm and you know lightning is going to strike?"

Of course, Anthony's hand was the first one in the air.

Ms. Keen smiled. "Anthony, let's give someone else a

try." Her tone implied the ending 'just for kicks'. "How about you, Kent?" she said, calling on one of my least favorite kids in the school. Kent was one of those annoying, egotistic jerks who still maintained that girls had cooties and were worse spies than boys. Which only went to show how much of an idiot he was.

Kent collapsed on the floor, lying sprawled on his back. I could see Anthony shaking his head before Kent was even all the way down.

"If you're like this you're not the highest thing in the field anymore." Kent smirked at Anthony across the room.

"*Hmm*," Ms. Keen said. "Kent, stay like that, for a minute, please. Anthony, could you show us what you had in mind?"

In response Anthony dropped to a crouch in between his desk and mine, wrapping his arms around his knees and tucking his chin to his chest. He balanced on the very tips of his toes.

Ms. Keen's smile broadened. "Good. Now, if these two were both in the field when the lightning hit, depending on how close and how powerful the lightning was, Anthony may never walk again."

"Ha," Kent whispered.

"But," Ms. Keen went on, walking over to Kent, "Kent, on the other hand, may never do *anything* again, and we'd all be planning a funeral right now."

"*What?*" Kent jumped to his feet. I saw Anthony grin into his knees.

The next Tuesday was when the dump truck hit. I'd made up that analogy when I was five, the week after I heard the news about my mom. It was perfect. Bad news was just like a dump truck, backing into you by mistake. And, sometimes, on purpose. First it hits you, and before you can absorb the shock it dumps its entire load on you so you collapse. Depending on the news, the dump truck could be carrying sand to bury you but not really hurt you, or it could be carrying bricks to bury you *and* leave a few bruises for good measure.

We were in science again. Anthony was grinning since he'd just won a double speed game of around-the-world about the atmosphere. I was settling back on the top of my desk for the next game, determined to make it to round three this time, when Shadow appeared in the doorway. He spoke to Ms. Keen for a moment, then called, "Mr. Luther? Can I...may I speak with you?"

I studied Shadow's face. There was a crease in the center of his forehead, his thin brown hair stuck to his sweaty brow, and his eyes were half-squinting in apprehension. A total dump truck face. Anthony's look of excitement vanished and was replaced by an anxious expression. *He's expecting something bad to happen,* I thought.

Anthony slowly made his way to the door. After a second's hesitation, I followed. Ms. Keen and Shadow both glanced at me, but neither one said anything.

Shadow walked silently toward his office. I fell into step beside Anthony. He didn't look at me. Instead, his hand curled around the bottom of his shirt like I'd seen him do the first day I ate breakfast with him. I wanted to say something, but at the same I time I found myself unable to speak. It was as if Anthony was a rubber band stretched near the breaking point, and anything I said would cause him to snap.

I stopped when we reached the office. A quick glance from Shadow told me I probably shouldn't go in with them. Under other circumstances I might have ignored him, but that day I did what I was supposed to do.

Shadow laid a gentle hand on Anthony's shoulder and led him inside. Anthony pulled his arm away, staring at

Shadow like he was a total stranger. At that moment I felt terrible. I must have been getting sick.

I sat down against the wall on the right of the door to wait. It was about seven minutes later when Shadow slipped out of the office.

"What happened?" I demanded in a low voice as I scrambled up from the floor. Shadow opened his mouth as if to speak, then closed it again. He gave me a long, serious look. I couldn't tell if he was sad or somber or upset, or if he was deciding whether or not to be angry with me. I raised my eyebrows in confusion.

"Amber...." Shadow let out a deep breath. "I just had to tell Anthony that his dad passed away last night."

I gaped, the sick feeling in my stomach deepening. Apparently Shadow noticed.

"I know. That's how I feel, too. But I can't...I'm not good at the whole comforting thing. I was wondering...since you...." He stopped again and stared at the wall behind me. "Since you know...what it's like...if you could...help Anthony...."

"Me?" I squeaked. "You think *I'm* good at that sort of stuff?"

"Can you try?" Shadow turned his gaze back to me. "Please? I know...that you can do it."

Shadow had always been more like a principal than an encouraging parent to me. I couldn't gather my thoughts for a moment. Then I shook my head. "I can try. But if it doesn't work, don't make me do it any more."

"Deal." Shadow sighed. "You have my permission to be absent from class. Go somewhere outside, in the fresh air..."

Shadow looked lost in his own world again. Giving me one last look, he retreated into the main office.

I saw the doorknob turn and Anthony stepped through the doorway. He stopped when he saw me standing there, and his hand instantly went to cover his eyes. I'd already seen them, though; they were red.

"Hey," I said, cringing at how awkward I sounded. Anthony stared at me from under his forearm. After a moment I continued. "Um…we don't have to go back to class."

"We don't?" Anthony's voice sounded thick, like he was speaking with a mouthful of cotton. I shook my head.

Shadow's voice intruded on my thoughts. *Go somewhere outside.* As I clenched my teeth I was struck by an uncharacteristic epiphany. I knew a perfect place. But I hesitated. It was my place, the old section of the wall out behind the piles of bricks and fencing that were used years ago when the building was a juvenile detention center. Now the school was a "Private Institution", but it still had enough reputation to keep normal people away. I went to the old wall to practice techniques I glimpsed when watching Red Group, or to read, or just think. I wasn't sure I was willing to share….

My contemplation lasted only a second. When I saw the obvious pain on Anthony's face, my defenses crumbled. I was pathetic, knocked to the floor with one blow, one *look*. I sighed.

"Do you want…to go…for a walk?" I was carefully choosing each word, like I was tiptoeing across an enemy hallway, testing each step for noises before I put my foot down (third grade, unit five).

It took Anthony a moment to reply. "I don't really want to do anything," he said, sounding somewhat like his usual frank self. "I honestly just need to get away from everyone."

"Okay." I felt uncomfortable, unsure if I was included in that 'everyone'. It was harder than I thought, watching the bricks from the dump truck slowly taking their toll. So I silently beckoned for him to follow me to the door. It was worth a try.

We stepped out onto the yard. The air was crisp and the April sun struggled to eliminate the lazy, drifting clouds. The light that did reach the grass gave it a yellowy, alert look. In other words, it was too cheerful.

I led Anthony around the building and out along the path towards the edge of the property. As we walked, Anthony strained harder against the weight of the bricks, or maybe they were even boulders this time, until he was struggling to even walk in a straight line. I was relieved when we reached the wall and grudgingly pleased that it was an ideal location. The old junk, like dilapidated desks, outdated refrigerators, and an old yellow teeter-totter, shielded the four-foot ledge from view of the school, and in turn, we couldn't see the school either.

Without invitation Anthony stumbled to the brick and cement wall and collapsed against it, sliding down like I had by Shadow's office. He pulled his knees to his chest and dropped his forehead to them, wrapping his arms around his legs to finalize the movement.

Once again, I didn't know what to do. When a minute passed without Anthony lifting his head, I slowly sat down in the powdery dirt five feet in front of him. I didn't know if Anthony was crying or thinking or trying to push away the boulders. I knew he would, eventually; I had as a five-year-old, hadn't I? But I knew it would also take time and pain and a whole lot of waking up. I felt a strange helplessness as I watched the uneven rise and fall of Anthony's shoulders. And indecision. Should I help him? Comfort him? Do nothing?

It was like that for fifteen minutes. Then twenty. It was going on twenty-five when Anthony finally raised his head and scrubbed at his eyes with his palms. I still saw the streaks tears had left on his cheeks. Then he slowly lowered his arms and stared at the ground. His dark red hair was a jumbled, carefree mess that stood out in huge contrast to the anguished pools of ultramarine that were his eyes.

I knew it wasn't really like that. It was impossible for eyes to actually look that animated, that extremely sad. But I guess my mind couldn't help imagining it, couldn't help comparing it to the hollow pain I'd felt five years ago.

"He knew it."

Anthony spoke so quietly I wasn't sure I was supposed to have heard. I didn't respond, allowing him a way out, but he went on, getting slightly louder.

"He must have known he was too sick, despite those stupid optimistic doctors. That's why he brought me here, somewhere I'd be safe. Surrounded by all these...all these amazing fighters and strategists. He was always concerned about my safety, like I was about to run into trouble around every corner." Anthony shook his head, as if to knock down cobwebs inside his mind.

"Well, Watson is a safe place." I was speaking with the aim of distraction now. "Only a few elite members of the government know about us. Well, them and our counterpart and companion facilities in other locations. All of the parents--well, except yours, I mean--the parents usually went through the school themselves and are involved in Intelligence or Counterintelligence jobs. You know, adult politics and stuff. They want their kids to be a part of their world, so they come here, and in the beginning it's kind of like they're being cared for while their parents are working and stuff, and at the same time they are being taught. Normal people think we're some private academy, religious or correctional or something. I mean, it's like the invisible school."

Anthony just stared at me, face expressionless. "What if the kids don't want to be here?"

"Well, they can always choose, when they're older, to pursue a normal career." I didn't see why anyone *would*, though.

"The way things work here, it's just weird." Anthony's voice was uncharacteristically harsh. "It's so different from my old school. I heard kids here talking about old students who actually died. And now it's supposed to be my home. Because my dad is dead." He swallows. "Oh, god, he's dead."

I reacted automatically this time and closed the distance between us until I was leaning against the wall right beside him.

"I know," was all I said. Anthony blinked, then nodded.

"That's right, you do," he said, his voice thick again with sorrow. "And you…lived. Did it seem like it at first, though?"

"No," I whispered. "It didn't. You really can't be prepared for it. Maybe it was even easier for me. My mom wasn't around all that often, but when she was…. But it's not like I had a dad to help at all. I don't even know who he is. Maybe he's dead, too." I heard Anthony make a noise in the back of his throat. "But…" I took a few breaths. "You still have your mom, right?"

"I guess." Anthony cocked his head. "Somewhere, I'm not sure where. But yes, I do."

"When you say 'I'm not sure where'…"

Anthony shrugged and traced, tracing a lumpy half-circle in the dirt by his foot. On second look I realized it was a cloud. Anthony marked it with 'sc', then said, "She's working on some project to do with her work, I think. I'm pretty sure I'm not supposed to know about it, though. I get letters about once a year. She mostly asks about me. 'How are you doing, Anthony?' 'Is school okay?' 'Are you studying hard?' 'Noticed any interesting weather patterns lately?' And then I have to send them back to someplace in Europe, but I don't think that's where she is. It just gets passed along, I think…because of that project. But…." Anthony didn't seem like he could go on.

"Tell me about something," I said quickly to avoid

another excruciating silence. And I knew it would help to get him talking about something else. The back of his mind would slowly be registering the news, but he wouldn't be conscious of it. And when he did become conscious of it again, it wouldn't hurt as bad. At least, that was my theory.

Anthony glanced up at me. "Like what?"

"Um..." I looked up at the sky. "I don't know. Something about weather. Tell me if I'm right. Those up there,"–I pointed–"are they cumulous clouds?"

"Yes."

"And those–way over there–are they cumulonimbus?"

"Yes."

"And the ones way, way up there, are they..." I contemplated. I had a good idea they were cirrostratus, but this was getting boring for Anthony. "Well, they're too big to be just cirrus, but too high for... Oh, high! I know, they're altocirronimbus."

"*Altocirronimbus*?" Anthony started laughing. "You've never heard that before, have you?"

"Why, haven't you?" I played along.

"No, partly because... I don't know, they don't *exist*, maybe?"

"Well, they do to me. If they're bigger than cirrus, and very high, there's no law that says it can't be an altocirronimbus cloud."

"No, there is a law," Anthony said with a snort. "It's called the law of science. And besides, cirro clouds are the high ones. Altos are medium height. So what you meant to say was cirrocirronimbus. Which still doesn't exist."

"You know what? I'm getting sick of clouds. Talk about something else, like lightning. How about that."

Anthony's eyes did that widen-and-light-up thing like when anything storm-related arose.

"Lightning! I'm good at that! See, okay, you know what

clouds are–"

"I thought we weren't talking about clouds."

"Well, you have to know this to understand lightning." Anthony settled his legs in a crossed position and swiped his hands across the dirt in front of him to make it smooth. "Clouds are evaporated water and other particles, like ice. During a storm the positive and negative charges in the cloud are separated." Anthony drew another cloud and put a "P" in the top half and an "N" in the bottom half. "The positive charges go to the top, and the negative charges settle at the bottom. Then during the storm they move around, creating buildup and discharge of electricity." He drew some lines around the cloud. "And then the negative leaders from the clouds and the positive streamers from the earth meet and the air glows. That's why you see it. The lightning."

"Do all meteorologists talk in gibberish?" I asked, not even trying to comprehend what he had just said.

Anthony shook his head. "That was a simple explanation! You should hear me about other kinds of storms, like tornadoes, or hurricanes."

"I'd rather not. God, how do you even remember *half* of this stuff?"

"I don't know. I honestly can't *not* remember it once I learn it. It's not like I'm spitting out facts and stuff. I'm *seeing* it inside my head and describing it. Because I can see it and understand it."

"Seriously? That's cool. And slightly weird. But mostly cool. For a meteorology geek, you know."

"Gee, thanks."

Anthony looked down at his knees again. Any other time I would've thought it was impossible for him to be getting bored of weather talk, but that's what it looked like now. And, of course, there were some exceptional circumstances.

I shifted my weight and stopped when I felt them in my

pocket. My emergency Vitamin C drink powder packets. I grinned and pulled them out.

"Here," I said, handing the Cheerful Cherry flavor packet to him. I myself kept the Obsessive Orange. The only thing I didn't like about this particular brand was their terrible taste in alliterations. Or assonances.

"What do I do with this?" He took it and flipped it over to read the back.

"You eat it, dummy." I ripped the top of mine off and threw back my head, draining the powder out in one shake. I swished the stuff around in my mouth a few times, then swallowed. "What's wrong?"

"Nothing, but don't you usually drink these?"

"It won't kill you if it's not watered down. I actually like it better dry anyway. Try it. Come on. Do you want scurvy?"

"No." Anthony fiddled with the 'tear here' cut, then managed to rip off part of the top. He shook a little into his hand and dumped it on his tongue. His expression was downright comical. "Oh my *gosh*!" he cried, and spit into the dirt. "That's *strong*!"

"What did you expect?"

"How did you *do* that? Eating the whole thing at once?"

"I've gotten used to it."

"Thanks for the warning," Anthony muttered, but the corner of his mouth twitched.

"You're welcome. Now eat. You don't get nearly enough Vitamin C as you should."

Anthony tentatively tipped a little more powder into his mouth. He made a face like he was sucking on a lemon (yum), but managed to swallow. "There. Am I good now?"

"No."

"Well, forget it. I'm not swallowing any more." But he contradicted himself and tipped the packet cautiously in his mouth to try again. Then he pocketed the rest of the pack and stared down at his hands.

I bit my lip. Now what to talk about? I really didn't know that much about Anthony, except that his birthday was April 14th, exactly a month before mine. And he loved weather. And was good at other things, and liked dogs, and his dad was dead now, and other stuff. But I knew nothing I could form into a good topic of conversation at that moment.

Luckily Anthony solved the problem for me.

"You're different, Amber."

"Is that supposed to be a compliment?" I asked.

"I'm not sure." Anthony leaned his head back against the bricks. "But, I mean, different than lots of girls I know. For one thing, your name doesn't even begin to describe you."

"Why?" I'd never given much thought to my *name*. I was usually more concerned with my skills and stuff.

"Amber is translucent. It has color, sure, but you can see right through it, everything about it. Even the little bugs in the center. You're not like that at all. I never can guess what to expect. You're like..." Anthony's eyes slid shut. After a minute he said, "You're like a melon."

"That's just about the weirdest analogy I've ever heard. Why am I like a *melon*?" I was wondering if he was nuts. It wasn't very often–well, actually, never–that someone compared me to a popular fruit. Most often I was being compared to a bomb or something.

"Because no one can see past your shell. Metaphorically. You put up a barrier so nobody sees the real you, inside, unless they get past the skin, like on a melon. But inside, you're different. Like, you can be sweet. Or sour. But still different." Anthony opened his eyes and glanced sideways at me. "I know. I'm going to call you Melon from now on! Mel for short, so it's not too weird."

I was still trying to work out the first part. I wasn't sure, but it seemed like an insult to me. I spit back the first thing that came to mind. "Well, if 'melon' is a nickname that describes me, I guess I'll have to call *you* 'turdmuffin'!"

Anthony raised his eyebrows. I crossed my eyes back at him just as I heard Shadow's voice calling from the back of the school. "Amber? Anthony?"

I opened my mouth to tell Anthony not to run out and give the spot away, but I didn't need to. He had already crawled to the edge of the wall and to the walking track behind it. I followed.

"Let's pretend we've been walking around the track," he suggested. I nodded.

"And when Shadow came out, we were walking on this side of the school so he didn't see us."

"Why do you call him 'Shadow'?" Anthony asked as we assumed a leisurely pace.

"I'm not really sure. He just pops up behind me all the time, like he's my shadow."

"You or everyone?"

"It seems like it's just me."

We rounded the curve and into Shadow's view. He hurried towards us.

"How…" he started to ask, but thankfully thought better of it. "I thought you might want some lunch. But Anthony, if you'd like to go up to your room, I'll send something up.

"Thanks," Anthony said quietly and slipped past Shadow. He walked quickly to the doors and disappeared inside. Shadow turned back to me.

"I thought you were going to stay out of it. At least for a whole hour or something," I said. Shadow ignored me.

"How did it go? How's he doing?" he asked.

"He seems like he's going to be okay. He's sad, but managing," I replied carefully. Shadow sighed with relief.

"Thank you so much. I'm really proud of you," he said, blinking. Another 'encouraging parent quote'. The administration must've been trying some new techniques.

I waited a moment, then ducked past him and headed to lunch. Shadow didn't follow me.

Anthony was the first from our table to arrive at breakfast the next morning. I grabbed my Friday special pancakes and two glasses of orange juice and headed for the table.

"Hello, Mel," he said quietly as I sat down across from him.

"Well, I've decided," I told him. I had. I'd come up with the perfect idea last night as I'd heard the teachers creaking by me outside, no doubt taking turns checking on Anthony. Lucky me had the only room on the third floor right next to the stairs.

"Decided what?"

"Your nickname."

"I get one, too?"

"If you get to label me as a melon it only seems fair I get to tattoo something on your reputation, too."

"I see. So what am I?" Anthony raised an eyebrow.

"Rain. Ray for short, so it's not too weird."

"And what is *Rain* supposed to say about me?"

"That you make everyone's day miserable." I crossed my eyes at him. "And I guess because you like weather, and rain is, like, weather's mascot or something." And because rain can be helpful, like with plants, and can cause some bad things to go away, like droughts. And his eyes were blue. Like rain, I guess. And because of the tears he'd cried the day before when the dump truck had hit. And it just seemed right.

"Ray," Anthony mused. "Well, it's better than *turdmuffin*, at least."

"So glad you approve," I said as Lyvia and Shay sat down. Anthony suddenly smirked at me. "What's with you?"

33

"Guess what I just realized?" he said.

"I'm dying of suspense."

"What?" Lyvia asked. Anthony didn't glance at her, but kept grinning at me.

"Your new name is *Melon Rind*," he laughed.

"Shut up." I stuck my tongue out.

"What's with *Melon*?" Lyvia demanded.

"It's Amber's new name," Anthony said. I groaned as Lyvia snickered.

"So I should call her Melon?"

"Let's keep it at Mel for now," Anthony told her.

"Interesting." Shay tried to catch my eye. I scrunched up my nose at her.

"Well, if you're calling me *Mel*, you have to call him *Ray*," I said.

"When did you come up with these names, *Mel*?" Looking puzzled, Lyvia shook her head. I didn't answer. Neither did Anthony. Lyvia waited a few more seconds, then dove into an account of what happened during seventh period the day before. As she chattered on Anthony caught my eye and gave me a small grin. After a moment's hesitation, I returned it.

2

Two Years and Six Months Later

"Bad news, Mel," someone calls as I head for the all-purpose room. I look over my shoulder and see Ray sprinting towards me, waving a paper in his hand, the stairwell doors swinging shut behind him.

"*There* you are. Sheez, I waited ten minutes for you. It's 8:27 already! We're *supposed* to be in the all-purpose room by now."

"My printer wasn't working," Ray says, catching up to me.

"Does your printer have something to do with the earth-shattering news you're about to tell me?" I ask as we continue down the hallway.

"Yup." Ray hands me the paper. "Read it and weep. I looked it up this morning. I *told* you too much Vitamin C is bad for you! Look! Proof!"

"Lies," I say, hitting the paper with the back of my hand. "I get, like, 1,000 milligrams of ascorbic acid a day and I'm perfectly fit. These people go crazy about 100. Give me a break. Besides, I read somewhere that even 3,000 is good for you. And I *don't* weep."

"You can't argue with the facts!" Ray exclaims, bumping me with his shoulder. "Anyway, I was right as far as our bet goes."

"You want a prize or something?"

"Sure. What do you have in mind?"

"A plaque. A really, really big plaque that we can hang up in the main lobby that says *Anthony Jonathon Luther was*

RIGHT…and nobody cares!"

Ray tugs the paper out of my hand, making a face at his full name. It took me forever to weasel his middle name out of him, but three months ago he finally told me. He hates it. Apparently every male on his dad's side of his family has the same middle name–Jonathon–and Ray hates being lumped with them, even if he never sees them, because they all laugh at meteorologists. And scientists. And engineers. And that's about all I can get him to disclose. But he still refuses to tell anyone else–not even teachers–his full name. He claims he doesn't have to; it's not on his birth certificate.

"I'll take this up with Shadow," he threatens, waving the article in front of him again. I see a grin behind his stern look. I smirk back. *Sure you will.*

"Well, anyway, I'm keeping the evidence." Ray folds the article and pockets it as we push through the doors into the all-purpose room. "Aw, great. It's another separated activity."

The all-purpose room has rows of chairs on the floor, separated into halves by a line of tape on the floor. Two signs lead boys to the left and girls to the right.

"See you on the other side, Rain-cloud," I say, walking off in the indicated direction.

"Same." Ray heads to the left. Before he's five yards away he looks back and calls over the chatter of the other students, "Expect scattered showers around mid-afternoon."

I give him the okay sign, and, shaking my head, continue on to the right. Shay's saved me a spot next to her at the end of the second row.

"This is the sixth Blue Group activity," she informs me as I sit down. "I've heard rumors that the exceptional students only need to go through ten before they're promoted to Red Group!"

I, of course, already know this.

"And we *are* exceptional." Lyvia flops across Shay's lap,

36

dark eyes looking up at me. Her chocolaty skin looks less radiant than usual under the full glare of the artificial lights above.

Shay grunts and shoves her back into her own seat.

"Ow, jeez, I just fixed my hair!" Lyvia runs her fingers through her ponytail and glares at Shay. Before she can start a five thousand year rant, Ms. Nailor starts speaking.

"Blue Group! Your attention, please?" Ms. Nailor waves our eyes to the front of the room. I glance at the boys' half of the room. Ray raises his eyebrows at me. I cross my eyes back, then look at Ms. Nailor, who's saying, "Are you ready for another activity?"

A cheer rises from the students. Rah, rah, rah. I'll do whatever it takes to get to the Red Group.

"Good." Ms. Nailor fiddles with the microphone on her shirt, then addresses us again. "This activity is an 'undercover research practice', the second one for some of you."

"Aww," Shay grumbles. "I wanted a 'normal' one again. Remember the first activity? At the roller rink? And the exploding soda all over Ray?"

I snicker under my breath, eyes on Ms. Nailor.

"For the new members of the Blue Group"–Ms. Nailor smiles at the small cluster of students sitting in the back row; I remember when that was me–"undercover research is exactly what it sounds like. You go undercover to do your research, meaning you retrieve information without being seen or leaving any traces. This particular activity is taking place in one of five malls. One in Webster, another in Fairport, one in Pittsford, the local mall, and one in Albion. We will divide you into large groups and then into smaller groups. We'll give each small group supplies and specific assignments."

Ms. Nailor pauses and I look over at the boy's side again, taking advantage of the silence. I see Ray is leaning back, watching her with slight interest.

Shay follows my gaze. "Why'd they separate us from the guys?"

"Probably so if we *are* spotted"—unlikely, at least for me—"we'll look like a bunch of friends on a dare. Boys and girls together would look slightly odd, because normal teen girls get weird around guys or something. We don't want the suspicion to snowball."

"Oh."

I finally catch Ray's eye. He shoots me a grin. *Are you ready for this?*

I roll my eyes, mouth twitching. *I* always *am.*

Ms. Nailor calls our attention back to her. "Your chaperones will choose groups and give you your assignments now," she says. Then she hurries from the microphone and into a gaggle of boys already rising from their chairs.

Mrs. Keen and Mr. Klein start moving through the girls. There are sixteen of us in Blue Group. There are twenty-six boys. Ten more boys than girls! Hopefully the numbers will even out in Red Group.

Mrs. Keen smiles as she walks up to us. She's balancing a clipboard. "Ready for your assignment?"

Why do people keep asking this? Everyone should know better by now. I am never *not* ready.

Mrs. Keen continues. "You'll be going with Miss Collins to the mall by Fairport. Your group's assignment will be to find out the year the second-floor bathroom facilities were last remodeled. The month of that year if you can. Extra credit for the exact date they were finished. And if you can find out the construction company they hired, you get a privilege each, like no curfew for a week, skip a homework assignment, et cetera."

Second-floor bathroom, prepare to meet your doom.

"Do we have to go *in* the bathroom?" Lyvia asks.

"That's up to you. You make up your own strategies on this one."

Mrs. Keen gives us our false names, so that on the off chance someone finds and interrogates us we are ready with an answer. Shay becomes 'Allie Sanchez', Lyvia is 'Justine Floyd', and I'm given the identity of 'Jess Carol'.

"Well," Lyvia says once Mrs. Keen's busy talking to Freida and Danielle. "We should introduce ourselves. Hello, my name's Justine. You can call me Teenie for short."

"Good thinking," Shay says.

"I'm sorry, have we met?"

Shay rolls her eyes. "No, my bad. I'm Allie. You can call me Allie. Not Al, not Alison. Just Allie. Do I make myself clear?"

"Quite clear," I say, and before either of them can scold me I add, "My name's Jess. Jess Carol."

Lyvia nods. "Nice to meet you, Allie, Jess. So, why don't you tell me about yourselves? Where do you go to school?" It's a prep question, so we won't be caught off guard in the unlikely event someone asks us. (They'd have to catch us first, meaning it's never going to happen.)

"My mom says I'm not supposed to tell strangers. But it's up by Lake Ontario, you know? Boarding school," Shay responds.

"Eh," I shake my head. "Leave out the last sentence unless someone asks specifically, okay?"

"Bossy."

"What about you, Jess? Where do you go to school?"

"Well, my mom says I'm not supposed to say that either. But I live in Union Hill."

"Oh, so how do you two know each other?"

"Summer camp," Shay and I respond at the same time. Though I'm surprised, and I bet she is, too, we don't show it.

"What about *you*?" I say. "Where do you live?"

"Just a few minutes away. I need a mall nearby. Have you ever hyperventilated? That's how I get when I'm too far from a shopping center," Lyvia responds.

Shay snorts.

"How do you know us, then?" I demand.

"I met you at a gymnastics meet–your sister competes, remember? And then we went shopping the next Saturday and you brought Allie and we've been bff's since," says 'Teenie'. "And you love my three cats, Squirrel, Fru-Fru, and Sparkles."

"Again, don't mention that unless someone asks." Which, again, is less likely than the earth spontaneously combusting.

"She *is* bossy," Shay mutters. How many times have I heard that? About five thousand times, if not more.

"My groups!" Miss Collins waves. The other teachers do the same. I notice Ray walking in the same direction as we are. I catch his eye. *You going to Fairport?*

He glances at Miss Collins, then back at me. *If that's where she's going.* Or something like that. It could've been *what does it look like?*, but I'm pretty sure it wasn't that sarcastic. Sometimes Ray's expressions are easy to read, but sometimes they're hard, like when he's angry, or upset. Or talking about weather. I *never* know what he's saying when he's discussing weather.

"You all look appropriate," Miss Collins says, nodding at us. We were instructed earlier to dress casually, not in our school uniforms, but in something flexible. I'm in my dark gray shorts and tan T-shirt. Lyvia hates my outfit choice, but I told her that tan and gray are the most inconspicuous colors in the spectrum, so she shut up. "Take a moment to ready yourselves."

Vanessa trudges up. "They're making me work with

Jaymee," she whimpers, naming a generically unpopular Blue Group newbie. "How am I supposed to survive this?"

Shay assumes an appalled look. I ignore Vanessa and pull my hair into a low half-bun. It's much harder to tell someone's hair length when it's like this.

Miss Collins calls our group outside to her dark blue minivan. It's the kind with two sets of three seats, so eight people total can fit. Lyvia, Shay, and I slide into the middle, while Ray, Owen Wingard, and Jaymee clamber into the back. Vanessa gives Shay a dirty look for not saving her a spot and climbs into the front passenger seat. Miss Collins hops in the car and backs out.

Shay, Lyvia, and Owen start chattering. Vanessa and Jaymee sit in silence. I'm quiet, too, for a minute, then I twist around in my seat to face Ray who, like me, has a window seat on the driver's side.

"So who are you?" I ask.

"Essel Franklin. My acquaintances just call me Es."

"Very original."

"What about you?" Ray raises an eyebrow.

"Jess Carol. Terrible to meet you."

"Dreadful to meet you, too," Ray replies with a wicked grin.

"I meant horrendous. Horrendous to know you," I edit, not to be outdone.

"Disgusting to be introduced to you." Ray's cheeks are twitching.

"Horrifying to make your acquaintance," I shoot back.

"Appalling to encounter you." Ray starts laughing.

"Repulsive to chance on you!" I laugh, too, at my own masterfulness.

Ray doesn't reply this time, but studies the sky critically. "*Hmm*. The clouds are dispersing."

"Brilliant observation," I say, though I hadn't noticed

until he brought it up.

"I was just thinking…"

"About what?"

Ray looks slowly back at me. "Altocirronimbus clouds."

Though we both laugh, I wonder why he brought it up. It must remind him of the day his dad died. The silence after the laughter confirms it. I shift uncomfortably as the others babble on. Ray studies his fingers, glances at me, then looks back at his hand.

"Are you reading your future or something?" I ask to break the tension.

Ray looks up, one eyebrow arched. *Why would you ask that?*

"I read somewhere that people actually make a living reading other people's palms. It's supposed to tell their future or something of the sort." I give him a look in return. *Yeah, get with the program, Ray.*

Ray laughs. "That's nuts. I bet I could, though." He drops his gaze back to his palm, feigning intense concentration.

"You can't do it to your own hand, dummy," I say.

"Do you have a rulebook or something? You're certainly acting like an expert."

"Forget it."

"No, I want to try. Give me *your* palm." Ray grabs my hand from where it'd been resting by the headrest and flips it over so it's palm up. I catch my breath. Ray raises an eyebrow. "Scared of my amazing powers?"

I glare. "Scared of your not-so-amazing brain, more like."

He sighs. *That's Harsh.*

Then he looks back to my hand and with intense focus, traces the lines on my palm. I try not to tug my hand away, which is the instinct I'm feeling. I'm also feeling like my stomach might disperse along with the clouds.

42

"Ohm…" Ray hums in a mystical voice. "A big storm is coming. Expect a sudden gust to knock you off your feet. It will rain on your spirits for many days. Then it will be overcast for a long time. But the sun will break through! And then the sun will evaporate some water and restart the normal water cycle once more."

"Is *everything* weather to you?" I ask, sliding my hand back into my lap.

"Sort of." Ray grins apologetically. "But I couldn't think of any other way to describe my prescience."

"How about 'I am going completely nuts?' That sounds about right to me," I say.

"What part of the mall will you be in?" he asks, changing the subject.

"Not sure yet. Near the main office somewhere. You?"

"In the food court."

"We'll steer clear."

"We have to steer clear of Vitality, too," Shay adds, leaning over to join the conversation. "That's where Vanessa's going."

Miss Collins makes a tight turn. She looks back.

"We're getting close, guys," she says. "I'll drop Ray and Owen off first, about a block from the mall. Then we'll circle around and drop off Vanessa and Jaymee on the opposite side, and Lyvia, Shay, and Mel, you're the lucky ones who get booted out at the main entrance."

Vanessa groans. I roll my eyes. Shay leans forward and pats Vanessa's shoulder sympathetically. Lyvia keeps on chatting with Owen (her most recent crush).

A few minutes later Miss Collins parallel parks by a sidewalk. Ray and Owen jump out.

"Later, *Jess*." Ray grins at me. *You're going to have an interesting time with Lyvia and Shay.*

"Get lost, *Essel*," I retort, pushing out my jaw. *Go stick*

43

your head in a fountain.

Ray laughs. Owen slides the door closed.

A minute and a half later Miss Collins announces, "Jaymee, Vanessa, this is you."

Jaymee exits the van quickly. Vanessa, on the other hand, climbs out as slowly as possible.

"Hurry up already," I grumble, feeling irritated. With Lyvia as an exception, I'm not that partial to drama queens. It needs to be a conditional trait if you're going to spend your life engaged in espionage.

"I am." Vanessa pouts and slams the door. Then she walks five feet away from Jaymee. Some secret agent.

"You know, Vanessa can be so dramatic, yet she's a terrible thespian," I comment.

Shay frowns. "Have some sympathy, Mel. What if that were you?"

"So what if it were? Even if I *didn't* like my partner, I'd still be a better *agent*."

"You know, sometimes it can be really hard to be friends with you," Shay says, defending *her* friend. "You think you're the best at everything."

I shrug. "Well, I am. So why pretend?"

Lyvia laughs, and after a moment Shay sighs in resignation. "You just wait," she says, attempting some dignity. "Someday you're going to encounter something that'll throw you like the rest of us."

"Until they make catapults that large, I guess I can just relax," I tell her and grin. No one can pitch me anything I can't throw back just as hard. Maybe even harder.

"Okay, ready?" Shay's looking around out of the corners of her eyes. Her recently cut hair falls around her chin, which would give her face a mysterious quality if she were sixteen instead of twelve. Now, though, she looks sort of awkward, and the childlike roundness left in her cheeks creates a sense of innocence. My own face is too sharp to look that way.

Instead of saying the obvious *of course I'm ready*, I say, "Just remember my plan."

"As always." Lyvia adjusts her sunglasses. "Thanks again for not making us go *in* the bathrooms."

"Shh."

"Sorry."

"Good luck, Mel," Shay says, as if I'll need it.

"Don't mess up," I reply.

"Gee. Thanks." Then, with a wave, they veer off towards the main office.

My job is the hardest. Lyvia and Shay are the ones going to find the bathroom information, but that only involves picking a lock and surreptitiously looking through paper files or a computer while no one else is around. We've been doing that since first grade.

I, on the other hand, have to trigger the alarm at Karisma Jewelers. It requires much more focus. One, it's electronic. Two, it's located on the door. It won't be hard, per se, but it will be a slight challenge. Which means a slight bit of fun.

I glance at the alarm and identify its type. If I remember correctly (which I do) we'd learned that this kind of alarm only signals when something is being stolen, not what item it is. And according to the employee code of conduct, the manager will get involved with any shoplifting of high value items. So if a mysterious valuable item is thought to be shoplifted, dear mall manager will be out of his/her office and occupied for the approximately three-point-seven minutes Shay and Lyvia need.

I walk into the shop and veer right along the wall. In front of me is the section with not-so-expensive jewelry, which is convenient for two reasons. One is the fact that it's the kind of stuff a girl my age would be looking at. The second reason is that the security stickers aren't very sticky on the cheap stuff.

I've had this idea for a long time, but have been saving it for something just like this. From my pocket I pull out a green glass marble and tuck it into my palm so it stays while I examine a large mood ring. It's so big that the sticker is across the smooth stone, not wrapped around the metal loop. Slowly, I run my thumb across the sticker, rolling it off the multicolored ring. Then, pretending to find it too flashy (and really...who wouldn't?), I replace the de-stickered jewelry and walk a little closer to the door, my fingers working the sticker onto the marble.

I drop down to tie my shoes. As I do I set the marble by my foot. When I stand up I give it a little tap. It rolls away across the linoleum, headed out to the main area of the mall. I walk away from the entrance now, feigning immersion in a display of beglittered watches. When the alarm goes off, I jump very convincingly.

In the orderly chaos that ensues next I'm able to slip away and find Lyvia and Shay, who are grinning.

"We got what we wanted," Lyv says casually.

"Oh, really," I reply.

"How did you do it?" Shay asks me eagerly as we stop outside a sub shop.

I hold up the marble. I'd found it at the base of a potted plant on my way over and scooped it up. Using my fingernails, I tear off the sticker, rip it in half, and drop the pieces into the nearby trash.

"I don't get it," Lyvia says.

"That's okay," I tell her. "It's an original Mel, so how could you?" Then I grin.

3

Ray knocks on my door at four-o-clock. Usually we do our homework together at the library, or do homework separately and hang out after. It's most often at one of our rooms or our special spot, the old wall behind the junk heap.

I finish tying my sneaker and open the door. "Hi. How was it?"

"Good. I would've told you about it, but Owen was talking about his terrible sandwich the entire ride."

"I know, I had to listen, too." I make a face and step back, letting him in.

"But, other than that, it went okay. Owen and I did fine. The lady taking the orders–what are they called, anyway? Clerkettes?–was really agreeable. We got the list of ingredients easily. And it's *gross*. Do you know how much sugar is in a Gargantuan Cheeseburger?"

"Let me guess–lots?" I say, turning on my TV. The Orange Group faculty gave it to me for my eleventh birthday. As far as I know I'm the only non-senior student who has a personal television set.

"*Tons*. Why are you doing this now?" Ray walks to my bed and sits on the edge while I start stretching. "We have the rest of the day off, you know."

"Days off make you go soft." I glance at the exercise DVD on the screen and switch positions, stretching my triceps now.

"As you've said a million times. Is this a new one?"

"Yeah, Shay got it for me online. It has more upper-body

training." I roll my head before moving straight into right hooks.

Ray watches me for a while, then murmurs something unintelligible.

"What?"

"I said, do you ever do anything for *you*?"

"Excuse me?"

"Do you ever just do something spontaneous, that you like to do? Personally?"

I gesture towards the TV, then resume alternating jabs. "Firstly, I *am* doing something for me." Left jab. "Secondly, this is spontaneous. I was going to do the ab DVD until I remembered this one." Two right jabs. " And lastly, who says I don't like it?"

"I mean, something that doesn't have to do with school, or your career."

Left jab. "Everything has to do with my career."

Ray sighs. "Sorry I brought it up. I've just been noticing lately…" After a minute he resumes. "You need to do something fun. And don't say 'this is fun' because I'm not buying you like to focus on school and work twenty-four seven. I mean…carefree."

Uppercuts now. "Carefree is a synonym for careless; careless is a synonym for stupid; stupid is a synonym for bad. And if something's bad…why would I do it?"

"Never mind," Ray sighs.

I choose a get-out-of-seventh-period pass as my privilege, since our group got the exact dates. Lyvia and Shay have chosen to skip the create-an-electricity-conductor-from-point-A-to-point-B assignment. Though it's easy enough, I'm always up for an assignment. I love getting A's. And seventh period today is all about steaming stamps off of envelopes. I've already read ahead about it, so I happily give my pass to

Ms. Meyer and escape to the empty hallway.

Well, not so empty. "Hey. What are you doing here?" I ask, stopping to let Ray catch up with me.

"I got the bonus on the task. Didn't I tell you that? But anyway, Ms. Nailor's doing some paper-pressing lab and she's in one of her rages again, so I figured today might be a good time to use my extra-credit pass." Ray stops for a breath. "So, yeah. Want to come to my room?"

"Sure. I can do my math homework. And we can get started on Klein's assignment. Or, I can get started, at least. You're already done, aren't you?"

"Yeah," he admits. "It's honestly not that hard for me to write a page on tornadoes. And he already graded mine."

"Let me guess. A?"

"A-plus," Ray replies, jokingly smug.

"Oh, shut up."

"You asked."

We reach the stairs and start climbing. Two minutes later we walk into Ray's dorm. A waft of chilly air washes over me. "Ahh. That feels *so good*," I say, collapsing on the small green couch. "You're so *lucky* to get a room right next to the AC. Mine's next to the water pipes, and they're worse than ever. When everyone got the flu last month all I heard at night was *gurgle, gurgle, gurgle*. It drove me nuts."

"I know," Ray says, flipping open his laptop.

"How?" I demand.

"Because you told me a hundred times. Here, you can use my computer. Hang on..." He clicks something, then hands me the laptop. On the screen is a blank word-processing program.

"Thanks. It's three paragraphs, right?"

"Yeah. How they form, what they do, and some conditions to look out for. Like, symptoms."

"Thanks." I open an Internet browser and search

'tornadoes'. The first page I click comes up with tons of text. I scroll down, scanning the writing for familiar words. After a minute I sigh. "Sheez, does no one in the scientific world speak English? I can't understand anything here."

"What?" Ray looks up from the notebook on his knees.

"Listen to this. *'Tornadoes are created mostly in supercell thunderstorms when a large amount of energy is accumulated. The energy is often a direct result of the condensation in the cloud...'* Yada yada, something about 'condensation nuclei' or whatever. *'600 calories of heat can be released from just one gram of condensed water and another 80 calories can be released when the water reaches the upper part of the cloud and* freezes. *When the temperature of the updraft is released as a result of this it is converted to kinetic molecular...'* Or something like that. *'Energy of...'* What the heck? *'Up and down movement of air...'* And now something about *'subsequently precipitated water'* and condensed and...my god, we're not even at the tornado part." I lean my head back and whack it against the couch. "Ray, translate."

Ray stands up and walks over to the couch. He sits down just two inches from me, leaning in so he can see the screen.

"*Hmm*," he says, then looks up. "Okay, in your paper you might want to throw in some fancy 'gibberish', but here's the simple version: this big supercell thunderstorm has all these water particles bouncing around, going up and down and creating changes in temperature, which causes a buildup in energy. If it's a *really* big thunderstorm, the energy could be, hmm, up to 100 times as powerful as a 20-kiloton nuclear warhead."

"Wow."

"Yeah. So all this energy makes *really* strong updrafts, which create, like, a whirlpool, only with air, inside the cloud. And when that 'whirlpool' is sucked down below the cloud, that's a twister, like we call it. Once it touches the ground, that's where the trouble begins. You know, the damage. I think you can get that part on your own if you want, though. Most of that's in normal-speak. You might want to stay away from any reports on a tornado hitting a meteorology lab. You might be overloaded by words like 'anemometer' and 'mercury barometer'," Ray teases. He slides the laptop back onto my lap.

"Thanks," I say sarcastically, then add in a slightly nicer tone, "thanks."

"Sure. It's not like it's a *challenge* or anything. Well, actually, explaining it to you...*that* is a challenge."

"You know what would be a challenge? Getting your foot out of your esophagus. Because that's where it's going to be if you don't cut it out in point one seconds."

Ray laughs. It's maddening he never takes me seriously. But I'm not exactly dwelling on that, not when Ray's leaning into me, still grinning, his hair tickling my cheek. The blood rushes in my ears. Crap. What's wrong with me? I'm not going to black out, am I? I hope I don't have to see the nurse. She's inordinately aggressive with tongue depressors.

"What's that all about?" Leaning away now, Ray looks at me like my hair's turning aubergine (a word I've unintentionally picked up from Lyvia).

"Um..." I remove my hand from my head, where it was previously massaging my brow. "It helps the blood flow to the brain so I think better." I lower my hand to my lap. "We learned about that in fifth grade. Duh."

"Interesting. But please don't do that anymore. If you were to think you think even better than you think you do, you'd think you think too good. You think that already."

I give up trying to make sense of that. "Okay, I have no idea what you just said, but I *think* it was an insult, so now I *think* you'd better *re*think or I'll *re*consider my offer to displace your leg."

Rain

Ray doesn't respond, just adjusts the laptop again so it's halfway on his knees too. Then he types in a website address and points to the screen. "Here's a good diagram, if you prefer pictures to gibberish."

"The more pictures the better, of course." I move his hand out of the way and open up my tornado essay document. But instead of starting the paper, I type, *so when do u think we're going to get a real End?* I lift my fingers off the keyboard and wait while Ray reads it. I'd sigh wistfully if I were a drama queen. But instead I just allow my eyes to slide past the screen and into nothingness. I'm getting more excited—not to mention impatient—as the days go by, waiting for there to finally be a crime suitable for a Blue Group member to End. My first End. We call them that because that's what we do—we *end* it. The crime. Not that I'd admit it, but I've put off sleep before just to imagine kicking butt and being promoted to Red Group.

when some idiot decides to do something stupid and our teachers realize we're the best blue groupers out there, Ray types.

they have to know that already, I key.

well, no offense, but u get on teachers nerves a lot

does that change the fact that i'm a straight-a student and the best in every subject?

except weather

yeah, well, the weather station is worse at weather than you are.

true

don't get a fat head— oops, too late

you're the one with the fat head

yeah but my fat head's not ugly

you're right, it's hideous

same thing, dummy

u-g-l-y. h-i-d-e-o-u-s. they sound different to me

that's because only you're that nerdy

As soon as I hit the *y* key there's a knock on the door. Then it swings open. Stupid teachers and their master keys.

"What are you kids doing?" Mr. Klein asks, a slight note of suspicion in his voice.

"Plotting a mutiny," I answer, not looking up from the computer screen. "Want to help? There are extra crowbars in the closet." I swear, ever since our birthdays the teachers have gone a little nuts over me and Ray hanging out. Every five seconds one pops in the room. I think Shadow is engineering the whole thing. He's paranoid, I swear.

"No, thanks." Mr. Klein raises an eyebrow and backs out. I glance at Ray's face. I can't tell what he's thinking. His eyes drop after a moment. I stare a second longer, then hit the delete button on the computer and watch our conversation disappear. And sigh.

"I guess I really should start the essay."

"I guess you should." Ray moves back to his bed and picks up his notebook again. I blink at the blank white screen for a moment, then glance at Ray.

"What're you doing?"

"I thought you were starting the essay."

"Please. I can spare a minute. I guess."

Ray writes something, crosses it out, and adds something short to the paper on his lap, then looks back up. "Writing to my mom."

"Oh. And...how is she?" I frown, like I usually do on the rare occasions Ray brings up his mom. I still can't believe that a parent would choose go without seeing her kid for years and years. Especially if that kid was someone like Ray. Meaning, well...his dad is gone, for gosh's sake! His mom should at least *visit*.

"I don't know. I haven't heard from her in a while. I'm going to try the address in Europe she sent with her last letter." Ray's pen hovers above the page for a moment. Then he sets it down, his forehead creasing. "But it's no big deal. I just wanted to make sure my last letter got through."

I know Ray enough to know that if it were no big deal he would've left it at 'I don't know'. So I let it drop. If he wants to talk about it, he will. Or maybe he won't. Either way I'm at a loss. Consolation isn't usually my strong point. Not that I'm *bad* at it. It's just not my favorite.

I sigh again and put my fingers to the keyboard. Better *really* start that essay.

4

"Aren't you excited? I'm excited! You should be excited. I'm so excited!"

I swear Lyvia has said the word "excited" five thousand times already. I'm not looking forward to our first *real* dance, if this is what she gets like for the first (and only) seventh grade "social". It's weird how we're not only divided into groups, but also divided into grades for peer assemblage. It's like, the higher the group you're in, the more advanced the classes are. So not only will Blue Group students be at the social tonight, there'll be some Purple Group kids as well. That's why I'm almost partly looking forward to this evening. I like the feeling of being a step ahead of people.

"I may not be excited, but I am sane," Shay says in response to Lyvia's babbling. "Take a chill pill. It's what, a bunch of kids sweating in a gym with really loud music playing?"

But even as she says this I see her glance at the outfit Lyvia made her lay out on a chair. Lyvia insisted we choose our outfits and congregate in her and Shay's room so we can "primp". That's her wording, not mine. I couldn't care less about "primping".

Lyvia shakes her head, rolling over on her stomach. I launch myself off my back and onto my knees, causing the mattress to bounce.

"Smooth," Shay compliments me, tossing a rubber ball at the wall and catching it as it bounces back. "Did you learn that watching the Red Group again?"

"Yeah. The younger members, at least, during their eighth period yesterday. Did you notice some of the older ones are gone? Three of them went to Switzerland."

"Switzerland? For an *End*?"

"Yeah. I heard Anne and Mark talking about it in the teacher's lounge. Anyway, the three Red Group members–Casey, Maddie, and Veronica–tracked down this con man and were about to close in at a coffee shop in Ozone Park when he disappeared. They spotted him on 678, but there was so much traffic that by the time they got to JFK and located his terminal, the man's flight to Switzerland was in the air."

"They didn't find a way to stop the flight? You would think Red Group could do so much better," Lyvia says.

"No, they chose not to stop him, but to look for him in Switzerland. He obviously wasn't Swiss, so they're going to find out if he has partners or a base over there."

"Are they working with another academy?" Shay asks.

"I don't think so–another reason why they're going. There isn't one we're in contact with over there."

"Cool," Shay says. "It'd be awesome to get an overseas End."

"Especially to Paris," Lyvia adds. "Or Madrid."

"It'd be awesome, period." I sigh and wiggle my fingers. "I swear, I'm never wearing nail polish again. It annoys me so much, not being able to use my fingers. Are they dry yet?"

"Probably," Lyvia says. "I still can't believe you chose *clear*." She wiggles *her* vermilion nails and blows on each finger.

"I wish *I'd* chosen clear." Shay glares at her sparkly citrine fingernails. "I only picked this color to shut you up."

"You guys can be so difficult. Would it kill you to go along with me once in a while?"

"It depends if that includes you smearing gloop all over my face. I'm *not* wearing eye shadow, not matter *what* you say." Shay scowls. Lyvia glares at both of us, then grabs her outfit and stalks to the bathroom.

"Get dressed," she orders. "And I don't care if you complain, I *am* doing your hair!"

This is stupid. I want to kick-flip the idiot teacher who thought this up. Not that a kick-flip is the best option. More like I want to strangle him or her with a tie or headband. Or trap them in a tuxedo. Or–

"Snap out of it, Mel," Lyvia grumbles, glaring at me in response to my less-than-satisfactory sour mood.

"Don't let me stop you from having a good time." I scowl and look around the gym again. The lights are purple and blue, spinning nauseatingly, and the music is killing my eardrums. Maybe the refreshment table will be worth my time. If not, I am going back to my room.

"Oo-kay everybody!" a voice booms. "It's time to open up the dance floor!"

Somehow strangulation doesn't seem sufficient anymore. I can't believe *Mr. Klein* is the DJ. I shake my head in despair. Of course, as the teachers have drilled into our heads a million times this week, it's not a 'slow-dance' floor, it's a 'dance' floor. Like it makes a difference to some crazy people. People like Lyvia, for example.

"Come on, Mel!" Lyvia tugs on my hand. I raise my eyebrows. *Are you kidding me?* But she's not Ray. She doesn't get it.

"N...O," I spell, sliding my hand effortlessly away. Lyvia spares me one last glower before grabbing poor Shay's unsuspecting arm and disappearing into the swelling mass of teens/preteens in the center of the gym.

Not for me.

"Alright, seventh grade, this next song topped the charts for three straight weeks." Mr. Klein continues his "cool"

façade. It's extremely sad.

I meander to the refreshment table. More boys than girls are amassing here, but it hardly matters. As long as I'm *anywhere* but the dance floor.

I bump into someone as I reach for a cream puff. "Hey, watch it," I snap, the evening's tension getting the better of me the slightest bit. Whoops. I should work on that. Something my teachers frequently remind me. "Sorry," I say quickly.

"Oh, I'm used to it." Ray plucks a pastry from the sticky tray and drops it on a plate. "So, have I finally figured it out?"

"What the crap are you talking about, Ray?" I grab a cream puff too and bite into it. Ice cream filling. At least the faculty got *something* right.

"*I trust everyone can follow along with this next song....*"

"Shut up, Mr. Klein," I mutter. "Right, what did you figure out?"

Ray swallows his cream puff, then grins. "The one thing you're not amazing at."

"I'm amazing at everything."

"*This song was nominated for a Grammy....*"

"Then why aren't you dancing?"

"Because dancing's for mental patients."

"*Come on, kids, do the steps!*"

"Admit it, Mel, you suck at dancing."

"Of course I don't. I won five thousand dance competitions in the past year. I just think it's stupid."

"Five thousand? Really?" Ray's eyebrows vanish beneath his bangs. Stupid, shaggy, too-long bangs like the models in Lyvia's stupid, airhead, superficial magazines. "That's thirteen-point-seven competitions a day. I didn't realize you were so busy."

"Multitasking. It's one of my very many outstanding

qualities. Hey...." I narrow my eyes. Ray's good at math, but not *that* good. "How the heck did you know that? Thirteen-point-seven? Where'd that come from?"

"You always use five thousand for everything. Especially when referring to number-of-times-per-year. I finally just calculated the number that would work out to be per day." When my eyes don't relax, he says slowly, "On. A. Calculator." His eyebrows reappear and he laughs. *Two steps ahead of you, Mel.* "You have to stop being so predictable. Speaking of predictions–"

"No one was speaking of predictions."

"Yes, we were. You. Predictable. Anyway. Heavy cloud cover to be expected tomorrow. Probably a lot of precipitation. Perfect time to take out the barometer and psychrometer and anemometer–"

"Not your weather kit again! I hate all those 'ometers'. And I am *not* predictable. *And* I'm in no mood to spend hours watching you watch little glass tubes. How fragile are they, by the way? Like, say I *accidentally* dropped one on the ground. Would the psycho-meter break?"

"*Psychrometer*. And yes. But shh." Ray suddenly holds up a finger. Around us everyone's jabbering over the music. They practically have to yell to be heard. I don't see how my shutting up makes a difference.

"What?" I ask irritably. Then it dawns on me that there might be a situation. "*What?*"

"Why isn't Mr. Klein talking?"

"You call that talking? More like screaming. Yakking. Trying to sound 'funky'." Then his meaning registers. "Oh. Huh. I don't know." I glance across the room to the epicenter of the small earthquake vibrating the building at the moment, a.k.a., the speakers. "It would appear our 'DJ' has stepped out for a mo. Mark Klein has left the building."

"Weird. It seemed like he was enjoying it."

"Yeah, he was enjoying torturing us."

"But," Ray says, turning back to meet my gaze, "all of this is irrelevant. I believe we were discussing your dancing?"

"Can we not?"

"Not until you prove it," Ray says, folding his arms across his chest. His stupid, not-ugly arms.

"Prove what?" I sigh.

"That you don't suck."

"I don't suck. Want me to prove Isaac Newton wrong and send you flying out the window?"

"Oh, you could do that in 50-ton gravity. I'm just curious about your dancing."

"I can dance."

"Then prove it," he repeats. Stupid boy. He knows I can't resist a challenge. Stupid, stupid boy.

"Mr. Luther?" someone suddenly says. "Mel?"

I look around. "Mark?"

Mr. Klein spares me a *look* before addressing us both. "You don't seem to be busy, but perhaps I'm wrong. Would you mind missing the social? We have an assignment for you."

"*Yes!*" I shout. "I mean, no! I mean, whatever I say to come with you! Of course!"

"What she said," Ray laughs. Mr. Klein almost grins and beckons us into the hallway. Ms. Meyer and Ms. Nailor are waiting outside. They lead us to Ms. Nailor's office.

"You think it's an End?" I hiss to Ray. He shrugs and grins. *Maybe. Hopefully.*

"Well, then, down to business," Ms. Meyer says, smiling at Ray and me. She's one of the only teachers not obviously certain that the two of us alone together equals trouble, therefore I give her some leeway. "Now, the two of you obviously work well with each other, that's why we picked you. But before we begin, do either of you object to being

60

partners? This would be your first End, after all."

Yes! *Yes*! It *is* an End! I share an elated look with Ray, then we both shake our heads.

"Good. Now, we'll make this short. You're obviously ready. At the top of every class you take. This will put you one step closer to Red Group–"

My mind seems to freeze. *Red Group.*

"–but nevertheless, we will be sending adult supervision. Mr. Klein has graciously handed over the DJ mike to Miss Collins and offered to come."

Oh, fun. Well, it's still an End!

"Okay." Ray nods.

"Well, here's the lowdown." Mr. Klein–still in hip mode, apparently–pulls out a page with three pictures. A head shot and two profiles. "David Cameron. He was released from a prison in Phoenix three years ago after doing two years for various crimes, the biggest ones being theft and arson."

"At the same time?" Ray guesses.

"You got it. So we've seen him around here. Glimpses on store security cameras and such. Not doing anything wrong…yet. But apparently last week he got into a huge argument with the owner of Chik-n-Wings."

"That tacky fast-food place by Brockport?" I say.

"That's the one. The owner couldn't identify him, but Gabe in Red Group checked out the security videotape on Tuesday and confirmed the man was Cameron. Gabe just reported to us that Cameron has left the hotel he's currently staying in and is heading towards Chik-n-Wings. The hotel is about an hour away from the restaurant."

"Tell us what we need to do, then," Ray says evenly.

"I can already tell you that," I say to him. "They'll tell us to–"

Ray shakes his head an infinitesimal amount. I catch it, but the teachers don't. It's one of Ray's small, but amazing in its category, talents. *Don't interrupt, Mel*, he tells me.

I heed the warning, something I only do for Ray. He can spot when to behave better than I can.

"The objective is to render him unable to escape. The less violence, the better. Anonymously, of course," Miss Meyer says.

"So if we can tie him up to, say, to the building," Ray says. "Or, if we need to, knock him unconscious, then call the police and let them handle it from there."

"Perfect." Ms. Nailor winks at Ray, who she inexplicably considers her absolute favorite student. *He* absolutely hates it, since it's cost him hours of listening to "You're such a suck-up" from me, though he never does anything to get off her good side.

Mr. Klein motions our attention to him. "Now, I want the two of you to get changed into…hmm…Mel, your dark red–"

"Garnet," I mutter.

"–technical sweat suit. And Ray, that gray one? Not the light one, the–"

"Pewter?"

"Yes, thank you, Mel," Mr. Klein shoots me a *shut-up-or-die* look. I cross my eyes back. "The *pewter* jogging outfit. With the matching sunglasses. And Mel, I want you wearing a hat. And…"

"No!" I pull my mouth down in a grimace.

"…makeup."

I moan in agony. "*Fine*."

"I want you back here in ten minutes, changed and ready." Mr. Klein motions for the door.

"Ten whole minutes? You don't need to be so generous," I say crossly. "I'm not in Yellow Group. I could be back in seven."

"Fine, then." Miss Meyer grins. "I'll be timing you."

"Great." I leap up and race to the door. I hear Ray's chair scrape on the floor as he also gets up. "I'll be done before Ray," I call over my shoulder, grinning in a special challenging-Ray way. "Make-up and everything!"

I sprint lightly to the stairs (it makes less noise and isn't as stressful on your legs: first grade, unit two) and take them one at a time, but quickly (it takes less force per stair: also first grade, unit two).

I'm glad I'm so sensitive to my surroundings. It helps me not slam right into Shadow as he steps out from behind the stairwell doors as I push through to the third floor.

"Amber," he says. I swear, Shadow's the only one who still calls me that.

"Um...yes? I really, really am in a hurry," I say, starting down the hallway again. "Can you tell me later or something?"

"No, wait." Shadow catches my arm. He glances down the hallway and back quickly and says in a low voice, "Look, the faculty obviously think you're ready for this End. But please consider waiting."

I momentarily forget my hurry. "You think I can't *do* it?" I say accusingly, angrily.

"No, I *know* you can do it." Shadow shakes his head. "But you don't...I mean..."

"No!" I yank my arm away. "I *am* going! I *can* do it. I'll prove it to you!"

"Don't get mad," Shadow pleads. "It's just..."

"It's just you think I'm a baby!" I stomp my foot down on the carpet. "Stop treating me like I'm in Green Group!"

That doesn't anger Shadow. Instead, he smiles. Not in a mean way, or in a ha-ha-I'm-going-to-get-what-I-want-anyway way, he just...smiles.

"I have to go," I say stiffly.

"Well, then, promise me you'll be careful."

"I always have to be," I mutter. "But, duh, I mean, I'm not suicidal. Sheez. Now can I go? *Please*?" I add sarcastically.

"You may go," Shadow murmurs, then disappears down the stairs. I check my watch. Crap. That cost me thirty-seven seconds.

I sprint the rest of the way to my room.

5

I arrive five seconds over seven minutes. Ray laughs and doesn't buy it when I insist it's Shadow's fault.

"You're just mad I arrived ten seconds before you," he says as we walk out into the evening. Mr. Klein had instructed us to get in his car while he gathered last minute information.

"In a million years," I scoff, and look around, excitement clenching in my lower abdomen. I finger the lump in my pocket that contains two plastic strips, much more compact and effective than handcuffs. "How are we supposed to get *into* Mr. Klein's car?"

Ray holds up his hand and swings the key chain on his thumb in circles.

"Are those his keys? Be still, my heart."

"He gave them to me five whole seconds before you showed up. He said you were too late."

"I'm sure."

"It's true." Ray walks ahead to Mr. Klein's little white sports car and opens the door. He slides in the back and pats the seat next to him. I swallow, shake my head to clear it, and sit down.

"Be very quiet," Mr. Klein says in a low voice, unlocking the back door of Chik-n-Wings. We walk (noiselessly) inside. Mr. Klein beckons Ray and me towards the back of the dining area. He tiptoes ahead, looking around. "This is the safe." He motions to a picture just inside the carelessly unlocked manager's office. "It's–"

"–Behind the portrait?" I finish. Mr. Klein glares at me. "Just a guess," I whisper innocently.

"Let's settle in," says Mr. Klein through semi-clenched teeth.

We get ourselves positioned in a shadowy booth out of the direct line of vision for anyone standing someplace other than directly across from us.

Frowning slightly, Ray glances over at me. *Convenient, isn't this?*

Almost too much, I nod. *He'll obviously look here, right?*

"Remain alert," Mr. Klein warns. I shift my gaze to the door. Ray watches the safe intently. Mr. Klein's eyes dart around.

It's almost an hour later. I'm glad I have the gift of patience. Lyvia would've been screaming by now. Or gone insane. I feel only slightly crazy. No, jumpy would be a better word. Ray, on the other hand, has hardly moved except to share a look with me about half an hour ago.

Five minutes tick by on the clock. The hands are shaped like feathers.

Ten minutes. The rest of the clock is shaped like a mushroom. A mushroom with feathers? Insane.

Like me. I *will not* lose concentration.

Fifteen.

Finally. My eyes relocate as I hear the sound of a bolt cracking on one of the windows. Ray shifts, but continues staring at the safe. Mr. Klein breathes, "Freeze."

A man climbs swiftly in after detaching the screen. As he straightens up, I blink. The intruder doesn't match Cameron's profile, yet this man is supposed to be Cameron. A suspicion clicks in my mind. Cameron's not the guilty one, only the one blamed. I can hardly stop a grin at my ingenuity.

Mr. Klein hits something on his cell phone. I know

enough that he's just sent a text message (convenient things) to the school. Soon the police will be summoned. We'd better get a move on if we want any action.

The-man-who-is-not-Cameron walks lightly to the safe, dropping a briefcase on the ground. Mr. Klein catches our eyes. Quickly, he points at the briefcase, then touches his wrist together to indicate the plastic strips.

Go, he mouths.

My heart nearly explodes into my mouth. But I swallow it back. This is it.

I slide silently out of the booth. TMWINC (acronyms make things so much easier) is busy with the safe's lock, just inside the office door. I dash for the briefcase and pick it up. Mr. Klein stands by the booth, ready to interfere. As if.

I sprint lightly back and deposit the briefcase with Mr. Klein. Ray nods in my direction. I think he's trying to communicate *I'll handle the plastic strip*. But a shadow hides his face, so I can't tell.

Now TMWINC glances back. He catches sight of us and leaps away from the safe. Ray's fist clenches. I'm sure he's swearing silently, and I join him. This complicates things.

But since when are complications a problem for me?

I move forward as Ray does. It *would* make it harder to put on the strips if both of us were over there, but I'm not waiting around if there's going to be a fight.

I half-crouch, ready, as TMWINC stares at Ray, probably in shock. That's another thing we have going for us—shock. Who expects kids? Or, teenagers, I correct myself.

But enough about that. My mind zeros in on the situation. I analyze TMWINC's face, waiting for a sign he's about to run, or, better, charge.

"If you give yourself up it will go easier when the police arrive," Ray says in a low, even voice, raising a plastic strip into view.

Rain

"Are you going to stop me?" TMWINC sneers and takes a step forward. "With your little piece of plastic?"

"If I have to," Ray responds. TMWINC's gaze flicks towards Mr. Klein, then back at Ray. Fury washes over me. What, I'm not good enough to be a threat? I tense. I'll show *him*.

TMWINC decides to act. He jumps towards Ray, swinging back his fist. I think he's pretty surprised to find Ray behind him, totally unharmed, when his fist whistles through air. I move closer and watch for a chance to join. It's better not to jump right in if I don't have to come to a defense. I can plan for a second. As I analyze the best way to get TMWINC's arms behind his back, the perpetrator throws another punch. Ray blocks it and pulls on TMWINC's arm. He stumbles. And glares. Boy, if looks could kill. I can't wait now, not when he's so angry. I rush at TMWINC as Mr. Klein moves closer. TMWINC tries to send me flying by thrusting out an elbow, but I catch it and spin him around, using his weight as a weapon. Weaknesses are so lovely when they're in an opponent.

"You're…just…kids," TMWINC gasps.

Teenagers, idiot. Before he can make another move I fling his wrist around to his back, and Ray grabs the other arm at the same moment. "Are you going to say this is just justice?" I ask as Ray quickly slides the strip onto TMWINC's hands. I see Mr. Klein nod approvingly. Just as he opens his mouth to speak, TMWINC moves.

Obviously he's not done.

Obviously he needs more persuasion. Gritting my teeth, I move around to his other side in less than a second, preparing to get him from the front as he tugs one arm free of the not-yet-fully-secured-strip. Then TMWINC yanks his other arm from Ray's grasp and the strip swings loosely on his right wrist too.

Ray makes a frustrated noise and begins to duck down to use "tackle-a-bigger-guy-move-three". TMWINC has other ideas. He puts his hands together and raises one, holding it flat. I see something glint on it. Mr. Klein starts forward in confusion, then panic, as TMWINC swings his hand down at Ray. Ray easily lifts a hand to block the attack.

And screams.

Automatically I spring forward, my mind only focused on one thing: Ray and TMWINC's hands, which are still connected. They could've been giving a bizarre high-five. But Ray wouldn't have screamed.

Shouldn't have screamed.

Something crashes into me and yanks me away. I twist around to find Mr. Klein's arms holding me back.

"Let go!" I shriek, kicking backwards. TMWINC doesn't look up. Ray's knees buckle and he drops to the floor, yanking his hand from TMWINC's. Something dark spatters on the linoleum.

"*Let me go!*" I yell again. How can Mr. Klein do this to me? I can take care of myself. I need to help Ray! Why isn't Mr. Klein *doing* anything? How can I make him let go if he knows all my moves? Has *taught* me all those moves?

TMWINC stays where he is for a moment, then backs up, grabs his briefcase and races for the door. Halfway there he skids to a stop. Flashing red-and-blue lights permeate the darkness in the restaurant. I barely notice TMWINC's form leaping out the window. Who cares? Who cares when Ray is…Ray is….

A moment later two police officers rush in. I finally manage to throw Mr. Klein off. He runs forward, calling out something I don't listen to. I stumble to Ray.

He's kneeling on the ground, clutching his forearm, his eyes squeezed shut in what's obviously pain. His left palm is dripping blood from four parallel gashes. As I crouch down by him, he lets out a moan that quickly turns into a cry and slips down even lower, doubled over. His hand is turning white and shaking uncontrollably.

"Ray!" I whisper, then louder, "Ray!" I reach out and brush his arm.

He opens his mouth to speak, but a shudder racks his entire body and all that comes out is a frantic gasp.

"Help!" I yell, staggering away. "*Help*!" How can the adults care about TMWINC? When something here is wrong...seriously wrong....

I dash toward the four men and slam into a policeman.

"Help!" I choke, grabbing his arm and yanking him with all my force over to Ray. Mr. Klein sprints after.

"What...?" The police officer exclaims, kneeling. Mr. Klein blanches and he pulls out his cell phone. In a few second's he's talking to a 9-1-1 operator. I hear the word "ambulance" before I tune out and focus on Ray.

"What can we do?" I ask. I sound small. And young. But for once, I don't care.

"I...what *is* it?" the officer says. "Can you sit up?" he asks Ray frantically.

Whether in response or not, Ray's arm suddenly convulses. With a cry he collapses on his right side, curling up, still clutching his left arm, only at the shoulder now. My fingers contract around my knees. I feel trapped. No, worse, I feel helpless. Utterly helpless. I'm *supposed* to help people. But all I can do is watch. I suck. I *suck*. Please, let the ambulance come, please let the ambulance come, please, let it come now!

The officer takes Ray's pulse. Ray doesn't seem to notice. Then the officer reaches gingerly for the injured, bone-white hand. As soon as he touches it Ray screams, and his body shudders again. I scream too and fall back in shock. My mind shouts at me to look away, but I can't tear my eyes from my friend. On the ground. In pain. Lots of pain. Too much pain.

After too many agonizing minutes I hear the wail of the ambulance. My shoulders slump in relief. Mr. Klein hurries out to meet the paramedics. A moment later I scramble out of the way as two rush in with a stretcher. Ray cries out again as he's placed on it. The EMTs force him to lie flat. I watch numbly as he's whisked out. Mr. Klein hurries after.

"Hey," I say, then heave myself to my feet and sprint after them. "Hey! What about..." I push through the doors. Ray's stretcher is being loaded into the back of the ambulance. Mr. Klein follows the paramedics inside. "Wait!" I start after him, but someone catches my arm.

I yank away roughly. "*What*?"

"Don't be unreasonable," Shadow says.

"Where did you come from?" I yell, backing away. "And don't tell me what to do! I'm going to the hospital. You can't stop me!"

"No, of course not," Shadow says. "We're going in my car. Come on."

"No."

"*Yes*, Amber, come on." I can see Shadow's agitated, but I still duck away when he reaches for my arm again. The ambulance starts driving away.

"Wait..." I say, my voice trailing off. Shadow takes the opportunity to lead me to his sedan. "Straight to the ER," I whisper. Shadow nods. "As fast as you can." He nods again. I turn and stare, dazedly, out the window.

We can't get there fast enough.

6

I almost break something–preferably a chair or one of the really large, floor-to-ceiling windows–when the doctors decree that no one can come in to see Ray. A nurse talks to Shadow for a minute, then disappears into the forbidden corridors. I dig my nails into my palms. When they start bleeding, I sit on my hands. That doesn't work either, so I settle for flexing my fingers on the wooden armrests of the pitifully uncomfortable seats.

A woman rushes into the waiting room. She spots Shadow and immediately starts talking a hundred miles an hour. "Mr. Syme? I'm Annette Robar. I got your call–"

"You're Anthony's aunt, right?" Shadow stands up. So does Mr. Klein.

"Yes. I came straight over. What happened? I've been worried sick. Can I see him? How bad is it?"

"No one is allowed in," Shadow says quietly. "The nurse says they can't tell what happened at the moment. The doctors think it's some sort of...poison." My blood freezes. "He's been given a sedative, but–"

A doctor opens the forbidden door and walks quickly to Annette Robar and the two teachers. "Are you the ones with the boy?"

I get up and inch closer.

"Yes," Mr. Klein responds quickly.

"I'm going to ask you to come with me," the doctor says quietly, beckoning the adults to the door. I follow. The doctor's gaze lingers on me as we file in. I stare back up at him with a *Yessss?* look. Stupid doctor. Unless he saves Ray.

Another white-uniformed doctor strides up.

"How is he doing?" the first one asks.

"Not good," the second one responds quietly in an almost-but-not-quite-British accent. If my brain weren't so stressed I could figure out what nationality the accent is (fourth grade, unit six) but my mind is latched onto the words. *Not good.* The doctor lowers his voice even more, but I can still hear. "He didn't respond to the first antidote. The whole left side of his body is numb now."

"Oh…" the first doctor says. I feel dizzy.

"Maybe you should leave," Shadow whispers, right behind me as usual.

"*No,*" I reply.

"I think our best chance is to…" the second doctor trails off. "I have some contacts where he might be helped. It's a long way off, though."

"Whatever-it-takes," Annette Robar speaks up. Shadow takes her elbow and leads her out of the doctor's earshot, not that they're listening. They're busy discussing something under their breath.

"I think it would be wise," Shadow says, "to not tell them Anthony's identity. His dad had specifically requested…"

"Of course," Annette says and nods. "I can…" She, too, lowers her voice. All I see is Shadow nodding. I turn back to the doctors as Annette approaches them. "I'm willing to do whatever it takes," she says again, "and as quickly as possible."

"Come with us, then, if you are–are–"

"John," Annette whispers.

"–John's parent?"

"Guardian," she says as she hurries off with the doctors. I only have room for a small amount of confusion. Wouldn't

Ray's mom be his guardian? But how can I even think about that now? I lean against a nearby desk, feeling dizzy and (mostly) sick. Maybe I need a doctor too.

"Let's go to the waiting room." Shadow guides me back to the land of uncomfortable chairs. I sit down, trembling.

And wait.

An hour later we hear the news that Ray's being flown in a private, and better yet, express, jet to this place the one doctor claimed might help. "Where?" I whisper, but no one hears me. I try one more time before collapsing back in my seat. My eyes slide closed. I try to force them open, but suddenly feel someone's arms around me, lifting me up. It feels nice.

"Go to sleep," Shadow's voice says, miles away, offering me a chance to escape the present. Without conscious permission, I let myself relax against him and let the steady motion of walking take me away from the night.

My eyes don't want to open, but I make them. Dull sunlight floods my pupils. It's afternoon. Late afternoon. Evening, even. Did I really need this much sleep?

"What happened?" I ask, struggling to sit up. I can sense another person's presence in the room. I look around. Miss Collins is sitting in my armchair. I'm in my room, in my bed, back at Watson. I force my eyes to meet Miss Collins'. "What happened?" I demand again.

"You fell asleep," she says gently. "It was a tiring night for you and–"

"No, with–" I swallow. "Ray?"

"We don't know yet," she replies, gently again, but the way she nibbles on her bottom lip gives it away. They aren't expecting good news.

I push back the covers and scramble out of bed. "You've heard *something*." That's in no shape or form a question. It's a

74

mandate.

"Yes."

"*What?*"

"Ray arrived at…wherever he was sent. They contacted Mrs. Robar at about five." Miss Collins brushes off the armrest. Five? It *is* late. It's very late.

"And? Stop stalling already!"

"And she was informed that it is poison."

"And? There's more, right?" I say despairingly.

"And…it is lethal."

A slow numbness spreads over my body. "Lethal?" I repeat, then shake my head. "Well…so? As long as they were able to hold it off…enough…and get help from this place…who are they, anyway? To say it's lethal? Do they have credentials?" I'm talking fast now. Almost like Mrs. Robar. I screech to a halt, breathing heavily. "Is…he…?" I whisper, unable to say anything more.

"We don't know yet," Miss Collins tries to calm me down again. "Please go back to sleep, Mel–"

"How?" I raise my voice. "Stop it! You and Shadow and Mark–" I feel a hot wave of resentment. How could he have stopped me? I could've helped Ray…I could've…"–and every other teacher are always treating me like I'm back in Green Group or something! How am I supposed to sleep when I don't…when I don't know…" I let my voice fade and sit down on the bed, squeezing my hands into fists, trying to stop them from shaking.

"I'm sorry," Miss Collins whispers.

I ignore her.

Shadow and Mr. Klein file in through the door what seems like hours later. I don't look at their faces. I don't want to see if they're dump-truck faces or not. So instead I stare hard at my feet. I've never noticed how weird feet are. Who came up with the idea for the long lumpy part and five little round things sticking out?

Unfortunately I can't block their voices. I wish I could. I wish I could put in ear buds, turn up my unopened mp3 player (too distracting before) really, really loud, and never take them out, because now that the news has obviously come, I suddenly don't want to hear it.

But I have to.

"Amber?" Shadow says softly, standing in front of me. I can see his boring, brown work shoes on the ground by where my bare feet dangle. When I don't answer, he turns around. Obviously he shares some sort of telepathic communication with the other two teachers, who get up and silently leave.

Oh no.

No.

They wouldn't leave for good news.

Shadow sits down next to me. I feel his arm around my shoulders. I close my eyes, waiting.

"Amber…"

Stop saying my name. Just get to it. I feel the dump truck revving up.

"The doctors…honey, they weren't able to stop the poison in time."

My brain doesn't process. What does this mean again?

"They weren't able to save Anthony," Shadow whispers.

Anthony? Who's Anthony? That annoying little ten-year-old? Who cares about him? What about *Ray*?

But my mind can't put it off for long. I feel my nose burning in advance, but before I can stop them, and for only the second time I can remember, tears slide down my cheeks. I pull away from Shadow and press my forearm to my eyes to absorb the wetness. I can just imagine if Ray were sitting here right now–"*Mel*? Are you actually *crying*? Isn't that sort of biologically impossible for you? Isn't that what you keep telling me? Are you undergoing a *mutation*?"–and he'd keep going until I was laughing.

But if Ray were sitting here right now, I wouldn't be crying.

Finally I force myself to stop. I can't afford to be this stupid. I need answers. I stand up and stagger away from Shadow, turning to face him, wiping my eyes one last time. He looks at me in concern. I glare back. *Like I want your pity. It's only making things worse.* Then I remember that it's only Ray who can read my expressions. I bite down hard on my cheek for a moment, then say, in a lower, rougher voice that apparently comes with crying, "What's going to happen to him?"

"He's dead, honey."

"*Not Ray!*" I yell. "The burglar! The safe robber! *The one who killed him!* Is he going to death row? The electric chair? Firing squad? *Huh?*"

"He was not apprehended," Shadow says carefully. My ears start to ring.

"Well, then, apprehend him! He's at large! How can we just stay here and be doing nothing? Why didn't anyone tell me?" I start pacing, my whole body trembling like a leaf in autumn.

"This has been determined a case for the police, not Watson," Shadow says quietly.

"*What?*" My voice rises.

"Amber, *calm down*." Shadow stands up. I shoot daggers at him with my eyes.

"Don't tell me what to do," I growl. "You're just like Mark." Fresh waves of fury wash over me, adding to the mix. "I'm going to kill him, too! How could he have–!"

"Amber, don't blame Mr. Klein," Shadow says. "I asked him to make sure you were safe. He did what he did to protect you."

My jaw drops. "How *could* you?" Warmth pricks at my eyes.

"It's my job," Shadow says. "I'm in charge."

"I don't usually put authority figures on pedestals, for your information."

Shadow sighs. "I know. I'm used to it."

No. No one knows but Ray. And no one's used to it but Ray. *No one.*

That's right. No one. Now, there's no one.

My dam breaks. Now, I'm sobbing. Embarrassment and tears flood over me as I cover my face with my hands. Then I'm leaning against someone. For a moment my mind races wildly—*Ray?* But it's too tall to be Ray. It's Shadow.

I slump against him, trying to stop, and making it even worse. After a minute the remnants of the dam crumble and a river comes surging forward, spilling over my eyelids, down over my cheeks, and before I can help it, down my neck, soaking into the collar of my shirt.

Shadow holds me the entire time.

The faculty just about forces me to stay in Lyvia and Shay's room tonight. I try to tell them all I want is to be alone. I'll be better if I don't have people crowding all over me with sappy remorse. But the teachers, especially Shadow, won't have any of it. They must think I'll turn suicidal or flat-out crazy if I'm left alone to mope the whole night. So I'm sent two hallways down to my two–remaining–friends.

Lyvia opens the door without a word, which must be a first for her. She and Shay watch in silence as I walk to the cot already set up for me, drop my duffel bag, and give it a kick before sitting down.

Lyvia clears her throat. When she speaks she sounds oddly hoarse. "I was thinking…you could sleep on my bed, if you wanted."

"No pity," I snarl, turning away. "For once, could you not be so dumb?"

Lyvia stands, shocked, in her place for a moment, before slowly sitting down next to Shay on the bed farthest from me. Out of the corner of my eye I see Shay pat her hand and whisper something, before getting up and coming over to me.

"I just want you to know...we're here," she mumbles, running a hand through her short, sandy hair. Five thousand dumb-blonde retorts run through my head. I bite my tongue so I don't spit them out.

"Okay." I still don't turn around, only scrutinize the back wall. "So, you're here." I want to continue with something that will get the message *and I don't freakin' care so leave me alone* across, but can't pick the right words out of my muddled brain.

"Do you want to do something? We could play Scrabble, or Clue..." Shay says.

"I want to sleep." Anything to clear my mind. I need to be sharp at all times. Especially if I ever meet TMWINC. I will be so sharp, I will shred him into a million pieces.

"We can do that, too," Shay says resignedly, and backs up to her bed again. I roughly unzip my duffel bag and stalk to the bathroom, slamming the door behind me. I know it's not fair to treat Shay and Lyvia like this, but *I just want to be alone*.

I quickly change and brush my teeth, but hesitate before pulling the door open. It's so *peaceful* in here, this quiet little azure-and-ivory tiled room. I step back and sink to the floor, leaning my side against the side of the tub. I lower my arms onto the rim, and drop the right side of my face into them. My eyelids slide shut. I feel unnaturally hot and sweaty as five thousand emotions pulse through me, trying to escape out of my veins.

I never would've expected it, but sleep comes easily.

* * *

Of course, Shay wakes me up an hour later, to make sure I haven't "drowned in the toilet or anything". She's only half joking. So I end up sleeping the rest of the time on the cot, in the too-loud room with the breathing of three different people and the fan whirring overhead and my nose burning and my head screaming too many things for me to make out. I wish I were back by the tub.

7

Now, days later, is by far the worst. I didn't want to come, but I made myself. I could just hear Ray if I'd stayed in my room like a coward: "Wow, Mel, I guess I feel a little misled. I thought you liked me at least enough to come to my *funeral.* Now I guess I know the truth. But don't worry, I'll just haunt you for eternity, no big deal." And the worst thing was, I knew it was true–he, or his memory, *would* haunt me if I didn't go. So I forced myself to put on my only nice pair of black pants (only idiots wear real skirts) and a black formal top and dragged myself out of my room, down the stairs, and into one of the buses waiting in the parking lot. It was filled with part of the Blue Group, the girls, all dressed in black or gray dresses or skirts (idiots). Heads turned as I walked down the aisle. I responded with glares–"lightning glares," Ray had called them, "powerful enough to kill with one strike." *Kill.* I sent a lightning glare upward for good measure before thumping down in the isle across from Shay and Lyvia. They both looked at me for a moment, then quickly looked away before I could start yelling. I slid down low in my seat.

As I stand in the waiting room, waiting to go into the main section of the funeral home, I fight back the nausea, dread, and helplessness that's come and gone in waves over the last few days. Helplessness, because, as terrible as I'm feeling, I know I can't *do* anything to help myself. Because it's all true, and this is all happening, and has happened, and I just have to learn to deal, though I'm not learning very well. Funerals have occurred before. Not very often, but they've been held for one or two older students who had accidents in the field or got sick and died. But there has never been a funeral for a murder victim. And there has never been a funeral for one of my friends.

This is the hardest thing I've ever done, actually, especially since I've barely accomplished anything in the past two days. But now is still the worst. Now, in this stuffy, overcrowded, sadness saturated little room, it's real with a clarity I couldn't even begin to feel before.

Annette Robar opens the doors and silently everyone stands and funnels in. The people waiting outside stop their hushed conversations and crowd the waiting room doors while the students take seats inside the larger room. As I step into the torture hall, someone pulls me out of line and gives me a fierce hug.

"I'm so sorry, Mel," Annette says softly. I try to pull out of her reach, but she holds on. "And thank you. I know you were a good friend to Anthony. I…even though I never saw him much…."

Since she's obviously in pain, I stay a moment longer than I normally would have. I feel strange–maybe because it's been eight years since an older woman's hugged me. But enough is enough. Not looking at her, I turn and keep walking. I find a seat in the back corner, as far away from the coffin as possible. Even though it's closed, and even though I know there's no body, only a flask of ashes (sent priority mail from who-knows-where, as it was apparently all they could do for the…body…at the end) it still makes me shudder.

Wordlessly, Shay, Lyvia, Owen, and even Sam slide into my row. I look away so she won't see the red gathering around my eyes. Shoot. The service hasn't even started yet.

After a millennium we get started. Ray's mom was Jewish, and so is her sister Annette, so there's a Rabbi to lead everyone. He asks us to sing. *Sing?* I can barely breathe. I keep my mouth tight as others murmur foreign words, somehow capturing a melody, too. My hands twitch towards my head, wanting to cover my ears. I hold them still with difficulty. It's as if five thousand nails are scraping over chalkboards in this room.

Next, as instructed, Annette Robar, Shadow, the teachers, Owen, Shay, Lyvia, and a few other students file to the front of the room to share things they'll always remember about Ray. I was asked, too, but I told them no. At least I was going, wasn't I? Wasn't that enough? And, I didn't add this, the biggest reason why not: there was simply no way to put down how I felt and how much I would remember about Ray. The way he'd transformed from the weird, weather-obsessed new kid to the best friend that I'd ever have (this coming from me, the least dramatic person on the planet). He's the only person I've ever met who actually *knew* me, and put up with me, and understood me, and changed my name–no, he didn't just change my *name*, he changed my *life*. I probably don't even know half the ways I've changed in the past few years– all because of him. Heck, I'm sitting here nearly crying my eyes out. Isn't that enough? And this is just from thinking these things. How was I supposed to get up and say them, when I can hardly form words in my head?

Annette Robar is first, still speaking surprisingly slow. "Anthony was the sweetest, kindest, and most caring nephew I could have asked for. Even before he attended Watson he was quick-witted, intelligent, and had a gift for meteorology. It's…a shame…he never got to pursue his dreams in that field…" At this point she appears unable to go on. Shadow pats her gently on the shoulder, and she moves over to let him have the floor.

"Anthony was an amazing student, but more than that, he was a good friend and peer to the other students at Watson." I see his eyes slide to me, and I quickly drop my gaze to my fists, which are clenched in my lap. "He's left an impression on the school and the people in it that will never fade."

Mr. Klein steps forward. "I was there...that night...and I'm sorry I could not have stepped in sooner and stopped the perpetrator before he...did what he did."

I raise my eyes to the front of the room and send him an ultra-crackling-lightning glare. *You* should *be sorry! Sorry you stopped me!*

Mr. Klein avoids looking at me and finishes up. Other teachers shuffle into the spotlight, each naming their favorite thing about Ray.

"Ray–I mean, Anthony–always did his best. His projects were not easy to rival."

"Anthony could always be counted on to help others."

"Anthony was considerate and well behaved." (Ms. Nailor was barely able to choke this out.)

"Anthony always applied himself in every class."

I take a deep breath. Somehow it's helping that they're using the name "Anthony", a name I hardly associate with Ray. "Anthony" is like a far-away speck, not close enough to be clear, or to hurt.

When the teachers are done, the gaggle of students redistribute so they're in the front now. Lyvia speaks first.

"I was always impressed with Ray's skills concerning meteorology," she says in a small, quiet voice, so unlike the Lyvia I'm used to. "But more so, I was amazed at how good a friend he was to Mel–" She stops, looking horror-struck. Her eyes search for mine, apology clearly etched in her face. I look at the ceiling, a new rush of emotion surging through me. "–And–and to everyone," Lyvia stammers, trying to cover it up. "Ray was...well, if we were all like him, the world would be a better place," she rushes and steps back, ducking behind the other eight or so kids around her.

If we were all like him? I repeat silently. *Dead, you mean?* I dig my nails into my knees, trying not to listen to the rest of them, and counting the seconds until the other students are finished.

When they finally are, candles are passed around. I stare at mine, a white stick of wax with a paper circle at the bottom. The lights are dimmed.

Beside me, Lyvia whispers an endless stream of apologies, none of which I hear. I only watch as matches are passed around, and slowly the room is filled with flickering, eerie light. A few are placed around the coffin. I choke down the burning rising in my nose as my wick is ignited and, as silently as I can (which is very silently, after a whole life of training), I get off my chair and slip back to the door behind me. I open it the slightest bit and dart through.

A shock meets me outside. Rain. Lots of it falling in torrents from the roiling clouds above. My candle goes out with a hiss. I let it fall to the ground and I stand where I am on the cement for a moment, taking in the irony, before stepping deliberately to the set of concrete stairs. I slowly descend them until I'm at the third one from the asphalt that makes up a jogging path. My hair falls out from my ponytail and sticks to my cheeks. I'm so completely soaked, I hardly even notice the new tears on my face, as the rain immediately washes them away.

I sit down and hug my knees to my chest, just sitting there, letting the rain pool above my ears and on my eyelashes and mouth and neck, soaking my clothes and streaming down me in rivers. It's better than being in the funeral home, at least, and maybe it will help wash away the stress, and the sadness, and the helplessness…

As I sit here, a human waterfall, I'm able to realize, in an almost safe way, that four days ago, the day of the social, the day of my first End…that End wasn't just *an* End, it was *the*

End. The End of my life as I know it. The End of my life as Ray's best friend. The End.

The deluge helps for a while. It's oddly distracting, and appropriate. But when it starts to lighten up and slowly fade to a drizzle, the feelings, without a river to escape on, start building again. Only this time, though it's a struggle, I control myself. No tears. No permanent grimace. I won't have the emotions outside of me, following like a demented black cloud.... No, they'll stay inside, locked in somehow. Somehow, I'll just have to live. I look up, shaking back my sopping hair so I can see the clouds that are dispersing now.

Somehow, I'll just have to live without Rain.

8

Two Years and Two Months Later

I shift ever-so-slightly to the side, putting table sixteen in better view while at the same time moving out of the direct line of vision of the one occupant facing me. I stir my soup and observe under my eyelashes, which are conveniently long now.

There are two people at table sixteen, a man and a woman, talking in low voices and passing a bottle of wine back and forth. Wine that has a very long name, unlike the one brand offered on the menu. It must be a bottle they brought with them.

I cock my head slightly in order to see the man better, taking glances in between sips of coffee, the only other food item on my table. He appears to be in his late forties or early fifties, older than the woman he's talking with by a good ten years. He has liver-colored hair, a kind of brown tinged with gray, and is wearing an avocado green suit with darker vertical stripes.

Maryanne, the woman I followed here, is sitting with her back to me, her raven hair twisted into an elegant bun, looking nice with her beige business dress. She's holding a briefcase in her lap. That's what I'm interested in. As soon as I see what's in there, I'll slip away and call the local police. In that attaché case should be the answer to why she was snooping around in New York Hospitals. I also found she was stealing quite a bit of money via online identity theft–but before I could secure her location and summon the Rochester police, she'd fled to JFK, bought a last minute ticket, and sped off. She was kind enough to accidentally leave a scrap of paper with her scribbled restaurant reservations in her motel room, so we figured out where to find her....

Ends don't thrill me like they once did, but I do feel good when I'm on one, especially a long one, tightening the noose with each new lead and scrap of information...it's nice and distracting, since it can fully occupy my mind. And since this is my first overseas End (and my second out of state, although the first barely went past the Pennsylvania border), I'm a little excited.

It was tough getting Shadow to let me go. All through the process of getting a next-day plane ticket, packing, and straight up to boarding time he was tailing me, reminding me I didn't have to do this. He said someone else, a senior Red Group member, could do the overseas part–I was only a year into Red Group, I was only just out of ninth grade, I was just fifteen...he even went so far as to suggest someone go with me, a partner. I'd told him flat-out–no, I'd started this End myself and, like every other End, I would finish it myself. I *don't* work with anyone else. I tried it once. That was enough. That's it. *End* of discussion.

He was worse still at the airport. "*Be careful*," he'd told me for the five thousandth time, giving me his 'please-listen-while-I-try-to-engage-you-in-a-boring-safety-conversation' look.

"I always am," I'd muttered. "Like I need to be, though. I could beat any idiot blindfolded."

"Just...*promise me*," Shadow growled. "I'll call to check up on you–frequently. So you'd better be doing okay. Okay? And be nice with Marvin Academy."

"Do you think there'll be anyone there I can actually *practice* fighting with?" I'd asked in a low voice, twirling the end of my ponytail around my finger, practicing being a silly, excitable girl on her first date at a fancy restaurant. Namely,

Amy Quinn, which is the name stamped on my passport and "birth certificate" tucked away in my wallet. Of course, this Marvin Academy will know who I am, but hopefully the lady I'm after–Maryanne–and her accomplice(s), won't. "Do they even have a hand-to-hand combat curriculum?"

"*Amber, please.* No, not exactly–Marvin's more of a research base than an action center. Can I go on now? Or do you want the population density of the surrounding area and a list of the faculty members as well?"

"How about you skip the monologue and I head for my terminal?"

"No. You're hearing me out one more time. After the plane ride you immediately head to the restaurant–you have the address in your purse–I've put the cab number in your wallet–and your reservations are for–"

"Seven-thirty," I finished, scowling.

"This will go a lot faster if you stop that. Now, about five–no, actually, ten–minutes before you'll need someone to pick you up, which will hopefully be after the police have left with Maryanne and her possible crew, call speed-dial-four"–he tapped the keypad of one of the school's foreign cell phones before handing it to me–"and someone from Marvin will come meet you. Or, if you need help, you'll get backup."

"*That's* likely. And I thought you said the Marvin people don't fight."

"I *said* they don't specialize in it–that doesn't mean they can't help at all. And lastly, make good decisions, all right? I don't know what the kids down there are like. If they start offering you drugs or beer–"

"You think I'm an idiot? Thanks, Shadow. Why would I want to *de*grade my senses–when I'm always trying to *up*grade them?"

"I'm just saying. And then about boys–"

"*Stop it!*" I'd exploded. "You *know* that's not going to

happen. It's even more unlikely than the beer. Not that'd I'd do that either. But, really…who needs the distraction?"

A few passersby, a middle-aged man and a few gossiping college students, turned and snickered. I must've look like the average run-of-the-mill teenager trying to avoid a dating talk from her dad. Ugh. But that was okay, all the better for my masquerade.

"You're just at that age, though–," Shadow had the nerve to continue.

"No, no, no." I had backed away.

"Okay. Fine. But call when you get there. And when you get to Marvin. And–"

"I get it! Enough! Since when did you become my father?" I swung my duffel bag over my shoulder and glared at him. The duffel bag was my only bag, and it was a carry-on. Nobody with any sense leaves their luggage in the care of others. "Besides, it's more than half a day ahead there. You'll be asleep most of the time I'm awake."

"Just be smart."

"I already am."

A voice crackled over the JFK loudspeakers. "*Flight D to Brisbane, Australia now boarding. Passengers with sections one through four on their tickets may now enter.*"

"That's you," Shadow said, but I was already hurrying away. He didn't follow.

"Are you ready to order?" a tall waiter asks, stopping by my table. His accent stirs something in my memory. I shake my head to repress it. It's painful.

"Not yet, thank you." I smile, fiddling with my hair. As if I would order anything else from this menu. It's sorely lacking Vitamin C. "I'm waiting for my date." I let out a giggle. The sound is completely foreign. If Lyvia hadn't made me practice before I left I may not have pulled it off.

"All right, then." The waiter moves off to his next table. My eyes slide back to Maryanne. Any moment now I'll see what I'm looking for and call the police. I sip my coffee and try not to fidget in the (shudder) dress I'm wearing. Of course it's necessary, but *extremely* inconvenient.

But...*there*. Maryanne lifts the briefcase up and opens it slightly, extracting a folder. It's a plain white manila folder, but as she hands it to the avocado man I see the top of a paper inside. I clench my teeth in satisfaction, recognizing the type of file. A birth certificate. This falls in with the hospital part.

So as not to be too obvious, I wait a minute–which seems like a very long time, if you're paying attention–before getting up and nonchalantly wandering to the bathroom. The skirt of the black dress ("Always in style, always pretty, but not in a stand-out way," according to Lyvia) swishes unfamiliarly against my calves. I can't wait to get out of this thing.

I push into the bathroom and head to the back corner, but not into a stall (outright suspicious, and it's idiotic to trap yourself in like that unless you really need to *use* the toilet). I glance at the door one more time before pulling Watson's Australia cell phone out of my hidden pocket and hitting speed dial four. The phone rings against my ear for a moment, then someone, a woman with a young, chirpy, yet still secretary-like voice, picks up. "Marvin Academy."

"Is this Ms. Rose?" I ask quickly.

"It is. How may I help you?"

"This is Amber Rind–Watson Institute–"

"Oh, Miss Rind–do you need me to send someone over?"

"Yeah, this'll probably be over in a few minutes, so if you could, please."

"Of course. It'll be a boy–he'll be wearing a gray three-quarter sleeve shirt and black pants. Do you have that?"

"Yes, thank you."

"See you later, then, honey."

I open my mouth to speak, and bite down a curse as Maryanne enters the bathroom. "Yeah. Okay, I know, Mom. Bye." I close the phone and clench it in my hand, pasting an irritated look on my face, going along with the charade of my-mom-just-called-and-she's-so-annoying-because-I'm-such-a-teenager. Not that I would know.

I step forward and turn on the faucet, washing my hands and then pretending to check my (nonexistent, they couldn't *force* me to wear it) makeup. Then I fiddle with my hair, adjust my dress straps, and tug on my pantyhose.

Maryanne doesn't leave.

When I'm done, and am about to head outside, and then onto the street to call the police, she seems to notice me. I happen to know she's been glancing at me the entire time since she walked in the bathroom. Foolish mortal. You can't deceive me.

"Oh, that's such a lovely dress on you," she says, sweeping her gaze over me. Obviously she's not assessing my dress–she's assessing me.

"Thanks," I twitter, pretending to be overexcited. My hands flutter around the waist, adjusting. Maybe I can trick *her*, though. If she thinks she's wrong, this can go so much smoother.

"Who are you here with?" she asks, moving one sink closer to me.

"I'm waiting for my date," I say, biting my lip and smiling in an excited way. If only she knew the excitement is me reveling in the soon-to-come fight.

"Is he cute?" she asks.

I cock my head. "*I* think so. Some of my friends don't agree, but he's totally sweet and an amazing golfer. You should see his arms. Wow." Ugh.

"I can imagine." She hops another sink. "Are you from around here?"

She must have noticed my accent. I remain at my sink, seemingly unsuspecting. "I live here now, but my mom and I moved here from Nevada when she remarried." I wonder whether I should ramble a bit more or not. I decide against it.

Maryanne pretends to scrutinize my dress some more. "You know what? I have a perfect shade of lip-gloss for that outfit. It would look *so* cute on you, sweetie."

"Really?" I raise my eyebrows. "Thanks! I'm wearing some, though." Not.

"Just try it." She pulls out a tube from her purse and uncaps it. She mixes the swab around and holds it out to me. I take it and pretend to sniff.

"*Mm*, vanilla," I say, but really detect something else–the smell of a sedative. I slowly lower the swab towards my lips, then pretend to fumble with it. It slips through my fingers and clatters down the sink drain. Perfect.

Maryanne turns blazing eyes on my face. I gasp in fake horror.

"I am *so* sorry! I can't believe I'm such a klutz–"

"Okay, honey, knock off the nonsense. You know and I know you're not a klutz." She moves closer. "And you're not waiting for any date."

I shrug. "Okay, then." I bring up my cell phone again and hit the speed dial, programmed à la Shadow, for the police.

Maryanne grabs my wrist and sends the phone flying. I roll my eyes and twist out of her grasp. She swings her leg out to trip me–typical. I hop over it without thinking and grab the phone before racing out of the bathroom.

Outside everything is like it was, only the man at table sixteen is staring at me. I dash for the front doors as I hear Maryanne barrel out of the bathroom after me.

Rain

Someone–a boy–is just coming into the restaurant. I notice vaguely that he's wearing a gray T-shirt and black pants. I sprint up the stairs and whirl around, stopping next to him and facing the dining area and table sixteen.

"Amber Rind. Call me Amy Quinn," I breathe.

The boy's eyes sweep the restaurant and stop on Maryanne. He nods. "Jonathon Carter. Call me Jon. Or maybe I don't want to associate myself with you. You seem to be some sort of target." His tone is both serious and joking at the same time.

I chuckle under my breath as Maryanne spots me and starts up the stairs. I pass the boy my phone. "Call the police, will you? Speed-dial two." He nods. I duck and dash down the wheelchair ramp as Maryanne gropes for me. Table sixteen is right by the wall that rises to the top of the stairs. I dodge between tables as Maryanne continues her pursuit. Waiters and waitresses start to converge, looking confused. Two try to stop Maryanne, but she jumps away and keeps following me. I look around. I have to get to that briefcase. I dance around people, moving closer–

Oof. Avocado Man spins around and grabs me from behind, yanking my arms around my back. I scream pretend to flail in terror, but actually throw in some practiced kicks– they work. He lets me go. The waiters go after him now. Avocado Man has other ideas–he grabs his briefcase and, throwing off some waiters, swings it at me. I duck, right into the path of his foot. He winds his leg back. I scramble to get up.

Suddenly Avocado Man staggers backwards. Jonathon's behind him, glaring at the older guy.

I make it to a standing position. Really, I could've taken care of it. To be polite, I nod to Jonathon. He meets my eyes and nods back. I go to take care of Maryanne.

Something stops me. The chaos rages around us, with

the waiters still trying to settle Maryanne and her partner, and the guests on their feet, shouting and staring. But despite this something makes me look at Jonathon again. Emotion surges through me. I gasp, shaking my head, trying to clear it.

Maryanne grabs me by the shoulders and yanks my body around. I elbow her in the gut, making her wheeze, and slam my heel down on her toes. She lets go. The next moment ten or so employees pinion her. Satisfied, I turn to take care of Avocado Man.

Where is he? I look quickly towards the other tables, but I don't see him there. He can't have gotten away. Impossible.

A voice reaches my ears. "Uh…Amy…"

I whirl around. Avocado Man, fist pulled back, is bearing down on Jonathon, who's forced against the wall that rises to the top of the stairs.

And he's clenching the bottom of his shirt.

An image fills my mind. A nine-year-old. With dark red hair. Sitting at a table in the Marvin cafeteria. Squeezing his fist around the bottom of his shirt.

I clamp my teeth together, forcing the image away. Jonathon raises his hand to block the oncoming attack. Oh, no….

Not again….

Adrenaline pulses through me. I dive at Avocado Man, knocking him off of his feet. About now the police–five of them–flood through the doors. Employees and officers crowd around table sixteen. I'm surrounded by adults, some running, others yelling as they hurry to arrest Maryanne. I jump up. Avocado Man is gone again. I look around wildly, but not for Avocado Man, for Jonathon. I start pushing through the crowd. My heart is pounding very, very loudly. I try to breathe normally.

A police officer stops me. "Are you the girl this lady was chasing?" She points to Maryanne. I nod. "What happened?"

"I was…" I try to remember. What's wrong with me? "I was…in the bathroom…and she offered me lip gloss…and I dropped it…and she flipped out and started chasing me." I lower my voice. "She sounded like she had a New York accent. You might want to contact the police department there." When the officer looks down at her clipboard I duck into the crowd and look around. I notice the briefcase is gone, too. Avocado Man must have gotten away–

"Amy?" someone says. I stiffen, and slowly turn around. Jonathon is standing by the stairs. "He ran out the door, Amy. I tried to follow him, but he took off in a car–I'm sorry. And thanks for helping me." He doesn't have an accent like the rest of the people do.

I nod mutely. It can't be. His hair's styled a little differently, and a little bit lighter, and he's taller, and his skin's slightly paler…but….

He's still squeezing the bottom of his shirt. Hard. And staring at me like I'm staring at him. He takes a shaky breath and slowly loosens his grip.

"We should go," he says quietly, gesturing towards the stairs. I stare at his palm. He turns and climbs up, fast. Then he stops at the top, leaning against the banister, eyes closed. I swear my head is spinning. I quickly run after.

"What's on your hand?" I whisper when I catch up to him. He moves his arm slightly behind him.

"What…?"

I grab his wrist and flip his hand over so it's palm-up.

Four white parallel scars cross his skin.

9

I look up, slowly. Oh. My. God. "Ray?" I choke.

His eyes widen at the word, and he pulls his hand away. I see his eyes are blue. Dark blue. "Ray!" I feel a burning in my nose. Before I can start to cry I squeeze my eyes shut and take a deep breath. Then I open them again. "How…but they said…you died."

"I died?" He takes a step back.

"It's been over two years. I can't believe it!"

"I…" He stares at me for a moment, squeezing his shirt again. "I don't know…what you're talking about…Amy. I…."

The confusion in his eyes throws me. My stomach feels strangely hollow. "You mean…you don't know who I am?"

He blinks. "Amber, right?" he says faintly.

"No!" I say, louder, but unheard over the hubbub. I take a step closer. "It's me! Mel! Aren't you…aren't you Ray?"

"Stop saying that!" he says, eyes wide and almost panicked. "Please," he adds. "I'm Jonathon."

"Why? Why are you pretending to be Jonathon? Is it Marvin? You're at Marvin, right? Are they… Won't they let you come back? Are you being held hostage or something?"

"I'm not pretending." He really looks scared now. "Yes, I'm at Marvin. But I'm not being held hostage! Come back to where?"

"But I *know* it's you! Why won't you tell me?"

"I'm not… I *am* Jonathon," he says, his eyes wide again. "Do you need to see a nurse? We better get you back to Marvin."

Frustration finally boils over. "Tell me the truth!" I scream. "Why are you pretending?"

"Shh! I'm not pretending!" He takes my wrist and pulls me outside. The moment we step through the doors and onto the evening-lit sidewalk, he lets go of me, as if my arm is burning. As I watch, dazed, he flags down a cab.

"You can tell me," I almost beg. This has to be Ray! Who else…who else can it be? It has to be. Even though they said he was dead, he *wasn't* dead…or who else would be standing here? A ghost? No, Mel. Ghosts don't exist. But then, who….

Maybe I'm delusional. Maybe I've been trying not to think about it so much that my mind has cracked and I'm jumping at this one, slight chance that– No. I'm perfectly sane. This *is* Ray. It *has* to be.

"I *am* telling you," he replies as the cab pulls up. Hesitating with his hand on the door, he looks back and says, "I'm not Ray." He takes a deep breath and holds open the door for me. I silently get in. Ray–no matter *what* he says– gives the driver an address. I try to listen so I can remember if I need to, but I'm too stunned.

Ray looks away for the short cab ride, and I don't speak, knowing the driver could be listening. When we pull up in front of a large, U-shaped red brick building, I get out and wait for Ray to pay the driver and come around.

"Are you feeling better?" he asks warily as he steps onto the sidewalk.

"No," I retort. "You won't tell me the truth."

"Please," he almost moans. "I am. I swear. Please stop!" He squeezes his eyes shut and clenches the bottom of his shirt again. His reaction surprises me. I watch as, slowly, Ray eases his eyes open.

"I'm sorry," I say, mystified.

"It's not…your fault," he murmurs, relaxing his hands.

"We really should get you to the nurse."

"I'm *fine*," I say fiercely. Ray's mouth twitches, then he shakes his head and leads me inside.

We walk into a maroon-and-magnolia tiled hallway. Ray leads me inside the central office. A woman in her mid thirties is typing at her laptop in the far corner, nestled in a large salmon pink armchair. When she sees us she closes the lid and gets up.

"Jonathon! Good, you made it back. And you must be Amber." She turns to me, smiling. She has straight brown hair just past her shoulders and a pretty smile. She holds out a hand. "I'm Ms. Rose."

"Actually, everybody calls me Mel," I say quietly, shaking the hand.

Ray glances at me when I say that, his hand curling back around his shirt. He stares for a moment, then drops his gaze to the carpet. I want to scream.

Ms. Rose doesn't point out that 'Mel' is an odd nickname for someone named Amber. Instead she asks, "How did it go?"

"It..." I replay the evening in my mind. "It went okay. One of the people was apprehended. But I'm going to be working on this project a little longer."

"Stay as long as you want," Ms. Rose says. "Do you need anything? It's Ms. Cedric's birthday today, and we're about to have cake. If you'd like–"

"I'm not hungry," I say quickly. "Did you get my bag? A 'TJ Davis' picked it up for me at the airport."

"Yes, it's already in your room. Jonathon, could you show Mel the way? It's guest room seven, please."

Ray nods and walks out. I follow as he heads silently for the other side of the lobby. There's an elevator and a stairwell. Ray pushes open the stairwell door and starts climbing. I keep up easily, even as I fight down the turmoil threatening to explode out of me.

On the first landing he stops. "Are you sure you don't want to see the nurse?" he asks.

"Positive." I glare automatically. "I am *not* mental."

"Sorry. You just seemed a little…unusual back there."

"I am always unusual. What's the point of being usual? I *know* the truth," I add. "I just don't know what happened."

"You probably overexcited yourself and–"

"Not me," I hiss. "*You.*"

"I'm not the one hallucinating."

"You're usually pretty perceptive, though."

"You've known me a half hour."

"Going by that, I've known you three and a half hours in dog time. Does that count for anything?"

Ray laughs. "Oh, definitely, if you were, I don't know, a dog?"

"My alter ego is a schnauzer."

"Well, mine's a rottweiler. So obviously you need to show me some respect." I can't help it; I laugh too. Then he gets serious. "Come on, let's get you to your room."

There is no doubt whatsoever in my mind that this is Ray. I've never been able to joke with someone else like that.

I'm suddenly aware that the building has come to life. The sounds of hundreds of students' footsteps rumble around us. A distant chattering fills the air.

"Late dessert. Cake for Mrs. Cedric," Ray explains. "Maybe you'll feel better after you get something to eat?"

"I'm not hungry." I give him the same automatic answer I gave Ms. Rose–the one I've been using the last two and one-sixth years. *Do you want to go out and get something to eat, Mel?* Or, in other words, *Want to do something totally unrelated to school and work and be a brainless citizen of The Land of the Stupid?* And I'd say, *No thanks, Lyvia…I'm not hungry*. Or sometimes *No thanks, Shay*, until she gave up and became stuck to Vanessa like duct tape. I've hardly spoken to her in six months. I guess I should be amazed she stuck with me for as long as she did. But I'm happier focusing on my work, anyway.

"I find that hard to believe," Ray's saying. "You seem like the kind of person who likes to keep their strength up. And enjoys food."

I am. Or, at least...I *was*. And that is a good point, but my head is practically spinning on my shoulders. Add jet lag into the equation; not the best. "I have a few things in my duffel bag to eat. And–"

New voices fill the stairway, their conversation bouncing down the walls to Ray and me. I listen attentively. The voices are high, giggly, and enthusiastic. I'd say four or five girls are coming down the steps towards us.

Four is correct. I watch as they round the corner. In front is a slim, agile girl with strawberry blonde hair tied back in a bouncy ponytail. She saunters down the stairs with an air of authority and slightly in front of the other three. My eyes flick to the second girl who's short and angular and bounding after the blonde. The third girl is obviously her twin–she has the same boniness and honey-colored hair. She's talking to the fourth and last of the procession, a patently pretty girl with a petite build and charming smile on her face.

The kingpin stops two steps away from our landing. A grin lights up her face.

"Hi, Jonathon!" she says cheerfully, waving and hopping to the platform. Her hand tucks a loose piece of hair behind her ear.

"Hi, Caidy," Ray says in a more subdued tone. "How are you?"

"I'm great, but you missed the lesson." The girl–Caidy–puts on an exaggerated pouty expression. I note her speech pattern. It's like a mixture of a British accent and a southern drawl. It's like everyone else I've encountered here–except Ray.

"What was it on? I'll read about it tonight," Ray replies.

"Radiation. Convection, conduction, and then infrared versus ultraviolet–like you don't know all about it."

"Maybe I won't read about it, then." Before Caidy can go on, Ray turns to me. I see Caidy's eyes slide my way too, and she frowns marginally. "Caidy, this is Mel." He glances at the other three girls. "Leah, Hale, Vivian, this is Mel." Ray turns back to me. "Mel, this is Caidy,"–he nods at the strawberry blond–"Leah,"–the twin in a dark blue tee–"Hale,"–the other twin, in bright yellow–"and Vivian." She's the pretty girl with long, blue-black hair.

"Hi, Mel," the twin in yellow says brightly. She resumes her conversation with Vivian, who smiles quickly in my direction. The twin in blue gives me a short wave and swivels back to Caidy.

Caidy hardly glances at me, but focuses her attention on Ray. "We were just heading down for cake. Coming?"

"I will later. Right now I'm showing Mel to her room." Ray beckons me forward. "*You* coming, Mel?"

"Of course." I slip past Caidy and resume climbing. The twin in yellow and Vivian continue down the stairs. The twin in blue and Caidy follow after a moment.

"Do you know them?" I ask when we're two stories away. Of course I know he knows them, but it gets the answer I'm looking for.

"My friends–Matt and Dan–were friends with them before I came here. So yes, we hang out sometimes."

"When did you come here?" I say in a quieter voice.

Ray looks at me for a moment. "Two years ago, or maybe earlier than that. I'm not sure. It's…a little fuzzy."

Of course it is. Poison will do that. So maybe that's why…

"Ra... Jonathon?"

"Yes?" He sounds a little apprehensive.

"What about before you came here?"

He doesn't respond as he strides forward and pushes through the doors to our left. He silently leads me down a maroon-carpeted hallway to the room on the end, guestroom seven. After fishing the key card from the plastic pocket under the doorknob and opening the door, Ray finally looks at me.

"I don't know."

Then, without meeting my gaze, he turns and disappears around the corner.

I stand in my doorway rounding up my thoughts and forcing them back into the far corners of my mind. He doesn't remember. That's what must have happened! And why we never were contacted, because he didn't know... But the place he was sent—wherever that was—said he was dead. But he wasn't, and if he wasn't, how did the place not know? I think walking and talking would be a pretty big giveaway. Idiots!

Getting a grip on myself, I step into my room and close the door. My duffel bag is on the bed in the far corner. Across from the bed is a desk with a computer on it, the screen black. A dresser is beside the desk. Next to me is another door leading to the bathroom. Opposite the main door is a window that looks out on a courtyard. The sky is dull evening gray. Back home in Rochester, it's about ninety degrees and cloudless. Here, it's overcast and semi-cold, ten to eleven degrees Celsius, though with an incredible view otherwise. But I don't take time to look.

The first thing I do is unzip my duffel and pull out some normal clothes, capris that were cut and hemmed to just above my knees by Lyvia, a flexible tee, and a zip jacket. It feels so good to be out of the black dress. It's specially made for Ends. At the restaurant, I was wearing technical shorts and a tank top underneath it. If I'd needed to, with one pull right over my sternum, the dress would've crumpled neatly to the floor and I'd have been ready to kick butt.

I start to unpack. As I move my duffel to the carpet, I notice some folded pieces of paper and an unopened pay-as-you-go Australian cell phone on the bed. I remember Shadow saying he'd preordered one for me. I turn the school's phone off and look for an outlet. Catching sight of one underneath the bedside table I kneel and examine it. Sure enough, it's different than the outlets used in the United States. This one has three equal-length rectangles, two perpendicular at the top and a vertical one at the bottom. That would explain why I'd need a different phone and charger.

Before I open the new cell phone, I look at the papers. On them are meal times, general information about the building, a staff list (ha!), and a map of the grounds and the first floor.

When I'm done programming in quick contacts and speed dials for Shadow, the police, emergency help, the hospital, and Ms. Rose's cell phone (not Marvin, or else it would be easy to trace where I'm staying), I close myself into my bathroom. It feels more private that way. I hit speed dial one and wait for Shadow to pick up. It only rings once.

"Amber? Are you all right?" he demands. "Is this the new cell phone number? Ms. Rose emailed—"

"Yes, of course I'm all right," I say, impatient and slightly irritated that he would think I wasn't. "This is the number. I'm settled in my room and everything. Not even a scrape. Though the stairs were very dangerous to climb."

"Amber, stop that. Tell me what happened."

I explain how Maryanne is in custody but her business partner escaped. "I saw what they took from the hospitals," I say. "Birth certificates. I couldn't obtain them, though."

"You will." I can't tell if Shadow sounds weary or

resigned. Neither one is the most encouraging attitude.

"Should I wait for instructions before I make my next move?"

"Should I expect you to obey them?" asks Shadow.

"It was worth a try, being good." I take a deep breath. "But Shadow, that's not why I'm calling, really."

"No? Then why are you calling?" He sounds confused.

"Because..." I take a deep breath. "I think...no, I know...I've found Ray."

There's silence on the other end. Then Shadow sighs. "Amber...." There's a note of sadness, mixed with stress, in his voice. "Ray died. He's not in Australia. Please. I know you want to believe he's there, but–"

"I don't *want* anything," I say furiously, "I *know*! Speaking of which, how do you *know* Ray's not here? How?"

"Calm down," Shadow pleads. "Don't get upset."

"Don't get upset?" I realize my jaw hurts from clenching it so hard. I loosen up to gape at the generic white wall. Why won't he believe me? "How? How do you know?"

"The...place...contacted us! They said the poison was lethal. They said he died! He's gone, Amber. Why are you doing this after over two years?"

"You always said not to believe anything unless you saw it for yourself!" I'd scream, but I have better self-control than that. Disregarding my lapse tonight, of course. "I swear, Shadow! I swear! He doesn't remember anything from before, that's why we weren't contacted, but it is him."

"Amber, go to bed," Shadow says in a low voice. "Get some rest. You'll feel better in the morning."

"I'm not tired!" I hiss into the mouthpiece. "I'm not delusional, either! I'm also not five years old!"

"I'm sorry. I meant you've had an exciting day and you should wind down some. You can get back to work tomorrow."

"Aren't you listening to me? About Ray? I'll work on my End as well, but–"

"Amber, listen to me. Drop this right now. I don't want you to hurt yourself."

"I'll be careful," I say, perplexed.

"No, I mean emotionally. Getting your hopes up and then..." Shadow pauses while I fume. "I'm sorry."

I yank the phone from my ear and hit end. Then I chuck it at the tub. It bounces off the side and clatters to the floor, unharmed. Of course. I kick it for good measure.

Then I slide down the door until I'm sitting on the tiles. I put my hands over my face. Not to cry–of course not–but to think. Only I don't get anywhere. And I'm probably getting sick. There's a lump in my throat.

Five minutes later I stagger up and grab the phone. I head out into the main room and get my bag of toiletries, return to the bathroom to brush my teeth and wash my face, go back to the main room to change into pajamas, and sit down on the edge of the bed. I check the clock. It's almost nine. My regular bedtime–9:30–isn't too far off. I lie down under the sheet and turn off the lights. The distant chattering of the students in the cafeteria should put me to sleep easily.

Only, it doesn't. I toss and turn for fifteen minutes before giving up and getting a mystery novel out of my duffel bag. It's guaranteed to make more sense than my thoughts.

I read until 9:42, when my eyelids finally start to feel heavy. I eagerly put the book down and close my eyes.

Still, it's another twenty minutes before I can finally sink into slumber.

10

I wake like clockwork at 6:30 and get dressed and ready in seven minutes. At 6:40 Shadow calls. I figure it's about 8:40 PM for him. I almost laugh thinking about how long a day he must've had, not wanting to call while I was asleep.

But, remembering our conversation last night, I hesitate. As the phone buzzes again my hand automatically picks it up. I sigh. "Hello."

"How was your sleep?"

"Fine," I say curtly.

"Good." He sounds relieved, but not repentant. "I'm calling because I was wondering what your plan is for today."

"I'm going to go into the city, around the restaurant. I'll look around and see if I can pick up on anything that might be useful."

"That sounds good." Shadow pauses for a moment. "And I was thinking…" his tone is apprehensive. "You might want to consider asking someone from Marvin to come–"

"No." I cut him off. "No way. Forget it."

"Be careful, then." Resigned now. "And report back."

"You'll be asleep."

"I don't care."

"Whatever. Look, I have to go. It's breakfast time," I lie and hang up. Since the schedule says breakfast doesn't actually start until 7:30–not that I plan on going, but Ms. Rose will definitely be awake then–I turn on the desktop computer and print out a map of Brisbane. With a red pen I find the restaurant and circle key areas around it to check out.

Then I pull a manila folder from the cabinet in the computer desk. With the red pen I label it with a "B", place the map inside, and slip the folder into the inside pocket of my duffel bag.

I still have thirty-five minutes. I pack my purse–might as well appear normal–with Amy Quinn's sparkly wallet filled with credit cards, hot pink ponytails, and my book. Then I redo my ponytail and adjust the technical sweatpants and windbreaker outfit. Easy to maneuver in.

It's better to go out around 7:00 anyway, I decide. Not that many people will be out so I can look for a trace. I need to find out where Avocado Man is staying, or where he's gone.

Though I hope he's still in Brisbane.

Ms. Rose answers five seconds after I knock. "Hello, Mel! How are you this morning? You're up early!"

"Not really," I say, nodding in greeting. "I just came to inform you that I'm going out to work on my assignment. I'm aiming to be back around twelve."

"Do you want someone–" she starts to say, but I'm already shaking my head.

"No. I'm going alone." I wait a moment, then say, "Bye."

"Good luck, Mel." Ms. Rose watches as I walk away.

I take a bus back to the restaurant, my starting point. First I go in and talk to a waitress, saying I'd dropped a necklace at table sixteen when I was here two nights ago. (This is entirely fictitious. I'd never wear a necklace; it makes it too easy for your opponents to choke you). The waitress lets me search around the table for five minutes until I finally determine I must have left it somewhere else (and Maryanne and Avocado man did not drop any evidence).

Next I check my map and, after a few minutes of

practice with an Australian intonation (Lyvia says I have a knack for accents), make stops at different places. Sometimes I pretend to look for my stepfather ("Have you seen him? My mum and I don't know where he's gone. We last saw him yesterday evening. He was wearing an avocado green suit. He's tall and thin and has brown hair with some gray in it."). I speak quickly enough that people don't have time to notice my rudimentary speech patterns, but not so fast they can't understand me. Other times I act like a lost tourist looking for my uncle, using the same description without the suit in case people have seen him today (and for this I don't need an accent).

I come up blank. Part of it I think is because I keep getting distracted. I can't stop thinking about Ray. I need to focus on my End. But if it really is him—which it is—should he come first? No. No, Mel. The greater good. That's what comes first. No matter what you want, you have to focus. And stop talking to yourself. It's annoying.

I turn into the first café I see and order an iced coffee, no cream. As I sit on the barstool, sipping my awareness enhancer, I keep arguing internally. Pretty soon, though, I tune myself out. What's the point? I'm not getting anywhere today. I've never done this poorly on an End. Avocado Man has left no trace. None whatsoever. And if that's the best I can do for today... Well, if that's the best I can do, I'm a pretty terrible secret agent. No, not pretty terrible, just terrible. I'm a terrible secret agent.

My nose starts to burn. Using the advance warning to my advantage, I press a napkin to the side of the coffee cup, soaking up the freezing condensation, then cover my face with it. I take deep breaths to stop the tears of frustration. In. Out. In. Out. In. Out.

When I'm sure I'm not going to have a meltdown, I lower the napkin and concentrate on finishing the drink while making plans in the back of my mind for tomorrow. I can't get anything else done today. I throw the drained cup into the garbage can. The ice cubes left inside rattle as they slam into the side. I think the garbage can rattles, too.

I amble out, the picture of blitheness, and catch the bus. It takes me two blocks from Marvin. I still walk in a casual manner, but the closer I get the more my feet itch to run and get through the doors...to what?

Something in the back of my mind tells me it's to see Ray. To make sure it wasn't all just a dream. As that thought takes hold of me, the itch grows stronger. I fight to stroll rather than run through the doors.

It's lunchtime when I arrive. I can hear a roar of conversation coming from the doors on the left side of the lobby, and through them I catch glimpses of round tables and laughing, chatting teenagers. My stomach rumbles, already unsatisfied with the coffee.

Ms. Rose sees me walk into the lobby. She says good-bye to the teacher she'd been having a conversation with and hurries over to me.

"Mel!" she calls. I look over. "How did it go?"

"I didn't die, did I?"

Ms. Rose hesitates, her smile slipping a fraction of a second. "No, of course not. Mel, you're so funny. Well, I just wanted to say, you're welcome to go have some lunch in the cafeteria. There's still a half-hour left."

"Thank you." I pivot away and walk stiffly into the noisy dining hall.

The food is pre-packaged and set out on shelves inside of the line, which is just an enclosed counter space off the kitchens. I eye the choices: plastic-wrapped PB&Js, bagels and cereals, salads, turkey hoagies, and a very unpalatable looking brown sandwich. On the bottom two shelves are side dish options, like fruits and vegetables, soft pretzels, pasta salads, bottled water, and cookies. This is a new and strange experience for me. The dining hall is like a real cafeteria straight out of the movies. Not that I've watched a movie in five years. I think I've read about six books for pleasure, total, in the last two years as well. So this really is foreign, and not just because I'm in an entirely different hemisphere.

I take a Caesar salad, skim milk, and two plastic cups of sliced strawberries. Strawberries are very rich in Vitamin C. And there's no juice selection. I'll either have to buy some or crack open an emergency Vitamin C powder packet. I finger my pocket while studying the water bottles lining the bottom shelf. Should I?

Seeing as everyone else had been through here fifteen minutes ago, I thought I was alone. But now I become aware of someone else in the lunch line. I turn my head slightly and see one of the twins I met the night before, Leah or Hale. Whoever it is, she's wearing a long bright orange T-shirt, white knee-length pants, and a rainbow Mardi Gras bead necklace looped multiple times around her neck. She reaches up to get a pre-wrapped moon pie and her hair shakes back. I see matching earrings swinging from her auricles.

After successfully obtaining the moon pie, the twin settles back on her feet and walks toward the other door. Then she catches sight of me and her eyebrows fly up in surprise. A second later a benevolent smile replaces the look.

"Hi," she says. I nod in reply and start to move away. "Wait," the twin says. "You're…Mel, right?"

"Yes."

"I know we met last night, but I'm Hale." The twin extends a hand. I vacillate for a moment, then reach out my own hand and Hale shakes it. "Nice to meet you."

"*Mm*." I retract my arm. Hale glances at my lunch.

"Doesn't this food looks so amazing?" she asks sarcastically, making a face. I blink, then shrug.

"It's a little different. Well, a lot different. At Watson, the food was cooked."

"That must be nice." Hale puts on the friendly smile again. My eyes travel over the lunch tables. My stomach seems to drop slightly as, after looking it over again, I don't see a trace of dark red hair. I feel the start of panic in my stomach. What if last night wasn't real? What if I didn't actually see him? What if Shadow's right and I'm just seeing things?

No. I am not crazy. There's a good reason for him not being here. I will find him later. I will find him. My eyes land on an empty table in the far corner, but suddenly I'm not seeing the table, I'm seeing a nine-year-old boy, hovering at the edge of the Watson dining hall, unsure where to sit–

"Mel?" I hear. I slowly look back at Hale. Her head is cocked, one finger wound halfway around a lock of hair. "Did you hear me? Do you want to come sit at our table? Or are you going out somewhere?"

"I…" I glance back at the empty table. Peace and quiet await; well, not quiet, but lack of conversation. However, I might learn more if I sit with Hale and her friends. About Ray, for instance, and about Marvin Academy. "Fine."

"Okay." Hale raises an eyebrow but sweeps ahead and shows me to a round table on the opposite side of the room.

Three people are seated at the table, the same girls from last night. The other twin–Leah, I deduce–is dressed in a dark green tank top with the word "Bonzer" stamped across the chest. She's deep in conversation with the strawberry blonde, Caidy. The pretty one, Vivian, is leaning back in her chair, eyes focused on a strand of silky black hair between her fingers. As I watch her fingers move, the strand twists into a small, perfect braid.

"Hey, Hale." Vivian looks up questioningly, letting the strand fall. It unravels before it hits her shoulder.

"Hey, Viv." Hale sits down in the chair next to Vivian, where a tray is already full of a half-eaten lunch. "Sit here, Mel." She gestures to the seat beside her. As I sit down Hale looks at the other two girls. "Remember Mel, guys?"

"Hi, Mel." Vivian waves.

"Hi." Leah pauses her conversation enough for a salutation. Caidy glances over during the hiatus.

"Hello." She quickly turns back to Leah and continues their conversation.

"So where are you from, Mel?" Hale asks, tearing open her moon pie.

"New York," I reply, uncovering my salad.

"The United States, cool. I spent a semester in California last year," Hale says.

"Oh." I pop the lid off of the dressing cup and start pouring.

"Why did you come to Brisbane?" Vivian inquires. She has a subdued, yet not toneless, voice.

"I have an assignment here." I put a piece of lettuce in my mouth so I can chew. I wait while Vivian asks Leah about her fourth period class, which they apparently don't have together, and Hale asks Vivian how her roommate issue is coming. I try to understand how their classes work from what I hear, but it doesn't add up to me; they don't give away enough information. After five minutes there's a slight pause in the conversation. I tentatively speak. "How do your classes work? What do you study?"

Vivian meets my eyes and smiles affably. "Everyone here has a certain area of expertise which they study. We call it our Pro, short for profession."

"Mine's design," Hale tells me. "I work on making better clothes to wear for reconnaissance and espionage. I have design class next. Our mornings are spent studying regular subjects, like math and science. But in the afternoon we take specific classes, straight from lunch until four."

"*Hmm.*" I take another bite of salad, then ask Vivian, "What do you study?"

She grins. "Forensic science and medical examination. You know, like blood spatters and autopsies."

"Wow." The word slips out before I can stop it. I quickly take another bite of salad.

Vivian's grin widens. "What were you expecting?"

I debate for a minute. "Maybe make-up, or design as well."

"Not dead bodies?"

"Not really." I look over at Leah and Caidy, still talking. "What–"

"My sister does geology," Hale answers before I'm done asking. "Caidy's into meteorology."

I fight to control a gasp. "Meteorology? Um…" I grip my knees under the table. "What does Ra…uh, Jonathon do?"

I notice Caidy's glance slides over to me. I stare back until she rolls her eyes and looks away.

Hale laughs. "Meteorology! I've never met someone who knows so much. Sometimes, he can just talk forever about different aspects of weather. But I never understand what he's talking about."

I squeeze my knees harder. I wasn't hallucinating! (Not that I thought I had been.) And of course she can't understand him. Not even I could. Which only proves… I have to find him again! But maybe, while I'm here, I can find out what happened. "Do Jonathon's parents live around here?"

Hale's expression sobers. "No, he was at an orphanage. I wouldn't ask him about his past. It's sort of a touchy subject for him, I think, since he always gets a really weird look on his face when we bring it up. Or I should say, brought it up. We don't talk about it with him anymore."

"Why is he at Marvin, then?" I find myself leaning in

eagerly and quickly straighten my posture.

"Um, I think the old weather Pro head teacher got him in or something." Hale bites her lip. "Should I be telling you this? Is it confidential?" She gives a nervous laugh.

"Believe me, it's okay." I respond with a bitter laugh of my own. "Not like I'll be gossiping. Even if I did know anyone." I close my mouth abruptly.

"Well, I think Jonathon got really sick or something. And then during the time he was at the hospital, the orphanage went bankrupt or something. Then, like, three Julys ago, he came here. When he was thirteen. That's all I know, honest," Hale adds, misinterpreting my skeptical expression.

So he got "really sick", huh? And his orphanage conveniently went bankrupt? Convenient that he was at an orphanage at all, right? And what was he doing in between late May when I sat at his immensely depressing funeral and July? And how did he get here? Who came up with the orphanage whitewash? Who said he died?

Vivian elbowing Hale under the table and whispering the word "typical" interrupts my mental cross-examination. Though I'm not paying strict attention doesn't mean I don't catch stuff like that. In fact, I practice catching stuff like that. It's only when I'm really deep in thought that I miss stuff. It's a weakness I work on constantly.

"What?" I demand, frowning. I don't usually refer to myself as "typical".

"Nothing," Hale says, too quickly. I glare at her and wait for another answer.

"It's okay, Hale." Vivian laughs, turning to meet my gaze, which I grudgingly admire. "It's just that all the new girls, or the exchange students, always ask about Jonathon."

"What? What do you mean?" I stammer, not comprehending. Hale stares at me like I'm insane. Vivian's eyebrows pull together, but she answers me.

"You know. They think he's cute."

I lean back in my chair, away from her words.

"Leah and I think it's because they like the strong silent type," Hale says, fighting a grin.

"Silent?" I say incredulously. I do not remember Ray being silent.

"He is, sort of," Vivian agrees.

"What do you mean?"

Hale stares at the wall, ruminating. "It's hard to describe. Like, he's in his own little world, but he's not really a space cadet. I don't see him much, so I don't really know."

"He always seems to be thinking really hard," Vivian offers. "Sometimes it looks like he's having these arguments with himself because he gets this real concentrated look on his face." She cocks her head. "Why?"

"Do you like strong and silent, too?" Hale snorts.

"No," I say quickly, at a loss for a better response.

Hale seems to take this as an invitation for more girly conversation. "Do you have a boyfriend?"

"No."

"Aw. Why? Not met the right guy?" She waggles her eyebrows.

I scowl. "I focus on my work."

"Oh." Hale pulls away a little, as if stung by my words.

"How do your classes work?" Vivian asks hastily.

"Nicely," I respond, keeping the smugness in my tone to a bare minimum. Vivian laughs. Funny, I hadn't meant that as a joke.

"Seriously," she says.

I stab a forkful of lettuce and chew for a moment. "We have math and science and English and history. Lots of it has to do with defense and the greater good and all, you know? Then we have our regular classes: martial arts, strategies, deductive reasoning, observation, survival, etcetera." I continue eating, looking around again. I suddenly remember something. "Where is Jonathon?"

"I don't know. Caidy?" Hale asks. Caidy looks up from her conversation.

"Yeah, Hale?"

"Where's Jonathon?"

It looks like Caidy's repressing a smile. "Mum had him stay through lunch. Not that he did anything wrong," she adds quickly. I nod. Of course Ray wouldn't have done anything wrong. He was all the teachers' favorite back home. "He's finishing up that tornado documentary. His is so awesome. It's even better than mine." I see Hale nod while rolling her eyes. Apparently, Caidy bragging about 'Jonathon' isn't a rarity. "Why?"

"Just wondering." Hale shrugs and takes a bite of her moon pie. Caidy hesitates, then turns back to Leah.

"There's, like, five minutes left." Vivian looks at me. "Hey, Mel! I have an idea. Cai reminded me when she said that about her documentary. I've already finished the project we're doing in Pro, so if you're free, after lunch, I can give you a tour of Marvin. If it's okay with Ms. Rose, that is. We can ask her."

I'm about to shake my head—no thank you, Vivian, I have work to do—but I stop. Maybe we'll see Ray. I don't think the teachers here would be too happy if I were wandering around by myself, but if I was on a tour....

"Okay."

11

Ms. Rose is enthusiastic about Vivian's idea. In fact, she strikes me as a very enthusiastic person altogether. Vivian seems pleased, too. She goes around the main building–the first two floors have wings dedicated to each Pro–telling me about each section. There's the design section ("Hi Hale!"; "Hey Viv! Check this out."; "Ooh, cute."; "Hi, Mel."; "Hello, Hale."; and so on until I impatiently clear my throat), and the geology wing (to Vivian's disappointment, we can't go in because the students are using hammers and there are flying pieces of sediment all over the place), and the medical classrooms, including the nurse's office (at Watson we have an infirmary), and her wing, forensics ("Hey, Ms. Kreiser. Here's a note from Ms. Rose. I'm giving Mel a tour."), and others, but at this point I'm just waiting for meteorology and file what I've learned in the back of my mind for later use.

Finally Vivian beckons to me and we exit the building through a back door. We step into dazzling sunlight. I squint a little, looking out at the green grass. I hear city noises in the distance. We're on the posterior lawn. Diagonal from our position is a small line of trees. I make out bricks behind it. And in front of the foliage is playground equipment, including a swing set, a slide, monkey bars, and a jungle gym.

"Is that a playground?" I ask, one eyebrow raised.

"Yeah," Vivian responds without hesitation. She's walking on the sidewalk right by the main building, following its inner curve. "The younger kids–we start enrolling around seven–go there for recess, and we older kids hang out there in the evenings."

"Oh." I try to wrap my brain around the concept of recess. It's another thing I've only read about or seen in one of the few movies I've actually watched. Why would the staff put a break in the curriculum? It's just an opportunity for kids to lose focus.

I follow Vivian around the sidewalk to a brick building behind the playground. Nearing the front doors, I see another structure beyond this one. Facing away from the trees, the second building is shabbier than the first. Connected to it is a brick wall. Though this wall is as tall as the building—maybe shorter—and thicker than the wall back home with an alley behind it instead of a walking track, I still catch my breath.

"That's the storage warehouse," Vivian explains, gesturing to the shabbier building. "This one is meteorology."

My breath catches in my throat again. I swallow hard and convince my feet to follow Vivian.

The meteorology lab is a long hallway with classrooms on both sides and a constant stream of chatter coming from everywhere. Vivian walks to the end of the long corridor and peeks in the last classroom. In here are little workspaces surrounded by partitions, like in an office. Judging by the few I can see into, each one is equipped with a laptop and a personal electronic weather station on the wall.

"Hi, Ms. Richards." Vivian waves to the teacher by the door. "Can we come in? I'm showing Mel around. Mel, this is Ms. Richards, Caidy's mum."

"Sure, Vivian, it's a free period." The teacher nods. She looks like she's in her early forties, tall with roan hair pulled back in a tight bun. "My daughter is in her cubicle, if you want to talk to her."

"Terrif. Come on, Mel."

I sigh and follow once again, fervently looking around for him. I hope this is his room this period—is it fifth? I think that's what Vivian said. Oh no. I should remember stuff like this. I need to–

As I round the corner after Vivian, I see him. Apparently, this *is* his fifth period. He's at the end of this row, working at his laptop. As soon as I turn the corner he looks up at me.

Vivian spots Caidy and bounds over. "Hey! Whatchya doing?" Caidy's cubicle is about halfway down, on the opposite side as his.

I rock back on my heels for a moment, then walk slowly to Ray's cubicle. The chair next to him is empty. I pull it out and hesitantly sit down. "Hi."

"Hi," Ray replies, hitting enter on his keyboard without looking at it. "How are you?" His mouth twitches. "Get a good night's sleep?"

"Yes. And I feel absolutely fine–like last night."

"Oh." Now he sucks in his cheek, looking apprehensive. "Um. How was your morning?"

"Frustrating."

"Sorry to hear that." He frowns. "Why? You really don't seem frustratable."

"I'm not," I grumble. "At least I'm not when I can control the situation. And 'frustratable' is not a word."

"Unfortunately, that rules out a lot of situations." He's back to almost laughing.

"Glad I can amuse you." A strange sense of release is flowing through me. It's like iron bands are relaxing around my chest. I haven't joked with someone like this in a long time, maybe too long.

"So you're getting a tour?" Ray glances down at his computer. He scrolls through something and hits the delete button a few times. "How long are you planning on staying?" There's something–some emotion–veiled under his tone. I can't tell if it's uneasiness or anxiety, or if maybe I'm just imagining it.

"Yes. And the plan now is two weeks. Hopefully I will have gotten a lead or two by then," I mutter.

"Is that what's frustrating?" Ray's eyebrows pull together. "The assignment didn't go so well this morning?" As he reaches up to adjust the screen I see the scars on his hand again. I swallow hard a few times to clear my airway.

"Yes," I say, and my voice sounds smaller than usual. I clear my throat, hoping for better results. "I can't find anything. It's as if that person–the man–left no trace whatsoever."

"That's rough," Ray says sympathetically. I nod, then change the subject.

"What are you doing now?" I lean in to see the monitor better. I notice that he has two–the one on his laptop and an extra one he can move freely between.

"Animating the start of a tornado," he replies. "See, when certain conditions exist in one region and–"

"Oh no, not gibberish." I kick off the floor and roll away a few feet (or, since I'm in Australia, approximately 1.75 meters). Ray actually does laugh now. I feel a prickling in my neck and glance behind me. From the middle of the row Vivian flutters her fingers at me before looking back at Caidy's computer screen. Caidy, though, is staring at me with an unfathomable expression.

"Yes, gibberish," Ray chuckles, but as I roll back his expression looks more confused than entertained. "Oh, never mind." He suddenly closes the program and leans back in his chair. "Tell me about your school."

I don't question his quick change of topic even tough I feel a slight lump in my throat. He needs telling.

I take a deep breath, then frown. "You honestly don't remember?" I ask quietly. I fight back the pleading that wants to accompany my words.

Ray's fist contracts around his shirt. "No." His eyes flick from the computer to my face, and back. "I'm sorry, Mel." His gaze drops back to his lab and he notices his hand. This time he opens his fist quickly and moves it back to the computer. "I'm Jonathon, not Ra–" He stops abruptly, swallowing something back.

"But you hate the name Jonathon," I tell him, still quiet and restrained.

Ray's head whips around. "How..." His fingers stiffen on the keyboard. "I mean, why..."

"How is the animation coming, Jonathon?" a smooth, authoritative voice interrupts. I look away from Ray to see the teacher–Ms. Richards–bending down and studying the monitor. "There's nothing on here. Did you close the program?"

"Yes," Ray says in the more subdued voice he'd used with Caidy and the others last night. "I was taking a few minute's break."

He glances at me. My response is automatic. I hardly– no, I don't–think before I shoot him a quarter smile. *Sorry.*

Instantly Ray raises one eyebrow and rolls his eyes the opposite way, his shoulders rising slightly. *It's no big deal.*

But it is. It's a huge deal. It's been so long since I last shot a look at someone, let alone have him understand it like only one person can and then react to it.

I feel a hand on my shoulder.

"Mel? You're looking a little pale. Do you want to go see the nurse?"

I move my shoulder away from Ms. Richards' hand. "No, I'm not sick, I'm–"

"You know, you've probably had a big day. I bet you're tired, too, from jet lag." Ms. Richards holds out a hand. To what, help me up? I glare in response. "I really think you should go get some rest."

"I feel fine." I clench my jaw.

Ms. Richards all but pulls me out of that chair. I twist away only semi-easily since I'm trying to tone down the defense so I don't make a big scene.

"Be reasonable," Ms. Richards says sharply. I can feel Caidy and Vivian and everyone else in the row staring at me. Obviously Ms. Richards is going to make this a big deal. What, am I a distraction to her prize student? Well, I will not be roped into making an idiot out of myself. Ray looks like he's about to protest. I meet his eyes. *Later.* Hoping this will get the Defensive One off my back, I turn away and walk down the row, not quickly, but not like a snail either.

Vivian half-stands when I reach her. "No, stay. I'm done with the tour," I snap. She sits back down, a worried crease in her previously smooth forehead. I make it out the door before I whirl around and let loose.

"Why are you following me? I'm leaving. I'm going back to my room. Look, I even found the door all by myself. What's—"

"Stop shouting." Ms. Richards pushes the door all the way closed. I give her a supercilious look.

"I'm as tranquil as a sage. And I am going. Exit stage left, do not pass GO, do not collect two hundred dollars. Did I miss anything?" I start to stride away, breathing deeply through my nose.

Ms. Richards' voice pulls me to a halt. "I've noticed, Mel, that it seems like you know Jonathon from somewhere."

My teeth grit together as I spin back around. "Tell me the truth," I demand, glowering at her face. It's impassive, save her lips, which are pressed together in a thin line. "The whole truth about him. Now."

"Mel, there really isn't that much to tell." She seems amused by my livid expression. She shakes her head. "I just feel you should know. He was very sick for a very long time.

He's only started to really recover in the past year. I think it would be unwise–unhealthy–for you to be playing with his mind like this." She pauses.

My eyes widen in surprise and indignation. Playing with his mind? If that's what she thinks…

"I–"

"Stop." Ms. Richards takes a deep breath. "Let me just give you this warning. I care about Jonathon very much. If you keep deliberately confusing him like this, I will have to ask you to stay elsewhere–or just away."

I fight with the urge to knock out all four of her incisors. Without responding I turn away and run around the corner. I keep running to the stairwell and up the stairs, letting my pent-up anger flow out through my limbs. Back in my guestroom I fumble in my duffel bag and pull out an exercise DVD. Quickly I shove it into the player and press play. Jabs, uppercuts, hooks, they don't help. But I keep going until the clock reads 4:15, restarting the workout four times.

Catching my breath, I take a shower before turning on the computer and logging into my email. I'll just write Shadow. It'll be easier than talking to him.

He's already emailed me. Five times. I scroll through the first four quickly. They're just how-are-you-doings and don't-forget-to-keep-me-posteds. The fifth one has a real message, though.

Amber. Just spoke with the big guys. Have determined our little friend has four, plus thirteen hundred and four. We don't know which four she has yet, but we'll play around until we do. Your big guys are alerted. They haven't noticed you yet. Be good.

Translation: Shadow talked to the Rochester PD and they've found that Maryanne stole four birth certificates total, but they haven't determined which ones. Also, the total money Maryanne obtained from identity theft is $1,304.

Shadow or the Rochester PD has notified Brisbane police who Maryanne is and that her accomplice may be in the city. But the police don't know about me, as usual. And I'm supposed to be good. Which is code for stay safe. Which loosely translated is, make sure you're careful. Which means he's still treating me like a five-year-old.

I write back.

Yeah. Great. I didn't do so hot on my test. But I'll retake it and try to do better. Other than that all's peachy. Tell me how everything goes. Mel.

Meaning: no results today but I will try again. And keep me posted.

I look back at Shadow's message. The amount of money catches my eye. I frown, open a new tab, and search the cost of a last-minute flight out of JFK airport to Brisbane. The cheapest is about $1,250, and that's with a five-hour layover in Japan, making it around twenty-eight hours total. The ticket I'd bought—a next day one—had been a twenty-six hour flight, so it was even more expensive.

So all but fifty-four dollars, assuming Maryanne went with the inexpensive flight, had been used on the flight. Fifty-four dollars that could presumably have been used to pay the check last night, or a cab ride and the bottle of wine.

Obviously, then, that was all the money was needed for. Whatever scheme Maryanne and Avocado Man have, it's financially secure. Otherwise, Maryanne would have stolen more money. She was done with that part by the time I started the End. It could hardly be a coincidence; it's too close to the cost of the plane ticket.

This would lead me to assume, then, that Maryanne and Avocado Man—him especially—are very far along in their plans. Which means I need to work faster, or just be smarter.

Though I am smart. Very smart. I should be able to do this.

12

I tie my sneakers and get up, ready to head down to dinner. I make it to the stairs before hearing Caidy's voice echoing down the stairway. I hesitate in the doorway, then duck back and close it until it's just barely cracked. I lean my ear closer so I can hear.

Someone–it sounds like Vivian–is asking, "What's got you so glum, Caidy?"

"Well, my mum asked Jonathon to stay in the lab during dinner. To work on his project, which she says is absolutely fantastic." Caidy's voice is admiring, but accompanied by a sigh of disappointment. "That means…"

"He's not going to be at dinner?" I think it's Hale's voice that finishes the sentence. "Soooo? There'll be lots more dinners, Caidy. Plenty of time for you to ogle the back of his head."

My palms sting and I realize I'm clenching my fists, pressing my nails into them until it hurts. I can't loosen them yet. I don't want to.

"I do not ogle," Caidy responds in a furious whisper I can hardly make out. (I wouldn't be able to unless I was specially trained for this sort of thing, which I am.)

"Stare, gaze, watch, observe, take your pick," Hale's voice says equably.

"None of them."

"Then what are you so upset about, if you don't ogle, stare, gaze, watch, obser–"

"Hale, shut up," Caidy says sharply.

"What happened, Cai?" a voice like Hale's—which I'm guessing is Leah, since Hale saying this would not make sense—asks sympathetically. Caidy lets her breath out in a huff. They must be almost passing the door by now.

"It's just…this is the first time he argued with Mum. I mean, not a real argument. Jon wouldn't do that, really."

Wait! *Jon?* Since when does she call him *Jon?*

"It was more like an…objection. Mum's like, 'Why don't you stay and work on your animation. It's getting so good, and I can see you're on a roll. You can have dinner in here,' or something along those lines. And Jon says, 'Um…no thanks. I think I'd rather go to dinner tonight.' Of course Mum won in the end, because Jon wouldn't really argue with a teacher, but still…. And then," Caidy continues in a furious whisper, "Jonathon was all distracted the rest of the day. Did you notice that, Viv, before you left?"

"Um…" Vivian's voice sounds a little apologetic. "Yeah, sort of."

"See? It was like that the whole day. Work for a minute, glance at the clock, look around, sigh, get back to the notes…."

"What's the big deal? You don't have to get angry over his mood swings, Cai. You don't control him." The voices are getting softer now. They must be moving away.

"Hale, you are so not helping. Why don't you go ahead and save a seat or something?"

"It would be pointless," Hale says matter-of-factly. "No one ever sits at our table."

"Except at lunch today, that girl…"

"You mean Mel?" Hale responds blithely. "She doesn't seem that bad. She's interesting."

"*Mel*. What a stupid name."

What a nice girl. I make a mental note to trip her next time I encounter her in the hallway.

Rain

It's Vivian who speaks next, faintly, but I can still tell her voice isn't as benign as usual. "You know what, Hale? I think we should save our seats. Let's go."

"Yeah, Viv." Hale sounds exasperated, and something else, but they're too far away. "Later, Caidy, later, sis."

"What's their problem?" Caidy asks a few moments later when, I assume, Hale and Vivian are out of earshot.

I can't make out Leah's reply, and after that the voices fade. I stand up straight, any desire to go to dinner gone. Scowling, I trudge back to my room and dig in my duffel bag for a granola bar or two. It hardly helps, and I have another late night trying to get to sleep with a gyrating mind and growling stomach.

I'm still able to get up early this morning. Not that I have a choice. My phone's vibrating incessantly on the bedside table. Forcing away wisps of fatigue I grab it, check the caller ID, and open up. "Hello."

"I–called–you–seventeen–times–yesterday," Shadows irate voice says into my ear, barely suppressing a yell. "Ms. Rose said you got back okay, but why didn't you answer?"

"Because I'm not attached at the hip to a cellular device?" I mutter sleepily, pulling today's clothes from my bag.

"Well, find some tape and append one, please. No, forget the please. This is an order." Shadow takes a few deep breaths. "How did it go?"

"I emailed you already."

"With the least possible detail you could possibly put into a message," Shadow replies exasperatedly. "Don't tell me that's all."

"That's all." I brush my hair in a few strokes and snap a ponytail back around it. "There was nothing–no evidence, no clues–around there. I'm going back today. I'll try some nearby suburbs and—"

"Wait, Amber. I was going to suggest that you wait until the police have finished questioning Maryanne."

"Oh, like take a break, you mean?" I cut him off, like he so rudely did to me. "I don't think so."

"Just listen—"

"Still not thinking so," I clarify, in case he's wondering. "I'll let you know how it goes, okay?"

"You better." Shadow's threat is slightly marred by the fact that he's sighing.

"Bye."

There's silence on the other end before Shadow finally says, "Bye," in a noticeably quieter voice.

I eat another two granola bars as well as a Vitamin C powder packet and leave the building just like yesterday. And, just like yesterday, everything starts as a complete waste. Waste of energy, waste of information, waste of time that could be spent figuring out the mystery of Ray's disappearance rather than searching futilely and despondently for nonexistent traces of—

Stop it! I literally stomp the asphalt beneath my feet after three hours of this. *Get the priorities straight. This is work. This is what's important.* Yes, this is what I need to be focusing all of my energy on.

But another irritating voice inside my cranium pipes up with something that occurred to me last night. *What'll happen when I leave, if Ray doesn't remember me?*

Shut up, I respond bitterly, even though I can't deny this is a problem. The likeliest outcome is that I'll—maybe—get this End finished, leave next Tuesday, and exchange email with Ray from then on. Phone contact is hardly an option since Rochester and Brisbane share few waking hours, most of which would be spent in school. But now that I know he's alive it's going to be doubly—triply? quadruply?—hard to go back to a life that doesn't include seeing him everyday and joking around and having that one person who actually understands me.

Toughen up, the responsible voice chides me. *You lived before him and after him. Can we focus now?*

No! I moan, then catch myself and mentally reply with a firm, *Yes*. Stifling a sigh I turn down the next alley.

An hour and a half later my phone rings. I find a nearby bench and scowl as I answer. "I'm fine."

"Good," Shadow says. "That's half of my conversation done with."

"What's the other half?"

"I just spoke with the police. They heard from the Brisbane PD that Maryanne refuses to give anything away."

"I wish I could interrogate her myself," I mutter.

"They don't know about you, remember?"

"Yes."

"Well, there's your reason–"

"Okay." I stand up. "If that's all...."

"Do you want to tell me about your first day there?" Shadow sounds uncertain.

"Not especially."

"Oh. Well, keep me–"

"Posted. Yeah, whatever. Bye." I hang up and start down the street again. After a block my prickling neck tells me someone's watching me. I scan the sidewalk out of the corner of my eye, determine it's not a pedestrian, and switch my gaze to the street. A small, dark green car hovering near a parking space draws my attention. Other vehicles are zooming by while this guy seems unable to decide whether he should park or drive on.

I move another block and check again. It's still moving slowly behind me. Fighting a grin, I walk straight into a large crowd. While the driver's vision of me is obscured, I duck into a hair salon and watch the car roll by. I've successfully confused my pursuer. I feign comparing the prices of two hair gels while still keeping an eye on the car.

"It's about time you arrived," a voice says behind me. I look over my shoulder and see one of the stylists staring at me critically. "What took you so long?"

"I don't believe I know you," I say, quickly but cavalierly. "And I don't see why you were expecting me."

"Not you, hon. Your hair." The lady rolls her eyes. "It's definitely due for a new style. Sorry, but do you always wear that ponytail?"

"Do you always wear that tawdry dye?"

"It is nice, isn't it?" She looks smug, patting down her hair. "Do you want some? It's on special."

Not *nice*, you idiot. *Tawdry.* Cheap. Ugly. Substandard.

"I do not." I turn away and stride to the entrance. "And you know what? Ponytails are practical." Then I slam the shop door and resume my work.

The car is a block ahead of me now. Keeping low, I follow behind, waiting for it to give up and go back to its home base. Hopefully it will give me a new lead. I feel excitement in my gut that comes from–finally–getting back on the trail.

Unfortunately, before I have time to seek out a cab, the car suddenly pulls out to the main road and turns out of sight. I run forward and see it disappearing down a road marked Edward Street. I grin. This is good. This means he–or they–are getting nervous about what I'm up to and want to know if I'm getting closer or not.

Now they'll be expecting me to follow them this afternoon. I grin as I get on the next bus. What they won't be expecting is for me to come back tomorrow after doing extensive research on the area.

Sure we're not just in a hurry to get back? the

annoyingly responsible voice asks.

Of course, I snap. *This is strictly business.*

Right.

It's a sarcastic retort, but at least I can now repress my own doubts.

No matter what I tell myself, I can't stop my head from turning to peer at the lobby. Ms. Rose spots me and shepherds me into the cafeteria, insisting I eat something. "We'll leave the lunch bar open for another half hour if you want. Or you can take something up to your room."

"The latter, please." I quickly slip through the doors, away from her too-sweet disposition. It's like eating a powdered and iced doughnut. Not that I've ever.

The cafeteria's mostly empty; a few students are straggling out the opposite door. I head for the lunch bar. I'm halfway across the room before I discern a movement out of the corner of my eye. I spin around.

Ray straightens up, the shoe he was tying sliding off the bench. "Hi," he says. "I was wondering if you were going to come back during lunch."

"You were, huh?" My voice sort of loses its usual hard edge.

"Yeah." He walks over to me. "Dan said you were here yesterday. Actually, he said 'that American spy girl ate lunch in the caf yesterday. She wasn't wearing black.'"

"I'm undercover, not Goth," I say, rolling my eyes.

"That's Dan for you." Ray shrugs while studying my face. "How's your..." His brow furrows, as if he's looking for the right word. He shakes his head. "I mean, get any new leads today?"

I grin. "Oh, yeah." I tell him in a low voice what happened with the car. His eyebrows move up an inch.

"That does sound helpful. What are you going to do

now?"

"Probably look at some more maps, figure out where to go next." I wait to see if he'll say something like "You better make sure you're careful", but he doesn't. How refreshing. "I guess I'll see if I can narrow it down tomorrow." I'm shocked to find myself sighing after that sentence.

Ray's also looking bemused. "You don't want to?"

"Of course I do," I reply quickly. It's supposed to have a 'duh' implication, but somehow that gets lost.

"Of course you do," he repeats quietly. "And—"

"Jonathon!" someone cries. I whip around and press my lips together when I see Caidy in the doorway.

"Hello," Ray intones, nodding past me.

"Jon," Caidy pants, running up and skidding to a stop by Ray. I feel a slight—well, no, large—twinge of annoyance. "Mum sent me to look for you. She's wondering where you are. We're doing a really fun lesson today, just for us."

"Okay. One moment." Ray looks back at me.

"You were saying something," I say, aiming at nonchalance. It comes out more like annoyance. The corner of his mouth twitches. "It started with 'And'."

"And you wouldn't admit it if you didn't want to go tomorrow, anyway," he says matter-of-factly. I clench my jaw, unable to deny his words and feeling strangely jovial.

Caidy looks furtively from me to Ray. I see her cheek trembling and I can tell she wants desperately to shout, "Admit what? Go where?" I grudgingly admire her self-control.

"I guess I'll see you later, then," Ray murmurs as Caidy gives a very non-blasé tap of her foot.

"Of course. I mean, sure. Yes." I come dangerously close to biting my lip, wondering why I sound stupid. Do I sound stupid? Am I just being stupid? This is getting very confusing.

Ray chuckles. "Are you coming down here for dinner?"

"Um," Caidy interrupts. "Um, Jon, I think this–" she glances at me with a trace of a smirk playing on her face, "–lesson, is going to go through dinner, so…"

The little jerk. I roll my eyes to communicate that I don't care what her covert little lesson is, but of course she doesn't pick it up.

Ray looks surprised. "Are you sure?"

"Quite." Caidy tucks a strand of hair behind her ear.

"Oh. And we can't…"

"We can eat after," Caidy says in a final sort of tone. I wonder when *she* became a member of the faculty.

"Whatever." I back towards the door. "Tomorrow, then. Or sometime."

"Bye," Ray says almost despondently.

I get in a few more exercise tapes before eating a Vitamin C powder packet and a protein bar. I reply to a few of Shadow's how's-it-goings so he doesn't go postal on me again and set out my phone so I can hear it if he calls.

I assume it's Shadow when the little device starts buzzing, but the caller ID only gives a number. I flip it open and say in a slow voice, "Hello?"

"You haven't called me in forever. What's your problem? I want to know about Brisbane! Am I missing anything? Like, any cute guys?"

This can only be one person. "Hi, Lyvia."

"That doesn't answer any of my questions!" Lyvia complains. "I had to ask Mr. Syme for your number cause you didn't call and give it to me. Why haven't you called?"

"I've been busy."

"With what?"

"My End, obviously."

"Oh." She sighs.

"What else would I be busy with?" I ask.

"Boys," she answers immediately. "Or new friends while forgetting about old friends."

"I haven't forgotten about you. And no. And no again."

"You didn't meet anyone interesting?" It's her turn to be exasperated.

I don't answer at first, wondering if I should tell Lyvia about Ray. She might pull a Shadow on me and tell me to forget it. But she's really the only person I can talk to. Other than Ray, of course.

"Ha! I knew it!"

"I haven't said anything yet."

"Silence speaks louder than words," Lyvia says sagely.

"My silence is saying 'Shut up, Lyvia.'"

"Ha!"

"Not ha. Really. Nothing much is going on."

Lyvia gives a long, drawn out sigh. "Okay, fine. Well, you could at least ask me how my life is going."

"How is your life going?"

"Well...." She goes off on a long spiel about her issues with the two boys she likes and the three that she knows like her and a lot of other senseless things. I do my best to "*Mm*-hmm" and "Huh" and "Yeah" at the right times, feeling a strange mixture of annoyance and gratitude. Finally she has to go.

"Bye, then," she says. "Call me more often, okay?"

"I'll try," I say, before hanging up. For the next hour I look over maps of Brisbane in and around Edward Street, plotting tomorrow's locations.

Finally I lie down on the bed, my head spinning enough that it makes me tired instead of maddeningly awake. Before I drift off I consider again something that's been bothering me: if Ray is here, then whose ashes are buried in the Rochester cemetery?

Rain
* * *

The spinning wears off around midnight, so I wake up late at seven, still tired. I automatically go through my morning routine. Instead of thinking about what I'm doing, though, I catch myself longing for more sleep. I quickly shake that off and look over–a.k.a. memorize–my notes for today's search. I force myself to concentrate so deeply that I'm surprised to hear the knocking on my door a half-hour later.

I look through the peephole and scowl as I crack open the door. What's she doing here?

"Hello, Mel," Ms. Richards says in a businesslike tone. "How are you this morning? I've come to ask you a few questions."

Interesting strategy to pretend she cares, asking how I am but not waiting for the answer.

I look at her aloofly and feel a spark of pleasure that she seems slightly thrown by my attitude.

"Yes, see, thinking back to our conversation yesterday–"

Oh, it's a conversation now? Not an inequitable accusation on her part?

"–I realized I never asked you for your story…about Jonathon." She leans in, as if eager for the next part, then catches herself and straightens up. I raise my eyebrows a little. "Um…well, Mel, who do you feel he reminds you of?"

"Well," I say in mock thoughtfulness, concealing reticence, "I think he reminds me of"–don't you think I'm not seeing that excited expression, lady–"Jonathon, right?"

Blank shock flits over Ms. Richards' face for a second before she recomposes. "You mean another Jonathon you knew, honey?"

I don't miss the use of past tense. "No, I don't know–nor did I ever know–any other Jonathon."

This time it's outright frustration on her features. "Well," she says, back to being professional, "thank you, Mel. I guess I'll see you around." She backs up a step. I'm ready to close the door when her voice stops me.

"Oh, sweetie?"

I stare at her.

She lets out her breath in a little huff. "Remember what I said. About Jonathon and his health."

Rage curdles in my gut. "I won't forget."

Now I really do close the door, still glowering.

But my mind is torn as my feet lead me to the bed. No one–meaning Shadow and even Ray himself–believes me about Ray. If I try to prove myself right and fail–my stomach lurches uncomfortably–people, especially Ray, will think I'm crazy. My stomach lurches again, even more unpleasantly this time. But then, if I don't try, what'll happen when I leave, which is inevitable? The third heave of my stomach is downright sickening.

I put my shoes on, still undecided, and head outside, making a split-second decision to go to the school breakfast today.

He meets me halfway down the stairs. Should my stomach have lurched again? Is this normal? I think not. I better not be getting sick.

"Good morning," Ray says pleasantly. He jumps down to the landing so he can walk beside me.

"That depends on whom you ask," I tell him, looking determinedly at the stairs in front of me.

"Why?" He glances sideways at me. "Having a bad one?"

I jerk my head noncommittally.

"What happened?"

"I didn't say… Oh, never mind." I shouldn't be surprised that Ray can see right through me. "It's nothing really. And don't ask again," I warn before he can open his mouth.

"Fine. What if I ask about your assignment?"

"That's okay. I've got a few more places figured out to go to today. And I am very excited." "*Hmm.*" He looks away, but I can still see his disbelieving look.

"I am."

"Whatever you say, Mel."

There's a moment's pause before I ask, "So how was your afternoon yesterday?"

Ray shrugs as we get in line. "Well, it was fun, at least. Late last night Ms. Richards showed Caidy and me this cool weather simulator. She let us experiment with it a little. I don't know why, but I think we're the only ones she's shown it to. It was pretty neat." He suddenly laughs. "I made up this new kind of cloud."

"What?" I ask as I grab a breakfast taco.

Ray grins. "I call it 'altocirronimbus'."

It's a good thing I have an amazing grip or I might have dropped the tray.

Ray raises an eyebrow. "Are you okay?" I realize my hands are shaking. He stares at them worriedly. "I–I'm sorry. I didn't–"

I steady my hands. "No, it's not you. I mean, yes, but not intentionally. You wouldn't have known."

Ray laughs again. "Do all girls speak gibberish?"

"That's 'meteorologists'," I correct.

"Ha. I've heard that before."

"Really? Where?" Instantly I wonder if I should have asked. Does this constitute as 'playing with his mind', all-mighty Ms. Richards?

"Shoot. I don't know. But, somewhere, a long time ago...." Ray chuckles nervously.

I open my mouth, close it, then open it again. "Oh."

We reach the drinks. Before I can get my own, Ray sets

two glasses of orange juice on my tray.

I'm a little too stunned to say 'thank you' right away. Finally I stammer, "Th-thanks. How did you... I mean, why?"

"Oh, come on." Ray gets one for himself. "Do you want scurvy?"

Before I can reply he turns and walks out of line, towards the tables. "Come sit with me," he says over his shoulder. I follow mutely.

Ray sits down with two other guys. I hesitantly sit across from him.

"This the American spy girl?" one fellow asks through a mouthful of hash browns. He has unkempt black hair and wears a rumpled gray T-shirt inside out.

Ray rolls his eyes at me. *See?*

"Why aren't you wearing black?" the boy demands.

"Ah," I say. "You must be Dan."

"Gosh." Dan looks impressed. "You are good."

I roll my eyes back at Ray. *W-o-w.*

"I'm Matt." The other boy stretches a hand across Dan to shake mine. Matt has neat blonde hair and a polo shirt covering his tan skin.

"Mel." I nod as I shake.

"Hi," someone says behind me. "Guys, mind if we join you?"

"Feel free, Hale." Matt grins and Hale slides in one seat over. She greets me with a smile.

"And Vivian?" someone else demands.

I look over. Vivian's raising her eyebrows playfully at Matt, one hand on her hip.

"I'll have to think about that," Matt says with mock contemplation. "Well, maybe, I guess, it might be okay."

Vivian plops down beside Hale. "Hello, Mel, Jonathon, Dan." She nods, pointedly ignoring Matt.

Before any real conversation strikes up, Leah and Caidy

join the table, Caidy throwing a disappointed look when she has to sit at the opposite end of the table from me. Of course, I have the feeling it's not me she's missing.

Chatting swells around me. I just watch, not taking anything in, trying to focus on work, but my mind keeps getting distracted. Most of the time I'm stuck between listening and thinking, which is defined as doing nothing. I jump when the bell rings signifying the end of breakfast, realizing with a start that I've just wasted an entire forty minutes.

"You sure were quiet," Ray says as we join the back of the throng crowding toward the doors. "Lot on your mind?"

"No," I reply, unable to keep the surprise out of my tone. Ray looks astonished.

"That's, like, impossible for you, though." He cocks his head. "Are you sure you're feeling–"

"Ugh! I'm fine." But I'm not sure. I mean, wasting an entire forty minutes!

"Okay, if you say so." Ray shrugs and breaks through a gap in the mass. I slip after him. "Well, I have class…good luck with whatever you do today. Try to be at lunch!" He waves as he's pushed down the hall. I return it too late; he's already around the corner.

When I'm back in my room, getting my purse together, Shadow calls. He basically tells me to take the rest of the day off. When I argue, he says it would be better to wait until Maryanne's answered some questions. I sigh pointedly a few times, but finally agree.

"Good. Tackle the area tomorrow. They really won't be expecting that. Just relax today," he says. Yeah, right. "Shadow…"

"Yes, Amber?"

I take a deep breath and say the next sentence very fast.

"Are you sure those were Ray's ashes in that coffin?"

"Amber Rind," Shadow says ominously. "I am going to come take you home tomorrow if you don't stop."

"Beg pardon?"

"I don't want you setting yourself up for disappointment like this!" Now he's irate. "You're going to make yourself miserable and unable to concentrate and then you'll get hurt and–"

"Can we stop with the logical fallacies, please?" I sigh. "Talk about a slippery slope. And no, that's not going to happen. I was just wondering."

"If I get one whiff that you're pursuing this...this fantasy..."

Fantasy? *Fantasy*? "You won't," I snap. "Not one whiff," I add to myself after hanging up. I feel like screaming in frustration.

Instead, I do exercise videos until lunch.

Ray drags me back to his table at lunch, where we're joined by Matt, Dan, and the four girls. This time, though, someone includes me in the conversation. Dan leans over the table, looking around Vivian and Matt to see me.

"So, do you fight a lot at your school?"

"Definitely." I nod and bite into a banana.

"You any good?"

Ray snorts. "I would not want fight Mel. If you like all your limbs where they are, I mean."

I think my racing mind just over-excelled the scientific speed limit.

"Why?" Dan looks confused.

Ray shrugs. "Well, it's your death sentence."

Dan sits back, looking at me warily. Matt 'coughs' over his pasta.

"I think that's really cool," Hale say, making eye contact

with me. I allow myself half a smile as Vivian nods as well.

"Of course, intellectual achievement counts more in the real world. But I guess if you don't have the capability for that then those fighting skills might be worth something." Caidy casually stirs her chicken-noodle soup.

"I agree," I reply seriously. Caidy's eyes fly up to meet mine in surprise. "That's why my school stresses academics the most. Physical education, fighting, and self-defense are just side focuses."

"Damn," Matt says in an awed tone. Dan quickly averts his gaze from me, as if afraid I'll gouge out his eyes if he stares.

After this normal conversation ensues, but Ray shoots me a grin from time to time. I return each one.

I put my tray on the conveyor belt and get ready to go do…something. Since Shadow's practically ordered me not to go into town, I should try to do something else productive, like thinking, which has been an issue today. Or exercise videos? I have that new one I haven't tried yet. Or….

"Don't you ever wait for anyone?" a familiar voice complains behind me. I stop in my tracks, and immediately a student stumbles into me.

"Watch it," I snap as a strawberry blonde ponytail whips me across the face. Caidy spares me a glance as we whirl around, both of us facing Ray.

"I'll wait for you, if you want," Caidy says, sounding confused. I resist the urge to snort and instead pivot on my heel. So they want to walk to class together. Whatever. I'll go do something important…

"Actually," I hear Ray say, "I was talking to Mel."

I turn back and study his face. He's grinning sort of uncertainly, but at me.

"Okay, talk." I cock my head. "I think I'm waiting. But I

could be mistaken. No, I'm really never mistaken."

Caidy rolls her eyes and brushes by me. I catch the words "egotistic freak" while struggling to keep my eyes on Ray.

He jerks his head to the door and I follow him out into the hallway. He heads for the stairs.

"I'm still waiting," I hint, matching his pace.

"Oh! Right. Sorry, I forgot I hadn't…" he stops and turns halfway towards me. "Well, I was just going to offer… I have a free period right now, and I was wondering if you want to…hang out or something."

Hang out or something. I haven't done that in who-knows-how-long now. But I do know. It's been two years, two months, and several days.

"Yes," I say before my responsible side can make an argument against it. Of course, it can't miss a chance to reprove me. *What about work? And exercise? Thinking? Ring a bell? Does this constitute as 'productive'?*

Shut up, I tell myself.

"Great." Ray grins and starts up the stairs again. His room is on the seventh floor. I notice a small metal box on the wall by his door. I remember I have one of those too, and I wonder vaguely what they're for as Ray unlocks his door. At Marvin, they have room keys like in hotels, flimsy little cards that you just drop in a slot, pull back out, and presto, you may enter.

"Security's sort of lax here, isn't it?" I stare at the lock as I enter the room.

"We don't really need it. It's just a school," Ray says. He throws his school bag on the chair by the door. "Go ahead, sit on the couch, or wherever you're comfortable."

The room is furnished nicely, with a large window on the opposite wall and thick carpeting under my sneakers. I sink into the plush armchair beside the bed.

"Fancy," I manage, still looking around.

"The old meteorology Pro head liked me a lot," Ray mumbles, shrugging. "No other room is like this. It's sort of embarrassing."

"*Hmm*," is all I can think of to say. My gaze wanders the room, finally stopping on something hanging on the wall. "What's that? It looks like one of those freaky weather instruments."

Ray follows my stare. "Oh, that? That's a psychrometer. It measures the relative humidity in the room because when the wet-bulb thermometer–"

"Ugh, never mind," I say, pretending to cringe. "I forgot about your gibberish."

Ray smirks jokingly. "The fearsome super-spy, scared of a few big words?"

"Big words aren't the issue," I inform him. "The issue is that you can keep track of them all. Tell me, were you ever diagnosed with OCD?"

Ray laughs instead of answering, which is funny, since I'm laughing too. Of course, stupid emotion chooses this time to invade my mind, so when I speak my voice is quiet and unsure.

"I haven't felt like this…in a long time."

Ray looks at me for a moment before answering. "Me neither. Actually, I haven't…that I can remember." He smiles. "It's funny that it's only been four days that we've known each other."

"No, it's been longer." I blink and stare at the fabric on the armrest. "It's been a very, very long time."

Ray nods. "Feels like it, huh?"

I'm a breath away from saying "That's not what I meant," but decide against it at the last second. Instead, I say, "So how did you get lucky and end up with your own room?"

Ray exhales slowly. "Well, I guess in the beginning, no

one wanted to share a room with a mental patient. And I've been lucky since."

"Mental patient?" I ask, raising an eyebrow.

"Yeah." He sits on the edge of his bed. "See, when I first got here–after I was sick, I guess–it was hard. I couldn't remember anything. I mean, I remembered how to talk and think and walk and breathe and eat and stuff, but other than that there was nothing. There'd be times back then when I'd feel almost insane." He looks away, out the window. "It was really, really frustrating, knowing I had a past but couldn't recall it, like I'd lost thirteen years of my life. I wanted to know what happened, but again there was nothing, no information other than that I was sick and I'd been at some orphanage before. I saw the school counselor and worked on meteorology–I guess weather had been a hobby of mine, because I knew a lot about it, but I didn't know how I knew–and I sort of got back into a normal routine, normal life. They convinced me to try to forget my past and focus on my future. Well, it must have worked, because I'm not in the asylum, right?" He attempts a grin.

"Yeah, that surprises me," I say. "Because anyone who can spend their entire day studying weather doesn't seem like a sane person to me."

There's relief and gratitude on Ray's face as he laughs again. I grin and dig around in my pocket, pulling out two plastic packets.

"Here." I toss him Smashin' Strawberry, while opening Crazy Cranberry. Ray catches his with a perplexed look.

"What…"

"You eat it," I remind him.

"Without–"

"Water? Yes. Just plain." I dump the concentrate into my mouth and swallow. Ray watches me, shaking his head.

"You do know that too much Vitamin C–"

"Is bad for me? Don't worry. I never go over a few tons. A day," I add.

"Very funny." Ray apprehensively shakes some powder into his mouth and makes a face. "How do you–"

"Eat it all at once? I've gotten used to it."

"Thanks–"

"For the warning, I know." I'm having some serious déjà vu issues.

"That's really–"

"Annoying?"

"Amazing." Ray grins. "Gotchya!" He swallows a bit more and makes a different, stranger face. "This is really bittersweet."

"The taste?" I ask, confused. Generally cranberry is the bitter one, not strawberry.

"No." Ray shakes his head. "The feel."

"The feel?"

"It reminds me of something." I notice his fist is clenched around his shirt again. "A time when I lost something, but got something as well." His brow furrows. I want to stand up and scream, *You had it the day your dad died!* That's the losing something. But what's the 'got something' part?

Ray shakes his head again. "Sorry. Well, there you go, the crazy part. Still think I'm compos mentis?" He's smiling now, but I hear the anxiety in his tone.

"Of course I do." I say it forcefully enough that his smile widens and his forehead relaxes.

There's a few short taps on the door. Ray stands slowly and strides across the room to open it. He's still grinning, and Caidy beams back.

"Glad I found you!"

I see Ray take a slight step back, his smile slipping into a polite expression.

"Why were you looking for me?" he asks.

"Well, it's about our project. Mum wants to show us something else."

I make a face. Does *Mum* have a slight enthusiasm issue? She's like a project aficionado.

"So she said if I could find you, I should tell you to come down to the lab."

"Oh." Ray's mouth pulls down in a slight frown. Then he brightens, turning away from Caidy to look at me. "Want to come, Mel?"

Caidy's eyebrows fly up as she peers around Ray and spots me. Her jaw drops slightly, but she recovers before Ray notices.

"Oh, sorry. Mum said it's just for us. Confidential, actually, was the word she used."

Ray stares at her for a second. "Really?"

Before Caidy can reply I slide off the armchair and stretch, as if bored with the proceedings. "That's okay, I've got my own confidential stuff to work on. You know, the greater good and all."

Caidy rolls her eyes. Ray presses his lips together to hide a grin. *Nice one.*

I lift the corner of my mouth in a half-smirk. *All my comebacks are nice.*

Ray snorts. Caidy looks from him to me, annoyance and confusion covering her face. What's confidential now, prissy?

Now Ray sighs and tilts his head towards the door, his expression saying something like *sorry about this, but I kinda have to...*

I shake my head, looking at the ceiling. *No, go have fun.* I sort of wave as I leave, walking casually until I turn into the stairwell, where I break into a run and bound down the steps, letting my frustration flow out through my limbs.

13

I reach floor four and skid to a stop, forcing my breathing to even out, then push out of the stairway and head to my room with every intention of doing work or exercise until dinner, when I run into one of the twins. And not in the sense that means 'accidentally encounter.'

"Ow," she says, sounding surprised to find herself on the ground, her legs tangled with mine. No, no, no. I really have to snap out of this. Clumsiness is not allowed. I pull my feet away and leap up.

"Sorry," I mumble, holding out a hand to help her up. She takes it and stands. I see she's wearing bright purple and those rainbow necklaces again. It's most likely Hale.

"That's okay. Isn't that funny. I was just at your room, but you weren't there. So I decided to go see what Viv's up to, but instead I find you!"

"You were at my room?" I slip around her and start walking. She falls into step beside me as we turn the corner to my hallway.

"Yeah, I was just going to stop in and say hi and see what you were up to, since all the tenth graders have a free period right now. Oh, and see if you needed anything, I was going to do that too."

"Wait." I frown. "You're in tenth grade?"

"Yeah, our school year started in March. Why? Oh, wait, you guys are like a half a year on one side. Are you ahead or behind us?"

"I guess we're behind," I muse, "since we're at the end of

148

ninth back at my school." It's alien, having someone be the same age as me but on a higher level. "But I guess that makes sense," I say, as much to myself as to Hale, "since we have opposite seasons. Like, our winter is your summer, or," I add, looking at the windows, "our summer is your winter."

We're at my room by now. I take out the key and run it through the slot, wondering if Hale wants me to invite her in. She keeps babbling behind me. That might be an affirmative.

"You're right. That's so interesting, like, it could be winter and then if I took a trip like you it'd be like, 'oh, wow, summertime! In August!' But then I suppose that is what it's like for you. Um, what's that smell?"

I've already held up my hand for quiet as I sniff the air as well. My eyes widen as I recognize the scent.

"Smoke."

"Smoke?" Hale asks as I rush into the room. She follows and gasps as I do when I see my bed, where flames are smoldering on the sheets. No, not just the sheets. My manila folder.

"Oh my god!" Hale cries as smoke alarms start to wail. "Were you smoking in here or something?"

"Of course not." I reach into the bathroom, grab a towel, and smack it down over the fire. "I was with you when it started, obviously. Get me a wet cloth or something."

Hale pulls another towel off the rod in the bathroom and shoves it in the sink, running water over it as fast as it will come. A moment later she pulls the sopping fabric out and tosses it to me. I drop the other towel and lay the new one over the burning folder. There's a hiss as the fire dissipates. Cautiously, I lift the material off and clench my teeth at the blackened remains of my research. Swearing under my breath, I shake out the towel, contemplating what to do next.

I realize my clothes are moist and look up, only to get a spray of water in my eyes.

"Ack! You have a sprinkler system?" I duck my head, watching the room grow soggy.

"Yeah," Hale says breathlessly, cautiously approaching the bed. Her shirt is also damp. "Mel, that was so cool how you put the fire out. You were just like, 'toss me a wet cloth!', like, you knew exactly what to do."

"It's what we train for," I say dismissively, frowning at the charred sheets. How did the fire start? No, who started it, on my folder? Which was conveniently out in the open, on the middle of my highly flammable bed, where I would never leave it.

"Oh, ouch," I hear Hale say.

"What? Are you hurt?"

"No, you are. Look, your hand!"

I drop my gaze to my right palm, which I realize is stinging. An angry pink mark decorates the base of my thumb. Hale darts to the bathroom and comes back with a dripping wad of tissue, which she presses on my thumb. I jump.

"I couldn't find any washcloths," she says apologetically as the sprinklers and fire alarm finally cease.

"Thanks," I reply distractedly. The door suddenly bursts open.

"What did you do?" An angry accusation rings through the drenched room.

"Ms. Richards!" Hale exclaims. "There was a fire on Mel's bed! But she–"

"I can see that," Ms. Richards says furiously. "I can hear it, too. You set off the whole building. How did it start?" She glares unambiguously at me.

"I didn't do it," I say angrily.

"We just came in and it was already burning!" Hale says earnestly. I get a sudden idea and move to the window. I run a finger over the crack where the sill meets the pane. A layer of dust comes off on my skin.

"Whoever started it didn't come in through the window," I determine.

"Whoever started it?" Ms. Richards eyes the room sarcastically, as though looking for someone hiding in the corner. I grit my teeth.

"That fire was lit about a minute before Hale and I arrived, probably less," I tell her coldly, "or it would have spread further, and burned through to the mattress under the folder." I point to where the folder had moved when I'd slapped it with the towel. The sheets underneath were only slightly singed. "Also, nothing else is out of place in here, except," I grit my teeth, "my folder, which was in my duffel bag, not on my bed. So someone deliberately took it out and burned it."

Hale's looking at me with an awed expression. Ms. Richards looks exasperated.

"Why wouldn't this someone just burn your duffel bag, then?" she asks.

"Well, I can hardly press charges for a folder full of paper, now, can I?" Today I succeed with my 'duh' implication.

Ms. Richards can't find an argument for that, so she just glares down at me. "If I come to find that is was you, Melanie, that started that fire, there will be serious consequences."

"My name's not Melanie," I retort.

"Is it Melinda?" Hale cocks her head.

"No."

Ms. Richards looks surprised a moment too late. I narrow my eyes.

"Well, I'm sorry, *Mel*. I'll tell a custodian to come clean the mess up." She retreats from the room.

"And what do I do in the meantime?" I grumble,

stomping over to my bed. After running the thumb and index finger of my uninjured hand over my tongue, I gingerly lift a corner of the folder. It's hot, but not searing. I note disappointedly that the folder's burnt beyond the ability to look for fingerprints or other such evidence.

The papers inside are too charred to make out anything on the paper. Good thing I've memorized the information.

And what does this mean? Well, one, whoever burned the folder has a room key or has figured out how to pick hotel locks. And two, either I'm on to something about their location or they want me to think that so I will go there, which is not where they are. Or they're using reverse reverse psychology and they're around there but they want me to believe what I was thinking previously.

Well, I decide, it can't hurt to look around the area.

And, I think, eyes narrowing, why was it Ms. Richards who barged in? Isn't she supposed to be showing Ray and Caidy something 'confidential'?

"How do you do that?" Hale waves a hand in front of my face. I blink.

"What?"

"How do you do that?" she repeats. "Totally space out like that?"

"I was thinking," I say, my tone telling her this is obvious.

"Woolgathering is more like it. Spacing, blanking, zoning–"

"Thinking," I say clearly.

"About what?"

"Well..." I feign thoughtfulness. "Maybe if there's going to be a full moon tonight, or if there's a correlation between puppies and rainbows. Or maybe I was trying to pick out a new favorite flavor of ice cream." I shake my head. "What do you think?"

"I don't know, you're the one thinking." Hale pauses, contemplating the wet carpet. "But I'm pretty sure the full moon's not until next week."

"And what about the puppies?" I roll my eyes and walk towards my duffel bag. I pull my eye shadow—a.k.a. fingerprint powder—out of my purse and head for the doorknob where I determine the perpetrator was wearing gloves. Shoot.

"Oh, jeez," Hale glances at my clock. "I have to go, Mel, sorry."

"Okay." I don't look up as I unzip my purse.

"Will you be around tomorrow?"

"I'm going to be working."

"For how long?"

"That depends on how well I'm doing," I sigh.

"Well, maybe I'll see you later, then," Hale says as she leaves.

"Let's hope not," I mutter, meaning I'll be on a lead and too busy, but she's already gone. The custodian arrives just after that, and another teacher comes to move me to guestroom six.

I decide I have to call Shadow or he'll surpass the decibel limit on cellular phones when he hears about this incident. I reluctantly dial and give him a modified version, but he can't ignore the fact that my bed was on fire.

"This is looking pretty serious," he says once he calms down. "Amber, did you—"

"Check for fingerprints? Yes I did, there aren't any."

"No—"

"Determine the method of entry? The doorway. The window still had—"

"No! Did you hurt yourself?"

"Um." I glance at the washcloth draped over my hand.

"You did."

153

Rain

I hear reproach in Shadow's voice. "I have it under control," I say quickly, defensively.

"You better have, Amber Rind."

"Don't worry. The little five-year-old can take care of her own boo-boo."

Shadow ignores my petulance. "So what's your next move?"

I explain my earlier reasoning and he reluctantly agrees it's a good idea. He's smart enough not to suggest someone else come with me. I finish the conversation as quickly as I can and get in my exercise and more thinking before dinner. Then I shower and head down to the cafeteria.

My mouth sets in an upset line when I walk in ten minutes after dinner has started and see Matt and Dan sitting by themselves, and, a few tables over, Hale, Vivian, and Leah. I walk to the girls' table.

"Hello, Hale," I say, coming up behind her. Hale jumps and turns around, smiling when she sees me.

"Hey, Mel!"

"Hi. Um, I was wondering...where're Caidy and Jonathon?"

"Working late in the lab," Leah says from across the table.

"Ah. Okay. Thank you." I start to back up.

"Wait!" Hale frowns. "Do you want to sit here with us?"

For a moment, I feel myself hesitate.

"Please?" Hale asks.

"Come on." Vivian pats the spot next to her.

My rational side takes over. "Sorry, but I have work to do. I have to prepare for tomorrow."

Hale pouts disappointedly. "Okay. Well, we'll see you around, Mel." Suddenly her face gets the 'epiphany' look I see on Lyvia when she gets an idea for a new skirt/tank top outfit.

I don't stay long enough to find out what the inspiration

is. With a quick wave I retreat into the food line, grab a plastic-wrapped sandwich–the kind with the strange brown spread–dart out the doors closest to the line's exit, and head back to guest room six. I eat dinner, reply to some emails, get chewed out by Shadow for not having my cell phone with me earlier, and mentally plan tomorrow's search. I go to bed early tonight, but don't get to sleep until past eleven.

I feel like screaming.

There's nothing–nothing as in nil, zero, zilch, goose eggs, nothing–to be found in any part of the area. I force myself to look from eight until past two in the afternoon when I finally admit momentary defeat.

Why is this so hard? There must be something I'm missing, something obvious. No End has ever been this hard. Heck, most homework assignments are harder than Ends for me!

But not this one.

Of course, my mood isn't much improved by the fact that Ray wasn't anywhere to be found at breakfast this morning.

Not that that should apply to the present. Now, Mel. This is important.

This is confusing.

As I ride the bus back to Marvin I rub my palms, which are throbbing where I'd dug my nails in too deep. There's no logic to this End. Maryanne won't talk, Avocado Man disappears, then a car follows me and I can't even scrape a lead from that.

I'm a failure.

No, something in my malfunctioning brain says. *Not yet.*

Yet, I reply miserably as I get off the bus two blocks from Marvin.

I've barely arrived in my room when I hear incessant

knocking on my door. Unwrapping a granola bar and shoving half of it in my mouth, I look through the peephole before opening the door.

"You're back!" Hale says. At least, I'm pretty sure it's Hale. It might be Leah, but judging by the way she's acting I'm pretty sure this is the affable twin.

I chew and swallow hastily. "Yes, I suppose I am. Hale, right?"

"Yeah, that's me. Are you staying?"

"Yeah, as far as I–"

"Great!" Hale exclaims. "Want to come down to Viv's room? We're hanging out there right now, and we think it'd be fun for you to join us."

"Me?" I ask.

"Um...yeah," Hale says.

Well, this certainly hasn't happened before. The last time I stayed somewhere other than Watson for an End–when the felon was apprehended in Erie–the track-and-field-boarding-school students barely said "hi" to me after the first day. Of course, unlike Marvin, they didn't know about Watson, so there wasn't really an explanation for my work-based behavior. But still.

"Um..." I try to decide whether or not to listen to the arguments my work side is presenting. They're the same as yesterday: work, exercise, think.

But I can work on the Ray mystery, a good spying exercise...I think.

"Come on," Hale urges. "Please don't tell me you have 'too much work to do'. After all the work you've done so far?"

She makes a good point. I really don't have anything new to go on that would constitute more work.

I close my eyes. "Oh...okay. Just...give me a minute." I turn away and retreat into my room, biting off another portion of granola bar. I quickly redo my ponytail and put away my supplies from town. On a spur-of-the-moment decision, I pocket my cell phone, thinking it's better to have the slight inconvenience than ignore another rant from Shadow.

Hale waits just inside the doorway, leaning against the wall, looking around with interest. She's wearing a lime green T-shirt with big dangling watermelon slice earrings. Her vivid pink capris stand out dramatically from the lackluster wallpaper. Last of all, she has on white flip-flops. I wouldn't ever wear flip-flops. The disadvantages are redoubtable: how easily they break, how easily they come off, how easily they can trip the wearer.

How can she want to spend time with me? She's the complete opposite of my personality. She's perky, optimistic, carefree; everything I'm not. Is that not sending the right message or something?

And why am I about to spend time with her? I'm serious, pragmatic, and focused. This is not part of my agenda.

I will be getting work done, I remind myself.

Not on the assignment, my practical side argues.

Work nonetheless, I counter as I whirl around and walk back to Hale.

"I'm ready now."

She gives me a thumbs-up and starts down the hall. I keep pace with her.

"Oh, you have a cell phone?" she says, noting the lump in my pocket.

"I don't really use it except to call my principal."

"I can call you," she says, and before I can respond 'No, thank you,' she's pulled out her phone–a much fancier model than mine–and is pressing buttons on the keypad. "What's your number?"

Sighing resignedly, I mumble it to her. Somehow she hears me and presses more buttons before pocketing the device again.

I follow her to the end of the hallway where she presses the elevator button.

"Um, no." I step back.

"Sorry?" She cocks her head. The elevator dings and the doors slide open, revealing the small area behind them. I grimace.

"I don't take elevators."

"Oh," she says, watching the doors slide closed again. "Okay. Do you take stairs?"

"No, I scale the wall."

"Oh." Hale looks uncertainly at the window.

I roll my eyes. "I guess I can make an exception today."

Hale sighs in relief. "Cool." She trails me into the stairwell, where I stop uncertainly.

"What floor?"

"The third. Number 390."

"Thanks." I fall back half a step to let her lead. "This is Vivian's room you're taking me to?"

"*Mm*-hmm. The four of us hang out there a lot."

"Who does Vivian share the room with?"

Hale leaps onto the third-floor landing. "Melissa Eren, Sarah Ellinsky, and Dominique Edenburgh. They're usually with their friends somewhere else, though."

"That's a lot of people for one room."

"Well," Hale says, pushing through the door to the hallway, "the rooms are a lot bigger than your guest room. But it takes up less space than if students were grouped in pairs."

"How are students grouped?"

"Basically, each Pro has it's own section of the dorms, and then it's alphabetical by last name for your roommates, only your roommates have the same Pro as you. But it hardly matters since no one cares, really, about Pros."

I raise my eyebrows incredulously.

"Friendship-wise," Hale elucidates.

"Ah."

"Yeah, like, look at me and Leah and Viv and Caidy. Design, geology, forensics, and meteorology, but we're friends."

Yet her mouth tugs down at the corner as she says that.

"What?" I ask, immediately curious.

"Huh? I didn't say anything. Look, here we are." She stops in front of the room labeled '390' and knocks. The door swings open.

"Hey," Leah says.

Hale jumps into the room, throwing her arms out to the sides. I can't tell if it's for balance or effect. "'Ello, everyone," she says in a throaty voice, going along with her dramatic entrance.

Vivian and Leah both laugh, but I'm watching Caidy, who's lounging on one of the bunk beds up against the opposite wall. She merely looks at Hale with an amused expression that has an air of superiority about it. Then she focuses on me and I cross my eyes at her. She looks away after a moment, but with the mien of someone bored with the proceedings.

Hale pushes me to the couch. I sit down on one of the moquette cushions, noting that the decor isn't as fancy as Ray's room. Hale plops down beside me and immediately earns the attention of Vivian, who's sprawled sideways over an armchair. "Hale, we were wondering. Have you changed your mind about the rainbow flats?"

"No," Hale responds, leaning back. "Everyone wears heels to dances. So what's wrong with being different? And you know me; heels are suicide. Plus, the flats go with my jewelry."

"Yeah, about that–" Leah swings her legs from the top of the second bunk bed.

"No! I'm not changing my mind," Hale says stubbornly.

"And you still think you're going to be stunning in a plain white spaghetti-sleeve dress?" Caidy asks cynically.

"Hey! You haven't seen it! How can you say it's plain?" Hale argues.

"Right, I forgot who I was talking to," says Caidy.

"But my socks are the coolest part." Hale grins impishly. Leah and Caidy both lean forward, mouths open in protest.

"Socks?"

"You've gone nuts!"

"Ha!" Hale raises a fist. "Psych!"

I fight down a smile.

Vivian leans her head back, laughing. "You're still nuts, Hale."

"Nuts with great style," Hale says, correcting her.

"I can't wait until Tuesday!" Leah bounces on the edge of the mattress. "It's going to be so much better than last year's dance."

"Which you've only said a thousand times," Caidy snorts.

"Does your school have dances, Mel?" Vivian asks.

"Yes," I sigh, feeling distinctly out of place with this topic.

"What are they like?"

"Well, Hale..." I contemplate my answer. "Well, my friend, Lyvia, says they're fun."

"And what do you say?" Vivian looks confused.

"I can't make an honest judgment," I tell her. "I've never been to one."

"Why?" Hale gapes.

"I never felt the desire to go."

"So you've never been to a single school dance?" Leah asks, making a face.

"I went to a seventh-grade social," I say defensively.

160

Three pairs of eyes stare at me. Caidy looks up at the ceiling.

"You have to come to the dance on Tuesday!" Hale exclaims. Caidy's head jerks back, staring at us. I can't see her expression clearly.

"Uh, thanks, but no thanks," I say hastily.

"Great idea, Hale!" Vivian says, winking at her friend.

I shake my head. "I think I'll probably have–"

"How do you know if you'll have work to do or not?" Hale demands. "Doesn't that depend on how your assignment thingy is going?"

How did she know I was going to use work as my excuse? "Yes, it does, but…well, I don't even have a dress," I stammer. Of course, I have the means to procure a dress. But they don't need to know that.

"That's not a problem," Hale replies.

"Is it open to non-students?" Caidy asks, frowning.

"Oh, you know Ms. Rose. Everyone's going to be invited," says Vivian.

It hardly matters, though. No matter what sort of invite I get, I will definitely have work to do Tuesday. Such school functions don't mix well with me.

My mind wanders to thoughts of Ray as the four girls start talking about trivial details like makeup and hair. I realize I could find out where he was this morning. Maybe he's gone other mornings, too. I don't know.

"Mel? Hey, Mel?"

"What?" I jump.

"You're doing it again," says Hale.

"Oh. Sorry."

"That's okay."

"But we were wondering," Vivian says, "what does Mel stand for? Hale says you told Caidy's mum it's not Melanie."

"Oh, yeah, it isn't." I look at the three curious (and one indifferent) expressions trained on me. "It stands for Melon."

"Melon?" Hale's eyebrows fly up. I'm expecting her to say something like 'why the heck did your parents name you Melon?' But instead she says, "That is so cool! I love it!"

"You do?" I'm surprised, but gratified. "Thank you."

"Is it your real name?" Vivian asks. "Or a nickname? Or–a code name? It's catchy."

"It's a nickname," I admit. "Not a code name. We don't have those. We have assumed identities. But not code names." I give an unwilling laugh.

"Cute." Hale nods, as Leah says, "Who nicknamed you after a fruit?"

I ignore her.

"Is your real name confidential, or can you tell us?" Vivian asks.

"My real name's Amber," I tell her.

"That's pretty." Vivian smiles.

"Mel fits you better," Hale decides. I can't help grinning.

"So I've been told."

Unfortunately everyone (but me) switches to a new subject before I can ask about Ray. I wait for a reasonable break in the conversation, wondering if it's even worth asking. Maybe I could leave and go find Ray and ask him myself. The idea's definitely appealing enough.

I notice there's a pause as everyone sort of looks at their laps–or the ceiling–aimlessly. I seize the opportunity.

"Hale?"

"*Hmm*?" Hale looks over at me.

"What–where did Ra–Jonathon go this morning?"

It's not Hale who answers, but Caidy, sitting up, wearing an expression I can only describe as smug. "Every Wednesday, Saturday, and Sunday mornings Jonathon helps this old lady–Mrs. Ilene–with her plants. She has tons of plants," Caidy adds, as if this is supposed to impress me or something.

"Oh," I say. I can imagine Ray volunteering to help some elderly woman with her strange fixation. Ray knows all about strange fixations himself. "Where?"

Vivian speaks up. "Down by Botanic Gardens. I guess Jonathon takes the bus to the corner of George Street and Alice Street or something. Mrs. Ilene lives around there."

"The bus?" I ask, to clarify. Alice Street, which turns off of Edward Street, is near the area where I need to go next. A plan automatically starts forming in the back of my mind.

"Well, yes, seeing as he's not old enough to drive," Hale says.

"Yet," Caidy says, quick to correct her friend. "Come April…"

Leah leans forward. "Ooh, Caidy, planning a romantic road trip already?"

Romantic road trip? My eyes narrow as I fight down a wave of nausea.

To cover up my impulsive queasiness, I say, "When's–when is Jonathon's birthday?"

"April fourteenth," Caidy answers immediately.

This time I fight down shock. How do they know Ray's birthday? They don't even know it is Ray. Even if Annette Robar had given the doctors his birthday, they thought he was dead as well.

Vivian's speaking to me. I pull myself back to the conversation.

"You and Jonathon seem pretty close," she says observantly.

"Yeah, we heard you were in his room yesterday." Hale glances at Caidy before grinning at me. I look at Caidy as well. What exactly did she tell them?

"We were just hanging out," I say firmly.

Vivian looks at the wall above my head thoughtfully. "He's, like, almost transformed since you came, though."

"Really?" I say, taken aback.

Caidy snaps, "Has not."

I ignore her and ask, "How?"

Vivian shrugs. "He seems more talkative, he laughs more. Matt was telling me–"

"The only thing I see different is he's more distracted in the lab," Caidy says, interrupting Vivian while glaring at me. "Are you trying to mess up his career?"

Vivian looks puzzled. "Caidy, what the hey?"

I return Caidy's glower. "I can be Jonathon's friend if I want to."

Caidy sneers at me. "You don't just want to be friends."

I rise and Caidy mirrors my movements. "Excuse me?" I say angrily.

Looking wary, Vivian straightens in her chair. "Caidy, calm down."

Hale's laughing on the couch.

"It's not funny," I say.

Caidy glares at Hale. "Shut up," she says sharply before turning on me. "Who do you think you are? You're just a guest here. You can't get involved!"

I scowl. "Look, I don't know what your problem is, but for your information, I can do anything I want. And I don't need your permission to do it!"

"You're so stuck up," Caidy retorts. "Just because you go to some flipping spy academy–"

"Whoa." Vivian pulls herself off the armchair, looking like she has half a mind to step in between us. "Mel, calm down. Caidy, cut it out, okay?"

"Gladly." Caidy's eyes stay concentrated on me. "And, with any luck, painfully."

"You know what would be painful?" I counter. "Your head up your–oh, wait. It's already there."

Caidy looks torn between screaming and punching

164

something. Me, probably. Finally she spits, "Freak," and stomps out of the room. She looks back from the doorway. "By the way, Melon is a stupid name."

I smirk back at her. "Tell that to Jonathon."

If she's confused she doesn't show it as she slams the door. I take a seat next to Hale again, who's looking at the closed door with an amused and slightly meditative expression. Vivian lets out a low whistle.

Leah glances from me to Hale, then to Vivian, then to the door before shrugging and sliding down from the bunk. "I'll go cool her off or something. Later." She leaves as well.

There's a few seconds of silence before I say, "Sorry…but what is her deal?"

"Caidy?" Hale turns to face me. "Isn't it obvious?"

"No," I reply, knowing I sound shocked. Well, I am, because, I never miss 'obvious' stuff, or unobvious stuff.

Hale lowers her voice a bit. "She likes Jonathon."

My insides feel like I just swallowed a few ounces of boiling water.

"She's kinda staked a claim on him." Hale giggles. "I don't think he has a clue. Or, if he does, he hasn't exactly returned the feeling, so Caidy likes to go with the ignorant theory."

"Oh," I say, an alarming idea forming in my mind. What if this is the thing I'm bad at, my weakness? This whole social mess, crushes and the complicated network of friendships and societal status among teenagers thing?

No, one of my little voices says. *I'm just not adequately informed. More research could help.*

"Don't worry about Caidy," Vivian's saying. "She'll get over it."

My potentially ineffectual social skills are telling me the little gathering is drawing to a close. I say thanks-for-inviting-me and goodbye, then I escape back to my own room where I collapse on the bed until my head stops spinning. I think this is a new record for amount of rotations my head has undergone in five days.

I really, really am starting to seriously detest Ms. Richards. Once again, Ray and Caidy are absent from dinner. I say no-thank-you to Hale and Vivian's requests for me to sit with them and instead eat my salad up in my room while looking over maps of Brisbane around Botanic Gardens and the corner of George Street and Alice Street. Shadow calls so I can assure him the little five-year-old hasn't got any more boo-boos, then I reply to one of Lyvia's emails.

As I fall asleep, I make a decision.

14

I leave Marvin at eight-thirty, wearing flexible capris and a zip jacket over my T-shirt, and, after eating a granola bar, catch the bus two blocks away. During the ride I try to center my attention on the End, but my mind keeps straying to that one possibility that maybe, when I get off by Botanic Gardens, I might meet him.

The bus screeches to a stop. The street sign outside tells me we're on the corner of George Street. I jump up, grab my purse and take a quick peek around the bus for anything suspicious, then join the queue of passengers fighting to get out the door.

I burst onto the street, jostled between a man jabbering on a cell phone and a woman lugging three children. I turn my head from side to side, but I don't see him. After a few moments during which I hesitate, unsure of where to go from here, I revert to my plan from last night and start down the road off of George Street. I spend about an hour there and the surrounding area, which includes the Parliament house and the Queensland University of Technology. On the opposite side from those buildings lies the Botanic Gardens.

Forced to accept there's nothing helpful here, I make my way back to the bus stop, intending to go somewhere else, like maybe up to Margaret Street. But just as I arrive I see the bus pulling away. Scowling, I turn and walk down Alice Street, intending to find the next bus stop on the route and wait there. I end up stopping on the corner of Edward Street.

I check my watch. It's nearly 10:00. I unzip my jacket

slightly, feeling warmer now. My hand hovers over the pocket holding my cell phone and I wonder if I should give Shadow a call. He must be going insane since I haven't contacted him yet this morning. I admire his self-control in not calling so far.

Before I can decide, I feel a hand on my arm.

"Are these just coincidences?" Ray asks. "Or do we both just have great minds?"

I spin around to face him. "Great minds? I mean, I do, but what's that supposed to mean?"

"We're thinking alike," he explains. He grins and brushes the hair off of his forehead. "Like that old saying: 'Great minds think alike.' What are the odds we run into each other out here?"

I don't tell him I knew he was helping Mrs. Ilene. Instead, I say, "Maybe that axiom is true, but the jury's still out on your 'great mind'."

Ray snorts and looks around. "So are you working here right now or what?"

"Just finished, actually. For the moment, at least."

"Really? Are you free the rest of the day?"

"That depends. Why?"

Ray shrugs. "I was going to take a walk or something. Want to come?"

A walk. That's good exercise. Fresh air. Ideal thinking setting. Good way to get better bearings on the city.

With Ray.

"Sure."

"Cool." Ray's smile widens. He beckons for me to follow him down a side road. Trees line the route for a little ways, then we come to a small parking area. There's even more foliage here.

"Where–?" I start to ask, even though I already have an idea.

"This is Botanic Gardens." We cross the parking lot to the trees on the other side, duck through them, and emerge on a pathway running right next to a river.

"Wow," I say in a low voice. My eyes sweep over the boats bobbing on the water and the Brisbane skyline in the distance.

"You should see it at night."

We stroll down the path, away from the bustling city. Trees and benches line the other side of the path, and between them and me is Ray. For the first time in a long time, I feel myself relaxing. The noises around me–sloshing of water, wind in the trees, distant city noises, chatting of the pedestrians we pass–register in my mind, but as insignificant. I realize I'm not taking in every detail. Instead, I'm letting my mind wander. I quickly shake my head to clear the feeling.

"So," I say, searching for something to talk about. I land on the last time I saw him, when I was leaving the room after Caidy interrupted us. "Are you allowed to tell me what your confidential errand was Friday?"

"Oh, right, that." Ray looks thoughtful. "It's not really confidential. It's more we can't tell the other meteorology Pro students what we're doing. It's a special opportunity, apparently, just for a few students. And I was chosen as one. Caidy's the other. But it was basically Ms. Richards showing us more on that simulator machine I was telling you about, the one where I made up that cloud."

"Fun?" I ask. He nods.

"Yeah, it's really interesting. See, we put in exactly what conditions are needed for something to happen. Ms. Richards gives us tasks–make a cumulus cloud, this many meters wide, this many tall, this many long, etc.–and we see if we can do it." Ray jumps to the side of the path as a bicyclist whizzes by. "But the best part is, it's perfect for me because I don't just memorize weather facts and stuff. I can see it in my head."

I resist the urge to say 'Yeah, I know.'

Ray shoots me a mischievous grin. "But you have to swear not to reveal the secret, or I'll have to kill you."

"You have my word! Don't shoot!" I pretend to cower in fear.

"Ah. I guess I can be merciful today. You want a mint?" Ray takes a container out of his pocket and passes me one. I accept automatically and put it my mouth, sucking pensively.

Ray sees my expression. "Don't tell me you've never had a mint."

"Not for a long time," I admit. It's true; I've made a point of avoiding such candy. It's too easy to breathe or swallow wrong and choke, which is a huge distraction when trying to concentrate on something. I tuck the confection in my cheek so I can keep up with the conversation.

"Are they really strict at your school or something?" Ray looks disbelieving, as if he knows my abstinence is self-inflicted.

"No, not really," I sigh. "But I find it...more convenient...to exclude anything that might detract from my work."

"Yeah, but, like, what about...fun?" Ray says disapprovingly. "Please say you haven't excluded that as well?"

"My work is fun," I reply, but even I hear the reluctance in my tone. I sigh again. "Look, I wasn't always...I didn't always...well, it's only been about two years..."

"Since what?" Ray asks quietly.

"Since I lost...a friend," I murmur.

"You mean..."

"Well, they say he died." I struggle to find the right way to explain it. It's still hard for me, but mostly out of frustration, not sadness now, because he's walking right beside me and he doesn't even know it.

"He," Ray muses to himself, before meeting my eyes. "Do you want to tell me about it?"

I hesitate for a moment. "Um..."

"You don't have to," Ray assures me. "But I'm guessing you haven't talked to anyone else about it."

"How..." I start, but shake my head. What I want to know is how he can understand me so well and still not remember.

"Feel like sitting down?"

I nod, and he steps off the path, me right behind him. He sits down on one of the benches. I lower myself down next to him, but still about a foot (or 30.48 centimeters) away so I can sort of face him. He turns towards me as well. I feel extremely aware of every part of my body, including the fact that my face is growing warmer. I avert my eyes and look instead at the river.

"Do you want to hear it?"

"If you want to tell me."

"Well, there was this boy named Anthony." It's easier to talk about Ray using his real name. It feels more like a separate person. "He came to Watson when he was nine. That's really old for new students, at my school, so Sha–Mr. Syme, the principal, asked me to sort of show him around. At first he seemed annoying"–I fight an unwilling smile–"but we sort of became friends. Well, I mean sort of for the 'became' part, because it was somewhat building up to it, and then...something happened. After that we just were friends. Really, really good friends." I watch the river without processing it, seeing instead a rush of memories from those two and a half years in between Ray's arrival and his...departure. "When we were thirteen," I force myself to continue, "we got our first End, and I was extremely excited. It was something trivial really, a restaurant safe-robber. But it turned into the worst day of my life. No," I correct myself, "the funeral was pretty bad, too."

"Funeral?" Ray repeats quietly.

I nod. "Anthony was poisoned. They tried to save him by sending him somewhere, but he...died." That part feels especially weird to say, since I'm contradicting my statement merely by looking at the other occupant of the bench.

"And that's why you changed?" Ray has an incomprehensible expression on his face.

"I found it easier, in the time after it happened, to focus solely on my work. It gave me less opportunity to think about anything else," I explain. "I guess I just kept it up."

Ray's silent for about a minute, examining the boats on the river. The sun sparkles off the water, but I don't flinch as the light twinkles into my eyes. I feel like I'm far away from the scene.

Finally Ray looks back at me. "I'm really sorry, Mel." He closes the small gap between us and puts his arm around my shoulders, giving them a short squeeze.

My mind goes totally blank for a moment and I'm at a loss on how to react. I can't say, "Oh, it's not your fault," because, even though I don't hold him responsible, it still has everything to do with him. Finally I settle on, "At least I have an excuse to try out the killing methods I've learned if I ever meet the person who did it."

"That still won't take back what he did." Ray says, almost dazedly. "To Anthony or to you."

"That's life," I sigh.

"That's rough."

We lapse into quietness, both of us lost in thought. Part of me is disappointed. I guess I'd secretly been hoping that my story would jog Ray's memory. But another part of me is relieved to finally have talked about it with someone, especially because that someone is the only one I ever wanted to talk to about it. Ray.

Some of the boats are moving now. I watch a group of kayakers paddle past.

"Do you want to walk some more?" Ray asks. "There's a better view down a little ways…"

"Yes." Some exercise may help.

We start down the path again, not saying much. I decide to break the silence.

"Have you ever gone on a boat?" I nod to the river.

"Of course. And I own my own pair of water-skis. I won the Olympics, you know," Ray replies.

"Oh, really? In what, kayaking or water-skiing?"

"Both," he says.

"And you're fitting in this special project. Truly amazing."

"Well, I am the reason for the term 'multitasking', after all." Ray half-grins.

"You're such an astonishing person. I'm surprised they haven't built a monument for you yet. Shame on your government." I shake my head.

"That's what I keep saying!" Ray throws up his hands. "And does anyone listen to me? No!"

"I can't imagine why," I say seriously. "Who wouldn't listen to a fibbing, weather-obsessed freak with…" I pause, trying to find something about him to make fun of, but I've just used my only idea.

Fortunately, Ray laughs, not noticing that I don't go on. "I'll have you tossed in jail for that. I'm next in line to be Prime Minister, after all."

"Do you want a prize or something?"

"Sure. What're you thinking about?"

I purposefully avoid mentioning plaques. "What if I bow?"

"*Hmm*," Ray pretends to consider. "No, a curtsy would suffice–for now."

Rolling my eyes, I bob quickly, then straighten up and cross my eyes at him.

"For that," Ray says, "you owe me two curtsies."

"Never."

"Do you want to end up in jail or something?"

"You'd have to fight me first." I grin imperiously. "Do you want to end up in the ER or something?" Disregarding the fact that he's already been there.

"I'm pretty sure that would violate some law or another. Aren't you supposed to be a lawful spy?"

"If lawful doesn't cover tyranny, then yes."

"Oh, yes. That will go over well with tyrants."

"See, it's not exactly supposed to," I explain. But his mention of my work brings me back–however reluctantly–to the present.

Ray must've seen the change in my expression. "What?" he asks. His attitude is suddenly serious.

"I have to work," I mumble.

"Just tell me, do you get a day off?" He looks upset.

"I don't usually take them. But I did this week. I took one Friday, and I took the afternoon off yesterday, and just now. But I have to work."

Am I imagining Ray's disappointment? Either way, I feel miserable.

"I guess I'll see you later, then."

"Yes." I nod, promising myself that I will. As I turn to walk away Ray's voice stops me.

"Mel…"

"Yeah?" I look back.

"Do you…want company? I have the rest of the day off."

My stomach plummets. "No," I say forcefully. Ray shrugs, avoiding my eyes.

"Okay, I was just offering."

"No, no," I add quickly. "I mean, yes, but no, it's not that

I don't want... Well, yes, I don't want, but... It's not you, it's just... I don't have company on Ends."

"Is that a rule?"

"No, not officially. But for me, it is. It's because of that Anthony thing. I have a bad feeling about... I'm not really superstitious, but..." I grapple for the right words to explain.

"It's okay," Ray says slowly, even though his expression is puzzled. "It was just an offer."

"Thanks, but no thanks." Ray still looks confused, so I quickly say "Bye" before I make a really big mistake. I duck to the side and go the long way through Botanic Gardens, up George Street, and to Margaret Street.

Where I am, again, unsuccessful.

My frustration builds as I ride the bus back to Marvin around three o'clock. I feel like I'm failing in all areas of my life, with my work and with Ray. The entire time I was searching, half my mind was consumed with the mystery surrounding him. How did he get here? Why did they say he was dead? Who is *they*? Did they really think he was dead or were they lying? Why would they lie?

By the time I walk through Marvin's doors, I'm ready for answers. I make my way down the empty hallway and bang on Ms. Rose's door.

"Come in!"

I push into the office. Ms. Rose, who's talking on the phone, waves at me from the other side before gesturing to one of the plushy seats just inside the entryway. I sit down and survey the fuchsia-infused décor as she continues her conversation. Finally she puts the phone down and smiles at me.

"Hello, Mel!"

"Hello." I fight to keep a nice tone in my voice while not giving into my choleric mood swings.

"Why don't you come sit up here now, hon." She motions to another plushy chair in front of her desk. "What's up? How's your day been?"

"My day's been..." I try to find a word to describe it: frustrating, then good but frustrating at the same time, then frustrating again, and now, downright upsetting. "Frustrating." I guess that's the best I can do.

Ms. Rose starts to say something like "Oh, I'm so sorry!", but I cut her off.

"Ms. Rose, I wanted to ask you about Jonathon."

"Jonathon Carter?" she asks, surprised. I nod, recognizing the name from when Ray met me at the restaurant. "What about him?"

"I want to know when he came here, and why, and how, and about when he got sick. I also want to know about his parents and his history before Marvin."

"*Hmm.*" Ms. Rose purses her lips. "I'm sorry, Mel, but we don't usually divulge our students' records to non-staff."

"It's a personal interest," I say quickly before scowling at the knowing smile that spreads across Ms. Rose's face.

"Ah. Well, then, Mel." She leans back. "I'm not sure you and Jonathon will find that much in common. But sometimes that's what makes relationships special, the fact that the people are different."

Stop. Talking. Now. I struggle to not jump up and scream in vexation. First of all, I am not looking for things we have in common. Secondly, I don't like what you're insinuating. And thirdly, *who said anything about relationships?*

"But, Mel," Ms. Rose continues, completely oblivious to my infuriation, "Jonathon's story is pretty sad. Are you sure you want to–"

"Yes," I say, cutting her off again.

"All right." She places her hands in her lap. "Jonathon

was an orphan before he contracted a disease that resulted in temporary muscular paralysis. He lost his memory, too. He can't recall anything about his life before he became ill. Peter Manifred, the doctor who diagnosed him,"–my ears perk up (figuratively)–"is an old friend of our former meteorology Pro head. He contacted her about a place for Jonathon here at Marvin. Mrs. Ilene, the former Pro head, helped us get Jonathon enrolled here."

"What about…where he was before?" I ask.

"The orphanage–Alison Orphan Childcare–went bankrupt. We couldn't trace them."

How convenient.

"But…" Ms. Rose gets up and moves to a closet. When she opens it I see a multitude of filing cabinets. She runs her finger along the sheet on the door labeled directory before pulling open a drawer. A minute later she removes a folder from the cabinet and comes back to the desk. "This is Jonathon's birth certificate, which we received with his medical files. The orphanage sent it with Jonathon to the hospital."

I lean over to see the paper she extracts. My jaw drops. Sure enough, his correct birth date is listed. Also, the category marked 'parents' is filled out as unknown. And it says his full name is Jonathon Lucas Carter.

"So," Ms. Rose continues, placing the certificate back into the folder, "does that help, Mel?" I don't miss her wink.

"Somewhat," I reply, thinking about the name I was given. Learning more about Peter Manifred is definitely my next step. Almost dazedly, I stand up.

"Have a nice day!" Ms. Rose says cheerfully. As I head for the door, she adds, "Oh, and honey? I'm not sure it would be the best idea to mention this to–"

"I won't," I say before stepping out into the hallway, still lost (for the second time today) in thought. Drat! Where's my compass?

As soon as I'm alone in my room I collapse into my armchair, tuck my chin over my knees, and continue thinking. I need to find this Manifred guy. If he's even a remotely good doctor, he'll know what the Rochester doctors knew: it was poison, not a disease, that caused Ray's problems. I need to learn his story and know why he said that junk about a muscle paralysis disease.

My phone chirps and I tug it out of my pocket.

"Hello, Shadow. Yes, I'm fine. No, I don't have any more boo-boos."

"Okay, then," Shadow says. "How did it go today?"

"Frustratingly." I don't waste time thinking of a new, more elaborate answer.

"Sorry to hear that."

What is it with people and saying 'sorry'? "Life happens. Do you have any more news up there?"

"Sadly, no." Shadow pauses, then asks, "Have you met anyone interesting?"

"Who are you? Lyvia?"

"No, I'm curious."

"Oh. Well, Curious, I've met a few girls, three of whom seem nice." Hopefully that will satisfy him.

"Are there some that are…not nice?"

"Petty females," I assure him. Still, I scowl at the thought of Caidy.

Shadow says more blah about being careful and taking it easy before we say good-bye. I slump back in the chair, vaguely aware that I should be exercising right now, but also aware that it's much easier just to sit here and think.

Still, I force myself to get up and do a few rounds of my new kickboxing DVD. Then I shower and halfheartedly look over a few maps of Brisbane. Finally I make my way back to the armchair. The clock reads 5:15.

A little while later I become aware of a vibrating on my thigh. I jump and pull out my phone, expecting it to be Shadow. Instead, the screen flashes *New Txt Msg*.

I warily open the message.

hi mel! it's Hale. just wanted to say...hi!

I blink at the words, and next thing I know I've hit reply.

Hello Hale.

I hit send uncertainly. A minute later she replies.

how was ur day?

Somehow 'frustrating' doesn't seem like the most appropriate response here. Instead, I press in, *I've had better. But I've had worse too.*

She writes back, *that stinks.*

I find myself agreeing with her, and thinking finally! Someone's not saying 'sorry'!

Yeah, it does. How was your day?

sry, its hard 2 understand u,

Why?

ur grammar is 2 proper

I gape. *What?*

why dont u use txt-speak? she asks.

Because I don't want to risk a misunderstanding.

Even as I send it I know it sounds pretentious. I quickly send a second message.

And I guess it's just a habit of mine.

Both are true. I used to write somewhat like Hale, in casual settings, but I've sort of reverted ever since....

After a longer pause this time, Hale writes back, *thats ok but just try to loosen up a little?*

I feel a small, grudging smile form on my face. *I would, but I don't think that's included in my cerebral composition.*

ahh stop i don't understand what ur saying!!!!!!! she responds. I grin wider.

Perhaps if you contemplate each individual term singly

before conjoining them you might be able to achieve comprehension.

r u trying to say something? im not 'contemplating' it

Do you mean 'comprehending' it?

whatever it is im not doing it!

Never read the dictionary, have you?

o god tell me that's not what u do 4 fun

It's quite a pleasurable pastime, actually...

MELON WHATEVER-YOUR-LAST-NAME-IS, U ARE SRSLY THE WEIRDEST GIRL I HAVE EVER MET!

I'm actually laughing now. *Weird in a bad way, or a good way, as in unique?*

Whatever the BAD way is. READING THE DICTIONARY, MEL????

Well–I'm not liable for any feelings of resentment, hurt, or extreme hilarity, by the way–I was actually joking.

GOOD! but any1 who can even JOKE about the dictionary is still weird!

I'm still chuckling as I enter my next message. *I think I was asking you about your day?*

oh yeah it was cool. better than caidys anyway.

My ears perk up again. It must be the schnauzer in me. *What's wrong with Caidy?* Other than the obvious.

o she was just a little miffed b/c jon came back late from helping mrs. ilene.

Was she? Why?

idk exactly. it's something like she and him r working on their project all day 2day and him coming back late cut into it or whatev

But he said he was free all day. And what is 'idk'?

u talked 2 him? o that means i-don't-kno

Um, yeah. I ran into him by Botanic Gardens and we took a walk, and yeah that clears things up

ohh! that is so cuuute!

Don't use the c-word. But it was fun.

cute cute cute cute cute cute cute cute!!!! what did you do?

Ahhhhh! We walked. And talked.

about what? she demands.

he told me about what he'd been doing Friday, I told him some stuff about me...

aww

Ack. Stop that.

awwwwwwwwwwwwwwwwwwwwwwwwwwwwwwwwww wwwwwwwwwwww

Suddenly something she'd said occurs to me. I type another message. *Wait. are Caidy and Ray going to be at dinner?*

um, she writes back. *caidys not. whos ray?*

I curse under my breath. *No one. What about Jonathon?*

no hes not r u coming?

For a moment I'm seriously tempted to say yes, but by thinking about Ray I'd remembered Peter Manifred and the unfinished research I have concerning him.

I have work I'm supposed to be doing. Right now, actually. Some other time, maybe. I hesitate, then add, *Sorry.*

And as I hit send, I really am sorry.

I try the online phone book starting with the present listings and going back five years, but I can't find Peter Manifred anywhere. Then I check out the websites of local hospitals. I finally come across his address in a list of retired staff from a nearby medical center. Satisfied with the results of my efforts, I go through my last two granola bars. I have to get more of them tomorrow.

Preferably I'll get some answers along with them.

First thing in the morning I board the bus to Spring Hill,

my desire for answers having intensified overnight and clouding my ability to focus on my End. Which I will do, of course…after I get answers about Ray.

The community Peter Manifred lives in seems like it would fit well in Florida. The closely packed homes with their solid-color roofs are all quite similar in size and shape. This is not a generic neighborhood, though, where every house is exactly the same. Evenly spaced along the block, each building boasts a unique design aspect that sets it apart in some way from its neighbors.

I walk about two blocks until I reach a low, basic gray-roofed house. The front is in shadow from the overhanging roof, making it difficult to see inside the windows.

I march right up and knock on the door. If he's not already awake, he should be; it's nearly eight-thirty.

A minute later a man answers the door. He has salt and pepper hair, the beginnings of a goatee, and creases around his forehead that indicate he furrows his brow a lot.

"Are you Peter Manifred?" I say immediately.

"Who are you?" he asks, staring at me. I don't miss the slight emphasis he puts on 'you'. He's avoiding the question.

"My name is Amy," I reply shortly. "Are you or are you not the retired doctor, Peter Manifred?"

The man purses his lips. "I am," he says finally. "What do you want?"

"I want," I say, "to know about an old patient of yours."

"I have had many patients, Miss Amy."

"Jonathon Carter."

I see Peter Manifred's face freeze for just a moment. Then he composes himself.

"I know of no such person."

"Oh, is that so?" I match his formal tone. "Two years, two months, and about two weeks ago, he arrived here, with some type of muscle paralysis disease, and you cured him."

Peter Manifred's mouth cracks open slightly. At the same time his gray eyes narrow. This expression could have been mistaken for annoyance, or incredulousness, or disbelief. I recognize it as disbelief, but not in a who-does-this-kid-think-she-is way. A how-does-this-kid-know-all-this-and-what-is-she-trying-to-do way. I feel the corner of my mouth pull up in a grin.

"Oh. Yes. Him," Manifred stutters, eyes on my face.

"Yes." I nod. "Him."

"Look, it was a rare disease. I'd never seen it before. It was a miracle I was able to treat it," he all but snaps.

So he's insisting on going along with the story. Fine. Something'll slip out eventually.

"Where did he come from?" I cock my head, looking intently back.

"Alison Orphan Childcare," Peter Manifred replies slowly, but immediately. "They went–"

"Bankrupt," I mutter. "I know."

"I don't know if this is for a school report or something," Peter Manifred says in a low, severe voice, "but these sort of undiagnosed cases are serious business." He glowers at me for a second before adding, "And that business is not yours."

I return his glare. "Is it my business if I want the truth...and know you're lying?" This'll help him slip up, now that I've put it out in the open like this. It's like someone playing the piano: they know they can do it in practice, but as soon as people are watching, they suck.

I see Peter Manifred's temple contract as he clenches his teeth. "Not even then."

Bingo. I hold his stare for one more moment before turning and walking back to the street. I've just stepped off his property when he seems to realize his mistake. "And I am not lying!" he yells before adding a swear word. Then he swears again because he's just sworn–and given his slip away.

Rain
* * *

I ride the bus for a few miles before getting off in need of fresh air. The stop lets off at the Roma Street Station. I walk up the side of the road, trying not to gag on the scent of car exhaust and thinking that this isn't much better than the bus, only less crowded.

I reach a turn off the main road and take it willingly. A sign tells me I'm entering Roma Street Parkland. I move in and end up on a walkway surrounded by intricate patterns of flora. After I walk a few meters it starts to smell better, too. I relax my shoulders slightly and walk, automatically turning corners and avoiding people while my mind mulls over Peter Manifred. I'll need to go back. It'll be simpler now to get the information since he knows I know, though it might be harder to get hold of him. I could start by calling him and making an appointment to speak with him. Then I'd show up an hour early, in case he'd try to hide. That strategy usually works. Or I could just go and surprise him....

Oh, yeah, I'll need to work on my End, too.

My feet pull me to a halt behind a family with a stroller as they wait for another group of people to pass. The twelve-year-old girl with the stroller family is arguing with her mother. By her accent, I guess she's a tourist here from the United States, probably around Georgia or the Gulf states.

"But Mom, everyone has a cell phone. Look around, okay? Everyone in my grade, everyone in my school, everyone here! Look, even *that guy* has one!"

That guy. That 'guy' must look out of place. I focus on the girl and where she's looking. Pretending to be observing the flowers, I pivot to see what guy she's referring to.

A middle-aged, slightly overweight man in khakis and a light jacket is standing casually a few meters behind me chatting on a cell phone. His hair is a dark roan. Something in my brain tells me the color is familiar, but I can't put my figurative finger on it, which bothers me. What bothers me more, though, is that he's not Avocado Man.

The mom is obviously impatient with her daughter. "Stop bugging me about this, Beth. We're on vacation and I do not want to be arguing with you. If you don't drop the subject right now…"

As my gaze sweeps past the man's face, I notice his eyes dart towards me, then just as quickly dart away.

Hmm. I must be getting close. It takes a few moments for my mind to convert to End mode before I switch directions. I stroll nonchalantly by the guy, looking for more information as to his identity.

His eyes automatically follow me as I pass. Then he hurries away, dodging through the now dispersing group. I know I can't follow him, but I do watch him jump into a car and drive out of the parking lot. My eyebrows come together when he races off in a direction opposite to the one I would've expected, more towards Marvin than to any of the areas I'd thought he might visit. I wonder if I'm searching too far away.

Before I can come to a conclusion my pocket vibrates. I grab the top of my phone and yank it out, the words "Yes, Shadow, I am all right," already forming in my mind. I stop in surprise when, again, my screen flashes *New Txt Msg*.

I hit View, not surprised when I see it's from Hale. On the chance that she might text me again, I'd programmed her into my contacts last night. Which brought me to a grand total of six contacts.

mel!!!! hi i hope im not interrupting or anything. but if ur all dun w/ whatevr ur doing do u want 2 meet me and viv and Leah at the ice cream place?

Before I can reply, another message pops up.

ps i kno ur thinking about saying u have too much wrk to do, but EVER HEARD OF BREAKS????

Rain

I scowl as she all but reads my mind. Which makes me scowl again as I acknowledge that.

Another text appears on my screen.

pps viv says she wants u to come too (hey look i used the right wrds!!!!)

I grind the toes of my right sandal into the concrete. True, I had—have—no plans for the rest of the day other than exercise, thinking, and all the other usual stuff. Well, I guess I should say I have no *work* plans.

Ice cream might take an hour, tops. *That won't cut into the day too much, will it?* part of me implores.

It might, another urgent voice counters. There's so much to do in preparation for Ray's case, and now this new development—

My other voice cuts me off. *I want to get ice cream, though.*

I swallow as my other voice snaps, *I don't eat ice cream.*

Maybe I should.

Maybe I shouldn't. What's wrong with me? I need to think!

That I do need. I feel myself walking slowly without a destination, not absorbing the view of the flowers. A different voice is speaking, faint and timid in the back of my mind. I struggle to listen.

You just think—the small voice says—*that if you go Hale and her friends will get to know you better...and not like you anymore!*

I stop listening, grimacing. This voice sounds less like me, but the words make a bigger impact.

Not true! the responsible voice is saying. *I just—*

You think you'll scare them away, the faint voice says miserably.

I can scare anyone, one of my voices says proudly. But my stomach is feeling less like organic material and more like lead.

Ugh, stop it, I snap to myself, but I feel sure that any second Hale's going to text back. I can see it–"sorry mel, but um we decided were not going to get ice cream. oh but dont go anyway. stay far away from the ice cream place. even if u knew which one 2 go 2. ummm how about u just dont get ice cream today."

I scowl harder.

My phone vibrates. I sigh and open the message.

plz?????????????????

I blink. Plz? Is this short for *sorry, didn't know what I was thinking earlier! Never mind!!!!* Though I can't imagine what words it could be an abbreviation for–

Buzz, buzz. My phone is like a wasp or something.

Plz=please, mel. PLEASE????

See? One of my voices says.

You're just afraid, the timid one whispers.

I am not afraid. Of anything! I retort.

So go.

The phone buzzes again. And again. And again. A flood of messages pops up.

Please? (look, i capitalized 4 u!)

Please?

Please? (im going 2 stop capitalizing if u don't reply!!!!)

Please?

Please?

plz??? (see now uve annoyed me lol)

plz???

PLZ???

I gape at the texts. She actually does want me to come. And…it feels good.

A new text fills my screen.

fine. i can take a hint. u dont like me. ok! sheesh! go find ur own ice cream

My eyes widen. I quickly hit reply.

No, wait, Hale! I'm sorry. I was reading your texts. I take a deep breath, then continue. *I'd like to meet you for ice cream.*

Her answer comes immediately.

lol mel ur so funny. i was just kidding about being offended (look another big wrd!) of course u can still come. yayyyy! cheering in background from viv

Below is the address of the parlor. I let out a long breath.

Thank you. I'll see you in a few minutes then.

c u!!!

I stare at my phone for about a minute as a few pedestrians pass by, ooing and ahhing at the blooms.

And then I remember I have to go.

Have to go meet someone–someones–who are maybe almost friends for ice cream.

As I hurry to the bus stop, I feel a small grin spread across my face.

15

"Mel! Hey!" Hale enthuses while bounding up to greet me as I walk to the outside dining platform of the small ice cream parlor.

"Hi, Hale," My small grin grows slightly larger. "And Vivian. And Leah."

"How's it going?" Vivian asks. She stands and stretches as Leah slides out of her seat as well.

"Okay," I reply, pretty much truthfully. "You guys haven't gotten anything yet?"

"We had to wait for you." Leah shrugs and rolls her eyes at her sister. In return, Hale sticks out her tongue at Leah.

"Of course we did. Why wouldn't we?"

I notice the two sisters are fashionably dressed, per usual. Leah's wearing a long-sleeve burgundy jacket and jeans while Hale sports a bubble-gum pink hoodie over waffle-print capris, her outfit complimented by a chocolate-brown beaded necklace. Vivian's the only one in a skirt; it's a solid burnt umber fabric that sort of floats around her calves and fits well with her tight sky-blue sweatshirt.

Vivian's working a twist into her hair absentmindedly as we head up to the counter. A tired-looking college student sighs down at us.

"Bubble-gum with chocolate sprinkles," Hale says immediately. "Waffle cone, size medium."

"She always gets what she's wearing," Vivian whispers to me.

"So, Saturday," I murmur back, remembering something

that stood out to me, "she would've gotten watermelon?"

"Exactamente." Vivian nods, smiling at me.

"Pecan," Leah says next. "In a dish, please, size small."

"You're so boring," Hale complains under her breath, as I suddenly realize I have no idea what I'm going to do. I haven't had ice cream since...well.... And I've probably ordered it only once outside of school. I think I was eleven, at the mall, on my first activity; it was my goal to find out what company the stand got their cones from. In the end, it had been Ray who'd gotten the answer, but we'd both planned and...

"*Hmm*," Vivian muses, pulling out a piece of paper. I see a long list of what look like combinations, about one fourth of them crossed out. "I'm on to...okay, size large dish of butterscotch, but with crumbled wafers as a topping."

"Why did you choose that?" I ask interestedly as the lady writes that down.

"I'm trying every single combination of ice cream and toppings available here and rating them," Vivian explains.

"Ambitious," I say.

"Well, I don't get cool missions like you–just dead bodies on a gurney. So I need some way to keep myself occupied."

"And you choose...ice cream?"

"Best invention ever." Vivian wiggles her eyebrows. "Want to help? You can try one of these and give it a score of one-to-ten–"

"Yes," I say instantly, to abstain from having to choose myself.

"Thanks! Okay...hmm...ok, here's a totally random one–will you try cheesecake with crushed peanut butter cups?"

I look up to find the ice cream lady staring at me. "Um, sure. I'll have that. A dish of cheesecake ice cream with a crushed peanut butter cup topping, small, please."

The lady writes that down and makes our orders. We take them back to the table where the three had been sitting. Leah slides into her seat and samples a dainty bite of pecan ice cream. Hale plops down and digs in, eating rapturously.

"Are they really related?" I ask Vivian.

"Well, we had their DNA tested in sixth grade, and the results said they were." Vivian shrugs and pats the chair next to her. "It's harder to eat ice cream standing, you know."

I suppress a smile and sit down on the painted metal seat.

"*Hmm*," Vivian says thoughtfully, tasting her ice cream. "Right now I'm going with a five. It's good, but boring."

"Mine's awesome." Hale grins brightly. "Have you tried this combo yet?"

"Yeah, I've been through all the sprinkles. How's yours, Mel?"

I realize I haven't tried my dish yet. "Um…" I scoop out a large spoonful and put it in my mouth. "A-ay-i!"

"Sorry?" Vivian says politely, while Hale laughs. A sudden headache attacks my skull.

I swallow, gasping. "Ow, ow, ow…" I clap my hands over my ears.

"Oh, brainfreeze," Vivian says. "Mel, do this." She presses her thumb to the roof of her mouth. I copy her. Instantly the pain in my head lessens.

"How does that work?" I ask after removing my finger.

"When the roof of your mouth gets cold, it gives you a headache," Vivian says simply. "It has to do with the arteries contracting and stuff, but it's not that important. The thumb warms it back up. Hey, what were you saying before you starting flipping out?"

"I was not flipping out," I tell her. "And I was saying 'amazing'." I take another tentative bite. "This is really, really good!" I'm surprised as well.

"Great!" Vivian spreads out her list. "How good, exactly?"

"Nine," I say.

"Wow! That is good." Vivian writes it down.

"Let me try," Hale says. I push my bowl across the table to her. She takes a spoonful. "*Mm*! Viv, this is awesome!"

Vivian and Hale both try it, then I start eating again. After a few minutes I check my watch. It's only ten o'clock, something that hadn't occurred to me earlier.

"You like ice cream early, I see," I comment.

"Ice cream is the perfect way to start the day," Hale replies sagely.

"But…shouldn't you be in school right now?"

"We have off this week," Leah says indifferently, looking down at her lap. I see a cell phone in her hands.

"Oh," I say, returning to my ice cream. It is *so* good. I had no idea ice cream could taste like this. I love it. I actually love it.

"Good thing, too," Hale says. "That means we have all day tomorrow to get ready for the dance."

Ah, the dance again. I tune out and focus on my ice cream, waiting for them to get bored with the topic. Though that could probably take weeks.

After ten minutes I realize I've emptied the bowl. I frown.

"What's wrong, Mel?" Vivian asks.

"I finished," I reply. "You know, I think I want more."

"Me too," Hale agrees. "Viv? Leah? Want to come with us to get seconds?"

"No, thanks," Vivian says. "I've still got to finish this. You know how slow I eat."

Leah snorts at Hale. "Do you know how many calories–"

"Oh, give it a rest." Hale stands up. So does Leah.

"Whatever. Um, sorry, I have to go now. Caidy wants to hang out." Leah taps her cell phone.

"If she wanted to hang out, she should have come along," Hale says, a little coolly.

"Aw, come on, Hale. That's not completely fair."

"It is so completely fair. Come on, Mel. Later, sis."

I follow Hale back to the ice cream parlor. "Why didn't Caidy come?" I ask once we're inside and waiting in line.

Hale rolls her eyes. "She's still mad. I can't believe her."

"Oh," I say, definitely surprised that Hale'd still want to get ice cream with me, even though her friend's decided to hate me.

"Yeah, it's completely stupid. She acts like she has this big legal claim on Jonathon, and she thinks you're trying to trespass on her property or something. Good thing I didn't tell her about you taking a walk with him. I mean, you should've heard the bull she was coming out with this morning. It annoyed the crap out of me."

"Thanks," I manage.

"No biggie. You want to order first or should I?"

"Go ahead." I pull out my wallet as she talks to the lady. Shadow'd supplied me with lots of Australian dollars. So far all I've used them on is the bus. Oh, and ice cream. But that reminds me; I need granola bars. Luckily this place is like a small convenience store too. I see a pack of multigrain snack bars and snag them before ordering my ice cream.

We head back to the table where Vivian's a little over halfway done with her butterscotch wafer combination.

"Those look yummy." Vivian nods at my granola bars, which I plunk in Leah's now-empty seat.

"They're useful," I correct. "And healthy. But actually, they're not that yummy."

"Then why don't you get some good ones?" Hale asks.

"Because these are the useful and healthy ones," I sigh.

Hale looks like she doesn't get it. Luckily Vivian cuts in.

"Hey, I was thinking while you were getting your ice cream, and Mel, you should go to the dance."

Okay, not so luckily.

"No, thanks," I say.

"Why not?" Hale says. "It doesn't matter that you've never been to one, if that's what you're worried about."

"That's not what I'm worried about," I respond, quickly adding, "I'm not worried about anything!"

"Please?" Vivian tries.

"I don't have a dress," I say, trying yet again to halt this conversation.

"I have extra," the two of them say at the same time.

"I'm taller than both of you," I point out.

Hale objects to my reasoning. "You're only taller than Viv by about an inch. "And I can fix that."

"I don't want to."

"What if we don't care what you want?" Hale raises an eyebrow.

"What? You're going to force me? I'd like to see you try."

"We have our methods," Vivian says in an ominous tone.

"Oooh! Chills." I pretend to quake with fear.

"Is that a yes?" Hale demands to know.

"Um, no."

"Come on…"

"No!"

"Please? Please, please, please?"

"No!"

"She'll change her mind," Vivian says to Hale.

"No, I wont," I tell her. "There is no absolute way I'm going to that dance."

Vivian and Hale share a significant look. They drop the subject, but I have a feeling it's not permanent.

* * *

I've been out of the shower for ten minutes when there's a knock on my door. I look through the peephole and quickly open it, my eyes wide.

"Hi," Ray says.

"Hi," I reply, stepping back to invite him in. I can't believe this is even slightly shocking, but I feel marginally unsteady. It's just...how long has it been since he's knocked on my door?

"How are you?"

"I'm okay," I say. "Go ahead, sit down wherever."

He chooses the armchair. I sit on the edge of my bed.

"Where were you this morning?" he asks while looking around my room.

I frown, choosing my answer carefully. I won't say anything about Peter Manifred, that's for sure. "Well, I just got back from having ice cream with Hale and Vivian. And before that I took a walk at the Roma Street Parkland."

"That sounds like fun," he smiles.

"The ice cream part was," I admit.

"Isn't the Parkland amazing?"

"Well...honestly, I'm sure it is, but I wasn't really noticing it. I was...thinking about other things. And then there was this guy watching me, and I have a feeling I should know who he is, but I don't! And he got away, and I still–" I cut myself off before I can say "don't have all the answers I want". Instead, I grit my teeth and stare at the carpet. "It's just so frustrating. No, I used that word already. *Hmm.* How about 'maddening'? 'Infuriating'? 'Vexing'? 'Irritating'? 'Annoying'? 'Exasperating'?"

"That bad, huh?"

"Worse. I just want to be done with this freaking End. But it doesn't want to be done."

There's a minute of silence. Then Ray says, "Mel, I was

just wondering…well, I don't really understand why you didn't let me come yesterday."

Instead of answering, my mind flashes to all the reasons. Ray on the floor in Chick-n-Wings. Ray screaming as they load him onto the stretcher. Shadow holding me while I cry. Seeing the closed coffin in the funeral home. Sitting outside in the rain. Things I haven't thought about in a long time.

I feel my nose start to burn and quickly look away, pressing my forearm to my eyes. My face is burning. I don't cry. Why am I crying? A mix of emotions–frustration, anger, embarrassment, sadness–flows through me. No, no, no. I will not cry. I will not cry. I will not–

Cry.

No. This has to be allergies. That excuse always works. Not that it's an excuse.

I feel the mattress shift as Ray sits down next to me. "Mel?" he asks softly. I squeeze the wetness out of my eyes and into my shirt, but it comes back. He doesn't say anything else; that feels better than the alternative.

Finally I gain enough control to mumble, "Because I don't want it to happen again."

He doesn't ask any questions.

After Ray leaves (and after I've gotten over my stupid allergies), Shadow calls.

"I'm fine," I say into the receiver.

"I have news," he replies.

"What?" I ask quickly. Maybe this will be the lead that's been avoiding me.

"The police have determined which birth certificates Maryanne took," Shadow says, almost hesitantly.

"Which ones?" I demand.

"Well, there were four total. They are completely unconnected to one another, as far as we can tell–Tara

Schnyder, Gregory Hopkins, Isabel Levitt..."

"They don't mean anything to me," I muse. "But, wait. Number four?"

Shadow hesitates, then says very quickly, "Anthony Luther."

I'm stunned into silence for at least two seconds.

"Again, I don't think it's a big deal," Shadow rushes on. "We even have a copy of it, all it says is date of birth, weight at birth, parents Jerry Luther and Bonnie Robar..." he trails off. I can tell he's afraid, because of my silence, that he's made it worse.

I force myself to recover, saying the first words, a question, that pops in my head. "Bonnie Robar–that's Ray's mom?"

"Yes, Annette's sister." I can almost see Shadow nodding, relieved at how I'm taking the information. He doesn't catch my use of present tense. And, luckily, he can't see my mind whirling. Why did they pick Ray? Was it just a coincidence? Are they in on the whole faking-his-death thing? "But it was all random, the police have said." There's a pause, then he adds; "Besides, what does it matter anyway?"

Do they want to know about his parents? Somehow the other data, like weight at birth, doesn't strike me as being likely candidates for the whole stolen-to-gain-information thing. So, then, what about his parents? His dad's dead, but his mom might not be. Does it have something to do with her? But why? Where is she anyway? She didn't contact us, and she wasn't even at the funeral! I gape as I realize this. I'd been so caught up on that day I hadn't even noticed. So maybe she is dead–or just an idiot or something.

"Amber?"

"Uh?"

"I was saying, since this doesn't seem to be going very far–and let's be clear that it is not your fault–you have permission to stop working on this End." My eyes widen in disbelief. As if he senses this, Shadow quickly adds, "I'm going to be there in a week, and I'll be able to have someone take it from there. You're leaving seven days from tomorrow. You can enjoy yourself until then."

He doesn't think I can do it? "I must have hearing problems. I'll pretend that was just a hallucination."

Shadow sighs. "I might have to order you to stop. Think about it, Amber. But for now, I guess I'll talk to you later."

"I will." I hang up, shaking my head. I will talk to him later. But I won't think about it.

All through dinner I'm impressed that Hale and Vivian don't bring up the topic of the dance again. And Ray doesn't say anything about my allergies, for which I'm grateful. It's actually just nice being at the same table with everyone, even though Dan keeps staring at me as if searching for traces of black clothing. He gets all excited when he spots my black sneakers. Ray and I share a couple of looks over that.

Dinner actually ends too soon.

By nine o'clock Tuesday morning I'm pacing in my room, still trying to decide what I want to focus on today– End or Ray? Well, I want to focus on Ray. So the question is...My phone vibrates on the bedside table. I topple across the bed on my stomach to reach it.

New Txt Msg. I half grin, hitting *View.*

b ready 2 open ur door!!!!

"What?" I mutter, sliding back off the bed. A minute later there's a thump from the doorway. I hurry over and pull it open. "What?"

"My arms are killing me," Hale moans. "Let us in already!"

I back up to let Hale and Vivian stumble in, both

weighed down by various boxes and huge plastic bags with coat hangers on top. They set the stuff on my bed and collapse on the floor.

"Why did you bring all that?" I splutter.

"Because we can't use it if we're here and it's back in Hale's room," Vivian says, propped up against the armchair.

"Duh," Hale mumbles, face down on the carpet.

"Drama queen," Vivian says, kicking Hale's foot. "Get up. Come on."

Hale gives an exaggerated sigh and rolls over. "I guess you're right. We only have..." she looks at my clock and gasps. "Nine hours and fifty-seven minutes!"

"Until what?" I demand, a suspicion already forming in my mind.

"I thought you were supposed to be the intelligent one," Hale jokes.

"The dance," Vivian says. "We're all getting ready together."

"Oh, no," I say, my fears confirmed. "No. I told you already! No. No. No. No. No."

"Um...Yes, yes, yes, yes, yes, yes," Hale replies, countering each of my 'no's.

"No."

"Yes," Vivian says brightly.

"Come on," I groan. "This isn't fair. I said I didn't–"

"You should know that sometimes what you want doesn't matter," Hale tells me.

"I do know that, but–"

"I brought a bribe," Hale warns.

"A...bribe?"

Hale scrambles up and tugs one of the boxes out of the heap on the bed. "Donuts!"

Sure enough, there are at least a dozen iced, glazed, and powdered pastries.

"You can have as many as you want if you agree to go to the dance," Hale says in a low, attempted hypnotic voice, trying to move the box tantalizingly in front of me.

"That's okay," I decline.

Hale's mouth drops open. "What? No one can resist donuts!"

"I've never had one, so I can," I reply.

"You've never had a donut?"

"Is that a crime?" I ask.

"Uh, yeah," Hale's still staring at me incredulously. "Viv! Come here and hold Mel down while I feed her a donut."

I snort. "You can't hold me down."

Vivian exchanges a glance with Hale, then stands up and stomps on my foot.

"Uh, ow," I say, turning on her, my mouth open in preparation to retaliate. Before I can tell her what I think of her, Hale's ripped a piece of chocolate-iced donut off the whole and stuffed it in my mouth. I stop, gagging, then stop again as I taste it.

Mmm.

I quickly swallow, but my mouth is watering. "Oh, come on, that's not fair," I complain. "You can't do that."

"All's fair in love and war." Hale smiles wickedly. Seeing my look, she says quickly, "This is the war part. We'll get Jon to do the love part," she teases. I scowl. "Or that Ray person you mentioned. Who is he?"

I don't have an answer for that.

"Does he go to your school?" Vivian asks.

"He did," I say truthfully. "But we're not talking about that."

"Right. We were discussing the war." Hale walks to my garbage can. "Say you'll go to the dance, or I swear I'll dump all of these donuts into the trash!"

"You wouldn't," I say confidently. Hale raises an eyebrow, plucks a white powdered donut from the box, and drops it cheerfully in the bin. Vivian sighs lamentably beside me.

"And I have more in store after this," Hale warns me. "We're not leaving. We have nothing else to do all day but get ready."

"I don't have a date," I try.

"No one has a date, except for those who are already boyfriend and girlfriend," Hale replies.

"Malicious little conspirator," I grumble. After a minute of internal grousing, I finally sigh. "Fine. Fine! I'll go. I'm not promising I'll hang around. But I'll go. Now give me one of those donuts."

Hale and Vivian cheer. Hale passes me the rest of the chocolate-iced one, which I chew on sullenly while Vivian and Hale eat their own donuts and at the same time, set up their miniature boutique. They have about three boxes of makeup, three of hair supplies, two of jewelry, one of what looks like shoes and stockings, and then the garbage bags with coat hangers which, I realize with horror, are dresses.

I'll have to wear a dress, a real dress. It's almost equivalent to claustrophobia to me. If I have to fight, it'll be extremely hard to do my best.

What am I going to fight at a dance? one of my voices asks.

You'll look stupid, the faint voice says glumly. I try to quiet it, to no success. *You'll look like an idiot while everyone else looks good. I don't want to watch this...*

I promised to go, the first voice says. *It'll be fun. I'll be with Hale and Vivian and maybe Ray...*

Ray'll laugh when he sees you, the quiet voice sighs. I frown.

Ray'll be happy to see me, my original voice snaps. I try

to agree. Who is this other voice, anyway? It's not me. The other voices are me, fighting for me, even if they are fighting with me. But this stupid little voice is talking to me, fighting against me. Grrr! I've never had that voice before. I want to scream '*go away*'! But I have a feeling it won't do any good.

"First you need to choose a dress," Hale says sunnily, unaware of my discomfort. "Try this one first." She pulls a layered periwinkle one from under the first garbage bag and almost pushes me to the bathroom. Resignedly, I pull the dress on and step back out.

"*Hmm*," Vivian says. "Not the best."

"I like it," Hale says, but forces another one on me, pink this time (absolutely no way), and steers me back to the bathroom.

They make me try on at least six dresses before they choose a knee-length midnight blue number. It's simple, with a layered skirt and a smooth sleeveless top. Luckily, though, it has something to hold it on, even if they are only spaghetti straps. I would not be able to pull off a halter-top.

Hale brings out white high-heels and a silvery pair of sandals. I choose the sandals immediately, because they're flat and somewhat practical. Oh, and they don't squeeze my feet half to death.

Next they show me their dresses. Hale's is a simple white spaghetti-strap dress, a little shorter than mine, but she somehow put glitter on it—thicker at the top, and thinning towards the bottom of the skirt—so that it fractures light and glints like a rainbow. Vivian's is a longer green halter-top dress with a flowing skirt and rhinestones around the collar. I give thanks that mine has nothing sparkly.

By now it's a little after ten. I wonder if I can slip away to work on my End until six or so, or if Hale would have a coronary.

Then I wonder if I should.

Of course I should. I have work to do, lots and lots of work to do. But Hale and Vivian came down and put this all together especially for me. Would it be rude to leave? Of course it would. But it would be irresponsible to stay, even though Shadow said I could take a break. But I don't take breaks. And I shouldn't, I need to work.

But I want to stay.

So? Need always overrules want in my life; it's routine. I press my lips together and begin to rise from the armchair. Just as I do so, Hale flashes a smile in my direction. I falter.

"What do you think, Mel?" Vivian asks.

"Huh?" I say.

"She was spacing out again," Hale laughs. "We were wondering what you thought about Marvin."

"Oh," I say. "I like it. It's definitely different than Watson, but it's also pretty neat."

"Cool," Hale says. I sink back into the cushions. What the heck, one day can't hurt.

Can it?

No.

I won't let it.

But right now, I can actually have fun.

At five-thirty, after we've discussed Hale and Vivian's Pros and Watson and various subjects from ice cream to cars, Hale says it's time to really get ready. My phone rings just as she's picking up her dress. I look at the caller ID.

"Oh, it's Lyvia," I say, looking at Hale. "You know, I think you two would get along really well." I flip the phone open. "Hello?"

"You haven't called," Lyvia growls.

"Oh–sorry! I've been busy, though."

"Like that's an excuse." I hear the pout in her voice. "Bryant asked me out! Can you believe that? And then Kent wouldn't talk to him for three days! And he and Nathan had a shouting match in the bathroom. No one could really understand what they said, but Lexi told me she heard my name said twice."

"Um...wow," I say.

"But anyway, what are you doing that's using up all your time? Other than your End, of course. That can't be taking up all your time!"

"Um...well, right now I'm getting ready to go to a dance."

I yank the phone away from my ear as Lyvia squeals. I wait fifteen seconds until deeming it safe, then bring the phone close again.

"That is awesome! What are you wearing? What's your hair like? Who are you going with? Is it at that school?"

"I think you better talk to Hale," I say.

"Hale?"

"She goes to Marvin," I explain, before handing the phone to Hale, who looks slightly puzzled but accepts it.

"Hello? This is Hale...Hi, Lyvia...yeah, she is...yeah, it was...I know, I can't believe it either! It took logic, persuasion, and donuts, actually. Oh, it's this really cute dress of Vivian's. It's like really dark blue and has different lengths...of course...heck, yeah! No, we have our ways...don't worry...oh, that's stupid...yeah...yeah!" Hale gets up and heads to the bathroom, carrying her dress. She's still chatting with Lyvia when she comes out, glittering like a disco ball. Without breaking the conversation, she points to Vivian and me and jerks her head towards the bathroom.

"Do you want to go first, or–" Vivian starts.

"Go ahead," I say. She shrugs, grinning, and grabs her dress.

Ten minutes later Vivian and I are fully dressed and waiting patiently for Hale to finish her conversation with

Lyvia. Hale finally closes my phone and puts it back on the table.

"Lyvia needs to come here," she says. "She'd fit right into design Pro!"

"*Hmm.*" I nod, not really paying attention to Hale because my dress is too distracting. It doesn't feel right. All over. I just want to rip it off and put on sweats. Whoever came up with the rule of wearing fancy clothes to dances was insane. Oh, and soon-to-be-dead, if I ever get ahold of them.

"Oh, let me fix that," Hale says, beckoning me over to her. I see a seam ripper, needle, and thread in her hands.

"Um, it's Vivian's dress," I object.

"She can put it back," Vivian assures me without looking up from her shoes.

"Okay..." I step over various bins and containers to Hale, where she looks me over once before making several swift tears in the closures. She takes a few measurements, moves her already threaded needle through the fabric, and adjusts the dress until it falls right. Ten minutes later she leads me to the full-length mirror behind the door.

"Well?" she demands.

"*Mm,*" I reply. It actually does look better, and it feels comparatively good. Still not comfortable, but I think that's a personal problem.

"Thanks! Viv, you need anything?"

"I'm good," Vivian says, working on the other shoe. She's wearing clear heels with complicated silver lacings that go to her knee. Hale hands me my shoes and I slip my feet into them, tightening the straps until they're secure.

"Viv's turn," Hale announces.

"What?" I ask.

"Viv is amazing with hair," Hale tells me. I remember the braid and the twist I'd seen Vivian doing with her own locks.

"I'm not amazing," Vivian objects. "I just know how."

"Yeah, what she said." Hale rolls her eyes, contradicting herself. "Do Mel first, Viv."

"I don't want anything," I say quickly.

Hale objects to my decision. "You're not going to wear that same old ponytail, are you?"

"What's wrong with my ponytail?"

"Please, Mel, let Viv–"

"No, no, I have an idea," Vivian interrupts. "Come here, Mel. If you don't like it, I promise you can take it out."

"Okay," I sigh. Vivian instructs me to sit in front of the bed while she sits on the mattress where she can reach my hair easily. I feel her pulling and tugging, but gently. It never hurts once. Finally I hear the ponytail holder snap into place.

"Well, it's better than a regular ponytail..." Hale admits. I run my fingers over the back of my head and feel a strange pattern of twists in my hair. I go to the mirror. Vivian holds a small mirror behind me so I can see. My eyes widen.

"It's a simple flipover ponytail," Vivian says nonchalantly, lowering the mirror. I spin around.

"Show me how to do that."

Vivian laughs. "Later, I will. We have to do makeup now."

I swallow. "Oh, no. I don't do makeup." That is one thing I will absolutely not stand for.

"Why not?" Hale demands to know.

"It's not compatible with my system. You want me to crash?"

"We're not going to poison you, Mel!" Hale says. "Please?"

"No, I..." I shake my head. "Look, I have bad memories of makeup."

"Don't force her," Vivian's still grinning. "But we'll have, like, a sleepover sometime so we can hear those horror stories, Mel."

Not.

"Lip gloss," Hale stipulates. "I insist on lip gloss."

"I can do lip gloss," I sigh, which gets Hale in a flurry about picking the right shade. The right shade of clear lip gloss. I roll my eyes. Vivian chuckles as she puts on eyeliner.

Hale chooses one at last and hands it to me. I swipe it on and hand it back. She sighs, putting it into a small purse. It's as shimmery as her dress.

"What are you doing with that?" I ask suspiciously.

"I'm putting everything we need for touch-ups in here," Hale says.

"I am not putting on lip gloss in front of your entire school!" I tell her.

"Fine." Hale replies. "I'll put it on you."

"You would not."

"I so would." Hale gives me her impish grin.

I am tossing that purse in the trash first chance I get.

I watch as Vivian and Hale finish their faces and give each other the once over. Then they turn on me. I expect a bunch of suggestions I'll have to ignore, but instead they both nod.

"She looks great!" Vivian says.

"Thank you." Hale takes a bow.

I let my shoulders relax and busy myself with helping put the scattered makeup and jewelry away.

"Hey, what are you doing?" Hale exclaims.

"Um…cleaning up?" I say.

"Don't touch the jewelry–you don't have any on yet!"

"Aw, Hale…"

"Nothing too fancy," she assures me. "Just a necklace and some earrings. And maybe an anklet–"

"Nooo. No anklet." Too easy to get caught on whatever you're kicking. "And no necklace." Too easy for someone to choke me. "Oh, and no dangly earrings." To easy for someone to yank them through my ear. Which is a very large and painful distraction. Not to mention messy.

"You, Melon, are impossible," Hale complains, throwing necklaces back into a bin. She extracts a smaller box and opens it, looking through the contents. "Here. Are these too much?" She shoves a pair of silver stud earrings into my hand. I turn one over. The front is a five-pointed star.

"Yeah, these are nice," I say, going back to the mirror to put them in. They sparkle when I turn my head.

"Well, that's the best I can do," Hale says.

"Muy bonita," Vivian says, putting in diamond earrings. Hale pulls out her own jewelry–some sort of mother-of-pearl beads that have a rainbow sheen–and slips on her rainbow flats. She has Vivian do an intricate six-stranded braid with a different-color ribbon braided with each strand–red, orange, yellow, green, blue, and purple–in her hair.

Vivian arranges her own hair in two braided, knotted bunches under her ears. Some hair sticks out from each, giving it a casual look, which makes her look amazing in a simple way.

Hale sprinkles glitter onto the top of her head and braid and makes it stick with hairspray. Vivian glues some green rhinestones into her twists.

I watch.

"You guys should do this as a business or something," I say almost jokingly when they're about done.

"Tempting, but my heart lies with deceased people." Vivian twists a loose strand of hair behind her ear.

"I might," Hale says seriously. "Maybe I won't go into espionage design. Maybe this suits me better."

"You have a choice?" I ask, surprised.

"Of course we do," Hale says. "Don't you?"

"I..." I've never thought about it, actually. I've just

known my career is in spying, now and in the future. "Well, I guess we do, technically...."

"Holy crap! Look at the time!" Hale yelps. "Six-fifty! We have to get down there!"

I sigh. I'd actually been enjoying myself here. But it was all for this, unfortunately.

"Let's the get torture over with," I mutter.

"Yup!" Vivian laughs. "We'll come back up after and clean this stuff up, Mel."

"Thanks," I say as Hale drags us out the door.

"Ready for your first dance, Mel?" she asks excitedly, throwing sparkles into my eyes as she bounds down the stairs towards the gym.

"No," I groan, as something makes my stomach swoop. Nervousness? Anxiousness? Regret?

Excitement?

Well, whatever it is it doesn't matter. Hale's hand is a steel trap on my wrist, and I'm headed for either a fun event or a nausea-inducing evening.

16

"Urgh." I grab the waist of the dress and yank it around again. "Are all dresses this difficult?"

"Stop messing with it." Hale rolls her eyes, trying not to laugh.

Vivian takes a more sensible approach. "Trust me, Mel. If you don't think about it, you won't notice after a while."

"How long is a 'while'?" I grumble, stopping by the food table. "Is the music always this loud?"

"Yes," Vivian and Hale answer at once.

"It's insane."

"It's a dance, Mel. Honestly!" Hale shakes her head to the beat. "Speaking of which, I wonder why they call it that? Maybe because at a dance…you're supposed to dance?"

Maybe she's saying this because we've just been wandering around since we got here. But I haven't gotten all of my complaints out yet.

"By all means, go ahead." I gesture to the mass of students already occupying the floor. The gym has been à gogo for nearly fifteen minutes already. "I'm not stopping you." As I speak my eyes dart around. I close them. Stop that, Mel.

"Come on," Hale says, pouting.

"Look, in case you haven't noticed, I'm really not the let's-go-party girl. Meaning, okay, I'll come and hang out by the food or something, but nothing else. I–"

I realize my audience's attention is somewhere else. I follow a line from Hale's narrowed eyes to somewhere around the center of the floor. My stomach feels funny all of a sudden.

"She's just bitter," Hale says to me, not tearing her eyes away.

"Conniving is more like it." Vivian corrects her friend with a more disparaging tone of voice than I've heard her use before. "She so knows he doesn't…you know…"

I swallow, then set my mouth in a hard line, still looking out of the corner of my eye at Caidy dancing with Ray. She's grinning–hugely–and somehow talking at the same time. I force myself to look away. My stomach doesn't want to see if Ray's enjoying it or not.

"I think I'm leaving," I say stonily. "I really do have work to do–lots of it. So–"

"Oh, come on Mel." Hale grabs my arm and yanks me back before I take two steps. I glower at her and twist free. "Are you just going to walk away now? You have to fight!"

I perk up. "I'm good at that. Fight who?"

"Caidy! Duh."

"That seems a little drastic," I say with a frown. "I wouldn't want to send her to the hospital or anything." Not that the idea's not intriguing.

Hale shakes her head. "No, not literal fighting."

What? "There's literal and verbal. I have to yell at her? Why am I doing this, anyway?"

Hale groans. "Don't tell me you have no clue."

"I…" I blink. Am I really going to say this? "…have no clue. What other kinds of fighting are there?"

Vivian chuckles. "Flirt fighting!"

"What?" I take a step back.

"I know you know how to flirt." Hale raises an eyebrow. "You do know how to flirt, right?"

"I've honestly never tried."

"Oh–my–god." Hale's eyebrows rise higher. "Then you

have to try! Come on Mel. Get over there!"

I feel a strange sensation in my gut. My feet twitch towards the door. What am I doing? I want to make a run for it? "I don't know. How…?"

Hale and Vivian share a look and laugh as the current song ends. I give a feeble "Ha, ha," and back away into the crowd milling around the food tables. Out of Vivian and Hale's view now, I turn around and start making my way to the door. I feel a part of my brain opposing my decision, and hesitate, confused. What is it with my brain and disagreeing with me? It's practically shouting, *Turn around! Go back! Idiot!*

Whose side are you on? I argue. *Mine! Okay? M-I-N-E.* I purse my lips and keep ducking through the crowd.

I can almost see the door when I feel a hand on my shoulder. I spin around, ready to say *go away, Hale/Vivian.* Instead, I stop with my mouth open partway.

"Hey," Ray says with a small smile. I snap my mouth shut.

"What?" I ask, too sharply to be en passant. Ray holds up his hands.

"Whoa. Don't shoot."

"Sorry." I frown. He shakes his head.

"It's okay."

No, it is not 'okay'. I open my mouth again to tell him that, and also ask (in a very indifferent manner) why he and Caidy were dancing, but he beats me to it. "I was looking for you."

"I–what?" I stammer. "Looking for me?"

"Yeah. Where were you?" he glances around, as if hoping to see a big, flashing arrow pointing to my previous location.

"We–Hale and Vivian and me–were just sort of walking around. By the snack bar," I clarify. "Why were you looking for me?" I put too much emphasis on the 'me'. I quickly look away in case he notices.

"Are you feeling okay?" Ray sounds concerned.

"No," I reply honestly. "I think I'm going to go…upstairs…" I trail off and start again through the crowd.

And again, he catches my arm. "Mel! Wait." I turn back. Ray's expression is unreadable. "You're not going to leave without dancing once, are you?"

"If I can ever escape, I am." I allow myself a small smile.

"Sorry, no such luck." He grins, too. And before I know it he's pulling me out onto the dance floor.

He puts one hand just above my waist and grasps my hand in the other. We start to sort of move in circles with the beat, which is conveniently slow. I try to control my feet and my breathing at the same time.

"So why were you going to leave?" he asks.

I struggle not to blush. "I…um…uh…" I shrug helplessly. Ray grins, stepping back, pulling me with him, so we don't bump into another dancing pair. I catch Vivian's eye, and she winks at me. I feel my face flush and silently curse. Hale, next to her, seems on the verge of hysterics. I look away as we continue to dance.

"Okay, I just want to clarify," Ray says, "but please tell me you've danced before?"

"Only under instruction," I say. Answering his look, I add, "We had to know how to do basic dances, like the waltz and stuff, in case we had to go to formal parties for our work."

"Ah." Ray nods. "Well, you're good anyway."

"Thanks," I say, surprised. We're both silent until the song ends. Ray slows and raises his eyebrows at me.

"Do you still want to go?" He gestures towards the door, indicating that I'm free.

"No," I mutter unwillingly.

"Okay, then," he says, grinning and holding my hand for a second time. "I guess you have to dance with me again."

I allow myself to smile as we start to move to the next song.

"So how was your day?" he asks at the same time as I do. I laugh. So does he. I catch sight of Caidy glaring at me from the side of the room. It's not quite in league with my lightning glares, but it's close. I smile wider.

"Mine was good," he answers. "I was working on my project for a while."

"I thought you were on break," I say.

"Yeah, me too, but apparently Ms. Richards wants me to keep going." A slight frown changes his expression for a moment, but he smiles again an instant later. "Not that it's not fun. I got to simulate part of a thunderstorm. It was so cool!"

"Electrifying," I say dryly.

"Yes, that too." Ray chuckles. "So how did you get roped into this?"

"Hale and Vivian," I mutter.

"Oh. Yeah, those two–especially Hale–can get a little over-enthusiastic. But I'm glad, because they made you come. You deserve to have some fun after all that work you do."

"*Hmm.* My wanting to attend didn't seem to factor into anyone's decision."

"Oh, of course you wouldn't want to come. But you'll have fun."

"Do you have a psychic license or something?"

"No, I read palms," Ray says, lifting my hand up and flipping it over. He traces one of the creases on my palm. "Ohm."

"That was very mystical," I say, ignoring my thudding heart.

"Ohhhhhm…"

214

"Better," I approve.

"Okay! *You* are going to have a very good time."

"Why?"

"Because I said so." Ray lowers my hand and resumes dancing with me. I see Hale dancing with Dan on the other side of the floor. Vivian twirls by with another boy I don't recognize, smiling at me as she passes. Leah's dancing with Matt, but Leah keeps looking at Hale and Dan and Matt's eyes follow Vivian and the other boy.

Ray and I lapse into silence, and somehow it feels okay. Good. Natural. We go through three more songs just dancing, and we both sort of smile the entire time. It's not until in-between the fifth and sixth song, when Matt taps Ray on the shoulder, do we talk.

"Hey," Matt says. "Can I have a turn with Mel?"

Ray looks at me and shrugs.

"Okay," I say, disappointed but slightly flattered at the same time. Is this how it usually is?

My eyes narrow as I see Caidy start off the sidelines towards Ray. But Ray quickly moves to Vivian, Matt's previous partner.

"Hi," Matt says as we start to dance. It's not as effortless as dancing with Ray, but it's nice in a different way, a friendly way.

"Hi," I say back. "How are you?"

"Good." Matt glances at Vivian.

"You guys dance well together," I tell him. He laughs self-consciously.

"Thanks." He looks at me slyly. "You and Jon make a good couple, too."

I glare back at him. "Are you trying to ask for it? Because you're asking for it."

"Whoa, whoa. It's okay. I do not want to fight you."

"Wimp," I snicker.

"Yeah, maybe, but like Jon said, I do like my limbs where they are. It makes it kinda hard to dance if your leg is sticking out your nose or something."

"I don't think anyone's ever tried," I say seriously. "You could be the first."

"I'll pass on that one."

"If you want."

"Dan might try, though, if you can get him to come close enough. He's sort of afraid to ask you to dance. He thinks you'll judo him or something."

"Why would he want to ask me to dance?"

"Well," Matt says, "he's a little awed that he's in the presence of a spy chick. Flabbergasted, actually. He's been watching too much action-thriller, if you ask me."

"Agreed. Not that my stupendousness isn't deserving of the reverence."

"But Jon's been hogging you the entire time. If I hadn't cut in, I doubt he would've danced with Viv. If he has his way, I don't think he'll dance with another girl all night, besides you. You should hear how he talks about you."

"Talks about me?" I say, fighting a blush.

"Oops–I probably shouldn't have said that." Matt bites his lip, looking sideways at Ray. "Oh well. I mean…never mind."

I don't respond, my mind flitting around, refusing to land on one coherent thought.

The song ends. Matt says good-bye and heads off to reclaim Vivian. I see Caidy make for the dance floor–or, more specifically, Ray–but before she reaches him he's in front of me again.

"Want to dance another song?" he asks.

"Sure," I say, taking his hand. Matt's right–Ray doesn't dance with another girl. He dances with me the rest of the night.

* * *

It's really hard to get to sleep tonight, but for a whole new reason. I lay awake analyzing the evening. I've done that before, but usually in an instructive way, like looking back and seeing what I could improve on. Now my mind replays every dance, some over again, each conversation, each smile, until past midnight. Even then, my stomach seems to have been left behind in the gym.

I'm up at eight this morning, still feeling floaty. I shower and dress and wander around my room aimlessly for a good ten minutes, picking up my cell phone first, then fiddling with my ponytail, then sitting in random places—my armchair, my bed, the floor.

I finally shake my head, attempting to focus. I pocket my cell phone and head to the door, maybe going to say hi to Vivian and Hale before breakfast, or head down to breakfast, or....

I step on something as I reach for the doorknob. I look down and see a piece of paper on the floor. Someone must have slid it under the door when I wasn't looking. It says 'Mel' on the outside. Curious, I unfold it.

Hey,

Last night was really fun. I have a field trip today, though, so I won't be around all day. We're watching clouds. Yeah, I know. It sucks because I'm on vacation, but I don't think trivial things like breaks matter to Ms. Richards. But I was wondering if you wanted to go around Brisbane with me tomorrow night? I know some pretty neat sights. It'd be fun to visit them with you.

If you feel like going, I'll meet you in the lobby at 7:30 tomorrow evening. Ms. Richards also scheduled me to work on my project all day.

Hopefully I'll get enough done that I can actually relax the rest of break!

    See you later,

    Jon

I gape, rereading it, before grinning. I put it in my back pocket along with my room key and head down to breakfast.

"Mel!" Vivian calls, beckoning for me to join her and Hale in line.

"Hi, hi," I greet them both.

"You," Hale says, jabbing her finger at me, "are going to tell us everything about last night. All we got out of you last night was 'fun, thank you'. That is not good enough. So right after breakfast I am marching you to Viv's room and–"

"Okay," I say. Hale blinks.

"Really? You're agreeing with me? Omigosh. Someone get, like, a reporter over here. Or maybe a video camera. Oh, wait, here." She pulls out her cell phone, presses a few keys, and holds it up to my face. "Say that again, Mel."

"Okay," I say slowly. Hale flips the camera back to herself.

"That," she says, "was Mel agreeing with me. This is now a national holiday. Complete with fireworks and everything! Ooh, and cake. Only not now, since it's breakfast time. But maybe ice cream later." She turns it back to me. "Okay, Mel. Tell us about your evening."

I move the cell phone away. "Not now, Hale!"

"Oh. Right." She closes her phone and pockets it. Vivian is trying not to laugh and failing miserably a few feet behind her. "But later. We will."

"But not on tape."

"Technically, it's a memory card."

I think that's the first time anyone other than Ray's corrected me with technicalities.

"Right," I say, getting a grapefruit and some bran cereal.

I don't miss Hale gagging to my left, and I fight a grin.

"You're in unusually high spirits today," Vivian comments as we eat.

"I'll tell you later," I hear myself saying.

"Ooooh," Hale says.

"Caidy says hello, Vivian and Hale," Leah says, looking up from her cell phone. "Her field trip's fun so far."

"Yeah, whatever," Hale rolls her eyes. "Tell her to say hi to Mel or I'm not responding."

"You don't have to do that," I say.

"After what she texted me last night, uh, yeah, I do," Hale says darkly.

"What?" I say.

"She's having issues right now, Mel," Vivian says.

"What did she text?"

Hale makes a disgusted face. "She was mad that Jon danced with you the entire time last night."

"He danced with her, too," I remember, my stomach twisting unpleasantly.

"I bet that was just as friends. Jon doesn't like Caidy in that way. She's just over-clingy."

"That's not—" Leah starts, but Hale cuts her off with a look.

"Stop defending everything she does, Leah! You know she's not being fair to Mel, and you also know she's being super jerkish right now."

"I'm sorry you feel that way," Leah says coolly, standing up. "I think I'll go sit with Melissa."

"That'll make Melissa's day," Hale scoffs. Leah gives her a dirty look before stalking off.

"Sibling rivalry." Vivian shakes her head.

"Stupid Caidy," Hale mutters.

"Okay, Mel, tell us why you're in such a good mood,"

Vivian says, closing her door behind her. I pull out Ray's note. Hale snatches it from me. Her eyes bug as she reads.

"Aw! That's so–"

"Do not say 'cute'."

"–cute!"

"Argh."

Vivian takes the note from Hale, scans it, and hands it back to me, smiling. "So are you going to go?"

"Of course she is," Hale says immediately.

"I am," I nod. "Do you have a piece of paper?"

"Yeah!" Hale rips a page out of a small notebook and hands it to me, along with a pen. I fold it in half, write ~~R~~ *Jon* on the top, open it up, and scribble:

Yes!

~Mel

"I'll go put it under his door!" Hale takes the paper and sprints off. For a second I wonder wildly why I'm trusting her with this, but relax after a moment. Besides, if she did drop it or something all it says is *Yes! ~Mel*. That would hardly give anything away.

Hale's back in a few minutes. "All done," she announces. "Now, on a more serious note…what the heck are you going to wear?"

After a half-hour of lounging on Vivian's couch, the guilt starts coming in full blast, making me distracted. I should be working on my End and Ray's mystery. I *need* to be working on my End and Ray's mystery. I want to stay here with Hale and Vivian. But I gave into 'Want' yesterday. Today should be about 'Need'.

Of course, that's not the only thing distracting me. My mind obviously didn't have enough of thinking about the dance, so occasionally it wanders to that, and I wonder what Ray's up to right now.

Oh, no. No, no, no. I am doing work today. I am not wasting the entire day again, even if it is 'fun'. So, despite Hale and Vivian's protests, and my own reluctance, I head back up to my room, choose a few points closer to Marvin, and head out for another day of potential failure and frustration.

Which, of course, is exactly what it is.

I see lots of tourists. I see amazing sightseeing spots. I see the grandeur of Brisbane City.

I see nothing of importance.

This is getting old. Maybe this End really is more than simple electronic theft and a few stolen birth certificates. I'm always able to track down other similar perpetrators....

If it is more, should I let Shadow deal with it, rather than beating my head against a brick wall for extended periods of time? The idea's tempting and unappealing at the same time. On the one hand, I wouldn't be beating my head against my figurative wall, but I would be admitting failure, something I never do.

As long as it's two o'clock and I'm not making any progress against the bricks, I might as well see if my friend Peter Manifred is home. Maybe today is a good day for answers.

I wait for ten minutes after knocking on his door, but no one appears. Either he isn't home, or he's avoiding me. Well, I'll get him sometime before I leave.

I make my way dejectedly back to Marvin, wishing I'd stayed with Hale and Vivian, for all the good my working did.

Vivian comes into the second floor landing a few seconds before I reach it, her nose in a thick book. She doesn't notice me until I come up beside her.

"Oh! Hi, Mel!" She closes the book on her finger,

marking her place.

"What are you reading?"

"This? My class is using it for a project. It's a murder mystery, and we're supposed to write hypotheses after each chapter and try to solve the crime before the protagonist does. It's not due till next week, but I had some spare time and decided to get started."

"Sounds interesting," I say.

"It is, definitely. Chilling, too. I was impressed that Ms. Kreiser was able to find a book I haven't read."

"You read a lot, then?"

"All the time. I've been busy lately, but usually..." Vivian trails off, pushing through the door to the fourth floor. I follow her to my room.

"Hey, look, you got mail," Vivian says.

"Huh?"

She points to the little metal container on the wall by the door. "See, the red flag is up. You have a letter."

"Oh, so that's what those are for." I open the top of the box and extract an envelope.

Amber Rind, Marvin Academy, it says above Marvin's address. Frowning, I inspect the envelope, narrowing my eyes when I see the slight folds and lumps under the flap that tell me it's been opened and resealed. Was someone reading my mail? Why would this be of interest to anyone?

Carefully, I slit open the envelope and pull out the letter. I unfold it and blink at the typed message. Who's writing to me at Marvin? And using the name 'Amber'? And typing the letter?

Miss Rind,

It would be extremely unwise for you to tell anyone what you know about Jonathon. It would be prudent for you to stop pursuing this matter altogether. But if that doesn't happen, something regrettable may occur, which is not the current

222

intention of anyone–yet.

Think about this carefully.

"Who's it from?" Vivian asks, eyes in her book again. I quickly crumple the letter in my fist.

"No one. Um, Vivian, I'm kinda tired. Do you mind if I just rest until dinner?"

"What? Oh, sure. Go ahead. See ya later, Mel!" She heads down the hallway. I open my door and make for my bed, still reading the note.

Judging by the content and the formal tone, there's only one person this is likely to be from–Peter Manifred. Somehow he found out who I am, where I am, and is threatening me if I don't drop the case. He must be an opponent–a bad guy, if I'm being melodramatic. Why else would he write this? It happens all the time, these notes, when the opposition feels you're getting too close. Lay off or get hurt. It only confirms my suspicions that something deeper than a misunderstanding is going on with Ray.

Now I need to figure out what I'm getting too close to. I need to take care of myself, but, more importantly, I need to take care of Ray, because somehow he's involved, even if he doesn't know it–which makes him even more vulnerable.

I go back to Peter Manifred's house around 7:30 AM, but he's still not there, or not coming out. Which means I once again do not get to interrogate him, or demand to know why he sent that note.

I take a few confusing turns on my return to the school, in case anyone's following me, like the man with the roan hair from the parkland. Normally, I'd want a follower--someone I could try to capture. But today I feel a more urgent need to get back to Marvin without complications–to make sure Ray's okay.

I arrive at the school in time for breakfast and confirm

with an unwilling Leah that Ray and Caidy are working on their project right now, which is why they're not here. I agree to a surprised Hale's insistence that I stay and hang out with her until it's time to go meet Ray (my stomach gives a funny swoop at that). I don't want to go out when Ray is here. After the note, my priority has switched to Ray's mystery. I may take Shadow up on his offer if it allows me to focus on this.

Throughout the day I ask Hale to text her sister and see how Caidy's doing, which means I know if Ray's doing okay in turn. For example, if Leah says 'caidy's fine but jon's sorta m.i.a.' then I know I'll need to look into something.

Hale texts Leah with a lot of grousing, obviously still mad at her about the whole Caidy vs. me thing. I feel guilty and flattered at the same time.

"I bet Jon's happy he's Ms. Richards' favorite student. She's even making him work on break!" Hale snorts sarcastically. "Oh yeah, I actually do think Caidy's loving it, though. All those hours alone with Jon..." she quickly trails off, matching my disgusted look.

Vivian heads off to the school library after lunch to work on her project, opening the book before she's three meters away.

"It's a miracle she doesn't trip," I remark to Hale as we climb the stairs to my room.

"Viv's practically developed an extra sense. She never runs into anything," Hale says admiringly.

"I can do that too, but I'm actually looking where I'm going, even if I'm not thinking about it." Maybe I should get Vivian to teach me how she does her version. "Hey! Text Leah again."

Shadow calls around three.

"I'm okay," I say immediately when I pick up.

"All right then." Shadow sounds weary. I guess he would–it's around ten PM for him.

"Anything new?" I ask, rolling a marble back across the floor to Hale.

"No. What about with you?"

Why does he have to be so interested in my life? I already said I'm fine. "Not much," I say evasively. "I'm taking a break, like you said."

"Really?" Shadow sounds pleased. "Have you been sightseeing at all? Seen anything interesting?"

"Um…I'm going out tonight."

"Oh." Shadow's voice is instantly suspicious. "With who?"

"A friend."

"What's her name?" I don't miss the emphasis on 'her'.

"Hale," I say quickly. Hale raises an eyebrow at me, flicking the marble back. *Sorry*, I mouth. But I'll avoid Shadow's reaction to it being a 'him' if possible.

"That's nice." Now he's relieved.

"*Mm*-hmm. Well, if that's all…"

Shadow sighs. "Bye, Amber."

"Bye."

I hang up.

"Who was that?" Hale asks.

"My principal," I reply.

"He seemed…"

"Nosey?"

"Uh, kinda. You his favorite or something?"

"Well, he's the only who still calls me 'Amber'. Does that count?" I'm not going to get into the whole guardian thing.

"Maybe." As Hale catches the marble my phone rings again. "Sheez. People want to talk to you, huh?"

"Huh," I say, seeing that it's Lyvia. "Hello."

"Hi!" she says brightly, and launches into an account of her day and her love-quadrilateral troubles with Bryant, Kent, and Nathan. Finally she gets around to asking me about how

225

I'm doing. And, more specifically, what I'm doing. I hesitantly tell her about 'Jonathon', swearing her to secrecy first, and have to tolerate five minutes of her reproving me for not telling her about him earlier.

"But he asked you out," she says approvingly.

"He said he'll show me around Brisbane."

"Just the two of you. Together. At night."

"The time of day has something to do with it?"

I hear her give a long-suffering sigh. "The time of day has everything to do with it." Then her tone brightens. "Hey, is Hale there?"

"Yeah."

"Put her on. I want to discuss your wardrobe."

Rolling my eyes, I pass the phone to Hale.

"Hello? Oh, hey, Lyvia! Yeah! Yeah! I was so ready to scream when he asked her to dance...oh, she didn't?" Hale gives me a disapproving look. "Well, he did, yeah. Yeah, for the whole time. I know! And...uh-huh, tonight...yeah, I was thinking, like, jeans. What? Oh, of course. Yeah, and then a long tee and some type of shrug...blue...silver, of course...well, I would, but she wouldn't let me...no, I don't have more donuts, unfortunately...oh, she wore earrings, but that's it...no, she looked good...yes, Viv did this really neato flip thing...oh, yeah...no, actually..."

I let my mind wander. I vaguely hear Hale start to discuss Lyvia's love quadrilateral and some new type of shoes. I wonder if Ray's having fun, working on his project with Caidy. I also speculate about Peter Manifred and who else he might be in league with.

Suddenly I realize that Maryanne had taken Ray's birth certificate. And this whole thing has something to do with Ray. So what if.... But wait, they didn't just take Ray's–they took three others as well. *Hmm*...so I'm just jumping to conclusions. Something I have to work hard not to do, or I end up seeing connections even when they don't exist. Just because I'm not working on strict work doesn't mean I have to get sloppy.

Hale finishes on the phone and checks the time. "Holy cow! We have to start getting you ready!"

"Hale, it's three-thirty!"

"Yes, but we have to make your outfit." She heads to my duffel bag and starts rooting through the main section. I'm glad I put my underwear in a separate compartment. Muttering to herself, she pulls out three pairs of jeans and about seven T-shirts. She pulls out two sweatshirts and a designer polka dot blue jacket with two large buttons down the front. I make a face. Lyvia must've thrown that in.

Hale forces me to try everything on before she selects a pair of light leans, a plain white shirt, and, to my surprise and horror, the polka-dot jacket.

"Put this on," she commands, shoving my arms through the sleeves.

"How about you do it for me?" I grumble.

"Well, I just did, so what's the point? *Hmm…*" She grabs her purse from the bedside table and pulls out her seam ripper and various threads and needles. Oh, and scissors. I eye those warily.

"Hale…"

"Do you like this jacket?" she demands.

"No, I hate it, but–"

"Would you mind if I accidentally destroyed it?"

"Not at all, though–"

"Then you really won't mind if I make it fabulous," she decides, and with that starts to cut, rip, and sew. I watch with a slightly dropped jaw. The garment becomes tighter around me, hugging my torso in an effortless way. Hale shears off the fancy collar and seamlessly sews on the hood of one of my white sweatshirts. Finally she steps back and looks me over critically.

"How bad is it?" I ask.

"Oh, it's fantabulous, but I'm debating whether or not to add rhinestones."

"Um…no."

"Well, then, I guess that's as good as it'll get," she sighs and leads me to the mirror. My eyebrows fly up.

It doesn't look fancy, but it doesn't look austere either. It looks…dare I say it? Cute. Ack. I have to wash my brain out now.

"Thanks," I manage.

"Oh, sure. Now where is Vivian?" Hale stomps to the door, vehemently pressing buttons on her cell phone. After a minute she relaxes. "Oh, good, she's on her way up."

Vivian arrives a few moments later. "Hey, Hale! Hey, Mel! Oh, great jacket!"

"An original Hale Williams," Hale tells her.

"Very original. It looks so awesome! Perfect sightseeing outfit."

"Perfect sightseeing *date* outfit," Hale corrects.

"It's not a date," I say wearily.

"Yeah, whatever, Mel. Viv, what can you do with her hair?"

"I'm not allowed to have a regular ponytail, am I?" I say resignedly.

"Heck, no. So what are you thinking?" Hale asks Vivian.

"I can do that flip thing again…or, no, I got it. Mel, do you remember what I did in my hair for the dance?"

"Yeah…"

"Well, what about one of those? Sort of at the base of your head here." Vivian pats the spot.

"Omigosh," Hale says. "Perfect! That so goes with the look! Casual-but-adorable. CBA Panache. That's my new line."

"Sit here," Vivian tells me, patting the armchair. I do so warily. Vivian positions herself on the right armrest, taking the brush Hale passes her. She starts to run it though my hair, along with some sort of cream, until it's actually sort of silky like hers.

"What is that?" I ask, touching it lightly.

"Dry-hair conditioner. I have it on the brush." Vivian continues to detangle my waves until she's completely satisfied. I feel her gather it to the back of my head and start twisting gently. There's some pulling and twirling, but soon she reaches out a hand for the hairspray and secures the style.

"Let me see." Hale jumps forward to inspect my head.

"There, all done," Vivian says. She shows the style to me in the tall mirror with her own small glass. Again, it's not elaborate, but not plain.

For a moment, I feel really, really grateful to both Hale and Vivian. I doubt I could've done half of this on my own, if I even knew what to do. I open my mouth to try to put this into intelligible words, but Hale cuts me off.

"Holy crap! You have to go!"

"What?" I say, spinning around to see the clock. "Whoa. How is it already 7:15?"

"Time flies when you're having fun," Vivian says.

"Or being tortured," I add, for the sake of my pride.

"We can discuss the sunny details later," Hale says firmly. "Right now you need to get everything together! Shoes! Lip-gloss! Purse! Hurry!" She shoves me around the room, overseeing the lacing of my sneakers, the refusal of my bringing a purse, and the unwilling application of lip-gloss. Finally she and Vivian escort me out the door and down to the lobby.

"She can sit on the couch here," Vivian says.

"And how should I sit, exactly?" I ask sarcastically. "Legs crossed or uncrossed? Lounging back or up straight?"

229

"Legs crossed, leaning sideways on the armrest," Hale instructs, starting forward as if to position me herself.

"We should go." Vivian catches Hale's arm. I shoot the former a grateful look, which she returns with a smile.

Then they're gone, and I'm alone in the lobby, with only my compulsively tapping foot and racing heart to keep me company.

Not for long, though.

17

I stand up as soon as he pushes out of the stairway, suddenly realizing how ridiculous I must look in that nonsensical position Hale has put me in.

"Hey," he says, walking up to me with a grin. "Oh, no. Hale got to you, didn't she?" He eyes my jacket.

"How'd you guess?" I laugh nervously. "She's scarier than a lot of criminals I've encountered."

"Her passion for design is her fuel," Ray tells me.

"And her scissors are her machine. Oh, yeah, and her seam ripper." I shudder theatrically.

"Another thing you're afraid of!" Ray says triumphantly, leading me to the door. "Meteorology terms and seam rippers. I need to start making a list."

"You need to forget I said that last part," I say, correcting him. "Or rather, did that last part. I'm just cold, that's all."

"Don't give me that. It's warm for August!"

"These differing seasons are getting on my nerves slightly. I think I need to propose a law that it should be summer at the same time everywhere. And the other seasons. Winter from December to March, spring March to June, summer June to September, and autumn September to December."

"Yeah, you do that," Ray snorts. "I'm sure that'll go over well with the whole world. Maybe you need to appeal directly to Mother Nature. Is she in the phone book?"

"Sure she is. Right under 'Father Nature'. Wait. Is there a

Father Nature?"

"That's 'Father Christmas', Mel."

"Oh. Really?" I don't usually get things confused. But then again, I don't usually discuss this type of thing. Imaginary, I mean.

"Yes, really." Ray laughs, brushing his bangs out of his eyes. We reach the bus stop.

"Where are we going?" I ask as the bus pulls up and we board.

"It's a secret." Ray winks, finding two empty seats. "I don't know if you've been there, but it's one of my favorite spots. Especially at night."

"I do remember you mentioning something about night," I say.

"So maybe you can figure this mystery out." Ray wiggles his eyebrows. I raise one of mine.

"Okay. So we were by the water. And I said..." I pause, hoping he doesn't see how easy it is for me to recall, having replayed it in my mind a few more times than necessary. "I said something about the river, and you said 'you should see it at night'. So...it might have something to do with the river."

Ray applauds, looking serious. "Good job, Miss Detective." A smirk plays around his mouth. "But you can't guess exactly where we're going, I bet." He leans back and props his feet up on the seat in front of him.

"Botanic Gardens?"

"Nooo..."

"Sailing? Because you're such an amazing sailor?"

"I am, I know. And closer. But no."

"*Um.*" I study the ceiling. "Ha," I say, thinking I have it. It's not exactly to do with the river, but he could be using reverse-reverse psychology. "Roma Street Parkland."

"*Hmm...*" Ray grins upward as well. "No."

"The Gallery of Modern Art?" I test my reverse-reverse

psychology options.

"Nope."

"A zoo?"

"Uh-uh." Curse the smug look on his face. *Humph.*

"Queen Street Mall?"

"Hardly."

"*Grr.*" I slump back, having exhausted most of my immediate sources. He hadn't said 'close' for any of them. So back to 'sailing'. "Kayaking? Snorkeling? Water-skiing?"

"No…no…*hmm*, no."

I clamp my mouth together, unwilling to say, "I give up." Ray senses it, though, and raises his fist in victory.

"So it'll still be a surprise. Actually, I'm surprised! I can't believe you didn't think of this."

"Just because I didn't say it–"

"–Doesn't mean you weren't thinking about it?" Ray guesses. "I'm so sure. Oh, yeah. On the subject of other things you don't know about, have you heard of Jack Frost?"

"I've heard of Robert Frost." Knowing this probably isn't correct, I still go on. "What? Were they brothers or something?"

"Ha, ha." Ray rolls his eyes. "Jack Frost is, like, frost. As in, evaporated water particles in the air that condense to form ice crystals on surfaces such as grass and trees when the temperature reaches the dew point. "

The topic of illusory beings gets us to Ray's preferred bus stop. I look around as we climb out. Already the sky is turning the dusky blue color of evening. Around us are tall buildings, busy streets, lit windows.

"We're in the city somewhere," I say.

"We're at 171 George Street," Ray says, pulling on my elbow to get me to cross the street when the little traffic light for pedestrians flashes green. We climb up onto another corner of a sidewalk, outside a more old-fashioned looking building.

"Why are we at 171 George Street? I don't see the river at 171 George Street," I say.

"We're at 171 George Street because I want to get coffee before we go to the mystery place."

"Oh. And why did you choose 171 George Street?"

"Because I like the coffee at 171 George Street. Why do we keep saying 171 George Street? I don't think 171 George Street is that amazing."

"We keep saying 171 George Street because we can't figure out why we're saying 171 George Street and therefore we can't figure out why not to say 171 George Street. And one of us has a little issue with being overly specific."

"You're not that overly specific," Ray teases, breaking the pattern. I roll my eyes.

"I was trying to be subtle, but apparently you aren't picking up on my hints. You're the overly specific one," I retort.

"Right," he snorts, obviously harboring a differing opinion.

"Right." I force my feet to move forward as he heads into a little coffee shop.

"You want anything?" he asks, approaching the counter. There's a very short line.

"I'll have whatever you get."

Ray turns to the lady at the counter and orders two of something almost exotic sounding. I watch people in the back make the coffee with mild interest. I've never been to a fancy coffee shop like this one. Usually I just get the beverages at drive-through restaurants.

"How's that look?" Ray asks when they're set down on the counter. The cups are fairly large and almost chic. If cups can be chic. I'll have to ask Hale.

Ray reaches into his pocket.

"Wait, I got mine taken care of," I say, pulling out some bills.

"No, that's okay," Ray says, shoving his own money at the employee before I can get mine in.

"I'll pay you back, then."

Ray hands me one of the coffees as we exit the café. "Get real."

"If you don't accept the money quietly, I'll knock you unconscious and force it on you," I threaten.

"Heaven forbid. Fine." Ray rolls his eyes as I force the money into his hand. "Now, I hope you don't mind walking a little."

"Pssh. My life story is walking." And, more recently, walking while failing.

Ray laughs. We start to stroll down the city blocks, more and more lights popping on. This is a different walk than the one I'm used to. More like this past Sunday's amble than anything. My usual walk is…purposeful. Focused. This isn't indeterminate, but it isn't hurried or precisely focused, either.

It's…nice.

So the walking takes longer than my habitual pace would. But I don't mind. Ray doesn't seem to either. We talk, we joke, we sort of grin at each other sideways sometimes, as if acknowledging the good time.

We're on the corner of a busy street and a quieter road when I recognize the location. I see trees on the other side of the smaller road, which catches my eye and makes me turn, and behind us is the entrance to the Parliament House. The sign on the streetlight next to us says Garden Point.

"Hey." I narrow my eyes. "This is Botanic Gardens. This is the corner of Alice Street and George Street. Where I came Sunday."

"Yes, but we're not going to Botanic Gardens," Ray says.

"Where are we going?"

"Nice try. Up for some more walking?"

"Of course." Good thing I was able to weasel into wearing my own shoes.

The topic of conversation turns to the present. Ray tells me about his field trip yesterday, and I tell him about being brutalized before the dance.

Ray turns off the road and onto a path, bordered by trees, which leads into more greenery.

"Hey," I say. "I thought you said we weren't going to Botanic Gardens."

"I said we're not going *to*." He grins. "I never said we weren't going *through*."

I frown. It's not like me to miss stuff like that.

We walk around the back of the Queensland University of Technology and finally come out at a large, paved area. A parking lot resides among trees to our left, but the rest of the scene is suddenly open–the city again. A highway rumbles beyond a grove of trees, but something else catches my attention.

"A bridge?" I say in surprise, peering at the entrance through the dusk.

"Goodwill Bridge," Ray says, sounding pleased. "Opened in 2001, named for the Goodwill Games. Pretty neat, right?"

"I can only see one end of it," I reply honestly.

"No duh. It's the view that's the best. Come on!" He beckons with the hand not holding his coffee for me to follow.

I warily enter the bridge after him. As we cross over the water, everything gets calmer. Almost…relaxed.

"See?" Ray says quietly, once we've reached the middle, pointing out at the city. I feel my mouth open in astonishment.

"Wow. That's…really pretty."

"It is?" He looks happy that I think so, so I grin and nod.

"Extremely pretty." It is, too. The lights from the skyscrapers are reflected in the water, making the river look like a sheet of black glass with splashes of color washing across it. But the naturalness of it–unintentional beauty–adds to the splendor.

Lots of things seem very far off. The city, noises, other people, any sort of hurriedness.

So it's silent again, but another nice silence. We both gaze out over the scene as the river rolls beneath us.

"Mel?" Ray says after a few minutes.

"Yeah?"

"When are you going back home?"

I'm not sure if he realizes this, but I definitely feel a sigh escape my windpipe. "Tuesday. Early."

"That soon," he says to himself. "And I haven't seen you that much yet, really, because of all this work we're doing."

"About that; why are you so busy all the time?" I ask. I find myself honestly wanting the answer, but not in a professional way, a personal way. "This project of yours…is it that important?"

"I have no idea. I guess since it's a special project, it might be. It's not like Ms. Richards to go overboard like this. She usually doesn't, for regular assignments and stuff. But I guess she just loves me that much," he laughs.

Her and her daughter both.

"So you don't get any time off?" I say indignantly.

"Look who's talking," Ray teases. "Taken a break lately yourself?"

"I'm here, aren't I?" Which is bad enough. Though I don't want him walking around Brisbane alone until I find out what Peter Manifred's issue is. But since I can't control Ray–which I know from years of experience–I have to work with him.

This is all disregarding the fact that I want to be here.

"Yeah." Ray looks away into the trees lining the bank. "You're here."

The shift in the mood from blithe to brooding disconcerts me. Which disconcerts me more, because it disconcerts me. I'm not supposed to get disconcerted.

"I must be feeling philosophical tonight," Ray muses. "I just made an analogy about myself."

"What is it?"

"See that tide? Well, this would work better with the ocean, the waves and all, but see how the water laps against the bank and is pulled back by the overall body of water?"

"Yes." I'm confused, a feeling only Ray could bring on.

"Sometimes," Ray whispers, "I feel like there's another person in me. Trying to get out. It happens randomly, like when I'm eating a melon or–" He cuts himself off. "But then I–the river, the body of water–have to pull it–the random wave–back down and cover it up. Ugh," he adds. "I didn't mean to bring that up. It's too easy to talk to you."

"I know what you mean," I say, watching the water slosh against the riverside with new eyes. "R–Jon, what if you...didn't pull it back, but let it out? If that's the right way to describe it?"

"I think I'd go insane," he replies. "When that happens, it feels like I'd lose myself completely if those 'waves' broke through."

I feel like this should tell me something. Give me some hint. But my mind doesn't seem to be able to grasp what that hint might be, so I let it go. For now.

The rest of the evening passes in a lighter mood. It's honestly the best time I've had in Brisbane, and I think Ray looks genuinely reluctant too when he announces that Marvin has a curfew of ten o'clock.

We head back to the road. When we reach the main street a taxi pulls up in front of us expectantly.

"What do you think?" Ray asks. "I don't mind."

I hesitate, not wanting to admit that I'm not liking the idea of walking any more. Ray grins.

"Okay, never mind what you want, I'm tired. Let's get in," he orders.

I smile back gratefully. We slide into the backseat. Ray tells the driver an address about a block from Marvin, then yawns.

"Tired?" I ask. He nods.

"I was up since six this morning, working."

I scowl out the window. What is it with this project? Why is it so important?

"That's not fair. Isn't it supposed to be holiday?"

Ray's reflection shrugs. "It'll be finished soon enough, I guess."

"Well, you should sleep in tomorrow."

"Don't know if I'll be able to. I'll try, though," he says quickly, answering my glower.

My forehead suddenly knocks against the glass as the car swerves to the side of the road.

"What?" I mutter. The cab lurches to a stop. We've only gone two, maybe three blocks. I'm about to question the driver when Ray's door flies open.

Another person—no, two people—are standing outside. Trouble. I immediately yank off my seatbelt. "Get out!" I command Ray, lunging at my own door. But it doesn't open, and the lock won't budge. A small sign on the window tells me cheerfully that the child safety lock is operable in this door.

I whirl back around, ready to knock the crap out of the people by Ray's door so we can leave via that exit.

Ray unbuckles himself and rolls away, towards me. Smart move. But he's yanked back immediately by one of the big, tall, and uglys.

I clench my teeth and my legs prepare to spring out. They can not touch Ray.

I'm so focused I don't notice the driver's arm coming at me until it catches my windpipe. I'm slammed back against the seat. For a moment, stars blink in front of my eyes.

That moment is enough. Ray's thrown out of the cab, onto the street. Before he can scramble up, the other two people have jumped into the cab.

"No! *Ray!*" I hear myself scream as the door is pulled closed. Two pairs of arms grab me and hold me down, one large hand covering my mouth and nose. I'm able to keep from getting suffocated, but it's hard to completely throw off two attackers when they're both twice as large as you and you're all in the backseat of a taxi. And they have the two window seats.

The car races through the back streets. The ride's over in three minutes, so I've made little progress with my captors. One will have quite a nasty bruise, though.

We're stopped in an alleyway. I'm pushed-slash-pulled out of the cab, one abductor on either side of me. They're wearing black ski masks. How original.

I don't struggle once we're out of the car, even as the driver gets out and approaches me. That would just waste energy. If I'm going to escape, I'm going to need to take these idiots by surprise. And I'm slightly curious about why I've been shanghaied in the first place.

But I'm more eager to get away. I need to make sure Ray's all right. I don't know where they threw him–in the middle of the street or just on a sidewalk–or if there were other people waiting for him on that side, or if he's hurt.

"Listen," the driver says in a low, controlled, and obviously disguised voice. "You are going to convey a message to your brain and overly-large ego, all right? Are you listening?"

I look back with an expression implying something negative about his intelligence. His shoulder jerks forward. I duck the slap easily. It lands on Captor Numero Uno's shoulder.

"Fine," the driver snaps. "You *better* be listening, you brat. This is it: if you try to look into Jonathon Carter's identity, you will be harmed."

Sure. Great. Heard it all before.

"If you get anyone else to try to look into Jonathon Carter's identity, you *and* that person will be harmed."

Why would I get anyone else to do it when I could do it myself?

"And lastly...if you don't listen to us, and if you tell Jonathon any...*lies* you come up with, *he* will be severely harmed."

Yeah, I– What?

That, if anything, inflicts some sort of fear. But I don't let it show.

"You won't tell anyone about this."

Then I feel my hands being tied up behind my back. I almost roll my eyes. Can't these people be any more imaginative?

After my feet are bound and I'm forced into a sitting position against the grungy wall of the building to my back, the three hooded people–all men, now that I can see their forms properly–get back in the car and drive off. I stay where I am for a minute, then rip off the ropes and pull out my cell phone.

I groan when I realize I have no idea if Ray even has a cell phone, let alone know its number. I decide my best bet is to get back to Marvin. I have a pretty good feeling that's what he would do if he couldn't reach me. He might have called the police, too. I hope he didn't.

So I'll have to wait a few more minutes to find out if he's

all right. I walk down two blocks until I find a sign telling me I've come upon Ann Street.

I wave down another cab. I tell this driver the same address Ray gave the last one and test the door as soon as I get in. It unlocks. Okay.

I don't even ask the driver to go around a long way to throw off anyone waiting to ambush or follow us. I know these kinds of criminals. They've delivered their message. They won't be taking any more action tonight.

I walk down the block to Marvin as casually as possible, but I'm itching to run, to find out if Ray's back yet. If he's not, I'm going to stay up all night, looking for him. I won't sleep until I know he's safe, I promise myself, because if he's not, it's all my fault.

I reach the school's front door and prepare to inhale in anticipation. Before my fingers reach the handle, the door's swinging open.

"Mel!" Ray gasps as he pulls me inside. Before I can catch my breath he's hugging me. Which doesn't help my lack of oxygen problem.

He lets go quickly, though, biting on his lip as he stares at me.

"Are you okay?" we demand of each other at the same time.

"Yes," he says.

"Of course," I tell him.

"What happened?" He sounds strained, dizzy.

"How did you get back?" I say evasively.

"I waited for you on the sidewalk, but then I just figured that if you got away, you wouldn't go back there, you'd come here. So I came here, and…"

"Did you call the police?" I whisper.

"No." He shakes his head. "I was arguing with myself the whole time, because I sort of knew you wouldn't want me to. But then I was thinking, if I didn't and you got...and it turned out bad because of it...I wouldn't...I'd..."

"You did good. Thanks," I say.

"What...?" He seems to struggle for the appropriate words.

"I can't tell you," I murmur, so that just in case anyone else is in earshot they'll miss this part. "You... Don't tell anyone either." In no way can he endanger *himself.*

"And now?" Ray asks.

"It's about curfew time, isn't it?"

"Past, actually."

"Now we go to bed, then."

"Mel..." He frowns.

"Trust me?"

"Of course," he says, sending my catch phrase back to me.

"To bed, then," I repeat.

Ray seems to know better than to push it and keep asking me questions, especially the annoying 'are-you-okay' kinds. He just silently walks me to my room.

"I'll see you tomorrow," he says as I open my door. It sounds as much like a promise as it does a farewell.

"You too," I reply in the same tone. I duck into my room, thinking how hard it was not to tell him about everything. Like he said, it's too easy to talk to him. Shadow, I can hide stuff from easily. But Ray...I actually *want* to tell him. And that makes it difficult. Which is a new adjective for me.

Speaking of Shadow...

Buzz. Buzz. I pull my cell phone from my pocket and debate whether or not to just let it ring. Pretend I'm asleep or something. But then he'd probably flip. And he's too old to be trying any acrobatics.

To keep his feet on the ground, I pick up. "Hello. I am

243

fine."

"Good," he says. "I was wondering how your evening was."

"Fun." Part of it, anyway.

"This Hale girl, she's nice?"

"Definitely." I frown slightly, thinking that this afternoon, when Hale was cutting up my jacket, seems like a pretty long time ago.

"Want to tell me about it?"

"Nope. I'm pretty tired, Shadow, so…"

"Oh. Okay." Shadow sighs. "Talk to you tomorrow."

"*Mm*-hmm." I hang up and get ready for bed, my mind reeling, trying to make sense of the evening. But that's the problem. It *doesn't* make sense.

My initial thought was that my friend Peter Manifred was behind my abduction. But then why did those men merely deliver a message? That's already been done, in the note. And another thing. The two events–the note and the taxi–each have a different ring to them. The note is a warning. The abduction, that's an outright threat.

Is it possible I have enemies from more than one side? Manifred and these goons from tonight?

Or they're trying to confuse me?

Or Manifred has a split–evil/eviler–personality?

I have to get some sleep. I wearily climb into bed, still thinking, but not getting very far since my thoughts seem to be unable to keep to a straight line. I only know that I'm not frightened for my own safety and I will not stop trying to figure out what's going on. But I am, however, alarmed.

For Ray.

18

I know as soon as I open my eyes that something's different. The light coming through the window is too bright, too cheerful for 6:30 AM. I sit upright and grab the bedside clock.

Nine? How can it be 9:00 AM? How can I have slept in? I can't afford to lose two and a half hours of my day! I need that time to think!

I rush around getting ready, but the problem is, I rush every morning, so it doesn't take me any different amount to time to shower, brush my teeth and hair, and get dressed.

Breakfast has already started when I arrive in the cafeteria. I quickly grab a breakfast taco and my two glasses of orange juice from the now-empty line, then make my way to Hale's table. I feel a wave of disappointment when I notice that, while Dan and Matt are both sitting there, Ray and Caidy are absent.

"Mel!" Hale cries as I sit down.

"Hi. Hi." I nod to both her and Vivian. "Sorry, um, I'm not staying." I start eating my taco. It's small and won't take more than thirty seconds. A minute at most.

"What?" Hale moans. "More *work*?"

"Yup," I say between mouthfuls.

"Your hair is going to go prematurely gray," Vivian says seriously.

"I'll dye it," I mumble, finishing up. I drain my orange juices and stand. "See you guys later."

Back in my room, I just throw myself across the bed. My

half-crazy dreams from last night blossom on the backs of my closed eyelids like on a projector screen. They don't help any, but they do make last night replay vividly in my mind.

I bolt upright in the middle of the driver's little monologue.

"If you try to look into Jonathon Carter's identity, you will be harmed."

That proves it! *That proves it!* I was–am–right! There *is* something going on with Ray! And other people *are* involved. I shake a fist in front of me, a symbol of *yes!-I-got-it!* and determination. Sticks and stones, ski mask dudes. I'm not giving up *now*!

"If you don't listen to us, or if you tell Jonathon any lies you may find...he will be severely harmed."

I freeze.

Right. That part.

Well, I can take care of myself and I can take care of Ray. No problem.

Right?

I shrink back, pulling my knees up to my chest. I feel an odd pain in my lip, and realize...I'm *biting* it?

Momentarily distracted, I look down to see if it's true. I think this is honestly a first. I've never bitten my lip before. My cheek or tongue, sure, by accident when I was little. But my lip, in anxiety? Never. How...weird.

So what does this mean? That I'm *doubting* myself?

Maybe.

No! No, no, no. I'm not *allowed* to doubt myself. I have to be confident at all times. In all ways. I've done stuff like this before. I can so take care if it.

Maybe.

Stop saying that! I wail to myself.

Maybe.

No! *NO.* I don't *use* that word in these cases. I. Am.

246

Sure. Of. Myself.

Maybe.

After a half-hour, I haven't come to a conclusion. I hate this! This stupid feeling of indecision! Not fair!

Ah. Yes. Life isn't, in fact, fair, is it?

Because first, I have to become stupid *fond* of that stupid little ten-year old, *Anthony*. Then he gives me a stupid *nickname* and I give him a stupid nickname *back* and we become stupid *friends*. Then we become stupid *best* friends. Stupid *close*. The he stupid *dies*. And *then* I stupid *find* him stupid *alive* and he stupid doesn't *remember* me. And now stupid *criminals* are going to stupid *hurt* him if I try to stupid figure this *out*, which is my stupid *nature*.

I fall back again, blinking at the ceiling. Frowning, I rub the back of my hand over my eyes.

I wouldn't trade him for stupid anything.

I spend another hour contemplating, but my mind is so stupid confused that I get stupid nowhere (and I'm stupid done with that now). I *know* there's something I'm missing. But I don't know what it is. Hence 'missing'. Ugh! This doesn't *happen* to me! Why? Why now? On the most important case of my life. Why?

Great. Now I sound like an arrogant, self-contained teenager.

My mind drifts to Ray. Like it does a lot these days. Like, a *lot*. This time the moment when he wrapped his arms around me flashes across my mental vision. I feel my cheeks heat up. I head to the bathroom and splash some cold water on them. I better not be getting a fever.

I look through my purse for something to divert my attention. I don't hit a winner until I come across the voucher for my return flight to Rochester, New York.

I'm not just diverted, I'm horrified. I leave Tuesday morning. Four days. *Four days* to get everything figured out, or I leave Ray here unprotected, oblivious....

I'm out the door in an instant. I need to know exactly what I'll be leaving him here to when I fly to Rochester. Assuming I haven't gotten everything under control, of course.

My feet take me to the office. I pound on the door, then push it open. Big surprise. Ms. Rose is on the phone.

"One moment," she mouths, smiling, then resumes her conversation.

I wait impatiently until she's done. Five minutes...ten minutes...eleven minutes...eleven and a half minutes...

Ms. Rose sets the phone down. "Hello, honey. How may I help you?"

"What sort of security do you have here?" The heck with preambles.

She blinks. "I'm sorry, Mel. I'm not sure I understand your question."

"Security. As in, how well are the students protected?" Speak English much?

"Well, there are the teachers, of course. Students are supervised in classrooms."

"What about outside?"

"Mel. Honey. It's a school." She looks honestly confused by my questioning. "Why do we need security?"

"Thank you for your time," I growl. I turn on my heel and stalk out.

"Mel...?" she calls after me, but I slam the door shut.

No security. None. No, that's it. I'll abduct Ray myself and drag him back to Rochester if nothing's been settled by Tuesday.

On the way up the stairs I pass Ms. Richards. I glare in front of me, purposely not meeting her gaze. I see her flash me a smug look as she passes, though. What? Is she happy that, because of her, Ray's spending more time with her precious Caidy than with me?

I stalk away faster, clenching my teeth.

I spend the afternoon doing some exercise, which I've been sorely neglecting. I need to stay completely fit, both physically and mentally. If I have to be on defense, well then, so help me God, I will be the essence of defense. If it's offense, then I will be the epitome of offense.

Hale texts about mid-afternoon.

r u STILL wrkng, mel?

I sigh. *Yes, I am.*

can u take a break? we want to hang out w/ u...

Not really. Sorry.

come on, mel. its friday! we only have the weekend left b4 classes start again and you leave!

My shoulders slump. I wish things could be that easy. But I doubt I'd be able to play the role of carefree when I'm so agitated.

Maybe tomorrow, I type to mollify her.

promise, she demands.

How can I promise anything right now? I sigh. *I'll try. I promise that.*

And I will. Try, that is.

I start building a case for tomorrow to let myself hang out with Hale and Vivian. If anyone's watching me, then it'll seem like I'm being...normal. That's a good one. Two, they'll probably be in touch with Leah, who'll be in touch with Caidy, who'll be all over Ray, because Ray most likely will have to work...again.

And maybe I can try a new angle of *not* thinking about it to let something come to me?

Okay, that's lame. Now I'm reaching.

But I will consider it.

My phone vibrates. I snatch it from the top of the television and look at the caller ID. Shadow. I swallow, then flip the phone open.

"Hello. I'm fine."

"What's new?" Shadow asks.

"I'm…uh…exercising," I say, searching frantically for the frame of mind that lets me lie easily to Shadow.

"That's good." He pauses. When I don't say anything, he asks, "So what's on your agenda for the rest of the day?"

"Not much." That I know of yet. Thinking, exercising, pulling some hair out…

"Good," Shadow repeats approvingly. "Glad you're listening to me, taking that break. The police up here and down there have been working on it nonstop, but no one's gotten any further. Judging by the look of it, it's obviously an extremely tough case," he goes on, like he's trying to convince me not to feel bad. "Some senior Red Groupers may take a crack at it. I'll see when I come in. You ready to get out of there Tuesday?"

No. That's insane. "Oh, I don't know. It's nice down here." I glance out the window at the gloomy drizzle.

"Oh. But I bet you miss Rochester, huh?" He doesn't wait for me to lie back. "Anything else you want to tell me?"

"No, sorry. I was sort of in the middle of a kickboxing DVD."

"Oh. Well, I won't keep you."

"Okay. Bye."

"Bye, Amber."

The rest of the day passes in the same fashion. Hale texts me again, grumbling that Caidy and 'Jon' are still working, working, working, which apparently is putting Leah and everyone else in a bad mood. Which gives me a good reason to skip dinner.

Okay, a bad reason. But I eat in my room nonetheless.

I start pacing after I'm done with my meal. My mind feels dizzy, labored, tense. All this unproductive thinking is getting on my nerves.

It feels like this day has passed in a rush. I shake my head to clear it, then shake every other part of me, thinking maybe it will help. I need to feel looser, like a flexible rubber band, not a rubber band stretched to the max and ready to snap at a moment's notice.

I take a deep breath, willing my rubber band to loosen, unwind, relax.

Tap. Tap. Tap.

An annoying rapping sound floats over from my door. I force myself to breathe again, my rubber band stretching again.

"Mel?" an insincerely friendly voice calls from the hallway.

Snap.

My hands ball up. What? Hasn't she hassled me *enough*? What does she want *this* time?

I stomp halfway to the door before I make myself stop and walk lightly. Not showing any weakness. That's right. No weakness shown. Not allowed.

I swing the door open, keeping my face impassive. She looks back, wearing the same guarded expression, but I see a flicker of anticipation behind it.

"Hello," Ms. Richards says. I raise my chin in a way that could be loosely interpreted into a nod, not blinking or moving my eyes from her steely ones. Actually, they're green, but the way they look down at me is steely.

She slides in–without invitation–forcing me to step back. She closes the door with her hand behind her, purposefully planting herself between it and me. Like she thinks she could stop me from getting out if I wanted to.

"Amber, Mel, whatever your name is," she starts, trying to bore her gaze into my cranium, "I have a few questions for you."

Wow. No kidding.

"My daughter informed me that you were talking about some 'Roy' person. Who is he?"

Immediately a swell of suspicion sweeps through me. I say back coolly, "I don't know what you're talking about. I don't know a 'Roy'."

"Actually, it might have been 'Ray'," Ms. Richards amends quickly.

Oh, really. "There's no one I know named Ray," I reply stonily. Named, no. Called, yes. Note past participle. No one calls him that anymore except me. Because they all think he's dead.

"You mentioned that name once, though."

I try to remember when I did. I know I let it slip to Hale once. Was she still speaking to Caidy then? Maybe. I can see Hale saying something about it as a joke. But would Caidy tell her mom? And why?

"I want to know who he is. Girl-to-girl, you know."

No, I don't, actually. "Someone I read about," I lie. "Detective. I like mystery novels, you know."

"I think you're lying. Come on, you can tell me."

I'm sensing some sort of falseness in that sincerity. I must have ESP. "I can't. There's nothing to tell." Nothing to tell *you*, that is.

"What's he like? Does he have good friends? A nice family?" she presses.

"I don't know. The book doesn't cover that. I think the character's dad was in the military." My rubber band is being irreparably damaged. So leave. Now.

"No, he wa–" Ms. Richards stops and glowers down at me. "See, honey, this is why no one likes you. You lie."

Funny how that doesn't bother me. "Why don't you mind your own business?"

"Rudeness isn't tolerated here at Marvin," she hisses.

"Nosiness shouldn't be, either," I retort. "But I guess when you have a nose as large as yours it's kind of hard to keep it to yourself. You should work on it, though. Some people like that thing called...is it *privacy*?" I reach around her and yank open the door. "Feel completely and utterly free to leave now."

"I'd work on your people skills soon," she says as she leaves, her green eyes flashing. "You don't have that long."

"Pardon me?" My eyebrows fly up.

"What, you think you're going to be a kid forever?" she says quickly. "Think again, Mel. If you can."

I am rubber and you are a sticky hole of dung. "Thank you so much for the advice," I growl. "I'm sure I will call upon it in times of great personal need. In the meanwhile, have a nice life." I push the door shut with a satisfying slam.

Ugh! She is so *annoying*. Obviously the conniving, megalomaniacal apple doesn't fall far from the conniving, megalomaniacal tree.

That on top of the earlier angst, I'm more frustrated than surprised to find that all I can do the rest of this evening is pace and mutter. Around nine the walls of my room start to feel too close for comfort, and with a ton of angry energy left in me, I feel myself stomping out of my room and to the stairs.

I just keep climbing, taking the steps two at a time, trying to burn off that adrenaline. But my legs are too used to stair drills at Watson to give in that easily.

The building around me is quiet, muted. Outside the sky is dark, cloudless now, and city lamps twinkle in at me. Yellowy light tries to brighten the stairwell without much success. Footsteps—my footsteps—echo around me as I ascend.

I feel my hands hit a door, and realize I'm on the last landing. No fair. I'm not tired yet.

Scowling, I spin on my heel, searching for something

else. Finding no more doors, my eyes pull upward. A square of ceiling catches my well-trained eye. It's a trapdoor. Yup, the sign on it says 'Maintenance Only'.

"That'll work," I mutter, spotting a stepladder in the corner. Reaching my leg out, I hook my foot around it, dragging it to me. I set it up under the aforementioned ceiling tile.

I spring to the top platform, giving my height another four-or-so feet (1.2 meters). I have to duck my head so it doesn't scrape the trapdoor. Then I find the latch and flip it open.

The inky sky stretches above me as I look through the opening. So this leads to the roof. Fresh air. That works for me.

I grab the edges of the square gap and vault myself through. I've done this hundreds of times through vertical hoops at Watson. It's the same basic principle, only my hands are at a slightly different angle.

I land sitting on the edge of the hole, my feet dangling down over the ladder, which I kick back against the wall.

Someone laughs.

I freeze, then whip around. "Oh," I say, surprised, but not really. "Hi."

"Hi," Ray says, still grinning. "You scared me."

You scared me too. Not that I'm going to admit that. "What…why are you here?" I ask, pulling my legs up onto the roof as well. As I do I push the trapdoor back down.

He's leaning back, propped up by his arms. Scattered around his right side are odd instruments, which I vaguely recognize as meteorology tools, like he had in that kit back at Watson.

"I should have guessed," he says, gesturing to a spot on his left.

"Should have guessed what?" I move slowly sink down

beside him.

"I've been coming up here for a while, and no one's ever found me." He looks up at the sky. "I just should have guessed that if anyone would stumble upon it by accident, it would be you."

"Why?" I say, mystified. Again, only Ray can do that to me.

"You're that different."

It doesn't sound like he means it as an insult, which perplexes me more.

There's a moment of silence. I fix my eyes past the edge of the roof. Lights of skyscrapers and cars on the highway glimmer back. They look very far off.

"You didn't answer my question," I say quietly.

"*Hmm*?"

"I asked, what are you doing here?"

"Oh." He shifts in my peripheral vision so he's sitting upright now, matching me. "Sometimes I feel like everything gets a little too much to handle. So I sort of…get away by coming up here. It's a good place to test relative humidity, and look at stars."

My mind flashes to an old brick wall, behind a junk heap. A place I've avoided for two years because my mind kept playing tricks on me, making me think every scuff in the dirt was his footprint, or any displaced rock was kicked up by him, every memory it brought to mind a painful one.

"I know what you mean about too much," I say. "But I didn't know you were interested in astronomy."

"I'm not, really," he responds. "But all the mysteries that aren't solved, about our universe and beyond, well…it makes me feel a little less alone."

My throat feels constricted for a moment. Alone? Ray should never be alone. He's too good for that. "Alone?" I repeat my thought before tact interferes, eager to understand, so I can try to make it better somehow. As I do, I turn my head to face him.

"In the world of unsolved mysteries, no, I'm not alone," Ray says, sighing. "But here, among other people, I guess, I feel alone. They all have a past. And I don't."

"You have a past," I say immediately.

"Not that I know of." Then he groans. "I'm doing it again! Poor you, having to listen to that. I never tell anyone else about that stuff. It's too depressing."

"It's fine," I say immediately. "I know what it's like, not telling anyone about what you feel." I take a deep breath. "Well, it's not fun."

"Because of Anthony," he says perceptively, then inhales sharply. "Sorry, I–"

"No, you're right," I say. I tilt my head back and try to pick out a few stars in the darkness. "But even before…he was the only one I could tell, about anything …"

"Oh." Ray's voice is quiet, controlling something. I don't listen, just keep on going with my sentence.

"…except for you."

There's a surprised silence.

"Really?" he asks finally. I nod, swallowing. "That's so strange. Not you–me. I mean, me too. With you."

"Really?" It's my turn to be shocked. I'd never realized the feeling was mutual.

"Yeah. It's been really different since you got here. Like another puzzle piece fell into place or something."

Funny, because it felt like half of my puzzle fell out of place when he died. I study the sky, trying to think of a good response.

Something blinks down at me. It's…pink.

"What's that? An airplane?" I ask. But the light doesn't move, just flashes some, like it's catching some light. "A star?"

"Where?"

I point. His head turns to follow my finger, and his expression becomes confused.

"Stars aren't pink," he says slowly.

"What is it, then?"

"No idea." He looks genuinely puzzled. "Never seen anything like it before."

"Me either. But then again, I don't really spend that much time looking at the sky."

"You don't? Really?" He cocks his head. "So you don't know any constellations?"

"Um…I think that's the Big Dipper," I say uncertainly, tracing a few of the shimmering spots above with my finger.

Ray laughs. "Every preschooler knows that one, Mel. And besides, that's in the Northern Hemisphere, so no." His hand reaches out and catches mine. "Do you know Aquila?" He shows me the stars with my own fingers. "Or Cygnus? What about Scorpius?"

I shake my head, but let him go on. After a few more he stops. "That's all I know off the top of my head, but it's all pretty interesting. The stories behind them, how they formed…"

"I bet it is," I say. "For you, at least. I'm not really into mythology. I prefer to keep my head in the real world."

"You would," he agrees, pulling his hand back down. But he takes mine with it, and they rest between us, still intertwined.

I feel like something in me is going to explode any second. We both stay still for several minutes. I wonder if he's struggling not to detonate as well.

He breaks the silence again. "I *knew* I was missing something."

"The normal part of your brain?" I joke, but it's halfhearted. I can't truly insult Ray now, even if it is playful.

257

"No, silly." He lets out a long breath. "I think…" he says, so quietly it's hard for me to hear him, "…that it was…you."

My breath stops for a moment. I force my trachea to open again, but I feel dizzy. My head droops to the side until it's resting on Ray's shoulder.

"I missed you, too," I whisper.

I have trouble getting to sleep tonight, more trouble than any previous night. But somehow I know it's for a different reason–different category, different *dimension* than my previous reasons.

I don't mind this time.

19

I have a fizzy, bubbly feeling in my chest when I wake up today. I actually like it. Does this mean I like getting sick? Definitely not. Sickness is a huge distraction. So I do not like it. Ergo, I shouldn't like this. Because it's a completely strange feeling, signifying sickness.

I can't manage to convince myself.

My focus seems to have gotten itself lost as well. I try to make a game plan, but concentration keeps slipping away. I feel content to just lie back on my bed, letting my thoughts swirl around in a jumbled mush. I'm vaguely aware that I'm not supposed to do this. I should be doing *something*. Doing nothing is not allowed. But it's too vague, at the moment, to matter.

When the clock tells me it's 8:50, I start getting ready. I space out again while brushing my hair and spend a whole minute on that before shaking my head (the fog doesn't quite leave) and pulling my hair back into a ponytail. On the way out of the bathroom, though, I catch sight of the front of my hair. Frowning, I reach up and twist the loose strands together so they hang down as a single loose curl on one side of my face, reaching my cheekbone. That little thing makes everything look so much neater, smoother. Feeling slightly surprised, I head out to get dressed.

I make it down to breakfast a little late, but there're still a few people in the food line, so it takes me another few minutes to emerge with my meal.

I look around when I come out of the line, gripping my

tray. I got my two glasses of orange juice, as usual, but also a fruit salad and waffles. There were waffles once in a while at Watson, but I haven't had them in a few years. They just...looked good to me today, I guess.

Spontaneous me.

Spotting Hale's hair glinting in the sun streaming through one of the many windows, I start towards her table. I guess sometime in the past day I'd decided to spend some time with Hale and Vivian before I leave. And also to be deceptive, that's a plus. I mean, that's the reason.

"Hi," I say, sliding into the seat next to Vivian.

"Hey!" Hale cries, leaning around to see me. "Are you staying today?"

"Yep," I reply, spinning a spoon around in my fruit salad.

"That's really great," Vivian says sincerely. Like she missed me.

"Yeah, spy-chick. We haven't seen you since the dance, as Dan pointed out." Matt grins across the table at me.

"Just observing," Dan mutters.

"Observation is the key to success in life," I quote Mrs. Keen, fighting the urge to chuckle.

"Of course it is," Hale says, nodding to me as Matt reaches over and grabs her still unopened syrup packet. He pops it apart over his own waffles.

"Mel!" someone says. I turn to face my front.

"R–Jon? Hi!" I say, surprised. "You're actually here for a meal!"

"Yeah, we're only working a little today, from ten till twelve," he says, smiling at me as he plunks down in the seat directly across the table.

"That's all? Really?"

"Yeah. I about had to beg for a break, but it's the *weekend*! We go back to class day after tomorrow!" He pauses, frowning. "And you leave Tuesday morning."

"I do," I say automatically, the weight of my responsibilities threatening to crush down on my shoulders. I struggle to hold it off.

"Hale! Viv!" Someone sits down at the end of the table.

"Leah," Vivian nods, but doesn't look over.

"Hey. We actually have mealtime together," someone else laughs. My teeth grit automatically.

Grinning–no, more like smirking–Caidy slithers into the seat next to Ray. I mean, Right. Next. To. Ray. I fight not to scowl. This is another new feeling. Not the scowling, but the source of the scowl.

I realize I haven't seen Caidy in person since the dance. In the past three days she'd seemed like nothing more pressing than an annoying memory. But now she seems like the number one pressing thing. No, that's just at the table. There are lots of things more pressing. Such as, Peter Manifred and his potential goons. Right, Mel?

I notice that Vivian and Hale don't respond to Caidy, only exchange a look with each other.

"Long time no see," Caidy continues, like she doesn't notice. "We're finally taking a break from the project today. And hey, I've been meaning to say, Hale, Viv, you guys haven't returned my texts in for-ev-er! What gives?"

Hale stabs a hash brown with her fork. Vivian shrugs, intent on stirring her cereal.

"Been busy, I guess," she says quietly, but not repentantly.

"You think *you've* been busy?" Caidy chortles. I glance up quickly, then look away. "Jon and I have worked three days straight! *You've* been on holiday!"

I realize I'm looking right at Ray. He catches my eye and scrunches up his nose. *And what a joy it's been.*

I stifle a snort. *She seems to think so.*

261

Rain

Caidy pauses, her eyes narrowing slightly, something I don't miss. I also don't miss as they flick towards me, but she barrels on without delay. "I mean, you do realize those are pretty much twelve-hour days?"

"*Mm*," Vivian replies.

"I wish I could tell you more about it," Caidy says, but somehow I don't feel the right sincerity in her tone. "But as I've said, we're not supposed to tell anyone."

Ray looks up at the ceiling, pressing his lips together. A laugh bursts out of me. I quickly clap my hands over my mouth. Everyone stares at me except for Ray, who stares resolutely upward, his mouth curving at the corners. Caidy sits back, her jaw flexing.

"Swallow much?" Matt asks, making the incorrect assumption that I'm choking.

"Sorry," I say, grinning sheepishly as I swallow another laugh. I'm not sure where this sudden hilarity came from, but it's as hard to control as…. My mind doesn't come up with a proper analogy, but something says it's probably not half as hard as Ray's 'waves'. The meaningless memories he has to control or lose his sanity over.

That sobers me up.

"*Me*-el," Hale sings, not giving Caidy a chance to continue.

"Ha-ale?" I respond.

"So you're not working today, right?"

Ray watches me, too, now. Does he want to know? He would want me to say no, I wasn't. He'd want me to take a break. Only I can't take a break. Not really. I have so little time left. So I have to lie, of course, to build on my decided pretense.

"Nope."

"Awesome!" Hale sounds infinitely more enthusiastic than when Caidy told her *she* had the day off. A smug feeling seeps through me, as well as another, nicer–*nicer?*–sensation, but I don't let either show. "Want to hang out this morning?"

"Okay," I say. "Sounds good."

Ray smiles, like that pleases him for some reason. Then his forehead creases and his mouth tugs downward, staring at my face, seeing the lie that only he could see. I avoid his gaze and instead share a cheerful expression with Vivian.

Okay, so my main purpose is not hanging out. It's a cover so no one will expect I'm actually working. But it's for Ray's own safety.

Caidy starts up this whole endless spiel to Ray about their 'confidential' project. How annoying. He keeps glancing over at me, like *how am I going to stand another two hours of this?* Or, at least, that's what I imagine him to be thinking. He would appear simply polite to everyone else.

When breakfast is over, I slip quickly over to the conveyor belt.

"Hey," Ray says, touching my shoulder as he passes on his way to drop of his own tray. "Later–when I'm done working–want to do something?"

"Yeah," I reply, flashing him a quick smile. The practical part of my mind rejoices. Perfect. I can get the immediate work done now and keep an eye on him after, when I can.

The not-so-practical part of my mind only feels. Happy.

"I'll stop by your room? Around 12:30?"

"Sounds like a plan," I say. "Have lots of fun in the meanwhile."

He snorts, waves, and moves on to the conveyor.

I duck into the entrance hallway. Almost instantly someone grabs my elbow. Hard. Rough. Aggressive.

She's on the ground before she or I have time to think about it. I open my mouth, ready to apologize, but stop when I see her.

Caidy glares up at me, lurching to her feet. "Touchy much?" she spits.

"I thought it was common sense that the predator pounces on the prey, not the other way around," I say indifferently, examining my nails. Not that I find anything interesting about them. It's just for effect–like she did my first night here.

"*Predator*," she sneers sarcastically.

"Prey," I tell her. "You are the prey."

Her mouth twists in a scowl. "Look, I don't like you either."

"Then why are you engaging in danger to confront me?" I challenge.

"Because I just wanted to tell you…" Her narrowed eyes flick across the busy hallway. No one glances at us. "I just wanted to tell you that if you're doing *anything* to make Jon mess up on his project, you better stop it. That will *not* happen if I can help it."

Who the heck does she think she is? "Firstly," I say icily, "if I wanted something, there is no way on Earth you would be able to stand in my way. And secondly, I don't want to 'mess up' his project. I would never do that. Ever." *Yours*, on the other hand…. Too bad they're working *together*.

She stares at me like she's trying to detect a lie. Pitiful mortal. Shaking my head, I whirl around and stride away.

She's in front of me again. She has issues, I swear. Of course, I knew that already. But still. This has gone beyond irritating.

"You want to do a butt slide again?" I snap.

"Back off," she says in a low voice.

"You're the one being overly assertive here," I inform her.

"That's not what I meant, idiot."

"Then please, enlighten me. Only, do it fast. You're

264

wasting my time."

"I meant, *back off.* Or you'll regret it."

Ooh. Chills. "Melodrama has been passé since the Mesozoic era, you know. Now, if you were to give me some *real* information, I might consider your proposal." Not. "In the meanwhile, please move. You happen to be in my line of vision. And that's making me unhappy, not to mention slightly nauseous."

"Don't tell me you're *that* stupid," she says, not moving. "You have to know what I mean. Don't you have a *life*?"

"The question is, do *you* want to have a life? Because right now it looks like you don't." I flex my fingers to keep them from curling into fists.

"I have to go," she says. "Think about what I said. You know what I mean. And if you don't listen…"

"Then we can have an epic battle of wits," I say. "I'm sure I'll show the proper amount of fear when the time comes. Now, honestly, I'm going to puke on your pretty little shoes in about two seconds."

Caidy makes a disgusted face and stomps past me, her dainty flip-flops smacking against the linoleum. Ahh, sweet relief. Caidy-free vision.

Hale and Vivian are waiting in the doorway to the cafeteria when I reach it. So I was right, they're still here.

"*There* you are," Hale says. "Where did you go?"

"Sorry," I reply. "I was…uh…" My mind, already starting to try to understand the confrontation with Caidy, takes a moment to think of something. "Talking to Jon for a minute."

"Oooh," Hale sings to the now-empty hallway.

"Please, don't."

"What is *up* with you two, anyway?" she asks. "It seems like you're bffs or something."

"Some people just click like that, Hale," Vivian says as

we meander to the stairway again. "Leah and Caidy, for instance."

"Shallow pools must attract," Hale observes. "Not that you're shallow," she assures me quickly.

"'Shallow' may be true for your sister sometimes, Hale," says Vivian, "but honestly, I think there's a lot more to Caidy than we know. She's like you in that way, Mel."

"What?" I blurt. There's a *similarity* between Caidy and me?

"Yeah." Vivian shrugs. "You both seem like there's a lot more going on under the surface than you let on."

"You read too many books," I mutter, though I realize that's probably true–for me. But Caidy? Deep? Deceptive? She can only try.

"Yep," Vivian says, unrepentant.

"So whaddya want to do?" Hale bounces ahead. "We have all day. Or until Jon's done working," she says, looking at me slyly. I drop my gaze to the floor. Then I catch myself and bring my eyes back up to stare right at Hale. She winks.

"Yeah, I guess until twelve thirty," I say, giving in.

"So are you two going out, or what?"

"Or what," I say. "And drop the subject, please."

She sighs. "Fine. You're no fun, you know."

"I know." Not sorry.

"So what are we gonna do?" Hale asks again.

"Do either of you have a laptop?" I ask.

"I do," Vivian responds.

"Can I use it?"

"Sure. Why?"

I shrug. "It has to be a better model than the desktop in my room. I want to check my email and such."

Actually, I want to use a computer that I'm pretty sure won't be hacked into. If my enemies know which room is mine then they could quite feasibly be monitoring my computer as well.

I angle the laptop screen away from Hale and Vivian, who are bending over some style publication. I join in the conversation as needed, so not to raise suspicion, and focus on the screen.

I pull up an Internet browser and search for 'Anthony Luther'.

Almost nothing comes up for Ray. Other Anthony Luthers, yes, but for Ray the only things are his name on an old Albany preschool roster and his obituary. His life is blank to the world from ages four to thirteen.

I frown, absentmindedly twisting a piece of hair around my finger. On impulse, I type in Jerry Luther.

He's there, on lists of staff or previous staff of this place or that, something about a tennis team at Eastland Rec Park, and other miscellaneous things. But it doesn't say anything about Rochester.

Bonnie Robar is next. She apparently received lots of awards for her work in meteorology. I see lists of places she worked, TV shows she broadcasted, scientific journals she contributed to. But then everything cuts off, saying nothing about her last eleven years of life.

Eleven years? That's the same with Ray. And his dad. No, wait, there's something else here. I frown as I read the small article. Something about Bonnie Robar retiring in California a year after everything else here stops.

To my well-trained eye, that looks like a cover-up. A story to deter suspicions. But why would there be suspicions in the first place? More information is key. I quickly replace Bonnie Robar's name with 'Jonathon Lucas Carter' in the search bar.

Nothing.

Everything that fills the screen is about some boring,

unimportant person. I even search more specifically for 'Marvin' or 'Alison Orphan Childcare'.

Ah. Here's something. Alison Orphan childcare comes up, but when I click the link I get only a 'Website Unavailable' notice. Like the website no longer exists.

Or never existed in the first place.

There's the Marvin home page. Watson doesn't have a home page. Marvin is obviously more of a socialite school. Watson is hidden in deliberate shadows.

No student records are available. After checking websites of places Bonnie worked and noting the prizes she's won, I'm forced to a conclusion based on the information here.

The Internet has everything. Anything. Each scrap of news, anywhere, gets pooled into that infinite resource; from blogs or newspapers or TV sites, if you search for anything it gives you back everything. Even the most commonplace people–all those faceless Jonathon Carters, other Anthony and Jerry Luthers, Bonnie Robars–wind up out there for everyone to stumble across, at random or not, without those faceless people even doing anything special. Ergo, faceless. Bonnie Robar didn't even have an obituary. Going by that, people would assume she's still alive. That small retirement notice, it doesn't fool me. Because other than that, there's nothing, *nothing* about this family. Not even a mention. They do not exist, even to the person trying to find them specifically. The only other person, or people, that have the same invisibility are...me. And Watson. We can't have records, of course not. No one can suspect we...exist.

But that retirement thing... It would seem like Bonnie was trying to draw attention away from herself and her family, to draw an official, though sketchy, conclusion, so no one would wonder if they disappeared. Why? Why was it that important? Why did Bonnie and Jerry end up getting divorced?

Bonnie went off on her own. Something tells me, my instinct, that it was because of this thing of importance, the reason for the disappearance. She *was* the reason. She had a secret, and if she were tied to her family, they'd slow her down.

Or they'd be in danger?

A random quote floats through my head. My mind ties it to that day, the first day Ray and I were at our spot together. The day his dad passed away.

"She was working on some big project when she left. Something to do with meteorology, I think. I get letters about once a year, but I don't know where she is, really."

So this 'project' was a cover up? Another fake story? Likely. The truth? Unlikely, unless it was reverse psychology. Only, then it could be reverse reverse psychology and be a lie again. Or reverse reverse reverse psychology and be the truth.

I think I have a fifty-fifty shot here.

And she could have died, too. Any number of times, any number of ways, Bonnie Robar could be gone. That *could* explain her obvious neglect for Ray. I always disliked her for that. I mean, yes, I live without a mom–*or* a dad. But the mom's the point here. And if Bonnie really *were* alive, well, she didn't even come back to see Ray after his dad *died.* She never got to know him. Probably doesn't even know he's 'dead'. For her sake, she better be dead too. Because if I ever meet her, and she's alive and healthy… She better watch her back.

I play another memory through my head. It's Anthony's voice, echoing from that day.

He knew it. He must have known he was too sick, despite those stupid optimistic doctors. That's why he took me here. Somewhere I'd be safe. Surrounded by all these…all these amazing fighters, and strategists. He always was concerned about my safety, like I was about to run into trouble around every corner…

Possible danger. That was prominent in their lives. Though it wasn't ever said directly to Ray, he could tell.

My eyes widen. Yes, the safety of Watson could have been a factor in Ray's being sent there. But more so, the invisibility? Like I thought earlier, Watson's hidden from the world. And if Ray's dad knew he was dying, he must have wanted some way for Ray to remain hidden after he wasn't there to do the job anymore.

20

I bid adieu to Hale and Vivian soon after that, knowing I'd have even more trouble keeping up the carefree façade now. Better safe than sorry, I think, as I lie back on my bed, trying to stop the room from spinning around me. Bad room, you're supposed to stay still.

"Ooh, she's gotta go get ready to meet Jo-on," Hale had said as I left, making kissy faces.

I think my response was something brilliant, like "Um, yeah, uh-huh."

Vivian got up and held the door for me.

"Are you okay?" she whispered as I slowly made my way into the hallway.

"I'm…um…sure."

"Okay." Her tone was doubtful. "Well, if you need anything, we're here all day."

"Thanks," I turned and ran for the stairwell. I'd left the laptop on, but deleted the evidence of my search, so they can't really figure out what's wrong unless they're psychics. Which don't exist. So I'm okay.

I realize my cell is in my hands, my finger pressing down on the number two button, the one I use to call Shadow. The back of my mind thinks vaguely that it'll be nice to tell someone about my problems. I haven't talked to Shadow in a while. I sort of miss him.

Then my hand drops the phone. Am I crazy? I must be crazy! Or the back of my mind is, anyway. Call Shadow? Tell him about this? I can't! I'd get Xpress flighted back to

Rochester by noon. And that's ten minutes ago. And he'd be in danger, and Ray might be in danger too, and I'd be ratted out to Peter Manifred and his cronies.

I can't tell anyone.

I draw in a long breath, shivering involuntarily as I realize this.

Why is that such a big deal? It's not. I've been here before. Everything about my life is confidential. I'm a pro at keeping secrets. At keeping my mouth shut. At keeping everything that hurts locked in a compartment somewhere below my kidneys.

But now it feels like every detail I've been keeping to myself, about this whole mess, is trying to make me explode into a thousand pieces. It wants to escape. It wants to make me weak. It wants to make me break. It wants to make me cry.

I have to get over this. What a great time for drama to kick in. Ever since I found out that Ray is still alive I've been...

...Vulnerable.

I shiver again. That word has never been used in the same sentence as my name. Unless there *is* a 'never' before it. But it's true. I've never, never before kept my word to goons and not said anything. I've always told someone–always told Shadow. Always gotten it figured out.

But with something much more important than my own safety on the line, I've given in. Not given up, but given *in,* and it sucks.

Ray knocks on the door when I'm sitting on the floor, still in an undecided sort of mess. I try to pull myself together enough to answer.

"Hey," he says, from where he's leaning against the doorframe after I've pulled open the entryway. "Sorry, sorry,

sorry I'm late."

"You okay?" I demand.

"Actually, I need your help," he says. My eyes widen. "I have a little problem…"

"What?" Would he be grinning if this were bad news?

"I figured you'd be the one to ask for this," he goes on oh-so-casually.

"Spit it out," I nearly beg.

"I need to sneak out of here." His grin widens.

That sounds like something he would say if someone were after him. But unless he *has* gone insane, he wouldn't be so calm. "Who did you shoot?" I ask, feeling puzzled.

"Might as well be Ms. Richards," he responds. "'Cause I'm cutting class right now."

I glance behind me at the clock. "It's 12:40. I thought you were only going until twelve-ish?"

He scowls. "Me too. In fact, she promised. But when we started to clean up at twelve, Ms. Richards asked if I was doing something fun today. I told her I had plans," Ray continues. "Then Caidy had this little coughing fit, and after Ms. Richards made sure she was okay she told us we're really behind and need to continue working."

No. That's over the line. I feel my toes curling up inside my sneakers in an effort to restrain my legs from marching down to the weather lab. "What? That can't be fair," I insist.

Ray shrugs. "Maybe we are far behind, I don't know. But I don't really care at this point. I mean, you're leaving soon. No way am I spending today holed up in the lab when you don't have to work."

"So you…?"

"Waited until it wouldn't be obvious, then asked to go to the bathroom. I think she's suspicious, though. Speaking of which…" He too glances at the clock. "I could really use that expertise of yours about now."

Rain

"What do you want to do?" I grab my key and cell phone, pocket them, and close the door behind me as I step out of my room.

"I don't know. Just get out of here." Ray looks at the stairwell doors down the hall. "They'll start searching the school in about thirty seconds, I bet."

"Well, then." I reach out to grip his wrist, but his hand flips up at the last second and I end up wrapping my fingers around his. Our eyes meet. He gives me a small, uncertain smile. I blink, then return it, trying not to look as confused as I feel. "Let's get going."

"I wish I knew how to do that," Ray says, shaking his head as we board the bus. "There wasn't even the *possibility* of us getting caught."

I wish he knew–remembered–how, too.

"Thank you," I say, taking an extravagant bow. "So, now that we've officially made you a delinquent, where do you want to go to utilize this new freedom?" As long as we're being extra-super-extremely careful, I'm up for anything.

"Why don't we just...do nothing?" he almost laughs, sliding into a seat.

Nothing? Do *nothing*?

Sounds great.

Right now, I could actually believe that life is good. I'm having my second ice cream of the week/month/year. I have no real purpose in walking through these city streets; ergo, I am not feeling frustrated. I'm actually taking in the amazing sights that surround me. And I am not dwelling on the little problem that I refuse to dwell on at this time.

I'm with the best person in the world.

Honestly, is there someone with a better personality than Ray? I contemplate this as the city swirls around me, happy and bustling. No one can be nicer. No one can be kinder, or more resilient, or in control.

Not even me.

"Oh! Let's go in here," Ray says, taking my elbow and leading me into a small store on the corner.

It's a cross between a joke shop and one of those fake-spy-tech stores. The credulous customers at these stores think they'll be able to do everything in espionage by wearing completely hideous and fake double-sided sunglasses. Give me a break. Even if he's forgotten his training, Ray should have enough common sense to see how completely ersatz it is.

"What's so amazing about it?"

"Not much," he admits, heading for the back. "Only this."

"The metal mushroom?" The thing Ray's pointing at is at the demonstration table in the back. It's a silver rod with a round sphere on top. Whoo-hoo.

"The Van de Graaff generator," he corrects. "It creates static electricity by taking the electrons in the air and–"

"Stop. Now." Then I laugh.

"How about I show you?" He walks up, ignoring the 'Have A Go At Your Own Risk' sign, and flips the thing on. "The neatest part is, it basically simulates lightning. Only on a much smaller scale."

"You're going to create a lighting bolt. In a joke shop." I hadn't *thought* the poison took any brain cells, but maybe I'm mistaken.

I realize I'm kidding myself, since I'm not leaving the Potential Scene of Trouble. Not even against my better judgment, I trust Ray too much for that.

"Watch," he tells me, holding his arm out to the sphere. Then he jerks back. I'm about to raise an eyebrow in an *are you scared all of a sudden?* look when he rolls up his sleeve and unclasps the thing around his wrist.

"Don't want this to get too near to the generator," he explains, but I barely hear through the roaring in my ears.

It's gold and blue, and almost too small for him. Without saying a word I grab the instrument and flip open the lid covering the circular part.

A small, wiggling compass stares back at me.

"Where did you get this?" I whisper.

Ray's chewing on his lower lip. "I don't know. I've always had it."

His mom's old compass. The one he showed me the very first time we ate breakfast together.

Not that I'd doubted myself, but this is proof. Solid, absolute, indisputable proof. It's the first thing I'll shove in Shadow's face when he steps off the plane Monday.

Except... I swallow as I realize I'm not sure if Shadow ever saw this. Or if he would recognize it.

Maybe there's an inscription. I flip the thing over. All that's on the back is a smooth, almost fluid blotch on the textured surface. Like someone melted it there to cover something up.

A name?

"You want to hold it?" Ray asks, forcing himself to release his lip.

"Yeah," I mouth, still scrutinizing it for anything, anywhere.

"I'll let you, only if you promise to watch. It'll be cool."

Only Ray could make me lift my eyes from the compass. I hold my gaze on him as his hand reaches for the metal sphere again.

There's an audible crack, then a blue spark flashes between Ray's hand and the thing. Though he jumps, he also smiles like he was just given a lollipop instead of an electric charge. "Cool, no? How amazing was that?"

"You think it's *amusing* to give yourself a visible shock?"

"Definitely." He moves to the side to give me a better view. "Watch. Again."

This time I do see the little lightning-bolt-resembling-phenomenon that arcs between the metal and his skin. He jumps again and shakes his hand out.

"You're going to hurt yourself."

"No, I'm not. Much. But only if I held my arm here for a long time," he assures me quickly. "Okay, next trick." He flips the machine off and places his hand on the sphere. Then, before I can object, he turns it back on.

He doesn't wince, only grins at me.

"Are you going to start flying or something?" I ask.

"Not me," he says, then crosses his eyes as he looks up. So do I, and my eyebrows shoot up when I see a good portion of his hair standing on end.

"It doesn't hurt?"

"Nope."

After another minute I shudder. "Okay, enough with the toys. Seriously. What you find amusing." I shake my head. Then I reach out to tug him away from his new best friend.

"Ack!" I yelp, jerking back as another visible spark of blue shoots from his shoulder to me. "Ow!"

Ray flicks the machine off and steps away, laughing as he rubs his arm. "*That* hurt," he says. "Very smart, Mel."

"What… But…" I clench my teeth to stop the inane yammering. Because I don't inanely yammer. I'm just slightly embarrassed. That's the reason for it. Not an excuse, but a reason. Even though electricity and weather were topics we study and have studied at Watson, they're maybe the only things that aren't strong points for me. Just regular. Not-at-the-top-of-my-mind-just-regular regular. That's why. "Here's your compass back," I say quickly. I shove it into his hand, needing something better to do than stutter.

"Relax." Ray grins at the ceiling, seemingly enjoying some sort of mental jest. Humph. At my expense, no doubt. Double humph. Fine. He can just go ahead and do that. I do not care. I'm just over here not caring. And definitely not being embarrassed. He can just–

Put his arm around my shoulders?

Now he's smiling over at me. No, not exactly over. More like down-and-over. Since, unlike when he–ahem–left Rochester, he is now more than an inch-or-so taller than me. Something like five-inches-or-so (12.7 centimeters-or-so). So now he's looking down at about a...hmm...forty-five-degree angle? No, fifty, going by our prox–

And now his head is facing my ear and he's whispering, "Don't be embarrassed. Not even *Caidy* gets it. In fact, I think you'd do better than she would."

How did he know? Well, that's a stupid question. My mask-of-composure is omnilost on him. And–what's that I hear? Better than Caidy? That I can live with, and die with, and just-stand-here-forever with.

He laughs one more time, quietly, still turned to look at my extremely interesting hair. Today I was too agitated to try that flippy thing, so it's in–wahoo–a ponytail.

I feel my neck turning. Um, hello, cervical spine? Did I give you permission to do this?

Whether I granted that clearance or not, the next moment I'm facing him. His dark, mysterious blue–oh, how fitting– eyes lower marginally to meet mine, that grin still on his face.

"Don't worry," he says.

Which brings me crashing down to thorny reality. Because if there are enemies intertwined with this whole mystery surrounding Ray's vanished memory, and said adversary is administering serious threats that Ray has no idea about, and me trying to help might end up being just the opposite and enact the menaces, and I have no backup since I'm supposed to be relaxing, and when I leave I'll leave Ray in danger because of something to do with his family even before he died, and to top off this not-even-complete list, Caidy and her mom are making every attempt to pilfer every last minute of Ray's time...how can I *not* worry?

Dinner's already started by the time we return. My eyes feel extra sore from constantly looking around and around and around at the thankfully and maddeningly clear coast all day. Ray's eyes might be a little sore, too, from watching me with sideways glances the whole time. He knows something's up. That I can deal with, just as long as he doesn't know what.

Theoretically I can deal with it, because honestly, I want nothing more than to tell him so he can help me, and be *aware*. But I *must* exercise self-control. (Fifth grade, that was all we focused on. They even had us learn yoga.)

"Be on your guard," Ray warns me. What? How redundant is that? My guard is getting muscle strains because I've been nothing *but* on it. "Fireworks liable to go off."

Ah, yes. The little issue of the megalomaniacal (what a wonderful word) Richardses.

"I'll be your Kevlar," I assure him. "Hungry?"

"Definitely." We'd had lunch at a little, innocent-looking diner a few hours ago.

"Let's eat, then." I turn the cafeteria door handle and step in, Ray right beside me.

Ka-boom.

Ray wasn't kidding about fireworks. In fact, he was underestimating, I conclude, as two hands catch my chest and shove me–forcibly–back into the lobby. I crash into Ray before I can react, and we stumble backwards. Well, he stumbles. By now I've regained my balance.

Caidy slams the door behind her. My mind flashes

between her and the potential witnesses in the cafeteria, in case she decides to go after us with a scalpel or something. Who might have seen she's the one who pushed us out here? Probably no one. There's a short corridor from the door to the actual dining hall, so we weren't in anyone's line of view.

Not that she'll harm us or anything. No, duh, of course not. I'd just so like to pin her for something. Figuratively and literally.

"*How dare you?*" she shrieks, her words echoing hollowly off the bare walls of the lobby.

Ah, the old 'how dare you' standby. Never fails, does it? Cease and desist, please. Your clichés are driving me nowhere but snoozeville.

"Calm–," momentarily naïve Ray starts, but Caidy keeps going. I glance at Ray with an *o-kay* look. He responds with a cautionary glance, or maybe just a half-exasperated-half-wary expression.

When she's done with a stream of profanities, Caidy spins to face Ray. Her expression melts into a histrionic pout. "We didn't know where you went. We were worried."

"I can take care of myself," Ray says mildly, but I can tell he's on the verge of annoyance.

"And if you were really worried about him, you might want to reconsider the whole burning the candle at both ends thing," I add, running a hand down my ponytail.

"Don't give me that load of bull. You remember what we talked about this morning?" Her hand jerks out and grabs the collar of my shirt. Ray makes a weird sound next to me, moving half a step forward in my peripheral vision.

I raise my eyebrows and slowly look down to peer at the half-fist pressed against my chest. My own hand, previously halfway down my neck as I trailed my hair, comes around and deliberately pulls her fingers away one-by-one, pushing the hand back at her when I'm done.

"Could you, maybe, *not* ruin my shirt?"

"I'm serious," she hisses, her slitted brown eyes wild, from what I can see of them.

"Am I not?" I ask innocently, holding my hands palm up at my sides.

"You think this is all a joke or something, right?" Her up-in-my-face expression has a bit of superiority in it. "And I say it again: get a life, Amber Rind."

"Get out of mine," I retort, flexing my hands to keep them from balling up.

"Caidy, stop," Ray says, his tone definitely harder than normal.

The guilty party's eyes travel over to him. Her jaw relaxes and she rocks back on her heels. Ahh, sweet, fresh, non-Caidy-contaminated air. Why thank you, Ray.

"I'll go tell Mum you're back," she mutters to him, still glaring at me.

"Yeah. Why don't you do that." He still sounds upset.

Caidy strides past me. She tries to knock against my shoulder—is your middle name 'cliché' or something? Caidy Cliché?—but I easily avoid her. Unfortunately I don't avoid hearing her hiss, "Don't forget again."

"I have a photographic memory," I call after her. "You can be sure any action I take is not a result of me 'forgetting'."

She slams the outside door. Sweet, benevolent temperament.

Wait. She called me Amber *Rind*. When did I tell her my last name? Of course, Miss Rose knows it, so it's not impossible for Caidy to find out, whether from her mother or by other means. It's what I would do if she were the guest at my school, try and find out everything about her.

But she's not me. Maybe she's trying to throw me with that huge, earth-shattering knowledge of my last name. Well, hmph. It won't work.

"Forget what?" Ray asks, looking at me when I turn around. It takes me a millisecond to get back on that train of thought.

"Oh. She told me not to mess up your project." I watch his face. He snorts.

"I doubt that."

"What? That she did?"

"No, that you would. You still hungry?"

"Starving."

And so we enter the cafeteria a second time.

"No! Do *not* argue." Hale fixes me with a glower.

"But–" I start, my jaw jutting out in exasperation.

"Mel!" Hale grips my forearm. Ten ways to shake her off immediately run through my head, but I remain still. "Please?"

I make a small, hissing grunt and tilt my head back to glare at the ceiling. "Hale, you don't underst–"

"I understand that you work *way* too much," she interrupts. "No, I don't understand the whole setup. But do you think I want my friend to have a coronary before she turns sixteen?"

"My heart is perfectly healthy. Anyway, I don't care."

Hale's eyes bore into mine as she scuffs her toes against the foot of my bed. The sky outside my window is dark and patchy, reflecting my mood. Clear, happy, lightheaded, then cloudy, confused, urgent.

"But I care," Hale says.

I fall back on my bed, one arm over my eyes. "Thank you, but I have too much going on right now to be *allowed* to care."

"Oh, come on," she says. I feel the mattress dip as she sits down. "How bad can it be?"

How bad? How bad???

I press my arm in harder, my face feeling unnaturally warm. "Bad," I say, but my voice sounds weird.

"Mel?" Hale whispers. "You all right?"

I try to swallow the lump in my throat. "Yes. Fine. No."

"Can I help?"

"No!" A student in *design*. She couldn't possibly defend herself against the waiting danger.

Silence.

The lump gets bigger. I sit up and immediately get a head rush. While I'm rubbing my forehead to clear my brain, I'm aware of something around my shoulders. It's Hale's arm.

"I bet I can," she says, and before I can flip out she continues, "I know just the perfect remedy for stress."

I take a deep breath to argue, but don't find the strength to do it. Could it be a good alibi? It's definitely a scary thought, but deceptive enough.

Hale interprets my silence to her liking. "See? You know I'm right. Pack your bags, sweetie."

I wince.

And wince.

And stifle a yelp.

Stick it out, I beg myself. *They can only torture me so long.*

"Stop fidgeting," Hale commands.

I'm on my back, my head resting on the pillow of one of Hale's roommate's beds while she attacks my toes with some sort of sandpapery sponge. A 'buffer'. All of the other girls who share the room are at their parents' for vacation. How convenient, all that space. Perfect for Hale's epiphany-of-the-day to occur.

A sleepover. That's her 'brilliant idea'.

Vivian laughs from the top bunk, watching upside-down. Her gorgeous, glossy hair tumbles around her face.

"It is a little uncomfortable," she agrees. I bite down my retort. "But the result is nice."

"Ugh!" I moan, pulling a pillow over my face so I can scowl without being noticed. The buffer resumes its buffing, and I resume the procedure we learned to ignore pain: focus intently on the tip of your nose. That way you don't notice the other injury–or, at least, it's muted. Of course, this only works for minor pain. And if your nose hurts, obviously that's not a good idea either. We have more cerebral methods for blocking out more intense pain.

"We're done, okay?" Hale's voice reaches my ears. "Quit the whining."

Whine? I do not 'whine'. I didn't even 'whine' when Hale announced that, to make be feel *better*, I would be given a full-scale makeover. (Okay, I objected, but that can hardly be counted as 'whining'.)

The one thing I will not let near me is makeup. Yes, okay, *fine*, they can give me a mani-pedi (whatever that is) and *okay* Vivian can do my hair and *yes* I'll participate in the pre-makeover yoga (don't ask). But *no no no no* makeup.

Vivian starts in on the hair. "Hey, Mel?"

"*Mm?*"

"Tell us more about you?"

"Me? I'm a spy. I've always been a spy and I always will be a spy. That's about it."

"Tell us about *Ray*," Hale suggests, her eyes brimming with curiosity as she lies on the floor, head propped upwards on her elbows so she won't miss me even blinking.

Aw crap. So she still remembers that? Lovely. "He was a friend."

"'Was'? 'Friend'?" Hale sounds both curious and skeptical.

I blow out a long breath. The gentle tugging on my scalp actually feels nice. My shoulders relax for the first time in days. "Yes. Was. Friend."

"Why?" Vivian whispers, her fingers trailing through my hair as she fans it out over the pillows. It's become a sort of golden color, definitely not blonde, but has a light tinge, so it's not fully brown, even though I maintain that it's brunette.

After a moment of vacillating, I feel the words come. It's the same story I told Ray at the park, the one about 'Anthony', only I add the part about the nicknames. Though Vivian keeps stroking my hair, Hale's jaw drops slightly and I can sense the near trembling in Vivian's hands. Is that because she's horrified? Weirded? Sympathetic? I don't know.

"Oh my god," Hale says when I'm done. "I'm so sorry I made those jokes."

"Don't be, it's whatever," I mumble.

"Thank you for telling us," Vivian says quietly. Her tone carries something else–understanding? Maybe now she knows why I'm always so incompatible. But no, that's impossible. Maybe she can understand tiny, unimportant things about me. But Ray's the only one who actually sees everything.

21

Too bright.

The light is too bright. It's making me see red behind my eyelids. But that's interrupting the dream I was having where I was thirteen at a Blue Group activity and Ray accidentally exploded the soda machine and–

My eyes open.

I bolt up, kicking off the bedspread. "What time is it?" I blurt out.

"Nine forty-seven ante meridian," Vivian replies from the carpet, where she's looking absorbedly through a *National Geographic* magazine. I frown, sidetracked.

"You get that at Marvin?"

"My pen pal in NYC sends them to me," she replies, flipping a page. "Hale got us muffins. They're on the dresser."

"How could you let me sleep this long?" I moan, coming back to my original topic.

"You can't deny you need the rest."

"The *rest*!" I mutter. "Where's Hale?"

"Hale and her sister are having some sort of profound, meaningful debate," Vivian says. "She's not going to be in a very good mood when she returns. You might want to hightail it out of here if you don't want to deal with it." I'm surprised by the way she says it; her tone isn't accusatory or sarcastic, but honestly advisory.

"What are they debating about?" I ask, reaching for my duffel bag. I dig through my hastily packed supplies, looking for the ones I need. Toothbrush, hairbrush, ponytail....

"Caidy," Vivian says. "Surprise, surprise."

"What about her?" I try to sound nonchalant as I find my outfit.

"Hale thinks she's being a total jerk, and Leah thinks she's completely justified in her actions."

"What do you think?" The words come before I can stop them.

"I think she needs to be more mature about all of this. And maybe stop relying on her mum to solve her problems."

"You've noticed."

"Yes, Ms. Richards is more than trying to spoil her daughter."

"In what respect?"

"In getting Caidy everything she wants that she is unable to get herself. Mainly, Jonathon. There has never been a project where two students have 'had' to spend so much time together to work on it."

That's seriously upsetting. Not that I hadn't suspected it, of course. But still. Megalomaniacal. Nothing potentially good about it except the satisfaction that I'm right, which is a feeling I get too often to take pleasure from it.

But then why is the fact that Vivian's taken my side making me grin as I head for the bathroom?

As I brush my hair back, I try to plan out my day. I grit my teeth when I find my mind balking against the thought of work.

Then it tells me why. *I don't have much time.*

Exactly, I reply, scowling.

With Ray.

Ray *needs to be safe*, I tell myself.

Ray wants *to be with me. I want to be with him.*

So? But I know right there is my biggest threat: want.

And, myself goes on, *I know the drill. Soon, the bad guys? Peter Manifred? Goonies? They're going to get curious why you haven't acted yet. And then they'll walk right into your arms.*

I blink. *True, that's how it usually works...*

See?

But it's not worth the risk! I shake my head.

But if I am actively working...it's so much more dangerous.

Not for me, right?

No. Ray.

I sigh, then slam the hairbrush down on the counter. *I'll decide later.*

I'm about to stalk out of the bathroom when my eyes catch the glare bouncing off the magnolia tub. Memories of my last sleepover come spinning back. That was with Lyvia and Shay, when she was still my friend, the night Ray died. How different this one is.

The two years that happened after that play on their little film reel inside my head. My forehead creases as I see all the times Lyvia helped me, or was nice to me, or was just there for me. Shay gave up. Lyvia stuck with me, forfeiting time with her other friends just to do that. And I can hardly recall any instances when I returned the favors with any sort of gratitude.

I slowly set down the brush. At the time I'd thought I was justified, that focusing on my work was more important, better, than being with friends–my one friend–and that it would save me from feeling that pain again, the pain when I lost Ray. If friends weren't that big of a deal, if I didn't care, then it couldn't happen again.

And Shadow. He'd always been trying to make sure I was okay, and still is, though he's been giving me space, now I recognize. Maybe it's a favor...or maybe he's gotten too fed up with me, like Shay. This makes me frown even more. I'd thought I was doing good, not letting myself hurt, just working….

But was I really just hurting everyone? Shay, Lyvia, Shadow…and myself?

I quickly pack my stuff back up and run out of the bathroom. "I'm going to make a call, I think," I pant to Vivian.

"Go right ahead," she answers, immersed in an article about defrosting a mummy preserved in a glacier. Somehow that's preferable, to me, than her being interested in my call.

I dig my cell out my duffel bag and slip into the hallway, which is empty. Scrolling through my short list of received calls, I find the one I'm looking for.

It rings five times before she picks up. "Mel?" Her tone is surprised.

I swallow. "Hey, Lyvia. What's up?"

There's a moment's silence. "Wow." Then she says, "I broke up with Bryant."

"You did? Really? Why?" I try to sound curious, interested.

"He's not my type." She sighs. "Nice, but nothing really between us."

I'm not sure how to sympathize. I'm not really the one to know about that something that's supposed to be between people.

I struggle to remember the other boys in the quadrilateral. One is clear, because I've never really forgiven him from petty Green and Yellow Group stuff, but the other one is…right. "What about Kent and Nathan?"

"I don't know about Nathan. But Kent's history, already asked out Cathie." Her voice wavers slightly. "Cathiodermie is more like it. Her face is so fake with makeup, it's hideous."

I blink for a moment, then something clicks. "Oh."

She lets out a long breath. "What?"

"Kent…" I start slowly.

"I know!" she wails. "I took too long. I chose the wrong guy. Now I'm too late and…" She trails off, breathing rapidly. "Tell me about you. Please. How are things with that Jon guy?"

"Um…good." Am I supposed to say it's 'good' when hers is 'bad'? "Not really anything really…complicated."

"Tell me." She makes it sound more like a command than a request.

"Um…we sort of hung out yesterday…and Friday…um, and Thursday…"

"Do you like him?"

My head spins on my shoulders. How many times have I been asked that? Why do people feel the need to know the inner workings of my soul? "Um…"

"Does he like you? Clarify 'hung out'."

"I don't know. 'Spent time together'?"

"Does *he* like anyone else?" she asks, misery lining her tone.

"I've not even been here two *weeks*, Lyv. How should I know?" Though the thought makes me grind my shoe into the carpet.

"Well, best of luck to you." Dramatic sigh. Then voices in the background. "Oh…okay, one sec," Lyvia tells them. Then, to me, "Mel? I have to go, okay?" Pause. "Thank you for calling."

"You're welcome. Thank you…too," I say.

"Bye-yas," she says somewhat cheerily, and hangs up.

I stare at the phone. Maybe, someday, our friendship can be saved.

The next call is similar. It rings a few times before he answers, his voice frantic. "Amber? Are you okay?"

"I'm fine," I say as gently as possible. Shadow takes a deep breath.

"Good. Good." Another exhale. "Why are you phoning?"

Kieryn Nicolas

"I don't know," I say. "Just…checking in."

"Really?" he says, his tone sounding happy. Then he clears his throat and adds, "Why?"

"I just told you," I snort.

"Yes, but…well, this is a first."

"It is," I agree. "How are you?"

"Well. You? Having a nice vacation?"

"Um, yes. Definitely. Superb. How are things at Watson?"

He gives the news–twelve students passing into Blue Group tomorrow, new piping being installed–and I sugar coat some things about Marvin before we end the awkward conversation.

Despite it being, as stated, awkward, I feel better as I head down to breakfast with Vivian. And that feeling only grows as Ray joins our table and Caidy and Leah find their own spot across the cafeteria to practice their voodoo or whatever. Hale's a little more subdued than usual, though.

"It'll be okay," Vivian soothes her, after Hale's continuous muttering of "jerk" under her breath. Vivian looks around, as if sensing, as I do, the high-strung nerves of most of the people at the table. "Why don't we all do something after breakfast? What say you to heading for the park?"

"Sure," Ray and I answer at the same time, and catch each other's eye. The next moment we're laughing.

And the moment after that I'm regretting my decision. I need to work. Well, actually, I need to figure out if I need to work or just wait in a crouch, ready to pounce. But after today I'll only have one more day to figure everything out. My breathing starts to become shallower.

Then Ray, still grinning, grabs my hand and pulls me after everyone. I feel the smile slide back onto my face. Well, parks can be good thinking spots, too. But just for an hour.

Or maybe two.

Rain

* * *

Apparently, I'm amazing at 'Aussie Footy', which is the Australian form of soccer. It must have something to do with my dexterity extraordinaire. After we've played for forty-five minutes, girls against guys, I've scored seventeen goals and am having abdominal pains from laughing too much.

As I flop onto a park swing, I realize my mind seems so much clearer. Like I'd been suffocating it before and not even noticing. Right now, I feel like it can breathe.

"You should have played soccer," Ray tells me, jumping onto the swing beside mine. I swallow. He's the only one, save me, that calls it 'soccer'.

"No time," I reply, inhaling deeply. The smells of city and brisk, late winter air swirl through my airway. In Brisbane, the seasons are relatively mild, though generally overcast. I only need a jacket to be comfortable.

"That sucks," he says, like he honestly thinks so. "You're really good. You should've been able to try it."

"What team would I have been on? There isn't one at Watson. Obviously we can't compete with other schools, and an outside team is nix. I'm not supposed to exist back there."

He shrugs, his eyes straying to follow Dan, Matt, Hale, and Vivian who are playing some sort of keep-away around the slide next door. I take a few more deep breaths, reveling in their freedom. The back of my mind is screaming at me to get back to work, but the majority of my brain is too rapturous in this new feeling, the weightless, liberated sensation, to listen.

The seconds seem to run together into one. My shoulders and brow relax for the first time in too long. I feel my hand tugging my ponytail out of my hair, and it swirls strangely around my face, catching the daylight in new ways. This brings a sense of spontaneity, and I kick off of the ground, pumping my legs to bring me higher in the swing.

After several minutes, I slow down, breathing quickly. The swing oscillates slightly, my sneakers trailing near the mulch.

"Having fun?" Ray asks in an amused voice.

Instead of retaliating, my thoughts pour in a jumbled mush out of my mouth. "This is so nice. I don't want it to stop. This from me, who never does anything unrelated to my job or school and always working and…. Well, it's just…" One hand twirls helplessly in the air, indicating a loss of words.

Ray's eyes shift from my fingertips to my face. "I don't want you to leave, either."

I sigh and glance up at the clouds blanketing the sky. They move lazily, unworriedly. I think I'd like to be a cloud.

"You could stay," Ray says suddenly.

"*Hmm*?" I pull my attention from the sky.

"You could stay," he repeats. "Here. With us. And me. You could study fighting." His voice gets faster, more excited. "It would be great. Ms. Rose obviously likes you. We all do. You wouldn't have to stress anymore and…" He looks at me expectantly. The eagerness in his expression almost pulls a yes from my lips right away.

Then I shake my head. "That might be great." *Would* be great. "Only…I don't think we could work that out. Especially with Shadow. He's paranoid about me being away for just two weeks." I let out a long, slow exhale. "At least, until I graduate… Then…"

"Then we'll have to get jobs," Ray says, facing forward again. "We won't have this." He pauses. "Freedom, maybe, is the right word. These are the best years of our lives, before we have obligations, jobs, huge responsibilities…"

"I already have all of that," I say, my frown starting to slide back.

Ray makes a face. "You always were a workaholic."

293

Suddenly he freezes, his eyes wide, still looking forward. I see his hands gripping the chains on the swing. Tight. "Always…" he murmurs.

The world seems to swoop around me. *No!* part of me screams. *He'll be in danger if he remembers! No!*

But the rest of me stays put, pleading, *Let this be it. Let it!* Because the only thing I want and will ever want is for him to remember.

I hear a faint whistling a moment before something hard and fast makes contact with my head, between my right eye and ear. I flip sideways off the swing in case there's another projectile. Instantly I roll to a crouch, my neck whipping towards the small line of trees separating the weather lab from the park. Wow. Who was the brilliant mind that put *trees* back here? Doesn't anyone have *any* common sense? Trees are too easy, too convenient for felons to make themselves unseen with.

"Mel!" Ray exclaims and pushes off of his swing to kneel beside me. One glance at his shocked face tells me it's over. Gone. His eyes are back to normal, though a bit startled. I silently curse at the person who threw whatever it was as I push Ray behind me, in case there are more.

My hand finds something that's not mulch on the ground. I pick it up. How original. It's a rock. More precisely, it's shale.

"Mel, what the–" Ray starts.

"Shh," I say. It sounds sort of choked. He was close, so *close*….

"Mel!" He grabs my shoulder and shakes me.

"What?" I ask distractedly. From the slide I hear laughing suddenly stop.

"Are you guys all right?" Hale calls, followed by a childish, "Shh, let them be," from either Matt or Dan.

"You need a nurse." Now Ray sounds perturbed.

"Okay… Good…" Slowly I get up, still shielding Ray, though it gets slightly harder when he stands up and is back to being taller than me.

"No, not good. Mel!"

"Later, Ray! We can take care if it *later*!" I snap back, leaning forward to get a better view around the trees. Shoot/phew. Whoever it was is gone.

I become aware of Ray's hand, still as a statue, gripping my shoulder. My words come back to me. "Oh," I breathe, driving my palm into my forehead. "Sorry! Sorry! I didn't… I mean…"

"That's okay," Ray replies, his voice sounding slightly strangled. Confusion races with chagrin inside my mind.

"No, no, no," I say to myself. If I can forget, and slip up like that, I need to get him out of here, back inside where it's at least more sheltered.

I guess it's good I think so, because Ray is already pulling me with him towards the door.

"Where are you going?" Hale demands, watching us.

"Nurse," Ray tells her before pushing open the door.

"I don't need a nurse," I mumble, letting my feet follow him anyway.

"I don't care," he says seriously. "A large piece of stone just grazed your head."

"So? I can handle it myself."

"It broke the skin."

I do feel a slight throbbing. I raise one hand to my head and see I'm still holding the stone. I hastily stow it in my jacket pocket and then probe where I felt it hit.

My skin stings beneath my fingers. I wince. If I were in any other company I would have automatically held my face still as marble.

"See?" he responds, sounding troubled. My fingers continue examining the wound.

295

"It's just grazed. Besides, head wounds always bleed more than other types," I say dazedly, my mind wandering back to the 'who' and 'why' aspects.

"Here we are." Ray leads me through yet another door.

Hmm. I've never been in a nurse's office before. It smells like antiseptic and rubber gloves. The floor is tiled pink-and-white. There're a few cots in the corner, and a middle-aged man sitting behind one of the desks, engrossed in a thick paperback.

"Hey, Jon," he says, looking up from his novel.

"Hi, Paul." Ray's hand moves from my shoulder to my hand.

"What happened?" the man—a nurse, according to his name tag—asks.

"Mel hurt her head," Ray replies, almost evasively. "Can you help?"

"Well, what am I here for? Come on over, Mel." Nurse Paul beckons me to one of the cots. I raise an eyebrow at Ray.

Are you sure?

He nods. *Of course.*

I lower myself onto the cot and Paul goes to work checking my 'injury'. Ray sits in one of the chairs in front of the desk, watching. I scowl at the floor.

Finally Paul finishes and voices his opinion. "It's just scraped, really. I'll just put a dressing on it for you."

Ha! "I can get it myself," I say, starting to stand up.

"Hey, it's okay. I have nothing better to do." Nurse Paul pushes me back down. I instantly shake him off, but remain seated, eyes on Ray. He shrugs.

"Okay," I mumble.

Paul pulls out a gauze strip and bandage and sets to work. I focus on the tip of my nose, not that it really hurts, just that it's something to do that's not staring too much at Ray.

296

"So what did you do?" Paul asks, pressing down the last section of bandage.

It takes me a moment longer to come up with something, since this is not the type of thing I normally encounter. But I answer with, "A swing hit my head. The side, the chain part."

Paul raises one eyebrow as he surveys the dressing. "That must have been one hell of a swing."

"Well, Matt pushed it," Ray says, casually jumping in. "What did you expect?"

"He *is* a league bowler," Paul replies, like he's agreeing. But he glances sideways at Ray, so I know he doesn't totally buy it. Oh well. Even if we've only leased our story, it's fine so long as he's not suspicious enough to put aside that novel long enough look into it. Or mention it to anyone.

On our way out, I see Paul clasp Ray on the shoulder and give him a small grin. Ray nods slightly, then follows me into the hallway.

"You know him well?" I assume.

"Yeah, sort of. Well…yeah." Ray pushes through the stairwell doors. "He's also Marvin's counselor." His eyes drop so they're staring intently at the steps.

"Awesome," I say.

Ray laughs quietly. "Thanks. I guess you could say he was my first friend here."

"He seems nice enough." It's true. Only I totally could have spared myself the indignity and applied a bandage myself.

"He is. Very." Ray looks at his watch. "I'm not completely off the hook. I have to work in the afternoon. But I have about an hour, so do you want to come up to my room?"

"Definitely," I reply, inwardly cursing the Richardses. We hike the rest of the stairs and hallway until we reach his door.

Rain

"No mail," Ray says after quickly lifting the lid of his little mailbox.

"Do you get letters often?" I step inside the room as he lets the lid drop back into place before closing the door.

"Sometimes," comes his answer. "Mrs. Ilene writes once in a while. She's completely computer inept, so she uses snail mail."

"Mrs. Ilene...the old Meteorology head?"

"Yep. And the woman I help with the plants. Meteorologist, resident botanist, and technology challenged."

"You haven't been there this week."

"No, I haven't." He shrugs out of his jacket and tosses it on his bed as I wander over to the armchair. "She gave me this week off, since I–was supposed to–have off of classes, too. I didn't want to, but she insisted. Her son was in town, anyway."

"Neat," is the response that comes out of my mouth first. "I mean, nice. Whatever."

"Yeah." Ray passes by his dresser, pulling out the top drawer. "I forgot to put on my compass this morning because Ms. Richards had me come in for a 'discipline meeting' at 6 AM. I'd better get it out now so I have it when I'm working later. Sometimes the compass helps me think." Frowning, he slides something in the drawer to one side.

"That's an early meeting," I comment. "What did she say?"

"She said I shouldn't have run off and it was irresponsible and a bunch of other very typical things." Ray's face suddenly darkens. "And then she tried to tell me I shouldn't trust you."

"Me? Not trust *me*? What's not to trust about *me*?" I say, the slightly joking tone covering shock and anger.

"You're from a spy academy, we don't really know anything about you, and you seem like you have quite a temper." Ray rolls his eyes. "Stupid. Though I did tell her she was right about the last one."

"Uh-huh," I mutter. "How nice of her."

"Exactly." He sighs, frowns, and crouches down, running his fingers over the floor. "What…" Then he looks under the dresser, stands back up, and pushes through the top drawer one more time.

"What?" I repeat. "What is it?" I swallow. "Jon?"

His hand is kneading the bottom of his shirt.

"*What?*"

He turns around to face me, biting his lip. "Mel, I think someone stole my compass."

22

"Stole?" I repeat.

"I always put it in this drawer," Ray responds, looking a little pale. I quickly run all the years I've known him through my mind. I can't recall him losing anything, especially not that compass.

I push myself to my feet and cross the room, feeling like I'm wearing blinders. The window fills my vision as I run my finger along the crack between the pane and the sill.

Dusty.

"Whoever it is, it's the same person who set my bed on fire," I murmur to myself.

"Mel? What is it?" Ray frowns as he watches me examine the window.

"They came through the door. They have a key," I say. "Who do you think…?"

"I don't know, I don't know," Ray whispers. "I've always had that…"

I spin around, intending to search for evidence in the drawer, but stop when I see Ray's face.

"Sit down. Head between your knees," I say immediately. He obediently curls up into the armchair I was recently occupying, hugging his legs to his chest, forehead down. His dark red bangs tumble down, shielding his eyes, but I imagine them squeezed shut.

"Sorry," he mumbles, gasping for air.

"Sorry? That's a stupid thing to say. Don't be sorry."

"It's just…I've always had the compass. It's sort of like a

lifeline for me," he continues, his voice muffled.

Instantly nothing else matters, nothing but making sure Ray's okay. I crouch beside the chair and place one hand gently on his right arm.

"We'll find it," I promise quietly.

Ray inhales deeply. After a minute, he lifts his head and props his chin on his knees. He stares straight across the room, but like he doesn't see the other wall at all. I feel the room sway around me. Is he okay? What's wrong? What am I supposed to do?

I almost faint when he snaps back to reality. His eyes focus again and he swallows. "That was so stupid of me."

"No way," I argue. "Never."

"Yes, it was," he insists. Before I can retort, he goes on. "I made it sound like the compass is my *only* lifeline. I forgot that I have two."

"Good. Where's the other one?" I ask, already half standing up to get it.

"Right here," he replies, dropping his legs and reaching out to grasp my hand.

"What?" I keep my arm steady so he can use it to stand up.

Instead of answering my question, he says, "Thank you," and puts his arms around me.

It's the first time I've really hugged Ray. My head rests comfortably on his shoulder, my own arms wrapping around his torso. I feel like I'm suddenly disconnected from my body, floating up with those gray clouds somewhere, while at the same time hyperaware of my surroundings. The confusion, the naturalness, the silence.

"This for helping you up?" I mumble.

"Silly," he whispers.

"But I…" I'm vaguely aware that I'm babbling, my thoughts too jumbled to form any sort of sense. "The compass...and you almost...and about the other lifeline..."

"Mel," he breathes, "*you* are my other lifeline."

I am? I am his other lifeline? *Me?* I'm having trouble processing the idea, partly because I'm trying to compare what that means to the way I feel about him.

Because, if we're defining lifeline as something that sustains life, something that keeps someone going, he's it. He puts more life in me and more in my life than anyone or anything else has. But what does lifeline mean to him?

We end up not reporting the stolen compass–yet. My excuse was that I wanted to track down clues without the nosey police in the way. The real reason behind me refusing any professional involvement was that, if this is something to do with Peter Manifred and the goons, and they hear the police were involved, it's potentially harmful to Ray.

I almost don't let Ray go to work on his (stupid) project. I want him in my sight, where I can be aware of more rock chuckers and take care of them. I want him safe. I don't want anything unexpected happening. I don't want him taken away again.

Then I realize I'm being paranoid and very self-centered. Ray is safe in the Meteorology lab, even if the company he's with leaves a lot to be desired. And he's good at this project. He enjoys it, even if he doesn't like the hours. And (not that this influenced my decision) I promised Caidy I wouldn't 'mess it up'.

So he leaves, and I make my way back to my room. Hale texts, asking if I'm okay, and I reply that I'm fine, absolutely fine, I just need to lie down and 'chill' for a little while.

Okay, a long while.

I'm still cross-legged on my bed, staring at my phone in front of me on the covers, ears straining towards the window and the Meteorology lab–though I can't hear a thing–when

Shadow calls.

"Hello." I bring the cell to my ear and tilt my head. From my room I can see the corner of the lab. Sometimes. If the wind is blowing the trees right.

"Hi, Amber. I'm just calling to check in before my flight leaves."

"Okay."

"I'll get there around eight in the evening tomorrow," he says.

"*Mm.*"

"You should try to be packed by then. You'll want a good night's sleep tomorrow. You have to get up early."

A good night's sleep tomorrow? What planet is Shadow living on? "Sure."

"Okay, then…" He takes a deep breath. "And while I'm on the plane and can't be reached…"

"*Hmm?*" I say distractedly, my eyes narrowing. Did I just hear a slight creak outside my door?

"…make good choices."

"Uh-huh. Yep. Okay. Gotta go. Have a nice flight."

"Amber?" He sounds sort of uncertain.

"Um, Lyv–I mean, Hale–is calling me. Bye," I say and hang up. Then I dash across the room and inch open my door.

Empty. Of course.

Cautiously, I edge out. No one's there.

I could have sworn they paused right at my door. The length of the creak proved it.

So what were they doing?

I pause, listening. No ticking–no time bomb. Good. Very slowly, I crouch down and examine the carpet and trim beneath the door, then the door itself. Nothing different.

The shiny metal mailbox catches my eye. Using the sleeve of my shirt, I gently lift the lid. Aware there might be something explosive in the box, I move back a step before rising on the balls of my feet to peer inside. People who put their eyes right up next to a crack are total idiots. You'd be blind before you could say "what the hey" if something blew up.

Nothing does, in fact, blow up. Me opening the lid only reveals the sheet of yellow notebook paper that is now inside.

So they were leaving me a message.

I pluck the paper out of the box and reenter my room, unfolding it as I go. Even though it's notebook paper, the words are typed.

Are you forgetting our deal? We are watching you, nosey. Closely.

I blink, then clench my teeth as my toes curl up in my sneakers. They're watching me? Well, of course they are. They're still there, and still threatening me. My breathing is shaky as I grind my molars against one another. And–*I'm* nosey? Excuse me? Who're the ones meddling in someone else's life? Before I'm fully aware, I've thrown myself down in the computer desk's wooden chair and am typing in the address of the site where I found Peter Manifred's information.

His number jumps out at me, and my fingers slam it into the keypad of my phone. It rings four times before his gravelly voice answers.

"Hello."

"Enough," I spit, "with the messages. And threats."

"Who is this?" he asks.

"Nice try," I retort. "Unless you're menacing multiple people."

"Menacing?" Pause. "Is this Amber?"

"That's another thing. How did you find out?"

"I asked. I thought you might have been staying there."

"Asked *who*?" I growl.

"That, like another matter, does not fall under the

category of 'your business'."

"Cut the crap and either answer or disappear off the face of the earth," I snap. "He never did anything to you."

"You–what? Amber, I fail to see your point."

"My point is, I'm going to figure out what is going on."

"I can't help you with that." His voice lowers. "But I've told you–don't try. I can't believe you're still following this. It could end badly."

"Like you've said a few million times. I am serious. I don't think you know who you're dealing with."

"Of course I don't. But neither do you, don't you see? Just listen to me, Amb–"

"I will if you tell me what you have against Jonathon."

"I have nothing against him."

"Really," I say sarcastically.

"Yes. Stop being impossible and just heed my advice, all right? Goodbye."

"Good*bye*? You are *so* not leaving until you–"

Click.

Muttering under my breath, I snap the phone closed and back open in one movement, redialing. He doesn't answer.

Well, says one of my voices, *I was right, at least. Something came to me.*

Great, I respond acerbically. Because, after that call, I now have more questions than answers. What was the not recognizing me about? Was it a trick? Denying everything, was that also a ploy?

It doesn't add up. For the first time, it seems like years of training have been wasted. They always said, 'get to the bottom of it, no matter what.' But what if it does matter? What if someone you care about more than words matters? And they're all in the middle of it? And it could–to quote Manifred–end badly?

What do you do then?

305

Rain
* * *

Breakfast is a quiet affair this morning.

Okay, it's not. It's loud and raucous. But Ray and I, sitting at the end of the table, are quiet. I'm too torn, too lost in thought, to speak. He doesn't seem to be too grounded either. And I think we're both aware that it's our last day, and we're wasting it with our silence.

But my mind is churning with yesterday's events–the frustration of discovering that, like the arsonist, whoever left the note was wearing gloves, and Peter Manifred's puzzling tones and responses, and the fact that tomorrow evening I might not be able to see Ray if I need to. That scares me the most, and I struggle to think about the first two.

Classes start right after breakfast, back on the normal schedule for the Marvin students. Hale and Viv make me promise to be at lunch. Matt says he'll miss me. Dan stutters something about me wearing a black shirt today and quickly runs away to return his breakfast tray. Leah nods at me.

Caidy smirks and looks away.

As we exit the cafeteria, Ray, books in one arm, beckons me to the side. We step away from the current of students.

He adjusts the collar of his dark blue sweatshirt, then says, "Today's it, then?" And sighs.

"Today's it," I say quietly.

"Does that mean you'll be really busy this evening?"

"Why?" I blink, trying to avoid falling into the pool his eyes seem to create.

"Well, I figured I'd put my idea in the suggestion box before you're booked." He grins. "I know it's overcast now, but I'm positive that by nine it'll be cloudless. Want to come up to my spot?"

"Yes," I reply instantly, using up the last of my oxygen. I quickly take a deep breath, wariness suddenly sweeping through me.

"Cool." His eyes crinkle up at the corners as he smiles, then waves, taking steps back towards the stream of kids. "See you at lunch."

"See you." I watch him head off to class.

The first thing I do next is head out to Peter Manifred's house. If I'm prepared, he and a million thugs can't take me. But I can get some sort of new lead.

I hope.

Oh, yes, that is a *great* plan. Only he's not *here*. I should have expected it, but it doesn't make me swear any less vehemently as I pound on his door.

Is he avoiding me? What's the point? He seems to think two idiots in a car can intimidate me. If he's that stupid, wouldn't he just answer? He answered the stupid *phone*.

I stomp my way back down the sidewalk, not saying sorry as I bump into some clumsy person. Not that I would anyway. No, I probably would, if I wasn't so upset. But I am, so I don't.

Something tells me wandering around the city won't get me anywhere, so I stop for a coffee and head back to Marvin. I spend the time until lunch packing and trying to figure out my next step. Police–out. Definitely would result in some sort of harm coming to Ray. Shadow–out. Same as police, and, besides, he's probably 3,000 miles (4,828 kilometers) over the Pacific right now. Manifred–MIA. Investigating–probably out too, since I'm 'being watched'.

Thinking–impossible.

With a huff, I flop back on my bed. Then I realize what I just did and swing myself back up. If nothing else, I can pack. Even though I don't plan on leaving at this point, it's something to do as well as avoiding a lecture from Shadow.

At lunch I am forced to swear I'll be at dinner, but other than that it passes similar to breakfast. Caidy continually smirks at me, which is irritating, but Ray hardly even glances at her, so that is gratifying.

More packing follows. Shadow calls, but I hardly register the conversation. All I know is that he's in Japan, and he's trying to engage me in some fluffy discourse, like should he get egg or vegetable sushi. I say "yes" and quickly end the discussion.

I need to get something figured out, but all I can decide is that, unless a miracle happens tonight, there is no way I'm leaving tomorrow.

I feel slightly better having resolved this. At least until I can get better bearings, if things stay at their normal level, some sort of stalemate, then it will be okay. I can have more time.

But still, by three o'clock I'm so tired of listening to myself trying to think that I do something I almost never do. I turn on the TV. The first channel is the news, which is fine with me. It sort of hums in the background as I scour my room for anything I might have left behind and then as I take a shower—well, I don't hear it then—and again as I absentmindedly reply to Hale's illicit texts. According to her, she is sending them under her desk as Ms. Daly 'goes on n on n on but i cant concentrate b/c the earrings shes wearing r just HIDEOUS'.

It's 5:51 PM when I actually look up at the TV again. Some dumb commercial for deodorant is playing. I snort at the utterly bogus spy portrayal in it and start to look away when the news show comes back on.

My eyes are drawn to the ambulance shown rushing up to the front of a hospital. A stretcher is unloaded, the patient rushed inside. The news anchor talks in the background. I reach for the volume and turn it up, interested in the crime. Then a name catches my attention.

Manifred.

Instantly I'm alert, leaning towards the TV. My mouth

drops as I hear more.

"Apparently he was driving his car back to his home in Spring Hill when someone fired at him. The shots did not injure Manifred, but he crashed into a street lamp as a result, and his shoulder is badly damaged."

Shot at? *Shot at?* Who was shooting at Manifred? Why? How? Is this live?

Yes, it is, according to the blinking red 'live' sign in the corner of the screen.

"Any news on the motive for the assault, Rosie?" The anchor asks his partner. They switch the camera view to her. She's standing in front of the hospital.

"None at all, Shen," she replies. "The local citizens are asked not to panic, the police are in pursuit, but anyone with information should call the number below."

More coverage follows, but none of the news stations can offer me any more. I begin to pace, waiting for a new segment to come on. Shot at? But not by the police. Manifred apparently has other enemies.

I watch eagerly as the next bit of news comes through. The police have identified the bullets. They're not from a pistol or handgun. They're from a shotgun. The would-be-murderers are serious.

I hear a ringing in my ears. No, wait, I hear a ringing because my room's phone is ringing. I dive across the bed for it. I don't recognize the number.

"Hello," I say in a low voice.

"Is this Amy?" A hoarse voice asks.

I narrow my eyes. "Maybe."

"Amber?" The voice sighs. "Good, I have the right number."

"Talk," I say sharply. "What do you want?"

"Amber, it's Dr. Manifred. I want you to come to the hospital to see me. I need to speak with you–now."

23

I walk straight through the hospital doors and to the room number Manifred gave me, ignoring the overly helpful nurses who attempt to get in my way.

I stop in the doorway of the room, though, when I observe doctors flitting around Manifred who is lying on a long bed surrounded by wires and tubes.

One doctor stalks over to me. "What are you doing here?" he asks, his eyes slit down at me, mouth and nose covered in blue paper.

My eyes widen. His sterile white outfit, the way he looks at me like I'm obviously not supposed to be here, and mostly his accent… Yes. He reminds me of the doctor who sent Ray away. The one who's brogue I couldn't place. But now I know: it was Australian.

"Let her in," a voice rasps from between the tubes and wires. The doctor barring my entrance glances over uncertainly.

"Dr. Manifred, I wouldn't advise…" he starts.

"I would," Peter Manifred counters. "Hear the 'Doctor' preceding my name, Phil?"

'Phil' glares at me once more, then steps back to let me enter. I walk over and gaze down at Manifred. His skin is ashy, brow drawn, salt-and-pepper hair damp with sweat. His shoulder is swathed in bandages.

"What?" I say.

"Could my niece and I have some privacy?" Manifred croaks. The doctors stare at him. He sets his jaw, looking quite formidable for a man of his condition. I am unwillingly impressed.

Once the doctors are gone, I fold my arms across my chest. "So, *Uncle*," I begin.

"I have to ask first," Manifred says, "can you shut up long enough to listen to a very complicated story?"

I scowl, somewhat out of surprise at the amusement I detect in his tone. "Shoot."

"Ironic," he says. "I was just shot at."

"Yes, *why*?"

"I'm not *sure*," he mutters. "But I think I know."

"Why?" I repeat aggressively.

"I am trying to tell you. This goes back to the shutting up part."

"So continue."

"I'm only telling you this because…you seem to care about Jonathon," he says.

"And you've figured that out from your little 'observations' of me, have you?" I sneer.

"Shush. I–" He stops. "*What?* Amber Rind, I have not been 'observing' you."

"'We are watching you, nosey,'" I quote bitterly.

"What the hell is *that*?" Manifred asks.

I blink. "What do you mean? *You* wrote it."

"I did no such thing." The furrow deepens in Manifred's brow. "It must have been them."

"Them who?"

"Them. The ones Bonnie…." He trails off, watching me. "*Do* you care about Jonathon?"

I swallow. "Yes. Very much."

He can't doubt my tone.

I'm half expecting a threat to follow, like "then stay out of it", but no such thing comes. Instead, Manifred takes a deep breath.

"Then I'm going to tell you. Because you need to know, all right? Maybe you can help. And besides, I have a feeling you'd try to find out anyway, which could land you in a lot of trouble."

I bite back the words, "Yeah, so? My *name* is practically Trouble," and let him go on.

"Two years ago," Manifred says, "when Jonathon arrived, I was working here at this hospital, in a certain wing. It's related to chemistry, only it's the study of poisons. It's not known to the public," he says, his voice still rough. My eyebrows inch upwards. Could it be I am getting answers? "At the same time, I was also dating Bonnie Robar."

My jaw drops. "His mom," I breathe.

Manifred doesn't hear, so he repeats what I said. "Bonnie Robar is Jonathon's mother. She was with me when he was brought in, sent by one of my correspondents in New York." My mind flashes to the doctor with the accent. "Jonathon was very sick, too sick for regular medicine, but I had the knowledge to try to do *something*. Bonnie persuaded me to treat him, but privately. She was sure someone had deliberately targeted him because of her project." Deep breath. "Even I don't know what it was, the project, just that she'd traveled to Brisbane to work on it with some partners.

"So I did what I could for him. It was about three days before he woke up. During that time I helped Bonnie fake his death and create Jonathon Lucas Carter. We sent word to New York that he had passed away due to the poisoning"–a shiver runs down my spine–"along with ashes from a gorilla's body that had been donated to our department." He laughs weakly at some memory, then his expression becomes solemn again.

"Bonnie stayed just long enough to see that Jonathon's–she called him 'Anthony'–memory had been lost, so her proximity wouldn't put him in further danger. But before she left, she contacted a former colleague of hers at the Meteorology department of Marvin Academy and smooth-talked Jonathon a position in the school. She knew he'd be well-cared for and safe there when she left." There's a gleam in his eyes as he talks about Bonnie. "She disappeared somewhere in Europe." Sadness tinges his voice. "I kept treating Jonathon–it took a month–and every day I hoped to hear from her, even after I got him safely to Marvin Academy. But I haven't corresponded with her in about two years." His eyes find mine and hold them. "Her parting words to me come back every day: 'Keep the secret, Peter–it could mean his life.'"

I fight to breathe, still locked on Manifred's eyes of steel.

"That's why," he says, "I was afraid, when you came around questioning. That's why I sent you the letter–the one warning you that something bad might happen if you pursued the issue." Another ragged breath. "But now someone else knows, too. I realized that when you told me about the multiple threats. I only sent one note, the one telling you to consider carefully. You've been caught, Amber, in the middle of me and the bastards who ruined my car."

"Thank you," I whisper. Everything suddenly seems to make sense. Except for the goons who are still threatening me, who still want something with Ray, and what the something is, and why. Okay, definitely not everything. But it's a big step towards it. "Is that why…you were shot at?"

"They know I know," Manifred wheezes. "That must be why. They know I know and they don't want you to know. Meaning, they already know, or they would've tried for information, not murder."

My head starts spinning. Not because what he said is confusing, but because it's upsetting. I'm the last to find this out. I still don't have all the puzzle pieces. And if whoever-it-is can shoot at an old doctor… I need to get back to Ray.

"Do you have any idea?" I ask. "Any idea at all who did it?"

"The ones who weren't supposed to know," Manifred says scratchily. "The ones Bonnie was afraid of."

I thank him again, wish him a speedy recovery, and leave as fast as possible, making my way back to Marvin with admirable speed. The cloudy twilight reflects my mood–some things are in shadow, others somewhat outlined, still others illuminated by the occasional street lamp. Every step and second that passes strengthens my resolve to stick right by Ray. Most definitely I am not going anywhere until this is resolved. You say I'm leaving tomorrow, Shadow? Bull.

I arrive back at Marvin around 7:20 PM. Sounds of dinner emanate from the cafeteria. I push through the doors and head for Hale's table.

She stands up when I reach it. "Mel, you promised you would be here," she huffs, putting her hands on her hips. "You're twenty minutes late and this is the last meal you're going to have here, so–"

"Hale," I say, fighting to control a sudden wave of irrational nausea, "where's Jon?" Because he's not here, sitting at the table where he should be during dinner.

Hale assumes a hurt expression. "How does that make a difference in the fact that you're–"

"He's in the Met lab," Vivian tells me, eyes on my face. "He and Caidy both."

Working. That's all it is. Working. "Okay," I mumble, backing up. "I need…I can't…I'm sorry." Before they can protest again, I turn and flee–I mean, run–from the room and back to my own.

I see that a piece of paper is taped to my door when I reach it. I grab it both eagerly and warily. It could illuminate something else…or it could be more 'conditions'.

But it's neither. It's from Ray.

Mel, it says.

We have to enjoy our last evening together. Meet me by the swings?

I immediately take it inside, my mind clouded with suspicion. The swings? Earlier he said roof. It isn't like Ray to change his mind, and especially not like him to not offer any sort of explanation for the switch. Also, there's no time on here, and that is most definitely un-Ray-like. He's pretty particular, annoyingly particular at times, never vague. And the note was taped to the door this time, not slid under it.

I rummage through my duffel bag and pull out the pair of pants I wore Thursday, the day we toured Brisbane, the day he left me the first note. It's still in the pocket—a deceptive way of storing things, because no one would expect a *spy* to be so 'careless' as to leave papers in dirty pants.

I spread the papers out and compare. My breath stutters when I find the differences; the *a*'s are more rounded in this one, the *m*'s aren't lopsided like in Ray's first note, and the crosses on the *t* 's are crooked while Ray's were straight before.

I suck my lip up to bite on, not even caring as I do so. So someone forged this new note, someone who has access to Ray's handwriting. Someone wants me at the swings.

Well, then. I'll be there.

Most people wouldn't realize that it's a fake in the first place. Of the minority that would, most of them would steer clear of the place indicated in the hoax, knowing it's probably a trap. Only a small percentage of aware persons would actually show up. And we're the smartest of all.

Because where there's a trap, there are trappers. And where there are trappers, there are answers.

I don't walk right up to the swings; that *would* be stupid. Instead, I loop around and move through the trees. I stop behind one and wait, casting my attention in all directions.

Five minutes later there's a rustle behind me. As I whirl around, a twig snaps. A figure emerges between the trunks.

That's when something grabs me from what is now behind. The figure in front of me lunges forward. I'm forced to duck him instead of twist away, and as a result my hands are strapped together with a plastic strip. Scowling, I start to—easily—twist them free, but in a split second something cool and smooth is being pressed against my wrists.

"This is a knife," someone says in a low voice. "If you don't stop fighting, we will cut you."

I take about a second to decide, then I stand still. I can always get out later. If I go along with them, I could be getting my answers. And that knife is positioned right over my radial artery. If I did get cut, it would be very distracting having to worry about all that blood while I'm working my way out of this.

"Good," one of the big-n-uglies says, stuffing a gag in my mouth. I make a face and reverse swallowing to push it away from my uvula. Gagging or throwing up would not be a good idea right now.

Forced to breathe through my nose, I try to appear slightly panicked. I'm actually pretty calm. I could spit this gag out right now. In fact, my tongue has already wriggled its way into position to do so. The strip will take hardly a second to remove.

The two men start to push me through the row of trees. I pretend to stumble, while actually trying to look at their faces. Damn! I think I'll sue whoever makes those ski masks. They're both wearing them, which leads me to conclude they're the same people who hijacked the taxi.

So now I wait and see what happens—whether I just bail when we get to wherever or stay quiet and listen.

They lead-slash-shove me to the edge of the trees and

beyond that, to a back door in a brick building. I twitch my head to the side, looking around. Even though I've never seen it from the back, I'm positive it's the Meteorology lab.

Inside is a small room with multiple storage crates that bear labels like 'barometers' and 'anemometers'. Oh, yes, it's the Met Lab.

Both doors–the one leading outside and the one I'm guessing leads back inside the building–are locked and the hands holding me loosen. I spin away to face the Masked Menacers, moving five steps backward as I do. Okay, fine, so yay for them. They have me locked in a room with my hands (temporarily) tied and them (temporarily) unidentified. But this infernal gag I will no longer tolerate. Hoping it doesn't tick them off *too* much, I force it out of my mouth and spit after it, trying to get the musty taste off my tongue.

"Do not scream," Masked Menace One says.

Scream? *Scream?* I almost choke on my snort.

MM2 grunts, tugging at the black cloth covering his face. "Damn mask itches. Can we just murder her now so I can take it *off?*"

"Go ahead, take it off, it doesn't matter," MM1 says, watching me. "Promise not to scream, kid?"

Ugh. I mutter something highly insulting under my breath, then nod once.

They both remove their caps. It takes me a moment to see their features in the dim light. When I do, my eyes widen. I recognize them both. One is the guy with roan hair who watched me at Roma Street Parkland.

The other is Avocado Man.

24

Both advance to stand on either side of me again. I discreetly place my thumb in the final position it needs to be to spring the plastic off.

"You're Maryanne's accomplice," I inform Avocado Man on the slight chance that, like in so many novels, it will launch him into a monologue.

He ignores me. Instead, the other man speaks.

"What is Jonathon's real name?" he demands.

That is both expected and unexpected at the same time. I'd assumed they knew. Obviously they don't. Which brings me to another question, what *do* they know?

My mouth is already one step ahead of me. "Well, I assume it's Jonathon, right? I don't know many names that 'Jonathon' could be a nickname for."

I feel the knife against my forearms again. How mighty you are with a blade, Avocado Man.

"Stop playing games," he snaps.

"You know and I know," the man with the roan hair says, "that you knew Jonathon before you came here. And you know his real name. *Full* name."

"I know his nickname," I reply immediately. "That's it. That's all anyone knew." Denying knowing him would be bad, since they obviously know that part and it would be pretty difficult to dissuade them without further knowledge of what else they know.

"Liar." Avocado Man presses the knife blade in harder. I feel a slight stinging before I block it out, focusing solely on the tip of my nose.

"It's true." I pretend to moan, hoping they'll think they're actually causing pain. "Anyway, what does it matter? I always used his nickname. So did everyone. It worked."

"What if I told you," Roan Hair tells me, "that none of this would affect Jonathon? It's just for a password. For...a project."

Project?

One more street lamp lights up. *Project.* Bonnie Robar's project? The reason she has enemies? The reason for...all of this. The reason Ray is in danger.

Ray, who will have no idea.

"Well?" Avocado Man's voice floats through my head.

"I've already told you," I say to buy time.

Roan Man crosses his arms over his broad chest. "Then tell me again. We know it's Anthony." I swallow down my surprise, hoping it doesn't register. "We just need...his middle name. Nothing too difficult."

Of course. Nothing of such little consequence would result in me being 'abducted' into this little room and threatened with laceration.

"He never told anyone," I say, then quickly switch off the subject, giving me some sort of time. "How did you find out, anyway?" Please monologue, please monologue...

"It was a nice surprise, actually. We had, uh, 'worked' with Bonnie Robar before–that's his mother, you know. But she was getting in the way. So I tried to kill Jonathon two years ago. Thought it would get his mother off our hands."

This causes my knees to go weak. I catch myself, fighting down nausea. I'm five feet away. Five feet away from the person who made life hell. I want to rip my hands away from Avocado Man's knife and use them to throttle Roan Hair.

Seemingly unaware of my murderous emotions, he

319

continues. "How nice it was when he showed up here, just after Bonnie was out of the way. Lucky, too. Of course, we weren't sure at first. But when you recognized him, it was a sure sign. Also, we saw he was wearing a familiar-looking compass. *Very* familiar looking, as we found when we borrowed it."

They stole the compass. Ray didn't lose it. Bonnie forgot about it, or... I recall the smooth blemish on its bottom. Or merely melted over an inscription?

"Let's try a new angle," Avocado Man suggests. "What if we promise to hurt Jonathon if you don't cooperate? Not kill him, obviously; he's the most skilled with the project. Would you talk?"

Swallowing down some bile, I work that out. So Ray has been working with the 'project' already. The project. The...project...that...Ms....Richards...has...been... making...him...do.

He doesn't know.

But they do.

I try to wet my lips, but my tongue is just as dry. "Why do you need his middle name...if he's already using the project?"

Roan Hair scowls. "He's only simulating. That's all we can do without the password."

"What difference will the password make?" I ask. Monologue, monologue, mono–

"Wouldn't you like to know," Avocado Man sneers. "So, what will it be?" I assume the knife digs in harder, but all I can think of is what if it were digging into Ray who never hurt anyone in his life and doesn't know how to block it out or even why.

"Jonathon," I gasp.

Roan Hair raises an eyebrow. "Meaning?"

"That's it. His middle name. Jonathon."

Silence. Then Avocado Man shrugs.

"All right," Roan Hair says. "Now, do we need to gag you again or can you be quiet?"

I clamp my lips together, glaring at the floor. My cheeks flush.

It's the first time I've ever given in.

They pull me down a hall and through a doorway into a room with a large machine in its center. Part of the device shields the room from view at the entrance. Roan and Avocado stop at one side of the door where we can see two people at the machine's controls.

Ray's back is turned to me. He doesn't know I'm here. *She* probably does, though she's not looking.

"Okay," Ray says, sounding slightly irritated. His hands are balled in fists under his chin, his elbows rest on the edge of the machine's control board, and he's staring up at the ceiling while his feet kick impatiently at the bottom of his swivel chair. He's clearly annoyed. "Can I go now? I need to eat dinner, and I have plans this evening."

It's completely irrational, but my heart lurches.

Ms. Richards shakes her head, leaning forward to tap on a key. One of the monitors above switches views. "Wait. Let's try one more thing."

Ray sighs and glances to the side, at the clock.

Look back! I want to shake his shoulders. *Look back and run!*

"I have an idea," Ms. Richards says. "What if you tried to set up a lightning bolt straight into the center of the Brisbane Airport?"

Ray makes a noise in the back of his throat. "Why would you do that?"

Ms. Richards shrugs. "It's just a simulation."

"I know, but still." Ray brushes his bangs off of his forehead. "I don't want to. It's not really the most humane way to be thinking. Besides, I told you, I have to go."

Ms. Richards exhales slowly, then catches Ray by the shoulder as he tries to stand. I freeze, completely still, as does he.

"And now *I'm* telling *you* that you *have* to do it."

"Do I?" Ray asks, his tone edging from irritation to anger.

"Yes," Ms. Richards says, completely serious. "You do."

Something in her voice makes Ray look up at her warily. "What?"

"It's not optional."

"I don't understand." Ray pulls away from her grip and quickly rises from his chair.

"Do it," Ms. Richards commands.

Ray backs away a step. "What's going on?"

"What is going on," Ms. Richards says slowly, "is you are programming that lightning bolt for me." She looks over at where I stand, flanked by my new bodyguards. "Do you have the password?"

Ray starts to turn, but Ms. Richards places a firm hand on top of his head, stopping him.

"Yes," Roan Hair says.

"Who's there?" Ray asks. He twists and reaches up to pull Ms. Richards' hand off of his head. She tightens her grip, entwining her fingers in his hair and catching his hand with her free one.

"Are you going to be difficult?" she snarls. "Do you need an incentive?"

"*What?*" Ray yanks his head away, wincing. Then his eyes widen as he turns and sees me. He gasps. "What the…"

His eyes hold mine for a moment. I try to arrange my face in an appropriate *RUN, YOU IDIOT* expression, but before I can he's started to leap towards me.

Ms. Richards reaches out and catches his wrist. Her iron

grip causes Ray to skid to a stop while still staring at me. Then he glances back at her, a look of fury on his face. "Let Mel go."

"The lightning bolt," Ms. Richards says.

"You do it," Ray says to her, his eyes focusing back on me. "Why do I have to?"

"You're just like your mum," Ms. Richards says. Ray's head turns automatically towards her again, his expression registering shock.

"My mom? You knew my mom?"

Know, I want to correct him. But I keep determinedly silent.

"Yes." Ms. Richards shakes her head exasperatedly. "You're both naïve. Stubborn. Can see weather in your head." Another long breath. "She designed the project that way. So only someone who saw it the way *she* did could use this thing."

"My mom *what*?" Ray gapes. "Designed…what?"

"The project. This. The simulator. Now it's your turn to use it." Her voice is smooth, her words Machiavellian and overall absolutely intimidating. If only she could scare me. Now she nods, still looking at Ray, and I feel Avocado man shift beside me. Light glints off of something, that something being the knife. He's menacing *me* with the knife.

Ray's eyes are almost inhumanly wide. My own eyes flick to the side. I see the blade is red. Oh. Well, I can understand how that might be a little unnerving.

I lock gazes with Ray. *Don't you dare do it.* I have only a vague idea of what would happen if he did, but I'm willing to bet it's not good.

"Come on, Jonathon," Ms. Richards says. She removes something from her pocket and sets it down on the machine keyboard, in front of Ray. His jaw drops as he stares at his compass. "You know that you want to make the lightning bolt."

"A *real* lightning bolt?" Ray says almost distractedly as he inches his right hand backward. I realize he's resisting the impulse to grab the compass. So instead, he looks to me "You can do that with this thing?" At the same time, his look says, *But what else can I do?*

"With the password, we can," Ms. Richards replies. "Unlike your mother, you can put this project, this compass, and your skill, to good use."

Run, I tell him. *Get yourself out of here.*

Ms. Richards' hand drags Ray into the swivel chair.

Are you crazy? he responds.

Just go.

No.

Slowly, while this is going on, I've slipped the plastic strip off my hands.

"Let's get rolling," Roan Hair says. He walks over to stand leisurely next to the machine to watch the proceedings.

Suddenly I realize why his hair color was so familiar–it's the same as Ms. Richards'. I look closer. Their noses have the same curve, both chins jutting, eyebrows all very straight. They're siblings.

"Will you do it?" Ms. Richards forces Ray to sit down again.

"No. He shouldn't be involved in the first place," I snarl at the same moment Ray says, "Only if you let Mel go. She's not a part of this."

"Yes, he should be involved, and no, we won't let her go, she knows too much," Ms. Richards replies.

Time. That's what we need. While I reassess the situation.

"Why do you want a lightning bolt in the airport, anyway?" I ask. "As long as he's doing it, he might as well know."

Ms. Richards settles herself in a sitting position on the edge of the machine. "Airports are ridiculously overprotected. The lightening bolt is such a perfect example of how our powers here can penetrate any defense. The bolt is strategically placed to cause extensive damage. No one could dismiss us as a fake threat."

Revulsion covers my face. "What do you have to gain from this?"

And not only that…. The room seems to tilt for a second. The airport. The airport Shadow will be arriving at any minute….

Ray's mouth widens. Clearly, he's about to protest. I quell him with a look. They have to keep talking. We have to prolong it as long as we can.

"Power, resources, wealth…. We could have anything." Ms. Richards shrugs. "Imagine Bonnie Robar's machine, with Jon at the controls, on our side. Certainly you *can* be imaginative here. Droughts, tornadoes, hurricanes, it's the unstoppable weapon."

"Bonnie…Robar?" Ray mouths.

"Your mum was a genius," Ms. Richards says to him. Seeing my raised eyebrows, she adds, "Well, we're going to tell him now anyway, and, frankly, the lying is tiring. Bonnie was so kind as to set everything up before she disappeared. The satellites, the magnets, the controls…"

Satellites? My eyes flick to Ray. His expression is stunned. *"Pink,"* he mouths. I blink. Pink?

Then I remember–that glimmer of pink I saw in the sky Friday. It was one of Bonnie's satellites.

Ms. Richards is on a roll. "All we need to do is work the machine and it will happen. Of course, we needed that password, which was very annoying to try to figure out. Bonnie made the clue something she thought only one of her colleagues could figure out. Like I said, naïve. Speaking of which, what is it?" she asks her brother.

"Jonathon," he replies. Ray's eyes narrow the same moment mine widen. This is why they couldn't risk him remembering. They didn't know how much he knew about the project before he was poisoned. If by some chance he remembered and recognized the machine and what it could do, he would never agree to program anything like the lightning bolt. If that had happened before the opportune moment, when they had the password and ability to make him do what they wanted....

"How did you know about the machine, anyway?" I demand. Time, time, time...

"Bonnie and I go...'way back'," Ms. Richards responds. "We used to be quite good friends...until her conscience got in the way. Or, rather, her blindness. She didn't see the true potential for this invention. It was only half-complete at the time, but she ran off with it. She left it in the hands of her colleagues at Marvin when, in an attempt to distract those who she thought were her enemies, she fled to Europe. Soon after, I located the project. Her colleagues, uh, took a permanent leave, so we have every right to be using Bonnie's project. As do you, Jonathon," she says, looking down. "It's rightfully yours...so long as you do what I ask."

This is Bonnie's project. This is why she was afraid for Ray, afraid of the enemies using him to get to her, or maybe she even knew about his ability to 'see' the weather in his head, and this is exactly why she took all the precautionary measures. Maryanne and Avocado Man, they were a part of it. They must have taken Ray's birth certificate for this reason. The other three they took were just to throw us off. I've been working on Ray's mystery all along. And now people are going to get hurt because of my idiocy.

Now we have to stop this. We have to get out of here.

What's first? I ask myself.

The knife.

I yank my arms upward. The blade flips against my skin so it's now resting flat on my elbow. Even if it does cut me, it'll only be a shallow scratch.

I spin around, out of Avocado Man's grasp, freeing myself from the knife in the process, and slide to his side. Before he can react, my hand flashes around and catches him just below the ear. He crumples to the floor.

Ray rises again. Ms. Richards jumps forward, making another grasp for his hair, but he knocks her hand away and steps back. I pivot to Roan Hair, feeling adrenaline spreading through me. I've been waiting for this opportunity....

Roan makes a lunge to recapture me, but I duck to the side. He crashes into a stack of old storage boxes, sending them careening and spilling their contents everywhere. Large metal objects, like old machine parts, skitter over the floor.

I quickly determine by the now-shallow rises of his chest, and also by his lack of rising from the floor, that Roan Hair has successfully taken himself out. I want to hurt him more. I want to poison him myself. But he is not the priority at this moment. There's still one more enemy.

My eyes move back to Ray and Ms. Richards. I suck a short breath through my teeth. Ms. Richards is leaning forward, poised to pounce. She won't, though, because Ray's crouched on the floor, one hand slowly closing around something that exploded from the boxes. With cool deliberateness, he stands up, raising the crowbar with him.

Ms. Richards' jaw drops.

"No," she says, like she can't believe Ray's actually considering what she thinks he's considering.

Ray sets his jaw, face harder than I've ever seen it. Then, eyes moving and locking on my face, he brings the crowbar over his shoulder and swings it down into the heart of the machine, irreparably destroying his mother's invention.

25

Within a split second, all of the monitor screens go dark, the light bulbs overhead fizzle and pop out, and a brilliant spark shoots through the now gaping hole in the machine.

Then everything's silent. Dead.

Before the shock has passed, Ms. Richards' furious shriek is ringing through my head. Ray has time to open his hands and release the crowbar, which is half-buried in the mess of metal and mechanisms, before she's upon him.

My feet push me over before my mind catches up. Ms. Richards slams Ray back against a pole. There's a flash of silver. A click. Then her surprised grunt as I grab her around the neck, pulling her away, choking off her oxygen. One second. Two. Five. She falls limp in my arms and I let go, sending her sprawling, unconscious on the ground.

Then I'm right in front of Ray, my hands on his shoulders, saying in a high voice, "Are you okay? Are you okay?" and one of his hands is grasping my arm as he says, "I'm fine, I'm fine. You, Mel?"

My hand has slid down his arm, to his wrist. A cool metal ring surrounds it. My jaw drops.

"She put you in handcuffs?" I say, my eyes dropping to them. His left wrist is, in fact, bound to the pole he slammed into.

"Thank god it's only that. Mel," he says one more time, his free hand resting under my chin as he looks at me, "thank you. I'm sorry–"

"Of course," I mumble. "Don't be, we don't have time.

We need to find the key for the handcuffs." I gulp and back away, almost unwillingly, then drop into a crouch next to Ms. Richards' limp form. The search of her pants and jacket pockets turn up empty. Since she's outrageously smart while she's so incredibly stupid, I'm seriously doubting she'd let, say, Avocado Man hold her keys. Now I'm debating between searching her brother (oh joy) and stripping Ms. Richards down to look for secret compartments in her underwear (even more fun) when someone runs into the room.

My blood almost freezes when I see Caidy, standing like a deranged (okay, pretty but psychotic) statue, in the doorway, gaping at the scene. I hear Ray inhale sharply.

"Mum," Caidy mouths, staring at her mother on the floor, then her face contorts with her signature rage, eyes burning into me. "What did you *do*?"

I'm still kneeling by her mom when she storms over. I see the lump in her pocket, right in front of my nose, and know where the keys are.

"Jonathon?" Caidy's saying. "Why aren't you…"

And I know she knows.

Her foot suddenly swings out, attempting to catch me in the face. I roll away in time, but she follows, towering over me, screaming now. "What did you do to my mum? Why did you ruin the project? You promised not to!"

Her bizarre forced promise comes back in a clearer sense. She was informed that this, forcing me to tell Ray's name, forcing Ray to make the lightning bolt, was going to happen.

And she didn't do anything about it.

Now I'm on my feet too, shouting over Ray's protest. "*Why?* Because I value the greater *good* over your stupid request, that's why!"

"You *idiot*!" she screeches. Her face is still twisting, going almost insane. I expect her to make a follow-up remark, but instead she draws back a fist and tries to punch me. I duck under her arm and push myself forward, sliding around her so I can reach my hand into her pocket and pull out a ring of keys.

She hardly seems to notice, just swings around, fist raised, trying once again to make a dent in my skull. I stumble backwards, surprised, but hold onto my balance.

"Caidy, *stop*!" Ray's insisting, trying to yank his hand free. But either Caidy doesn't hear or doesn't care, because she just keeps coming at me.

I honestly think she has cracked.

Which is when I realize the danger of having her madly trying to bludgeon me around Ray. He could get hurt.

And she wouldn't even notice.

After ducking another advance, I make my decision. To get her out of here and take care of her elsewhere, then come right back for Ray. I take a deep breath, estimate my distance, and throw the keys.

They skitter over, just beyond Ray's feet. I'm standing in the doorway. Our eyes lock for a brief moment before I dodge again.

"Mel," he mouths, starting to shake his head, guessing what I'm about to do–take on Caidy alone–but before he can finish Caidy's in front of me, unintelligible, dangerous.

I turn and run up the stairs.

She follows. She's away from Ray. She's madly rushing after me.

Good.

Outside in the cool air, everything starts to feel different. The sky is clear now, just like Ray said it would be. The stars cast little light down on the short area between the building, the trees, and the brick wall blocking off the alleyway. Shadows add to the darkness.

Normally, my opponent would stop, hesitate, and assess

the situation. Caidy doesn't. She just runs at me, like I'm a magnet. In the split second I have to act, my only choice is to leap onto the junk next to the wall and propel myself up on top of the bricks.

And she's right behind me.

The exertion of the climb should have slowed her down, but it hasn't. I work out regularly, and I feel a slight burning in my arms from the last heft. Caidy seems to be too full of adrenaline–or stupidity–to notice this.

She comes at me again. I can almost imagine her foaming at the mouth. I hold up my arms, blocking, moving, keeping my balance on the wall. My foot hits something metallic, and I realize there's a metal ladder propped up against the wall on the other side, the side of the alley. The deserted alley.

"Caidy," I say, "Caidy, stop, give up."

"No!" she yells. "No! You can't take everything from me! I won't let you!"

I have to block three more strikes before I can say, "What? Take everything from you?"

"You took my friends!" she cries. "You took Jonathon! And now you took my future!"

"You can have a different future," I tell her.

Any further conversation is suspended by one of her hands catching my windpipe. I stagger back, sucking in air, head spinning.

And she's everywhere. This is nothing I've dealt with before. There's no reason, no logic in her moves, only a reckless, violent frenzy. I can't anticipate anything. I'm using all my energy trying to block, not getting in any offense while she continues to break through and I'm spinning like mad trying to find her, but she's here then there and not anywhere while she's all over. We've only learned to anticipate the next move of our opponents and block it, then attack, which is second nature for me.

I stumble and fall, tearing a new cut into my forearm. It hurts, and I can't concentrate on my nose because I have to concentrate on Caidy. But I can't find her though she's still finding me, and now my jaw is aching and my shins are screaming and my collarbone is throbbing–

I try to stand, but my knees buckle, and I can't force them back up. The onslaught pauses for a moment. My eyes pick out Caidy's face inches in front of mine. Her eyes glow in the dim light, mad, savage, triumphant. Her hands are on my shoulders, pushing. I reach up to yank them away, but suddenly the world is spinning, a blur of darks, and my head is colliding with something hard and metal, and the rest of me is tumbling against the ladder until the ground rushes up and meets me, forcing every last particle of oxygen from my lungs.

I struggle to remember how to breathe. Now all of me hurts and my skull is too wrapped in pain to tell the rest of my body to move–not that it would listen, anyway. I can only lie here, on my back, trying to breathe as I stare at the stars–the same stars Ray showed me a million years ago Friday night when we were both safe and uninjured–and wait for Caidy to find me. My mind casts around for something, anything, to focus on, something to motivate me to get up.

My mind lands on Ray. Immediately I'm lost in memories, one's I've been suppressing for years, and they flash through my mind with more clarity than the pain in my body.

Once the film reel in my head is done playing, I blink. I can–no, I *will*–get up. And when Caidy comes, I'll be ready.

What's taking her so long?

Struggling to suck in enough air to push myself up an inch without succumbing to dizziness, I move my arms and slowly arrange myself in a sitting position. I become aware of sharp pain in my spine. But I have to ignore it. I crawl away from the end of the ladder, propping myself up against the wall, in a shadow. Next to the wall on my left are numerous dumpsters and bags of garbage. The wall of the building to my right is solid brick.

Deep breath, I instruct myself, which is immediately followed by *ouch* as my diaphragm protests. But, inch by inch, I raise myself up, using the wall for support, until I'm standing.

Which is how Caidy, bounding down the ladder, finds me.

She's breathing heavily, too. Still? After her nice little break? But if she has any ailments, she doesn't seem to be aware of them. She walks towards me, rapidly, but not in the same frenzied manner. Maybe she's calming down enough to kill me nice and slowly.

No, I contradict myself. *No. She won't kill you.*

Because what would happen to Ray? He doesn't know the full story. It's his word against Ms. Richards and her brother and Avocado Man. Ms. Richards could easily lie and say that Ray's story is a product of his 'condition' as well as overstress. They'd be too smart to leave my body in plain view, and by the time it was found it could be too late.

No one would ever know what they did to Ray.

I'm able to use determination to counterattack. As Caidy starts to come at me again, I hook my foot around her back leg and shove. Unable to catch herself, she topples over. But something's wrong. Somehow she's grabbed me, too, and I'm crashing to the ground again with Caidy on top of me. One of her knees is on my chest, suffocating and restraining me. Her other knee is on my right arm, cutting off its circulation. I feel my hand grow cold, then start to tingle, as Caidy points the knife she's clutching straight at my temple. *What is it with knives tonight?*

"See," she says, her voice low and shaking from either adrenaline or anticipation. The frenzied look in her eyes is evident even in the darkness. "Training, your stupid skills, they can't save you. Fighters don't always win." She licks a fleck of saliva off of her lips.

I bite my tongue in case a retort rises to the tip of it. Provoking a potential murderer–never a good idea. My head spins with a thousand lessons, each of them seeming more useless than the one before. Caidy is right. Caidy is right.

Caidy's head whips to the side as the ladder rattles. A shape stumbles down the rungs.

"Jon," she whispers.

"No!" I scream, fear suddenly engulfing me, fear because Ray is once again within range of Caidy.

"Be quiet," Caidy warns, eyes flashing as I struggle to get up, despite the knife, despite her on me, despite the fact that I could die any second.

Ray's bent over, gasping for air, hands clutching his ribs. But lower, not where a stitch would be. No. He's already hurt. No.

"Stay where you are," Caidy commands him.

Ray's face, etched with horror and fury and shock, takes in the scene. Me on the ground. Under Caidy. With a knife to my temple.

"Caidy, don't," he gasps, obviously still too stunned to understand that Caidy is beyond reason. I try to communicate this with my face, but it's too dark and my face hurts too much to do it properly.

"I have to," she retorts angrily.

"No," he says, his voice hoarse, exhausted, scared. "You don't."

"Yes I do!" She sucks in a breath. "As long as she's around, you'll...you'll go away...you'll go back...you won't...be with...me," she splutters.

"But nothing could change the fact that..." Ray stops himself. He's looking at me. "That..."

His expression is changing. Changing from restrained to outright pain and–something else. "That I already..."

"No, you don't!" Caidy's shouting again. "If she were out of the picture–"

This is about Ray and me? Simply about her obsession for Ray reaching the point of murdering me because we spend too much time together, are closer to each other than to anyone else, and maybe even...?

Ray puts a hand to his head, pressing his palm against his cheek, fingers twining in his hair.

The other hand is clenching the bottom of his shirt.

"No..." he protests, still staring at me, still wearing that expression.

"You can change your mind." Caidy heaves a few deep breaths. "Or...I can change it for you." She glares down at me. "It never would have come to *this* if *you'd* stayed in *America.*"

But it's not her wild accusations that save me. It's one word, so completely familiar to me that I don't have to think anymore.

"Mel," Ray says, his voice ringing with lost recognition.

My adrenaline finally kicks in. My eyes flick around the surroundings again, looking from a different angle–strategy. I finally notice that Caidy's leaning forward, her knee–which is currently half-suffocating me–supporting most of her weight.

Her voice, whatever Caidy's saying now, is just a buzz. It doesn't matter. Not if she sees me flex my arm like I'm about to move it. Not if her eyes are drawn there like I want them to be. Not if, as soon as she looks, I'm successful in snapping my own knees up and ramming them into her back.

Her displaced weight sends her tumbling forward, over my head. In her surprise the knife slips from her grasp. I feel it slice down my cheek, and with it, the accompanying rush of warm blood that spills out.

As soon as Caidy's off of me I struggle to my knees, but that's as far as I get. Ray's already moved forward and grabbed Caidy, yanking both of her arms behind her back. She hardly notices, only rips away and looks around wildly, stopping when her eyes alight on the knife resting on the asphalt next to me.

Ray grasps her arm again, flinging her away, towards the other wall. Caidy stumbles backwards over the garbage bags and disappears, landing somewhere among them with a dull thud.

She doesn't stand back up.

I try to rise, but find my muscles unwilling and unresponsive. My legs shake like mad. So I can only sit here, listening to Ray panting a few yards away, waiting.

Nothing.

Caidy must be unconscious. Which means, for now, we're safe. Ray is safe. I start to droop back down in relief.

Instantly Ray is kneeling by me, his arms wrapping under mine, supporting me. I feel my hands lock automatically behind his back. My head is resting against his shoulder. The sweatshirt he has on is soft. Warm. Safe. I squeeze my eyes shut.

"I'm sorry," he whispers.

I shake my head, trying to tell him that it's stupid to apologize. But, feeling this isn't adequate, I mumble, "You saved my life." And I don't feel the shame that should accompany those words, only a deep, burning gratitude. And more.

"You need something...for your cheek..." he murmurs, wrapping his one arm more tightly around me, freeing the other. He lifts it to my face and gently presses the sleeve of his sweatshirt to my smarting cut.

As he does, he feels more important, more significant, more treasured to me than anything else. I've had the feeling before, but now it just overwhelms me, intensifying as I realize how close I came to losing him.

I clench my teeth against it, trying to build the barrier, trying to hold off the flow. I'm so preoccupied I don't notice I'm crying until the first tear reaches my lips and I taste the salt.

Another drop slips down, then another. I struggle to stop, but my breathing is all shaky and my stomach feels hollow and I can't even see anything except for a wet blur of color.

I do *not* sob. But I can't stem the gush of tears, since my hands don't want to unclasp. So, one-by-one, and then in twos, and then finally too quickly to count, the drops fall, creating a stain in Ray's shirt.

And he doesn't say a thing, only presses me closer to him, offering all the support I need. Because he understands. He understands everything.

It only takes a few minutes to spill out every tear I've held back since the funeral, but it seems exponentially longer to me. Finally I can lean back to look at him again, pulling one arm out to wipe away the last stray droplets.

"Aargh," I mutter, my throat feeling swollen. The cut just above my wrist from when I scraped it is caked with dirt and gravel along with blood.

"What?" Ray asks quietly. "I didn't see that."

"You didn't see it," I say in a fairly steady voice, "because it was behind your back, bleeding into your sweatshirt." I push up onto my knees, my hands on his shoulders for support, and look at his back. A dirty brown and burgundy stain streaks across the material. "Shoot. Sorry."

Ray shakes his head, his hair brushing my cheeks as I struggle to keep my face composed. "You're *bleeding,* and all you can worry about is my *shirt?*"

"Well, I..." My words of defense are lost as my gaze travels across his face, taking in the details through the dimness. A welt beneath his cheekbone. A crimson-lined tear in his sweatshirt over his lower ribs. A clumped section of hair, dried blood making it stiff. A bleeding lip.

"I'm fine," Ray says too quickly, seeing where my eyes are pointed. I cautiously probe under the bloody part of his hair, wincing when he does.

"How?" I demand, only it comes out as more of a plea.

"I..." he hesitates. "Caidy..."

"You were fighting with Caidy? When?" My mind reels. If she beat me, then Ray, who hasn't had training in nearly two years....

"Right after she pushed you." Ray's voice is tight. "I tried to come get you, but she wouldn't let me."

I'm glad I'm sitting, because I need all my energy to repress the scream of rage building in my chest. *She got what she deserved,* the rational side of me says, glancing over at the trash bags. But the rest of me almost feels like picking up that knife and going over and giving her *more* of what she deserves.

Almost.

Because I've seen too much blood tonight. And a tiny, infinitesimal part of me feels...sympathy. Because in reality I *have* taken everything from her, even if unintentionally, even if I had to.

Especially Ray.

Ray.

He's the reason I'm alive now. If he hadn't said that one word, my name, then I would never have had the strength to...

The moment he said my name rings through my mind. I gasp, my head jerking up, to look him in the eyes. What I see makes my jaw drop, my fingers contract.

"Ray?"

"Mel," he mouths back.

My limbs start to feel like butter, but I force myself to keep my head upright, still astonished. "You...you know that it's you, that you're..." My voice sounds oddly strangled. He nods slowly. "How..."

"I let him out," Ray whispers. "Me. I let me out."

"The tide," I say. "The one you were fighting against."

"That was him...me...Ray.."

The silence stretches for a few seconds before the emotion swoops down on me and the tears come again, this time accompanied by odd gasps–sobs. But I don't do anything to stop them, just let myself cry into his shoulder, his arms around me, telling me it's safe and he's back and I finally have my best friend again.

26

I'm still crying, squeezing the life and probably death out of Ray, and hardly making an effort to control myself, when we hear it. The clang, the unmistakable sound of the ladder moving.

Ray's head jerks around, instantly looking at the trash bags. There's no disturbance there. I struggle to lift my head so I can look too, irrational trepidation engulfing me.

A light swings around the alley. Ms. Richards? Avocado Man? Roan Hair? Have they come to find us?

Ray catches his breath.

"Them?" I try to speak louder than a whisper, my voice broken by unsteady breathing.

"No." I feel Ray's arms contract in surprise, but I don't mind—it's better support, being closer to him. "It's...it's...." He gasps.

"W-w-what?" I stutter, the words not coming right. I try to squeeze the water out of my eyes so I can see. Before I achieve vision, the clanging starts again, and I hear the thud of someone jumping onto the asphalt. Then a frantic, uncontrolled shout.

"*Amber!*"

I free a hand to rub over my eyes, head spinning in confusion. As I begin to straighten up in Ray's arms, someone else—a tall someone—falls to their knees beside us. "Amber— what—why are you—*what happened to your face?*"

The person's hands are yanking Ray away and he falls back unresistingly. But I want to protest. I want Ray to tell me why and who is pulling me against them, cupping my face in their hands, fingers searching over it for injury....

"I...told you...to be...careful," the person says, more breath than voice.

"Shadow?" I mumble.

"Amber, what?" he demands. "What made this cut?" His thumb softly traces the edge of the knife slash, but I can feel how stiff his fingers are. "And...." There's a low, slow inhale as he sees everything else on my face. I move my arm slightly, rotating it so the cut on the inside is hidden against my jacket.

His torso turns when I don't answer, his eyes now glaring at Ray. Groundless fury causes him to spit, "What did you do?"

Ray stares at him, then mutters, "I was too good at meteorology."

I don't think Shadow even hears, his attention already sliding back to me.

"Amber, please tell me," he begs, pushing my hair gingerly away from my facial injuries. The flashlight he holds illuminates the side of my head, but not my eyes, which is good. I'm sure they must look crazy as I try ineffectively to focus on his face.

"I was attacked," I manage. The words sound too low.

"Attacked?" The meaning sinks in. "By *who*?" Shadow's eyes snap to Ray.

"No!" I shake my head, feeling it pound. "Not Ray. It was Caidy–a student–"

"A *student* attacked you?" Shadow's voice rings with anger and incredulity. "Where is she?"

Silently, Ray points to the garbage bags.

"And you," Shadow says to him. I can tell he's trying to keep the hostility in his voice to a minimum. I squirm slightly, wanting to move back, to have Ray hold me again.

341

But I recognize that I need to stop sniveling and find a way to support myself. "What part did you play in–" Shadow stops, looking from me to Ray. "Amber… You said *Ray*."

I nod painfully.

"I thought I told you," Shadow says, sounding almost scared, "to drop that."

"But I was right," I argue, though feebly.

His eyes narrow. "You were right?"

I nod again, forcing my head to stay steady.

"You *are* Anthony?" Shadow demands, looking again at Ray.

Ray hesitates, brow furrowed, then says, "I am."

Shadow makes no effort to keep the skepticism off his face.

"It's true," I say with more force than before, moving so he is only holding me and I'm no longer leaning against him.

"But how…"

"Not now," Ray pleads. "Mel needs a doctor."

"Right," Shadow says after a moment. "And we need to do something with…Caidy."

Suddenly he lifts a trembling hand and pulls me closer to him. The gesture surprises me. As far as I can remember, Shadow's never really hugged me. In fact, I can remember only one time he did, the day Ray died. But that wasn't like this. That was an embrace meant to comfort me. This hug is more urgent. Comforting him more so than me. Reassuring himself by holding me as close as he can. Saying I'm so glad you're okay. Saying I care about you.

It's only a moment later when Shadow pushes me away slightly. "Now. You need medical attention."

"Ray too," I say, trying to blink the world into focus.

"Him as well?" There's surprise there. I set my jaw indignantly.

Shadow turns the flashlight onto Ray, who winces away

from the brightness. I try to free an arm to lower the beam, but Shadow has me pinned to him. I watch his eyes widen as they take in Ray's injuries–and then his features.

"You didn't believe me," I accuse.

"I didn't." Shadow lowers the flashlight and stands up, gently raising me with him. One arm supports me while I unsteadily find my footing.

Shadow extends the other hand to Ray, who accepts and stands, cautiously but steadily.

"I'm sorry," Shadow tells him, still staring.

I open my mouth to tell him he should be sorry, sorry for not believing me, but as my gaze finally focuses on the trash bags, another sentence comes tumbling out.

"What about Caidy?"

I see Ray grimace in the slight glow that reaches his face, sharing the anger that makes my voice shake. Shadow perceives the tremble as fear and squeezes me closer.

"We can't risk her getting away," Shadow says. "She needs justice. And some psychiatric help. What…what did you do to her?"

"She tripped," Ray replies. "She's unconscious."

Shadow purses his lips, a struggle going on in his mind. After a minute he speaks, forcing the words out, though clearly unwilling to say them. "Maybe if…" He hesitates. "Anthony? Do you think you can get Amber–and yourself– back to your infirmary? And when you get there, call the police and tell them where I am."

"And where Ms. Richards is," I add, though I'll be there. Ray's already nodding.

Shadow braces himself. Then he reluctantly loosens his hold. I step back.

My face twists with pain as my spine supports my upper body. When I fell off the ladder I twisted something the wrong way.

Instantly, both Ray and Shadow are next to me. Someone's hands are against my back, helping me stay up, but someone else's arms are wrapping under my shoulder blades. I lean towards them, into Ray, gritting my teeth.

With a nod to Shadow, Ray moves out of the alley and around it, back to the street, and through the park to the door of Marvin, supporting me the whole time.

He's always close by. Throughout the blur of calling the police, having Nurse Paul check me over and dress my wounds, and being forced to lie down while people come and go, I just let myself drift, eyes locked with Ray's.

Police come, flooding the infirmary. Shadow is back, telling me that Caidy has been taken away and an officer says they have the three adults from the Meteorology lab in custody. Police start talking to Ray and Shadow, asking for the full story of events, and I suddenly remember that only I know everything that happened.

I have to use energy to shout to make myself noticed above the chaos. Everyone in the room turns to look at me.

"I know," I say.

An officer kneels by the bed I'm on. I push myself up on my elbows. Ray stands and pulls a pillow from another bed, sliding it in behind me. I lean back, taking a deep breath.

"You know what happened," the officer clarifies.

"Yes," I say. And slowly, carefully, I give them the details. How Avocado Man (who I describe as the taller man) is Maryanne's accomplice and they were trying to get information on Bonnie Robar in New York. How Roan Hair (the shorter man) attempted to murder Ray ("Jonathon") and how he and Ms. Richards (the woman) were trying to use Bonnie's invention for personal gain. How Caidy (Ms. Richards' daughter) attacked us because she was infuriated that we ruined the machine.

I leave out the parts that are most important–the parts

about Ray. The part about him being the only one who could work the machine, the part about him being the reason I could finally knock Caidy off of me, the part about him coming back.

After I'm done, I feel far away, a million miles (1,609,344 kilometers) from the room. I lay my head back, staring at the ceiling. Someone moves a glass of water into my line of vision. In his other hand is a pill. I shake my head, pressing my lips together like a child.

Ray's face takes the place of Paul's arms. "Mel," he says distantly. His fingers rest on my forehead. Comfortingly. "Please?"

For Ray. I slowly move my hand up to take the pill and place it in my mouth, and swallow the water. Then I watch Ray until the world dissolves into the weightless state of a drugged sleep.

The only things glaringly different are the lighting–this time grayish, muted–and the position of the bed–head facing the door rather than the left wall. Otherwise it's almost exactly like waking up the night after Ray was poisoned. Like then, I have no recollection of being placed in my bed. And, like then, there's someone waiting for me.

It's not Miss Collins, though. It's Shadow.

Seeing my eyes fluttering open, he moves to sit on the edge of the bed.

"How do you feel?" he murmurs.

"Beat," I say, my voice cracking on the words. The word has both meanings for me. Tired and defeated.

"I'm sorry," he whispers, reaching out to tuck a stray piece of hair behind my ear. His fingers brush the long bandage running from my temple to the edge of my chin that covers stitches I received in the ER. My memory of that experience is fuzzy at best. Everything that occurred after I

345

swallowed Ray's pill is more like a mass of colors and sounds swirling through my brain than actual remembered facts. I figure I must have been seen by a doctor, though—who else would have stitched me up?—and I kind of recall getting X-rays.

"Anything I've missed?" I ask weakly.

"I'm not sure how much you remember about the hospital," he says. "You tore some muscles, and there's severe bruising to your spine." I automatically shift my back and realize I'm wearing a thin plastic brace that limits my movement from side to side. "The cut on your face will leave a scar, but it's not deep enough to affect the nerves. The rest of your wounds are minor." Shadow's face says he isn't happy—understatement of the year.

"Oh," is all I come up with. Then, "Ms. Richards? Caidy? Roan—I mean, Ms. Richards' brother?"

"Being detained while awaiting trial. Caidy will probably have to go to a juvenile detention center. And who knows about the others." Shadow's scowling, upset. "They have also located another man, Greig Prentiss, who claims he was only doing work for pay and knows nothing about this."

That covers everyone—Avocado Man, Roan Hair, Ms. Richards, Caidy, and even the third man who helped 'kidnap' me at Goodwill Bridge.

It's quiet for a while. Then I find myself asking, "Do Hale and Vivian know?"

"What?" Shadow asks.

"My—my friends. Do they know what happened?" I think about Leah, too, and how the Caidy news will affect her, because I don't believe Leah was involved with any of this.

"I think Ms. Rose is planning to talk to her students later this morning," he says.

"But Hale and Viv, they probably went looking for me early this morning." I can see them doing just that, running around, up to my room, trying to catch me before I leave so they can say goodbye. The idea makes me feel a bit better.

"There were a few teachers walking around the school then. They might have run into your friends and told them to stay away," Shadow says. "We wanted you to be able to sleep."

"Where's Ray?" I ask.

Shadow's still not adjusted to the news of Ray's reincarnation, thus the rapid blinking. Then he answers, "Anthony is also sleeping–at least, that was the plan. He needs to heal as well. You've both had a big night." He pauses. "How awake are you?"

"Awake." I feel like talking, getting all the foggy confusion cleared away.

"Do you mind telling me…. There were some things you didn't say last night, weren't there?"

"To the police?" I ask.

Shadow nods.

"There were." And then I let everything out, telling Shadow the most important parts, a pressure lifting from me as I do.

His breathing is tight when I'm done, trying to process this. Finally he takes my hand.

"I am so sorry," he apologizes for the millionth time. "Sorry I didn't believe you, that this happened, that you had to go through this. I never wanted it to be this way."

"Who did?" I ask.

He shakes his head.

"How did you do it?" I ask. "Last night, how did you find us back there?"

"I'd gotten off my plane and found Marvin," he says, "but you weren't in your room and no one seemed to know where you were." He winces. "I was almost going crazy. Then this girl asked if I was your principal. And when I said yes, she told me you might be with someone, but she didn't say who."

I imagine Hale trying to assure Shadow that I was all right without giving it away that I was with 'a boy', and I feel a rush of gratitude.

"Then the lights flickered. I waited for you for another ten minutes after that, but then I couldn't stand being inside, so I went out. I walked around those trees behind that park equipment, and saw the junk by that wall strewn all over the place, and just thought, what if..." He shudders. "So I looked. Thank god."

"Thank you," I say. "Though...well, I guess it would be pointless to tell you that you were overreacting."

Instead of a snappy comeback (not that he's good at those), Shadow leans forward, still holding my hand. "I don't know what I would have done if I'd lost you, Amber."

My snappy comebacks aren't very quick today either. So I blurt out something I've been wondering for years. "Why do you do that?"

"Do what?" he asks, and sounds almost wary.

"Call me Amber. No one does but you."

Shadow looks at me for a long time. Then he says quietly, "Because when you were born, your mother held you in her arms and said to me, 'Isn't she a jewel? My little piece of amber. She fits her name perfectly.'"

There's a pause while I try to absorb this never-before-heard piece of information.

"She had a bracelet," Shadow continues, "that had amber beads. It was her favorite stone."

"You were there?" I say finally. "When I was born?"

"How could I not have been?" he seems to ask himself.

I stare at him, the underused part of my brain that tells me when I'm missing very obvious things screaming at me. But it's incoherent.

"How did you meet my mom?" I ask. I never have before. Usually I avoid talking about my mom, especially with Shadow.

"I was a professor at UCLA," he says. "When we first became acquainted, I thought she was taking night courses there for a third bachelor's degree in education. That's what she wanted me to believe." His eyes stay focused on my face as he speaks. "She pretended to be enamored by the attention I gave her, though who wouldn't have paid her the same attention? Smart, witty, beautiful as she was... Just like you," he tells me. "We spent time together during the days. She always asked me about my work, about the school. I was happy to give all the answers I could. I never dreamed she was really investigating, trying to solve a homicide connected to our university. We didn't even know it *was* connected. Only your mother could have determined that." He's smiling now, just slightly.

"Then it was solved. She'd finished. Her work in California was done. We met one last day. Took a walk in one of the community parks. And then...she told me everything."

"She told you?" My eyebrows fly up in surprise. I've only ever heard my mother described as smart. Certainly telling Shadow that she was a top-secret-off-all-records spy would be under the category of 'dumb'. "Why?"

"Because...." Shadow grimaces, eyes dropping to his own lap. "She loved me."

"She...." I'm unable to finish the sentence.

"Loved me," he repeats. "And I her. She convinced me to come back with her, use my credentials to become a teacher at Watson so I would become a part of her network. She helped me seem like the perfect candidate for a job there."

I blink very slowly, trying to fit all of this in with my

image of Shadow. "And then…how…."

"No one ever knew about our relationship." He's whispering now. "Her job was so completely off the record that we could only be 'friends'. But we broke the rules." His eyes lift back to my face. "Our anniversary is April nineteenth."

"Anniversary?" I swallow.

"There were no guests at the wedding," he resumes. "And we destroyed the certificate afterwards. We used false names, but to us it was important to have the ceremony. It was as official as it could be." His face is lost in the past. "She was wearing a simple beige dress, and her hair in a bun. Her hair was lighter than yours–blonde. You have her mouth, though, and her chin, the proud chin. Her eyes were so similar to yours, only yours have flecks of gold in them. Hers were just green, like the sea after a storm." One of his palms swipes quickly across one of his own eyes. "And no one was there to see her.

"She wasn't supposed to have kids. It wasn't written in her job contract, but it was an unspoken rule. When she realized she was pregnant, your mother took a leave and came to stay at Watson. We played our parts well. No one suspected we were more than friends. Miss Collins was there–I think the only remaining teacher who was. She helped your mother after classes had ended. I was grateful, and even more so when I overheard her and an old teacher, Mrs. Osbourn, discussing whom the father might be. Miss Collins unknowingly made a very good argument that would deter suspicion away from me or anyone at the school."

My head is starting to spin. I squeeze a fistful of blanket with my free hand, unable to take my eyes from Shadow's face, or he from mine.

"You mother decided to leave you at Watson when you were born. She liked the community, and you would be with me. At the time I was only a teacher, not yet principal. That's how it was when she went back to her job." Shadow's eyes are reflecting the grayish light. "She loved us both. But she felt an overwhelming commitment to the greater good, and could never be happy unless she was working for it. She died the way, if she had a choice, I'm sure she'd have wanted to. Taking down a threat. Her murderer died, too. She sacrificed herself to save the victims of that felon." He shakes his head.

"I never knew that," is all I can manage as the street lamps flood on.

"The story is horrifying," Shadow replies. "Not right for a five year old. And I could never bring myself to tell you after. I was going to tell you when you were fourteen, I had promised myself. But after Anthony was gone, I felt like I lost you, too." He doesn't need to tell me the magnitude of pain he felt. I can see it clearly on his face.

"So you…" I murmur. "So you…you are…my…"

"Dad," Shadow says in a tight voice.

"I always thought…he didn't…know," is what I come up with.

"I knew," Shadow says, like he's trying to assure me and not cry at the same time.

"Why didn't you tell me before this?" I fight the waves of chaos raging through my mind.

"At first you were too young," he says. "Then I was too afraid. Afraid you'd be upset, angry, alienated. Even if our relationship wasn't Kodak, I still cherished it. And I thought you might hate me if you found out."

"I don't hate you," is all I can reply before my throat seems to close off. I turn my head away, not wanting an audience.

"I'll…let you sleep now," he says in a low voice, hands releasing mine. He stands up. Then hesitates. And leans down and kisses me on the forehead.

He's out of the room by the time I've come out of my daze.

I don't go back to sleep. Instead, I get up and slowly, gingerly, brush my teeth and hair and lay out my clothes. Then I tug up the bottom of my pajama shirt and frown at my brace, contemplating how long it will take me to dress.

There's a light knock from the door. I let the shirt fall back down and make my way over, look through the peephole, and immediately open up.

Hale's mouth drops open. Vivian's a little subtler with her shock. But I'm happy to see them both.

"My gosh, Mel," Hale says. "Ms. Rose said something about…" She tears her eyes from my bandages and tries to focus somewhere around my nose, which is unscathed. "We didn't know." She starts to back away. "We'll…we'll come back later, if you want."

I'm already shaking my head. "No, that's okay." My voice is slightly hoarse. "Actually, I need your help." My mouth twitches into a small smile. "Please?"

27

Shadow–should I start calling him Dad? He still feels like just Shadow to me, except, well, less secrets–arranges for our flight to be moved to tomorrow instead of today. I'm pretty confused right now, but I do know that I don't want to leave yet. Shadow's not familiar with Brisbane; he only associates it with foreignness and my bad experience. He wants to be back in Rochester. But for me, the city of Brisbane holds not only those things, but a sense of discovery, friendship...Ray.

For once I don't protest and try to make it work out my way. I just nod and accept it.

Shadow/Dad has called Annette Robar and tried to explain as best he can. Her talking rate exceeded the natural speed limit, so Shadow says he *thinks* she's very excited and can't wait to see Ray, but he can't be positive. When I heard the original plan was for Ray to stay here until Annette came down to settle things, I protested as forcefully as I could. So did Ray. We want to stay together. The idea of leaving him behind, even for a week, makes my head spin. What if he disappears again? He's only just gotten his memory back. It seems too fragile to risk.

Peter Manifred calls at eleven.

"Amber?" he asks, his voice still weak when I pick up the phone.

"Yes," I say. "What? What's going on?" My voice is starting to rise in panic.

"Nothing. Calm down," he says quickly. "I've just read

the paper. All it says is that Ms. Richards, her brother Manuel, and a Mr. Hallow were taken into custody last night. And it mentioned Marvin Academy. I have a feeling that you were involved."

"Yes." I sit down on the edge of my bed, looking around the momentarily vacant room. Shadow's just gone to get some food, and Hale and Vivian had to leave for class, which they had been sort-of-maybe-skipping. I run a hand over their email addresses in my pocket and smile.

"Are you...all right?"

"I will be," I say slowly. "You?"

"Healing well enough."

The conversation past this is fairly pointless, except for when he thanks me, and asks me to let him know if I ever find out where Bonnie Robar is. I say sure, but the back of my mind rebels against thinking about it. But still, as I hang up, I'm grateful. He helped me. Without him, I might not have been as aware as I was. It could have turned out much, much worse than it did.

I eat lunch in my room, with Shadow. The soup is good and the orange juice fresh, but both seem bland on my tongue. I hardly even register the usually rejuvenating Vitamin C content. We're both silent, Shadow mulling over something or other, and me battling with an almost frenzied need to see Ray, and soon.

It's like he reads my mind. He shows up at the door before I'm even finished eating. I quickly gulp down the rest of my potato leek soup and set it aside, standing as quickly as possible.

He hugs me briefly and gently under Shadow's hawk eyes, then stands back to give me an almost sad smile.

"Want to go up?" he asks quietly, leaving it entirely up to me. Am I so inclined? Willing? Able?

I nod yes.

"Where…?" Shadow/Dad asks, starting to get up.

"To the roof," Ray tells him. "The view is incredible."

I plead with my eyes, already thinking of ways I can sneak out if he denies me. But it's not necessary. After a moment, he nods. His face says 'be careful,' but he doesn't actually form the words. I allow him a smile as I follow Ray out of the room.

Our journey to the roof is slow. I still won't use the elevator, so Ray, who is in much better condition than I am, has to put up with my pace all the way up the several stories. He doesn't seem to mind, though, just smiles and talks and helps.

On the actual roof I feel better. The air is fresher, the sky wide if not clear, the view, as stated, incredible. And the company…invaluable.

Ray has a blanket with him. He spreads it on the concrete and we lie back, beside each other, gazing up at the lazy clouds above. We don't feel the need to talk for a long time.

The evening sky is beginning to take over when I finally speak. Just one word, to reassure my paranoid self.

"Ray?"

"I'm here," he whispers.

"You don't know how happy that makes me," I say. "It was unbelievably frustrating that I knew and you didn't…" I trail off, thinking maybe that was something like what Shadow felt about me, only mine was five thousand times worse.

"It makes me happy, too," Ray says. "Finally realizing that you are…you."

"What changed the tide?" I ask quietly, seriously.

"When she"–he doesn't have to say Caidy's name–"was talking about how I would never be with her, I knew it was, as she implied, impossible. Because…" The back of his hand rests against mine. I see him swallow. "Because I already loved you."

His words make my heart feel like it's twice as big and about to fail any second. "You do?" is my ridiculous question.

"Yes." He stares intently up at the sky, remembering. "And as soon as I admitted that to myself, the tide became waves. Ray came back."

I think I might be crying again, but all I can really notice are my words, which are "I love you too. I love you, Ray," and how I'm struggling to push myself up so I can see him and he's doing the same thing and then I'm in his arms and we're kissing.

Something I've been waiting for for years, which only a small, hidden part of me, the honest part, would admit. And I never listened until now.

I think he might be crying, too, when we lay back down, hands entwined between us. The clouds are darker, blending in better with patches of indigo sky.

After a while Ray says what I'm thinking. "What now?"

"I don't know. I know you and me and Shadow..." I trail off.

"*Hmm*?"

"I didn't tell you about Shadow," I say.

"What about him?"

"He's...he's my dad." Though I haven't told anyone yet, I know it's immensely easier to tell Ray than anyone else.

"Really?" Ray sounds surprised, but not shocked. "I actually thought it was something like that."

"You did?" I'm surprised as well, but then again, not really. If Ray can see who I really am, he can see just about everything.

"He did, I did...Ray did," he replies.

"It's still confusing?"

"Getting clearer."

"Better than before," I sigh.

"Much."

"So we go back and let everyone know you're not dead..." I wince with him, imagining the awkwardness, the disbelief, the questions. "And then..." I hesitate, wondering if that little honest part of me is telling me something sane.

"And then?" Ray asks, because he knows there's more.

"And then... I don't want to go to Watson for this school year," I whisper. Ray nods, covering slight amazement. "I think I want to spend a year...at a regular school. And be...not a spy. Just for one year. To try it."

"I think," says Ray, squeezing my hand, "that sounds like a great idea."

"But if you're at Watson..." I trail off unhappily at the idea. Of course I would choose to be where Ray is. But I balk at the idea of immediately going back to the pressure, the danger, the stress.

"I'm not sure I will be," Ray says very quietly.

"What do you mean?"

"I mean, now that I know my mother might be alive," he murmurs, "I want to try to find her."

"You mean...go to Europe?"

"With Annette." He nods again. "And see if there's any way to...track her down, tell her I'm..."

Back, I supply in my mind, while the rest of me shudders at the idea of him leaving again. But if it's what he wants...

"Not for long," he goes on. "And not right away. But I feel like...I have to."

"I can come," I offer.

"But I want you to have your normal year." His words aren't commanding, but his tone says he really does want it. For me.

"But I don't want you to be..." *So far away.*

"We don't have to decide yet." Ray's voice is barely

audible. "Right now, we can just…relax."

"Relaxing sounds good," I respond, my voice even quieter than his. His thumb strokes the length of my hand. I feel my shoulders unclench, my eyes slide closed, savoring every part, as I do what I've never done before. I put the future away for later. I stop worrying about it because, right now, I don't have to. Right now I can relax. Right now I can let all the leftover street lamps turn on in their own time.

Right now I can be with Ray.

Kieryn Nicolas resides in central Pennsylvania with her parents, younger sister, their lovable yellow lab, black cat and ten hens. Kieryn was a competitive figure skater for nine years and is currently working hard to advance in Taekwondo. She is considering a career as a forensic scientist or crime scene investigator, and has eleven novels in the works. Kieryn enjoys spending time with her close friends, and also loves to read, write, eat chocolate and travel with hopes of someday seeing Brisbane, Australia for herself.

Visit Kieryn at

www.kierynnicolas.com

www.kierynnicolas.blogspot.com

Breinigsville, PA USA
13 March 2011
257508BV00001B/1/P